**Praise for the novels of *USA Today*
bestselling author Lynn Kurland**

When I Fall in Love

"Kurland infuses her polished writing with a deliciously dry wit, and her latest time-travel love story is sweetly romantic and thoroughly satisfying." —*Booklist*

"The continuation of a wonderful series, this story can also be read alone. It's an extremely good book." —*Affaire de Coeur*

"One of the best romances that this reviewer has ever had the pleasure of reading! It is enough to make even nonbelievers believe in the power of love." —*Love Romances & More*

"*When I Fall in Love* is a wonderful tale. Ms. Kurland's fans will find plenty to enjoy in this latest novel." —*A Romance Review*

"Lynn Kurland has surpassed even her personal best with *When I Fall in Love*. This is a book that will haunt you long after the final page is turned." —*Kwips and Kritiques*

"A sweet story of love across time. There's plenty of humor and romance to entertain . . . a splendid way to escape reality, even if it's just for a few hours. Highly recommended." —*MyShelf*

"Revisiting Ms. Kurland's world is always a joy . . . a cheerful, positive, feel-good romance that will make your heart glad." —*The Eternal Night*

"Delightful . . . Ms. Kurland knows how to deliver a heartwarming romance and remarkable characters." —*Romance Reviews Today*

continued. . .

Much Ado in the Moonlight

"A pure delight."
—*Huntress Book Reviews*

"A consummate storyteller . . . will keep the reader on the edge of their seat, unable to put the book down until the very last word."
—*ParaNormal Romance Reviews*

"No one melds ghosts and time travel better than the awesome Kurland."
—*Romantic Times*

Dreams of Stardust

"Kurland weaves another fabulous read with just the right amounts of laughter, romance, and fantasy." —*Affaire de Coeur*

"Kurland crafts some of the most ingenious time-travel romances readers can find . . . wonderfully clever and completely enchanting."
—*Romantic Times*

A Garden in the Rain

"Kurland laces her exquisitely romantic, utterly bewitching blend of contemporary romance and time travel with a delectable touch of tart wit, leaving readers savoring every word of this superbly written romance."
—*Booklist*

"Kurland is clearly one of romance's finest writers—she consistently delivers the kind of stories readers dream about. Don't miss this one."
—*The Oakland Press*

From This Moment On

"A disarming blend of romance, suspense, and heartwarming humor, this book is romantic comedy at its best."
—*Publishers Weekly*

"A deftly plotted delight, seasoned with a wonderfully wry sense of humor and graced with endearing, unforgettable characters."
—*Booklist*

My Heart Stood Still

"Written with poetic grace and a wickedly subtle sense of humor . . . the essence of pure romance. Sweet, poignant, and truly magical, this is a rare treat: romance with characters readers will come to care about and a love story they will cherish." —*Booklist*

"A totally enchanting tale, sensual and breathtaking . . . an absolute must-read." —*Rendezvous*

If I Had You

"Kurland brings history to life . . . in this tender medieval romance." —*Booklist*

"A passionate story filled with danger, intrigue, and sparkling dialogue." —*Rendezvous*

The More I See You

"The superlative Ms. Kurland once again wows her readers with her formidable talent as she weaves a tale of enchantment that blends history with spellbinding passion and impressive characterization, not to mention a magnificent plot." —*Rendezvous*

Another Chance to Dream

"Kurland creates a special romance between a memorable knight and his lady." —*Publishers Weekly*

The Very Thought of You

"A masterpiece . . . this fabulous tale will enchant anyone who reads it." —*Painted Rock Reviews*

This Is All I Ask

"An exceptional read." —*The Atlanta Journal-Constitution*

"Both powerful and sensitive . . . a wonderfully rich and rewarding book." —Susan Wiggs

WITH EVERY BREATH

LYNN KURLAND

JOVE BOOKS, NEW YORK

THE BERKLEY PUBLISHING GROUP
Published by the Penguin Group
Penguin Group (USA) Inc.
375 Hudson Street, New York, New York 10014, USA
Penguin Group (Canada), 90 Eglinton Avenue East, Suite 700, Toronto, Ontario M4P 2Y3, Canada
(a division of Pearson Penguin Canada Inc.)
Penguin Books Ltd., 80 Strand, London WC2R 0RL, England
Penguin Group Ireland, 25 St. Stephen's Green, Dublin 2, Ireland (a division of Penguin Books Ltd.)
Penguin Group (Australia), 250 Camberwell Road, Camberwell, Victoria 3124, Australia
(a division of Pearson Australia Group Pty. Ltd.)
Penguin Books India Pvt. Ltd., 11 Community Centre, Panchsheel Park, New Delhi—110 017, India
Penguin Group (NZ), 67 Apollo Drive, Rosedale, North Shore 0632, New Zealand
(a division of Pearson New Zealand Ltd.)
Penguin Books (South Africa) (Pty.) Ltd., 24 Sturdee Avenue, Rosebank, Johannesburg 2196,
South Africa

Penguin Books Ltd., Registered Offices: 80 Strand, London WC2R 0RL, England

This is a work of fiction. Names, characters, places, and incidents either are the product of the author's imagination or are used fictitiously, and any resemblance to actual persons, living or dead, business establishments, events, or locales is entirely coincidental. The publisher does not have any control over and does not assume any responsibility for author or third-party websites or their content.

WITH EVERY BREATH

A Jove Book / published by arrangement with the author

PRINTING HISTORY
Jove mass-market edition / June 2008

Copyright © 2008 by Lynn Curland.
Cover design by George Long.

ISBN: 978-0-515-14470-3

JOVE®
Jove Books are published by The Berkley Publishing Group,
a division of Penguin Group (USA) Inc.,
375 Hudson Street, New York, New York 10014.
JOVE is a registered trademark of Penguin Group (USA) Inc.
The "J" design is a trademark belonging to Penguin Group (USA) Inc.

PRINTED IN THE UNITED STATES OF AMERICA

10 9 8 7 6 5 4 3 2 1

Acknowledgments

To Lynn Rowley and Mike Forbes, for patiently telling me everything I ever wanted to know about the ins and outs of stocks, bonds, and boutique trading firms.

To Derek Anderson, M.D., for answering my endless, kooky questions about potentially dire medical scenarios.

To Charles Bleakley, for the medical discussion on a wonderful spring afternoon in Devon last year.

To David and Claire Bleakley and Joanna Pratt, who unflinchingly discussed all sorts of British slang with me, also on a wonderful spring day in Devon.

To my brilliant accountant, John Schleuter, for all sorts of useful ideas on off-shore accounts and the delights of Swiss banking.

No book would make it out the door without my wonderful editor, Kate Seaver, and my fabulous agent, Nancy Yost. Thank you, ladies, for more things than I can mention here. I'm also very grateful to my publisher, Leslie Gelbman, who has been so consistently supportive and gracious. I am truly fortunate to rub shoulders with three such terrifically talented women.

And last, but not least, to my family, who has made my life so much more wonderful than I ever dreamed it could be.

*To my grandmother, Ramona,
and my great-grandmother, Violet,
who taught me how to love things that grow.*

*C*hapter 1

S*cotland* in the rain.

There were, Sunshine Phillips decided, not many other words that could conjure up more romantic imaginings than those. She pulled the exercise studio door shut behind her, then lifted her face to the sky and closed her eyes. The rain that fell on her wasn't particularly warm—it was the end of March after all—but it was still the sort of rain that made a woman want to curl up in front of the fire with a cup of something hot and listen to it falling softly on the roof. She smiled in pleasure. It was perfect.

She absolutely loved Scotland. She loved how the sky pressed down against the land and left her feeling grounded. She loved the cycles of the earth, the seasons in the Highlands, the family her sister had married into.

But she loved the rain most of all.

She'd had her first taste of Scottish drizzle the year before when her sister had invited her to come to the Highlands. She'd happily left her hectic life in Seattle behind for a visit that had stretched all the way through her sister's pregnancy and delivery.

And somehow during all those months, she'd begun to wish she had a reason to stay in Scotland for quite a bit longer than a single spring and summer. She hadn't dared hope for it, though.

Then, unexpectedly, she'd been offered a little moss-covered cottage that looked as if it had come straight from some Highland fairy tale. She'd accepted it without hesitation and happily spent the previous winter sitting by the fire and dreaming.

Then spring had hinted it might arrive and she'd grown restless. She'd even thought about going back to the States to pursue that raw-food catering business she'd been ready to start before Madelyn had come home from Scotland with her life turned completely upside down. But going back to Seattle would have meant leaving the Highlands and she couldn't bring herself to even consider that. Her lovely, crooked little house was full of herbs, the forest around her house was full of quiet, the meadows and mountains outside the forest full of flowers and heather. She couldn't give that up. Not yet. Not until she was certain she wouldn't find what her heart wanted the most.

All of which she could think about later, when she was sitting comfortably in front of her own fire. For now, she really needed to get out of the wet. She wiped the rain off her face, then started toward the corner. She jumped in surprise at the sight of a woman standing not twenty feet away from her wearing dark sunglasses that were completely unnecessary for the day. Actually, it wasn't just the woman's sunglasses, or her jet-black hair that was so disconcerting. There was something about her aura as a whole that was rather dark and forbidding. The woman gave her the creeps, and she wasn't unacquainted with things of a spooky nature.

Madelyn would have had a field day with that admission.

She gave herself a little mental shake and decided promptly that too much time in the rain had rotted any good sense she had once possessed.

"Can I help you?" she asked.

"I'm waiting for someone."

"From yoga class?" Sunny asked, puzzled. "But I'm the last one out."

"So you are," the woman said, without any inflection at all to her voice. She stood there motionless for another minute, then turned suddenly and walked away.

Sunny watched her go, then considered. Maybe the woman had been stood up by her boyfriend, or been pulled over by a cop on the way to the village, or was waiting in the wrong place and frustration had gotten the better of her. Whatever the case, it wasn't her problem. She shouldered her bag and walked up the alleyway between buildings, putting the woman and her potential troubles behind her. She rounded the corner of the building and paused to take in the view.

The village was not large, but it suited her purposes. There was a post office, a greengrocer, and a few other stores that sold goods that one might not want to make a trip to Inverness for. It also boasted an herb shop where she worked a few hours a week to kill some time after teaching yoga in the studio attached to the back of the shop. It was a charming place.

Well, the village was. The herb shop wasn't.

She looked at the shop front. *FERGUSSON'S HERBS AND SUNDRIES* was announced in precise, unforgiving letters. If it had been her place, the letters would have swirled and enticed and invited the would-be herbal shopper to come inside, have a cup of tea, and sniff the herbs and sundries. Her brother-in-law, Patrick MacLeod, offered on a weekly basis to buy the place for her, but she declined just as often. She had money enough to buy at least part of it herself, but she hadn't wanted to. Her heart was not in being a shopkeeper, even a shopkeeper of things she loved. She had other things in mind for herself.

She ducked under the awning and walked into the shop. Unfortunately, remaining on her current side of the Pond would probably require marriage and marriage would require that she find someone within a fifty-mile radius to date. She was still working on that—and not having much success. She glanced at the man behind the counter who sported the enormous shiner under his right eye.

Case in point.

"You're late."

Tavish Fergusson didn't even look up at her as he spoke. He was obviously very busy tallying up something on that sheet of paper in front of him. Perhaps he was making a list of all the bottles she hadn't arranged on the shelf precisely so. Perhaps he was counting how many flakes of peppermint tea one could reasonably subtract from a prepackaged bag yet still have it taste remotely like it should. Perhaps he was calculating how many seconds had elapsed between the time when he'd first attempted to grope her in the storeroom yesterday and the precise instant her fist had connected with his eye.

Not very many, by her count.

She walked behind the counter and set her bag down on the floor. "What do you need me to do?"

"Go restock soap."

"I did that yesterday."

He shot her a dark look. "Do it again."

She caught her breath at his rudeness. All right, so he'd never been much of a gentleman. At least he'd pretended to be civil. Obviously there was no need for it now.

She pursed her lips and went off to see what he'd managed to sell during the day. She checked the clinical, silver shelves stocked with unimaginative bits of soap, then headed into the stockroom to gather a lone bar to replace what had apparently been purchased.

She walked around the store, looking for other things to do. Perhaps it had been a mistake to even take the job in the first place, but she'd needed something to keep herself busy. How could she have refused, especially when Tavish had offered her a job in spite of the fact that she was related, by marriage, to those evil MacLeods up the way. It had seemed like a gesture of good-will to accept. Besides, she'd been certain that even after Tavish had ignored her less-than-subtle hints—and in spite of the fact that he tended to unbutton his shirts too far in a misguided attempt to look sexy—she could avoid any entanglements with him.

Of course, that had been before last night. After four months of knowing her, he'd suddenly decided it was time to know her quite a bit better. She glanced at him briefly as she went to throw a carton in the trash. That black eye was a good one. Patrick would have been proud.

It had been Patrick who had insisted that she learn to defend herself—and quite ruthlessly, actually. She'd gone along with it because she'd suspected he might be right. She and Madelyn had spent a good part of the previous summer learning various useful things. Well, *she* had learned various useful things. Madelyn had spent most of her time with her very pregnant self reclining in a chair and her feet propped up on a stool in front of her, calling out encouraging words as Sunny had practiced repeatedly fending off Patrick's merciless attacks.

She had put in extra effort, just in case she had needed to take care of herself and Madelyn both. Then she'd put the knowledge aside, figuring she wouldn't need it except in a pinch, sort of like tenth-grade geometry. Who would have thought that she would need to use it when she realized Tavish Fergusson wasn't inter-ested in discussing any inclines other than horizontal?

She spent a pair of hours helping the odd customer and gener-ally making herself useful. She was, however, unusually happy to see the clock strike six.

"Want me to lock up?" she asked.

Tavish looked at her coldly. "I wouldn't trust you to."

She rolled her eyes. "Get real, Tavish. I may not appreciate your advances, but I'm perfectly capable of appreciating the value of your sundries. I wouldn't leave the store unlocked."

"You definitely won't because you won't be here any longer to do so."

She stared at him for a minute until she realized just what he was getting at. "Are you *firing* me?"

"Aye. Nessa Paine can teach the yoga classes."

"Who?" Sunny asked in surprise.

"Nessa Paine," Tavish repeated with a smirk. "She's young and *very* beautiful. Just what we need. Why don't you go back up the hill where you belong and be grateful I don't file a complaint against you for assault."

"Assault?" she echoed.

He pointed to his eye.

She shut her mouth and started across the room. She was marginally satisfied to note that he backed away when she came behind the counter to pick up her bag. She dug around in it for the key to the store, then laid it carefully on his papers.

"I suppose you could call your brother Hamish and whine all about it," she said, slinging her bag over her shoulder, "but then you'd have to explain why you got my fist in your eye, wouldn't you? I think you might not want to bother."

"There will come a day when you won't have MacLeods about to save you," Tavish muttered.

She stopped halfway to the door, then turned slightly so she could look at him. "Is that a threat?"

He glared at her. "Just go."

There were half a dozen comebacks clamoring to get out of her mouth, but she was nothing if not disciplined, so she bit them all back and left. She pulled the door shut behind her and stood there for a minute, trying to let the chill cool her temper. No wonder the MacLeods disliked the Fergussons so much. They had good reason.

She took a deep breath and walked away only to find herself suddenly sprawled on the ground. She groped for her bag before it disappeared with her attacker, then realized that her purse wasn't going anywhere. The things inside certainly were, though. She lay there for a moment, too stunned to move any more, and listened to things rolling out of her bag onto the wet sidewalk.

"Watch where you're going," a female voice said sharply. "I almost tripped over you."

Sunny didn't have a chance to even push herself up before the woman stepped on one of her hands. It hurt so much, all she could do was gasp in pain.

"Unsurprising," the woman said in disgust. "She's probably drunk."

Sunny wondered what sort of person didn't at least stop to see if a drunk needed help to her feet. Well, at least Miss Stepper hadn't been wearing stilettos. Things could have been much worse.

Sunny sat up and rubbed her palm absently, then realized the woman hadn't been alone.

There was a hand in front of her, a hand that was being offered by a man. She couldn't see his face thanks to the fact that Tavish had already turned off the store lights, but she could see the hand. She reached up and took it.

And felt as if she'd just stuck her finger in a light socket.

She pulled away with a gasp. The man's hand shook briefly, then steadied and remained outstretched.

"Oh, Mac, will you come *on*!" the woman demanded. "Stop being Sir Gallant."

The man sighed lightly, then reached out and pulled Sunny to her feet. The electricity of his touch was no different from what it had been before, but she was expecting it this time.

"Are you all right, lass?" he asked.

Sunny felt a little breathless. All right, so her life was full of manly Highlanders with their lovely trilling *r*'s and cascading consonants and lilting cadences. One more shouldn't have been so overwhelming.

Yet, somehow, he was.

The man took her hand in both his and ran long, callused fingers over her palm. "No blood, at least—"

"Mac, *now*! I want to be out of this bloody rain. And I want to find somewhere besides this *village* to have a decent meal."

The man muttered a curse in Gaelic, then stooped and collected Sunny's things. He put them back in her purse, put her purse in her hands, then put his hand briefly on her shoulder before he stepped around her to catch up to his girlfriend.

Sunny turned and watched them walk away. The man was tall, several inches over six feet, and broad-shouldered just like all those finely built MacLeod men she was surrounded by. She closed her fingers over the spot on her palm where he'd touched her.

All right, just what else weird could possibly happen to her that day?

Deciding that it was probably better not to know, she turned away and walked unsteadily toward her car. Her hand ached abominably and she indulged in a few unkind thoughts about that woman who had stolen a perfectly good Highlander.

At least her car started up right away, though she probably shouldn't have expected anything else. It was a modest little Mini, but brand-new. She'd inherited money from her great-grandmother the year before, which had enabled her to not only buy a car but live without working too hard for a while.

Actually, she could have lived for quite a while without working after she had sold what she'd owned of her very small house in Seattle and moved to Scotland. A car had seemed a rather permanent thing, but the right thing at the time. It didn't compare to the hundreds of thousands of dollars worth of very fast cars her brothers-in-law owned, but she was happy to let them get the tickets while she just puttered home at her own pace.

She had just gotten onto the main village road when a low-slung, dark sports car blew past her, honking. It wasn't Jamie, Patrick, or Ian so she felt not even the slightest obligation to be polite. She laid on the horn because there wasn't enough time to flip him off. Then, feeling as if everything was now right with the world, she turned off onto the road that wound up through meadows into the mountains.

And promptly had a flat tire.

She didn't bother pulling off the road. No one came this way except family and the odd intrepid tourist capable of ignoring the rather prominent *NO TRESPASSING* sign she'd just passed fifty feet earlier. It wasn't that the MacLeods weren't a friendly, welcoming group. It was just that their land was loaded with potholes.

Of a sort.

Sunny sighed, then pulled the parking brake up and got out of the car. She fished around in her trunk for her emergency kit and found the heavy-duty flashlight Patrick had insisted she keep. It was a decent light, enough for her to change the tire by. Now, if she'd only agreed with him that she really should have a cell phone, she could have called for a rescue. She'd never thought she would need one.

Famous last words, apparently.

She had no idea how long it took her to get the tire off, but by the time she'd done that and gotten the other one into place, she was absolutely soaked. She squatted down and fitted the tire to the wheel studs, though it didn't go on as well as it should have. She chipped two fingernails, sat down unintentionally in the mud, and bloodied her knuckles before she managed to get the lug nuts back on and the other tire into her trunk. She got back in, then carried on in her best the-rain-doesn't-bother-me fashion, driving past Patrick and Madelyn's castle and on through the woods to the little house that was now hers.

Moraig MacLeod had been born in that house, then died in it ninety years later after a long life spent doing exactly what she wanted to do—which had mostly included puttering in her garden, drying herbs, and reminding the laird down the way that he was fortunate to have his own witch. Jamie had invited Moraig to dinner once a month in appreciation.

Or perhaps he did it just so she wouldn't put a hex on him.

Sunny had met Moraig shortly after she'd arrived in Scotland and in her she'd found a kindred spirit. She'd spent the greater part of the previous spring and summer doing for Moraig what needed to be done and learning things she had never considered. She now knew how to feed herself during any season of the year in the Highlands, how to treat all sorts of wounds and infections, and how to brew a love potion.

She hadn't used that last one quite yet.

When Moraig had insisted on her deathbed last fall that Sunny be given her house and her things, Sunny had been touched beyond measure. She'd also accepted Jamie's invitation to stay in Scotland and take over Moraig's place in the clan. Clan witch was better than fighting Seattle traffic.

All of which left her, a year and a few months after she'd first come to Scotland, parking her own little car in front of her own little house and thinking that her life was fairly perfect.

She walked inside, then shut the door behind her. She turned on the lights, one of the few concessions to the twenty-first century, and leaned back against the door and smiled. Herbs hung from the rafters, pots and wooden bowls were stacked on shelves that might have been level at one time but now leaned along with the rest of the house, and a substantial fireplace dominated what could have been considered a great room. She stood in the middle of the house and felt a deep contentment wash over her. It wasn't what she'd expected from her life, but she wasn't unhappy with it. After all, she had Scotland and its rain. What wasn't to love about that?

A smart rap on the door had her jumping in spite of herself. She put her hand over her chest, took a deep breath, then went to open the door. A gorgeous Highlander stood there with a smile on his face.

Too bad he was her brother-in-law.

She smiled anyway. Patrick MacLeod was a prince among men, doting on his wife and baby daughter until Sunny wondered how he managed to get anything done.

"Dinner?" he asked.

She nodded. "Always."

"Sunny, you're covered in mud."

"I had a flat tire," she grumbled, wiping her hands unsuccessfully on her leggings.

"If you'd had a mobile," Patrick began wisely, "you could have called me."

"Spoken like a man who only began charging his cell phone after he found out his wife was pregnant."

Patrick pulled her out of her house, reached in and shut off the lights, then shut the door as well. "Aye, and now that I've seen how useful they are, I recommend one for you."

"I won't need one because I don't have anywhere to go anymore."

He looked at her in surprise. "Did Tavish sack you?"

"He did."

"Must have been the black eye you gave him," he said, unsuccessfully fighting a wicked smile. "How did it look today?"

"It was ripening nicely."

"Good gel." He put his arm around her shoulders and pulled her along the path. "Don't fash yourself over it, Sunny. We won't let you starve."

"I have money, Patrick," she said dryly.

"We'll still feed you so you don't spend it all." He drew his jacket up toward his ears. "'Tis bloody cold out. Let's run. We'll be soaked to the skin if we don't hurry—och, but you are already, aren't you?

She glared at him, but he only laughed.

"Not to worry; you can raid Madelyn's closet when we get home. I'll buy her something extra to make up for it."

"You already buy her too much," Sunny muttered. "She complains endlessly about it."

"Aye, I know," he said with the contented smile of a man who knew his wife adored him. "Let's hurry just the same. Did I tell you that Madelyn made dessert? Something with chocolate, just for you."

Given the day she'd had, she thought she might just have to

give in and partake. She nodded, then hurried with him down the path.

Several hours later, she sat in front of her own fire with a cup of tea in her hand. There was no point in going to bed early when she had nothing to get up for in the morning. She wondered if she was making a mistake staying in Scotland.

She quickly came to the same conclusion she always did: she wanted to stay. She loved the heather on the hills, the fire in her hearth, and the rain falling softly on the roof above her.

Her hand ached briefly and she realized that she'd forgotten about what had happened earlier. She looked down at her hand and wondered how it was that crabby English gal had snagged a solicitous, Gaelic-speaking Highlander. Would he be tempted to dump her for a perky, herb-loving American?

She smiled to herself. Probably not. If he had that high-maintenance sort of girlfriend, he was probably just as high maintenance himself and that wasn't the sort of man for her. Even Tavish Fergusson with his very proper, very pinched way of looking at life wasn't for her. She wanted a laid-back, re-laxed, private sort of man who would be happy with his nine-to-five. She could supplement their income with veggies grown in the backyard and an occasional stint as a midwife.

Or perhaps she would just content herself with being the MacLeod healer in residence. She would get up in the morning and think about the book on herbal medicine she'd been wanting to write for years. She would go to Jamie's that next evening for the witch's appeasement meal. Maybe she would open the door and find Jamie's minstrel Joshua standing there, come to escort her to the MacLeod keep—just as he'd done every month for the past year. And if he actually got up the nerve to ask her out in-stead of hemming and hawing about it, she might even say yes. At least she wouldn't have to punch him in the eye.

But for now, she would be grateful for what she had and let the future take care of itself. It always seemed to. She washed out her cup, banked her fire, then put herself to bed.

She fell asleep to the sound of rain on her roof.

Chapter 2

R obert Francis Cameron mac Cameron stood up to his ankles in blood and muck and cursed.

The day had not gone as he'd planned. He was surrounded by dead and dying, which wouldn't have troubled him any other day but today too many of those poor souls were his own kin. Damn those bloody Fergussons to hell.

He'd never liked them. He liked them even less than he liked the MacLeods to the south. At least a MacLeod would come to a battle with a sword in his hand and a grin on his face. He had yet to meet a Fergusson who wasn't lying in wait behind some bloody bush, ready to cry foul for some imagined slight and demand a fight to settle it.

And they tended to stab in the back.

His youngest brother had discovered that first-hand. Sim lay facedown in the mud, a wicked-looking dagger haft sticking out of his back. His next youngest brother, Breac, had just fallen to his knees, clutching his belly where a sword had recently resided.

"Cameron, ride for the MacLeod witch."

Cameron looked up. "What?"

His cousin Giric stood in front of him. "I said, ride for the MacLeod witch. 'Tis a rout for us here anyway. I'll see Breac back to the hall. Go fetch a healer before he dies."

Cameron looked about the field and saw that his cousin had it aright. There were more dead Fergussons lying before him than he'd ever had the pleasure of seeing before. Of course, his clan had paid the price as well, but not an equal one.

Unless he was to count the loss of one brother who was already dead and the other who would be dead before midnight, and then the price had been high indeed. And for what? Yet another imagined slight.

He stood there in the rain and stared down at Sim, that braw, fearless lad who had seen but twenty winters. Where was the justice that he should meet death on a soggy spring day? There was a girl waiting for him behind in the keep, a girl he'd planned to wed in the summer, a girl who would likely now end her own life in despair.

And then there was Breac. A score and four years sat upon him, years full of laughter and maids fighting each other to have him. He had a wife, a young son, and another babe coming in the fall. How would Gilly react when Breac was brought back, bleeding from a wound that no power on earth could heal?

At least he had no one waiting for him inside the hall. He was too sour, too demanding, too brusque. There was the occasional wench willing to warm his bed, but nary a one willing to touch his heart. Perhaps it was a pity that he alone of his brothers remained on his feet.

"Cam!"

He looked at his cousin. "Do *not* call me that," he growled. "'Tis Sim's name for me."

"Very well, *Cameron*," Giric snarled, "go fetch that damned MacLeod witch before you kill another of your brothers." He spat onto the bloody ground. "You shouldn't have faced this challenge openly."

"I am no Fergusson," Cameron said coldly. "I don't creep up behind those I intend to slay."

"Aye, and your brothers are dead because of your precious honor, aren't they?

Cameron knew he should have used the blood-drenched sword he held in his hands a final time to slay the whoreson standing in front of him, but as Giric was his first cousin—and the only one left him—he supposed there was reason enough to allow him to draw breath a bit longer. "See Breac safely to my chamber," he commanded.

"I will. *Go.*"

Cameron nodded, then caught sight of his priest wandering through the mud, bending every now and again to close eyelids or feel for a heartbeat.

He turned away. He wasn't ready to watch the man close either of his brothers' eyes, not when he might be able to save one of them.

He turned and sprinted for his hall. He resheathed his sword in

the scabbard strapped to his back, swung up on his horse, then
wheeled around and thundered south.

He would fetch the witch and hope.

He could do nothing else.

*F*or almost two hours he rode as if the very devil himself were
on his heels. He slowed only when he crossed onto MacLeod
lands and only because it behooved him to be careful. He might
have had a chance to tell them why he was borrowing their
healer; then again, they might have killed him first and wondered
what he was about later. He had to admit that was the one thing he
liked about them. He wasn't one to pause and contemplate where
action served him better, either.

But he needed their healer, so he was careful.

He knew where he was going, for the most part. 'Twas rumored
that the healer's house was to the north of the keep, north and a bit
east. Surely he could slip past their scouts, snatch the woman
whilst she was stirring her pot, and make off with her before she
could sound any alarm. With any luck at all, the MacLeods were
just as afeared of her as he was and they wouldn't be guarding her.
She would be by herself and easily carried off.

He left his horse tied to a tree on the edge of the forest, then
melted into the shadows. He heard nothing, but that wasn't
reassuring. Scouts were, by nature, very silent lads. If they weren't,
they were usually dead.

With that pleasant thought to keep him company, he continued
to creep through the forest. He would find the old woman, convince her to come with him by promising her some reward she
wouldn't be able to refuse, then spirit her back to his horse. For all
he knew, she would be able to work a miracle and Breac would be
whole once again. He wasn't pessimistic by nature, his sour dis-
position aside, but he supposed he would be surprised only if his
brother lived long enough to allow the witch to look at him.

He turned away from the thought of being the last of his father's sons, partly because he would miss his brothers and partly
because it would change nothing for him. He would still be laird
of an unruly and feisty clan. Giric would still slink around behind
him, waiting for a chance to slip a knife between his ribs. He
would still hold on to power by the sheer force of his will alone.
Hadn't his father done the same, ruling with an iron will and

heavy hand long after Cameron's mother had fretted herself into an early grave?

Cameron had always known that he would take his father's place—and not just because he was the eldest. His father had given him his clan's name to remind him who and what he was.

His mother had given him another unprecedented pair of names to remind him that whilst he was his father's son, he was also hers and came from a line of fair, reasonable men. His father had called him nothing but Cameron, likely out of spite. His parents' marriage had not been a happy one.

It was, he suspected, why he was still unwed.

Or perhaps 'twas that he hadn't yet found a reasonable woman. He didn't want a shrew like Gilly, Breac's wife, who would blame him for everything that went awry in her life, and he didn't want an immature, unsteady girl like Heather, Sim's lass, who would no doubt sob herself to death over Sim's lifeless body. He wanted a woman who would stand up to him but not screech at him, who would respect him but not cower, who would love him and not betray him. Obviously, he was doomed to die without an heir.

He continued to walk silently through the woods until he saw a clearing. A little house stood there, listing to the west, with a pale, unholy sort of light spilling out the rounded windows. The air around it shimmered with some sort of magic that he couldn't quite see but he could certainly feel.

Apparently he had come to the right place.

He dragged his sleeve across his suddenly sweaty forehead and pressed on. It was just a woman, and an old one at that. He was weary and that had led him to imagine things that were not so. He had nothing to fear.

He hesitated in front of her door for far longer than he should have, then put his shoulders back and reminded himself that he'd seen a bloody score and seven autumns already and he wasn't about to die on the hearth of a woman who was—despite the rumors—nothing more than a brewer of potions to cure warts.

He took a deep breath, then rapped smartly on the door.

And for the briefest instant, he wondered if he might be so fortunate as to have her not answer.

The door opened suddenly and a woman stood there. Cameron

couldn't see her face, for the light from her fire was behind her, casting her into shadow.

"Are you the MacLeod witch?" he demanded in his most brusque tone. It wasn't that he was nervous; he was simply in haste. 'Twas best the witch understand from the start who was in command.

She tilted her head to one side. "Aye, I am," she said slowly.

Cameron found himself unreasonably relieved to find her Gaelic was intelligible. He wouldn't have been surprised to have had her babble in some sort of evil tongue that would cast a spell on him immediately.

If he believed in that sort of thing, which he most certainly did not.

"Did Jamie send you to fetch me?" she asked.

He considered giving her the truth, then decided against it. If she was expecting to be summoned by a Jamie, a Jamie he would be until he'd gotten her home. He was already going to hell for consorting with a witch. A bald-faced lie or two wouldn't make things any worse for him.

"Aye," he said briskly. "Come with me now."

"All right." She stepped back. "Let me get—"

"Nay," he interrupted. "Now."

"I have to bank the fire."

He would have done it for her, but he found that he couldn't cross her threshold. He stood in shadow with his hand extended into her home and fought the urge to shiver. To distract himself, he watched her move back across her floor to tend her fire. When she turned back toward him, he felt his mouth fall open.

Why in the hell had he thought the MacLeod witch would be an old hag?

Her hair fell over her shoulders in a riot of curls, framing a face that surely the very angels of heaven envied. She moved with a lithesome grace that left his mouth suddenly and quite appallingly dry. Well, at least she was dressed in black. That was something he'd expected and for some reason that made him feel slightly better.

Until she extinguished her lights with a loud click.

He swore to cover what would have been a gasp of horror, crossed himself quickly, then reached out and grabbed hold of her hand.

"Wait," she said, digging her heels in. "You didn't let me get my shoes."

"No time," he said, pulling her out of her house and around the corner. "I brought a horse."

"Do we need a horse?" she asked.

"I thought it might be useful," he said. "He's waiting for us just up the hill."

"But Jamie's is down the hill."

Of course. Who else would come for her but a MacLeod? He squeezed her hand. "Up the hill for the horse, *then* down the hill," he amended. "Hurry. We're late."

He pulled her after him before she could answer and quickly enough that she apparently lost her breath for any more questions. She didn't protest the haste or the path, though he felt things crunching under his boots and supposed those things hurt her feet. She didn't complain, though he heard her catch her breath a time or two.

She tripped and fell suddenly. He tried to save her, but he was not at his best and didn't manage it. He helped her back to her feet, then swung her up into his arms. She flung her arms around his neck and one of her hands hit some part of his sword. He felt her stiffen immediately.

"Put me down," she said in a low voice.

"Nay," he said without hesitation. "I need you."

She struggled, but he held her tightly and continued on.

"Do I have to draw your own stupid sword and clunk you over the head with it?" she demanded. "Put me down!"

"Be silent," he hissed, "lest you draw every MacLeod in Scotland down upon us. I've no intention of hurting you. I *need* you."

She stopped struggling. He knew she was glaring at him, but he ignored it. At least she wasn't drawing a wee dirk forth from some part of her witchly costume and plunging it into his eye. She said nothing, not even when he reached his horse and let her slide to her feet.

Once there, though, she turned immediately and bolted.

He caught her quickly, because he'd expected the like. He took her by the arms and drew her out from under the eaves of the forest. The clouds were too thick to allow the moon to give much light, but he could see her well enough just the same.

She was absolutely terrified. He could see it in her eyes.

"I need your aid," he said firmly, shaking aside the sudden pity he felt for her. "I give you my word I will return you to your hall, unharmed. Now, come. I've no more time to waste."

"Who are you?"

"I have no time—"

"Tell me who you are or I don't come."

He looked at her sharply. Terrified though she might have been, she certainly had spine.

And she was so fair, it hurt him just to look at her.

He loosened his grip on her arms slightly, so he didn't leave bruises. "I am Robert Francis Cameron mac Cameron," he said impatiently. "My healer is dead and I need you to see to my brother. *Now*."

She shivered, once, then she took a deep breath. "When were you born?"

"Why the bloody hell does that matter?" he asked in surprise.

"Answer my question, or I go home."

"Do you actually think you can?" he asked. He heard the edge to his voice, but it was too late to stop it and he didn't have time to apologize. He would try to be more respectful later, when Breac's life wasn't hanging in the balance.

"Actually, I do," she said coolly, peeling his fingers off her arms.

By the saints, had he thought the woman afraid? She was passing bold and seemingly unimpressed with the peril of her current situation. He snorted at her. "Get up on the horse, wench. I'll not answer anything."

"Then I won't come with you."

He folded his arms over his chest. "Actually, I think you will."

She opened her mouth to speak, then coughed instead. He thought it a ruse until she truly began to gasp. She turned away from him and gestured frantically to her back. He saw his chance to save his brother slipping through his fingers. Damnation, what next? Fergussons, MacLeods, and now a witch who was apparently so weak-constitutioned that she couldn't keep from choking herself to death? He cursed, then patted her back as gently as he could.

"Harder," she wheezed.

He obliged.

Then, before he realized she was far cleverer than he'd given her credit for being, she had elbowed him so hard in the ribs that *he* doubled over with a gasp. She took his arm, backed into him, then with a mighty heave, flipped him over herself.

He landed flat on his back, looking up into rain that seemed to have begun just for him.

He lay there, stunned, for a handful of moments until he could breathe again. He heaved himself to his feet with a string of curses, then looked around him.

The witch was very fast, he would give her credit for that.

But so was he. He had to sprint to catch her, but catch her he did. He snatched her around the waist, then slipped on the wet grass. He rolled, taking her down to the ground with him with far more care than her treatment of him merited. He pinned her underneath him and glared down at her until he realized he had knocked the wind out of her. He heaved himself up and leaned over her with a hand on either side of her head.

She tried to knee him in the bollocks.

He leapt up, then stood—well away from any of her limbs—and watched her until she caught her breath. When she finally sat up, he held down his hands for her, only to have her try to sweep his legs out from under him.

"Bloody hell, woman, cease!" he bellowed, reaching out and jerking her to her feet.

"Let me go!" she shouted back at him.

He was almost surprised enough to do just that. He had never in his life had a woman speak to him so rudely.

Then again, he'd never abducted a witch before.

He hauled her into his arms and held her close where she couldn't do him any more damage. He tried to be gentle, truly, but he was afraid he hadn't been. She made no sound of distress save a squeak, but she was stiff as a sword in his arms. He supposed he couldn't blame her for that. He relaxed his embrace, but not overly. The wench was canny and surprisingly resourceful. He would do well to be on his guard around her.

"Well?" she gasped finally. "Are you going to answer my question, or do you want me to leave you unable to get up this time?"

He would have smiled if he'd had it in him. By the saints, she was an audacious wench. And she smelled very good. He was distracted enough by that to find himself giving an answer he'd not planned on giving.

"1346," he said. "Late in the autumn of that year, or so my dam claimed."

She went still. "And what is the year now?"

"Are you testing my wits?" he asked with a frown. "'Tis Year of Our Lord's Grace 1375, just as it was yesterday."

She pulled away far enough to look up at him. He was dumbfounded at the look in her eye. It was mixture of equal parts horror, surprise, and resignation. She looked at him for another moment, then bowed her head.

Something akin to a sob escaped her. It was just a little one, immediately stifled. He might not have noticed it if he hadn't had been holding her so tightly.

It was that small noise that undid him. He took his blood-caked hand and put it against the back of her head and held her close to him. He had no idea why the date should trouble her so, but perhaps there was an especial meaning to it that he couldn't divine.

He closed his eyes. The saints pity him, he was a fool. What he should have done was knock her over the head and carry her home like a sack of grain. Instead, he stood half an hour within enemy territory and held a witch in his arms while she gasped repeatedly for breath she couldn't seem to catch.

He realized at one point that she had put her arms around him and was holding on to him as if he were all that kept her from sliding into the yawning pit of hell.

He stroked her hair for quite a bit longer than he should have, then knew that they had to be away or they wouldn't be able to leave. He cleared his throat. "What's your name, lass?"

"Sunshine."

He almost smiled. It was certainly not the name for a crone, but what did he know? Perhaps her mother had had a well-developed sense of irony. "Are you the MacLeod witch, Sunshine?"

She let out a shuddering breath. "Aye."

"Will you help me?"

"Aye."

He shouldn't have felt such a sense of relief. After all, he was the Cameron and she was but a simple MacLeod clanswoman. She would do what he wanted because he demanded it of her.

Though he couldn't deny that the thought of her coming willingly, and without putting some sort of vile spell on him, was welcome indeed.

"All right, then," he said. "Let's be off."

She nodded, just once.

He pulled away, but kept her hand in his. She didn't try to pull away or stick him or fell him again. He swung up onto his horse, then held down his hand for her. She put her foot on his, then pulled herself up behind him.

"Hold on," he said.

"I will."

He put his heels to his mount's side and galloped toward home. Well, he had her.

He could only hope that the trip to fetch her would be worth the trouble.

Chapter 3

B *e careful what you wish for; you just might get it.*
  Sunny contemplated the truth of that as she held on to
Robert Francis Cameron mac Cameron and rode through the
dark and the rain toward what she could only assume was his ancestral home.

His *medieval* ancestral home.

Well, she had wished for a Highlander, hadn't she? She just
didn't remember wishing for a medieval one who instead of asking
her to go to dinner at the pub would demand that she go with him
to his hall and use her mystical powers to save his brother who was
probably already dead 650 years in the past.

Maybe she should have put her foot down about that monthly
appeasement meal Jamie insisted she attend. She'd tried to argue,
but apparently since Jamie was her laird and she was his healer,
that relationship necessitated the observation of certain formali-
ties and traditions. He'd made that quite clear when she'd knelt in
front of him, put her hands in his, and pledged him her fealty in a
particularly medieval way. She'd never dreamed it would lead to
her answering an unremarkable knock and finding herself pulled
back into the past.

She supposed she shouldn't have been surprised. Rumors of
spooky happenings on MacLeod lands were standard fare down
at the pub in the village. She herself believed in all sorts of Highland magic. She had seen ghosts. She was almost sure she'd seen
a fairy or two peeping out from the bunches of herbs she had had
hanging from her ceiling. She was also a firm believer in time
travel—along with everyone else in Jamie's family.

And why not, when Jamie had a map in his office that showed
all the places on his thousands of acres where one might step and
suddenly find himself in a century not his own?

She certainly didn't remember seeing her threshold on that
particular map, or any of the copies of the master map Jamie
made by hand for anyone who stayed any time at all on his land.

Obviously, an update needed to be made. She would tell him about that, just as soon as she saw him again.

Assuming she saw him again.

She shook her head in disbelief. How was it she had gone across Moraig's threshold literally thousands of times over the past year and never had it be anything but ordinary, yet tonight a Cameron—and she could only assume he was *the* Cameron—had reached into her house and pulled her back to 1375? She hadn't felt anything odd until she'd touched his hand. That was the second time in as many days that she'd touched a man's hand and gotten zinged for it.

She decided that thinking about it any further at the moment was probably a little unproductive. Her kidnapper, or borrower as he could perhaps more properly have been termed, was patting her hands, so perhaps she was sounding a little more panicked than she realized. She rested her forehead against the scabbard of that six-foot broadsword strapped to his back and tried to relax. Not even her all-purpose stress-relieving mantra was going to touch an event of this magnitude, apparently. She would just have to make do with a few deep breaths.

They rode like bats out of hell, but she was certain at least a couple of hours passed before she saw the faint outline of Cameron Hall in the gloom. She knew what it looked like in the twenty-first century because she and Madelyn had driven all the way there one day the summer before. It had been spectacular, retaining much of its medieval character but obviously having been added to and modernized with a very careful, thorough hand.

The medieval version was smaller, but no less sturdy. She looked at it by moonlight breaking through the clouds as they rode through the village and under the castle's outer gate. Her host jumped down off his horse in front of the hall door, then held up his arms for her. She let him help her down because she wasn't sure she could manage it with any grace by herself.

She was immediately towed after him into the great hall, across to the stairs, and up to the floor above. He led her into a large chamber with an enormous hearth. A fire burned brightly in it, which was nice because she was absolutely freezing. A man was lying motionless in front of the hearth with a woman kneeling next to him, rocking back and forth and keening.

Cameron looked at her. "Well?"

Sunny swallowed. "That's your brother?"

"Aye. What will you have me do?"

"Get rid of the woman," Sunny said without hesitation, "then bring me all the herbs you have and whatever you have to drink that's strong. I'll also need a knife."

"Can you save him?"

"I don't know yet," Sunny said.

Cameron pulled a knife out of his boot, handed it to her haft first, then strode over and hauled the red-haired woman up and into his arms. He said nothing, not even when she scratched him and cursed him and beat on him with her fists. He merely carried her out of the room without comment.

Sunny walked over to the fire and knelt next to Cameron's brother lying there on a plaid, his arms crossed over himself. He looked a great deal like Cameron, with dark hair and exceptionally handsome features. There were no lines of pain on his face, so perhaps he was past feeling anything. That was a blessing, no doubt. She set the knife down on the floor, then set to work. She placed his arms down by his sides, then gingerly pulled away the cloth that covered his belly.

There was a gaping hole in his abdomen, as if someone had skewered him with a sword, then twisted the blade several times. Even if by some miracle he lived, he would probably never walk again. Her knowledge of anatomy was excellent, her experience with herbal medicine was extensive, and her theoretical familiarity with dressing field wounds was as complete as Patrick MacLeod had been able to make it, but none of it was going to save the man lying before her.

But she would do what she could anyway.

Cameron burst back into the room, carrying several small cloth sacks in his hands and a leather skin full of liquid under each arm. He set everything down next to her on the floor.

"What else?" he asked.

"Boil water in a pot," she said. "Bring me needle and thread. Put more wood on the fire."

"What do you plan?" he asked.

"I'll sew him back together and pray he lives," she said in frustration, then she remembered whom she was talking to. She looked up at him. "I'm sorry. I was too frank."

He shook his head. "I prefer frank. I'll see to the water and the rest."

Sunny nodded, then set to sniffing the sacks of herbs he'd

brought her. The herbs weren't fresh, but in all honesty, she just didn't think it would matter. She set aside several things that would be useful, made another pile of things that wouldn't be, then got up and tended the fire herself. She paced impatiently until Cameron came running back into the chamber. He had shoved things into her hands, then barked at a serving lad to place the pot in the middle of the flames. Sunny waited until the boy had gone before she looked at Cameron.

"I'm going to do what I can," she said. "Help me when I need it. Stay out of my way when I don't."

He nodded grimly.

Sunny took a needle that looked more suited to mending saddles than flesh, held it into the fire, then wiped off the blackened end. She set it aside, then cut her skirt and worked several long threads out of it. They would be stronger than what Cameron had and marginally more sterile. She braided her hair, then tied the end of it with a strip she also cut from the hem of her skirt. She waited until the water was very hot before she dipped a cup into it. She singed her fingers on the fire licking the sides of the cauldron, but she didn't complain. She dropped herbs into the cup to steep, then washed her hands in the rest of the hot water. Not sanitary, but the best she could do. She took the needle and threaded it.

"Wash your hands," she said to Cameron, "then rip up clean cloths and soak them in the hot water."

He washed his hands in the water as she had, though he cursed as it burned his fingers. He then pulled up the hem of his long saffron shirt and started to rip it into strips.

"I said clean," she said sharply.

"This is all I have."

She closed her eyes briefly. Of course. "I'm sorry. Just use the cleanest part, then." She paused. "What's your brother's name?"

"Breac."

She shot him a faint smile. "Only one name for him?"

"My father had better control of my dam the second time around."

She smiled, then looked down at Breac and felt her smile fade. She put her fingers to his throat and couldn't believe he still had a pulse. It was a testament to either his strength or his stubbornness.

Cameron handed her the dampened cloths she'd asked for. She took one, sponged out some of the gore in Breac's gut, then set to work. She first sewed his intestines back together, then she turned to his belly muscles. She paused at one point and dragged her sleeve across her forehead. She picked up a bag of dried plantain.

"Make tea from that," she said wearily.

Cameron did so without question.

By the time she'd finished sewing muscle to muscle and closing the belly skin, Breac's pulse was very, very weak. She put her bloody hand on his forehead and bowed her head. Hot tears ran down her cheeks.

There hadn't been any hope, of course. Maybe there would have been if he'd been in a modern emergency room where the docs could have given him bag after bag of his proper blood type, put him on life support until he regained his strength, then pumped him full of antibiotics to kill the massive infection she knew he would have if he managed to survive the wound. But he was in fourteenth-century Scotland and his life was ebbing away.

"Sunshine? The tea is ready."

She put her fingers to Breac's neck, then looked at Cameron.

"We won't need it," she said very quietly.

He tightened his mouth, then took a deep breath and blew it out. He set the cup aside, then took his brother's other hand in his own. Tears were running down his cheeks, but he didn't seem to notice. He put his hand over Sunny's resting against Breac's neck.

Breac's pulse slowed.

And then it stopped.

Stillness descended. It wasn't unlike what she felt surround her at the birth of a child. The worlds of seen and unseen seemed for a moment to mesh and become one. Sometimes it was a peaceful meeting, sometimes a loud, noisy collision. With Breac, though, it was very quiet and very sad, as if heaven was sorry that it had to be so. Sunny looked down at a very handsome young man and wondered why it was that he had died while others lived.

"Is he gone?"

Sunny leaned over and put her ear against Breac's chest. There was no heartbeat, but she hadn't expected to find one. She remained there for a minute or two, then sat back on her heels and looked at Cameron.

"I'm so sorry," she said quietly.

He shook his head. "I didn't expect him to live." He looked at her. "I had to try."

"Of course you did."

He reached over and closed his brother's eyelids. He stared down at him for several minutes in silence, then looked at her. "Thank you."

"I wish there was something I could have done," she said very softly. "He was very strong to have lived as long as—"

She was interrupted by the door being flung open behind her. The woman who had been screaming before burst inside, came to a teetering halt, then began to scream again.

Sunny stood up to get out of her way, but found herself borne back to the ground with the woman's hands at her throat. Perhaps Patrick should have taught her how to defend herself against a grief-stricken, half-crazed medieval clanswoman.

The woman scratched, kicked, bit, and shrieked like a banshee. Sunny heard Cameron shouting, then felt him pulling the other woman off her. She managed to disentangle her hair from the woman's fists, then sat up in surprise.

"She killed him!" the woman shrieked, her eyes wild with grief and anger.

"Stop it, Gilly," Cameron said, pinning her arms down to her sides. "Of course she didn't."

"She's a witch," Gilly said, fighting against him. "I'll kill her in return for this!"

"Enough," Cameron said, struggling to keep her under control. "She is no witch and your husband was dead before he left the field."

Sunny watched Gilly continue to thrash about as if she were truly on the verge of losing her mind. Her fiery hair was long and stringy, and it hung down in front of her face, giving her a truly crazed appearance. At one point, she managed to get Cameron's hand close enough to bite him. Cameron bellowed and cursed her, but he didn't let her go.

Sunny listened to Gilly grow increasingly incoherent and wondered if now would be a good time to be heading home. She got to her feet and hesitated. It seemed disrespectful to ask Cameron if there was anything else she could do, but she didn't think she had a choice.

"If you don't need me anymore," she began slowly.

He nodded toward the door. "Go find something to eat downstairs. I'll see to her."

Sunny hesitated. "I'm so sorry about your brother."

That sent Gilly into a new round of shrill accusations. Cameron shook his head and nodded again toward the door. Sunny sighed and crossed the uneven wooden floor. She paused at the doorway and watched as Gilly finally freed herself from Cameron's arms and threw herself onto Breac. She shook him, as if she thought by doing so she might bring him back to life.

She stopped, then shot Cameron a look full of hate. "This is your fault," she said coldly. "You've ruined everything!"

Cameron folded his arms over his chest and merely looked at Gilly, silent and grim.

Sunny shut the door softly before she had to hear any more, then made her way back along the hallway. She found a garderobe and made use of it quickly, then went to look for water to wash her hands.

She stepped into the great hall and found that it went silent quite suddenly. Men in plaids looked at her suspiciously. One man crossed himself before he spat over his shoulder. Others followed suit.

Well, even she knew that wasn't good.

She went in search of the kitchen before she was the object of any more scrutiny. Why *wouldn't* the men think she was a witch? She was dressed in a leotard, with a long flowing skirt of modernly loomed linen, and she was covered in blood. If she hadn't known better, she would have been frightened of herself. All the more reason to be on her way as quickly as possible.

She found water, washed her hands, asked for and was given a bowl of the dregs of supper's soup and a hunk of stale bread. She ate and considered her next move. Obviously, the first thing to do was get out of Cameron's hall. She could hide in the woods and walk south when the sun came up. After all, dawn couldn't be too far away, could it?

She thought about going back out to the great hall, then thought better of it. If the men were already crossing themselves against her, it didn't make any sense to keep herself in their sights. She would simply wait for dawn, then be on her way. It could have been worse; she could have found herself in Cameron's dungeon.

She wrapped her arms around herself and shivered. She'd forgotten how cold a medieval castle could get when the fire had burned low. She looked up into the darkness of the kitchen and thought warm thoughts. It wouldn't be long, then she would be sitting in front of Moraig's fire after having run out the tank of water in the shower Jamie and Patrick had built her in the fall. She might even go so far as to indulge in a small cup of hot chocolate. She never kept things like that in her house for herself, though she did humor Madelyn by stocking them for her. When she got home, she thought she just might have to raid the stash.

She took a deep breath, then closed her eyes. She heard the hall beyond the kitchen settling down and she could no longer hear Gilly screaming upstairs, though very far off she thought she heard another woman weeping.

What a brutal life.

She would be very glad to not be a part of it for much longer.

Chapter 4

Cameron sat next to his brother, who lay dead on the floor in front of the fire, and listened to the absolute silence. Gilly had finally fallen asleep next to Breac, her bloody hand resting on his chest. Her accusations during the night had been shrill and unending. Cameron had said nothing to her out of respect for his brother and how that brother would have wanted his wife to be treated, but now that she slept he could admit that he was exceedingly relieved not to have to listen to her anymore. She would no doubt wake and begin to scream again, but he supposed he couldn't blame her.

He felt a little like shouting himself.

His first instinct had been to wrap his plaid about himself, stick several dirks down his boots, then slip into Simon Fergusson's hall and slay him in his sleep. He supposed that he could have sent quite a few more Fergusson clansmen to hell after their laird, but he supposed he couldn't kill the entire clan single-handedly—though he might just attempt it the next time they dared raise a sword against a Cameron.

He turned away from thoughts of revenge and looked at his brother. He watched Gilly sleep next to him and wondered absently how Breac had borne being wed to her. She was unpleasant, argumentative, and plain. Cameron generally didn't judge a woman by the fairness of her face, but he would have thought that since she had all those other faults, she might have at least been easy to look at. Cameron knew Breac had thought wedding Gilly Fergusson would bring a measure of peace to their clans.

A deadly miscalculation, to be sure.

Cameron rubbed his hands over his face and dragged his mind back to what needed to be done. He would have to see to the burying soon. He would need to send a message to the Fergusson and let him know how many he'd lost so he would understand what his arrogance had cost him. Generally that was his favorite part of a battle. Today, though, he had no stomach for such grim details. It wouldn't matter how many men they lost, those bloody idiotic Fergussons would continue to come against him, continue to waste the blood of their young men to appease the egos of the old, continue to receive his messenger with the number of their dead. Nothing would change.

Only he wouldn't have his brothers fighting with him anymore.

The door opened. He half expected to see Sim come bounding inside, all smiles, frothing at the mouth about some ridiculous adventure that would involve glory, cattle, and potential death. But it wasn't Sim, it was Giric. Giric looked at Breac, looked a bit longer at Gilly, then leaned back against the door frame.

"I thought you might want to see to the burying now."

Cameron blinked. "Is it day already?"

Giric frowned. "Didn't you notice?"

Cameron shook his head wearily. "I hadn't, actually. How many dead on the field?"

"We've lost six men. Fergussons lost twenty-five. But that isn't all."

Cameron grunted. Too many of his own lads dead for his taste, but there was nothing to be done about it now. He contemplated that for a moment or two, then the remainder of Giric's words sank in. He looked up. "Who else, then?"

"The witch."

Cameron nodded absently, then he realized what his cousin had said. He looked up in surprise. "The *MacLeod* witch?"

Giric lifted his shoulder in a half shrug. "They're trying her right now down at the loch—"

Cameron leaped to his feet. "And you didn't stop it?"

"Her beauty alone is suspect—"

"Giric, you're a bloody fool," Cameron snarled as he strode across the chamber and pushed past his cousin.

The sun was coming up over the eastern hills as he ran across the courtyard. He cursed as he sprinted through the village and across the meadow. If he found her alive, 'twould be a miracle, and if he found her dead, 'twould be his fault.

It was only a handful of moments later that he was pushing his way through the cluster of men at the edge of the water. He didn't even bother taking off his boots before he waded in himself. He jerked a pair of his men away so he could see what was happening.

Well, Sunshine MacLeod was half drowned, that's what was

happening. She might have been able to keep her feet if she hadn't been having them continually kicked out from underneath her. Perhaps the lads thought it would be easier to keep her underwater that way. He knew all this because he watched it happen once more before he could get to her. He clapped a hand on Brice, his fourth cousin twice removed, and shoved him out of the way. He had to dive under the water himself to get Sunshine back up. She didn't even cough as she surfaced.

He bent, put his shoulder against her belly, then straightened. She was completely limp, damn Giric and the lads to hell. He fought against the water and hurried to the shore, stumbling as he did so. He snarled curses at the villagers, whom he didn't blame, and his men, whom he most certainly did.

"Give the gel room to breathe," he snapped.

They all backed away, crossing themselves.

Cameron swept them all with a look. The villagers turned and scuttled away. His men followed suit, though certainly more slowly. Soon only Giric was left there, watching him silently.

Cameron laid Sunshine gently on the ground, then turned her over onto her side and whacked her firmly on the back several times. She coughed up water enough, to be sure, but she didn't rouse. He continued to force more water from her by pressing on her belly, but there came a point where he could see that his efforts weren't going to be of any more use. At least she was breathing. Perhaps that was all he could hope for. He looked at his cousin.

"Well done," he said coldly.

Giric only shrugged. "The safety of the clan is *my* first thought, as always. I never would have brought such a creature into the hall—"

Cameron shot him a look that had him, for a change, shutting his mouth. Giric was a dangerous fool, but a stupid one and perhaps all the more unpredictable because of it. It was no secret that Giric believed he should have been leading the clan. He conveniently forgot that Cameron's father, not his own, had been the laird before him, and that his own father had thought him particularly unsuited to leading anyone anywhere but astray. Cameron didn't trust him, but he kept him close. It was easier that way to see when he would strike.

"I wonder that she's still breathing," Giric said suspiciously, obviously unable to keep his mouth shut. "Surely that says much."

"She's no witch," Cameron said with a snort. "If she had been, Breac would be alive, wouldn't he?"

"Perhaps she's not a very good one."

Cameron looked up at him evenly. "If you want my sword going into your belly and out through your back, keep talking."

Giric smirked. "You don't have your sword."

Cameron realized with a start that his cousin had that aright. "Then I'll just use yours."

"Will you?"

Cameron stood up. "Aye. Care to test it?"

Giric only folded his arms over his chest. "I would be more careful where I laid my blade, cousin, were I you. You never know when you might find it being all that stands between you and many hands wielding death."

"I'll remember that," Cameron said blandly.

Giric gave Sunshine another very long look, then turned and walked away. Cameron watched him go, wished rather acutely for the comforting weight of his sword strapped to his back, then decided there was nothing to be done about it. He had knives in his boots and two wits to rub together. He would gain his hall without trouble.

He picked Sunshine up in his arms and quickly walked back the way he'd come. The village streets were empty, but he was sure he was being observed. His people were no doubt crossing themselves furiously and looking for whatever charm of ward they might have had lying about their houses to use in protecting themselves against evil—all whilst a beautiful, innocent woman lay unconscious in his arms.

He entered his great hall, glared at his men as he passed them, then made his way up to his bedchamber. Gilly was no longer there, but Breac was still lying in front of the fire. Cameron sincerely hoped he wouldn't be placing Sunshine next to him come sunset. He laid her on his bed, then looked down at her. She couldn't stay as she was; she would catch the ague and die. Obviously, her clothes would have to go.

Unfortunately, he could hardly bring himself to touch them.

Her skirt was made of a sort of fabric he'd never before seen in his life, not even in Edinburgh on the one occasion he'd traveled there in his youth. He wasn't overly superstitious, but he couldn't deny what he faced at present.

Magic, obviously.

But he wasn't a squeamish gel, and the woman before him would catch her death if he didn't aid her. He drew his knife out of his boot and slit her skirt from waist to hem before he could think about it anymore. He pulled it out from under her, then quickly cast it into his fire before he had to touch it overmuch. He cast more wood onto the fire to build it up, then took a deep breath and turned and walked back over to the bed.

Sunshine's remaining gear covered her from wrist to ankle and was made of cloth equally magical and unusual. He cut it all from her. He didn't even allow himself to wonder about what she was wearing under that layer of cloth. He cut those things from her as well and consigned the lot to the fire. He didn't look at her as he put her under the covers.

Well, not much.

He went and stood next to his brother's body and watched the flames consume with difficulty what Sunshine had worn. He didn't want to think about what he'd just seen, but he couldn't help himself. There wasn't a soul alive who wore clothing so fine—or so odd. Perhaps she was a witch after all and he had put his hand to something so unearthly that he wouldn't escape unscathed.

Then again, he was fairly certain that no witch alive could possibly be that beautiful under her clothes.

The soft knock on the door behind him startled him. He turned and saw one of his wee serving maids standing just inside his bedchamber.

"My laird, do you need aught?" she asked timidly.

Cameron forced himself to smile reassuringly. "Food, Brianna, if you would. Food and drink. Also, find Brice and send him to me, won't you?"

The girl bobbed a curtsey, then fled. Cameron watched her go, then turned back to the fire. It was smoking terribly as it strove to consume Sunshine's clothing. He threw yet more wood on, ignored the unsettling smell the cloth produced as it burned, and waited. Finally, he heard a man clear his throat uncomfortably.

"Cameron?"

Cameron turned and smiled. "Was it your idea, Brice?"

Brice shifted uncomfortably. "What?"

"The idea to drown a woman whose only crime was to agree to help me try to save Breac? Did you think that up all on your own, or did someone help you?"

"Ah," Brice began, "Gilly and Giric wondered and that led me to wondering . . ."

Cameron motioned for him to come in. He went to stand by the bed and waited for his cousin to join him.

"Look at her," Cameron said mildly. "Look at what you almost killed because you're stupid."

Brice spluttered. "But she's a witch—"

Cameron grabbed a fistful of his cousin's hair and forced his head down close to Sunshine's face. "There are no witches, you dolt," he growled. "Just beautiful women, like this one. And if she dies, so do you." He released him with a shove. "Go think on that. Don't let me see you until I'm sure she won't precede you to your grave."

Brice shot him a look of hate, then stomped from the chamber, cursing him viciously.

And all was yet again right in Cameron Hall.

Cameron sighed, then put his cousin out of his mind. No sense in wasting any more thought on that one until he was forced to. He pulled up a stool next to the bed and put his hand on Sunshine's face. She wasn't cold, which meant she lived still, and she wasn't hot, which meant her fever hadn't begun yet. She was breathing. He supposed he couldn't ask for more than that.

He pulled the blankets up to her chin, then rested his hand on her forehead and waited.

Brianna returned, carrying a tray which she almost dropped as soon as she saw him. Cameron jumped up and caught it before she did. She was trembling badly. Cameron looked at her for a minute, then shut the door with his foot.

"What is it, Brianna?"

She wrung her hands in her apron. " 'Tis Giric," she said miserably.

Cameron looked at the tray in his hands, then at her. "Should I drink the soup?"

She nodded.

"The wine?"

She looked very pale all of a sudden.

Cameron set the tray down on the floor, then pointed to the stool. "Sit. I'll return."

She sat down and looked at him, mute, her eyes wide with fear.

Cameron picked up the cup and went to hunt down Giric. He

found him standing at the entrance to the kitchens, chatting up a buxom serving wench. Cameron handed his cousin the wine.

"Drink."

Giric paled. "I'm not thirsty."

"And I say you are," Cameron said in a low voice. "Drink, or I'll pour it down your throat."

Giric reached for the cup, then flinched suddenly. The goblet slid through his fingers and clanged against the stone of the floor. He smirked. "Thought I heard someone behind me."

"You did."

Giric blinked. "Who?"

"Death," Cameron said distinctly. "And believe me when I tell you, he will come for you long before he comes for me." He leaned in close. "Don't try to poison my wine again or you'll find yourself staring up at the sky with my knife in your belly."

Giric laughed loudly, though not easily. "Poison your wine? What a fanciful imagination you have, Cameron."

"It keeps me alive," Cameron muttered. He walked into the kitchen, fetched wine for himself, then gave his cousin one last lingering look of warning before he retreated back upstairs. He shut his bedchamber door and bolted it, then looked at Brianna sitting on the stool. "You'll remain here tonight, gel. And I'd suggest you stay away from Giric."

She nodded, then went to sit on the floor near the fireplace. She looked away from Breac and shivered.

Cameron ate, tasted the wine himself, then wondered if he dared try to force any of it down Sunshine.

Her breathing was shallow and rapid. Cameron set the wine aside, then put his ear to her chest. He could hear gurgling inside her, but he'd done all for her that he knew how to do. He pulled one of her arms from under the blankets, then took her hand in both his own and bowed his head.

All he could do was wait.

Three days later, he sat in the same place and still held Sunshine's hand. She was burning with fever. He supposed that was better than being cold as death, which she'd also been. He smoothed her hair back from her brow, then took the cloth Brianna gave him and bathed her face with it. It didn't do much to relieve the heat that burned within her, but he had nothing else to try. He had no healer. The last woman who'd dared call herself one had met her fate in the loch.

His clan was, he had to admit, a damned suspicious brood.

He thought back over the past pair of days. He'd buried his brothers, buried Sim's betrothed, then stood silently as the rest of his men had been laid to rest. He'd seen so much death that for the first time in his life, he'd seen enough.

He had finished with the priest earlier that morning, then retreated upstairs and actually knelt beside his own bed and prayed for deliverance. And he'd prayed for the woman in front of him who had been willing to help him but had been repaid with harm.

He turned to look at his hearth. Breac no longer lay there and the floor had been scrubbed. The herbs, though, remained where Sunny had left them. He rose with a groan, then went to fetch them. He sniffed, but that didn't help him overmuch. It wasn't that he didn't have some knowledge of healing and such. He could find plantain to take away the sting of nettles. He could survive for quite some time on whatever he could gather from meadows and forests. Trying, however, to identify the contents of bags of very old weeds that had surely lost any virtue they might once have had—and attempting that on the handful of hours of sleep he'd had in the past three days—was just more than he could manage at the moment.

"We'll make tea," he said to Brianna, selecting a bag or two at random. "I'm sure it will help."

Brianna nodded and went to fetch him water. He knew she would return instantly. She ran everywhere she went when she was outside his chamber. If she didn't return within minutes, he went to fetch her. He'd only found her once being cornered by Giric. He'd shoved his cousin out of the way, sent Brianna back upstairs, then snorted at the suggestion that he was bedding Brianna and the witch both.

Giric grew bold, it seemed.

He waited at the door until he saw Brianna hastening down the passageway toward him. He took the pot of water from her, tossed handfuls of dried herbs into it, then put it on the fire to boil. He had no idea if it would serve Sunshine, but it couldn't hurt.

"My laird, she stirs."

Cameron spun around and watched Sunshine turn her head. It was the first thing she'd done in three days. Maybe it was the smell of the herbs instead of death. He had to admit it cheered him as well, no matter which herbs had been responsible for it. He looked at Brianna and smiled.

"Well," he said, pleased.

"A good sign," Brianna offered.

"Aye, lass," he agreed.

Of course, Sunshine moving could have been the last throes before death as well, but he didn't say that. He drew out a cup of tea, fished the herbs out with his fingers and threw them into the fire. They hissed and smoked, but the smell was a far better one than what Sunshine's clothing had produced, so he didn't complain.

He carried the cup over to the bed and sat down on his stool. He slipped his hand under Sunshine's head and lifted it up, then put the cup to her lips. She managed to drink a few sips, before she turned her head away.

"More, my laird?" Brianna said hesitantly.

"Give her a few minutes, lass," he said, more hopeful than he'd been in days, "then we'll try a bit more."

"Of course, my laird."

Cameron looked at the woman lying in his bed and sighed deeply. A pity he hadn't met her before the battle, before he had a duty to wed Breac's widow and raise his brother's son as his own. A pity he couldn't have met her when he had been free to love where he might have desired it.

A pity she was a MacLeod.

Unfortunately, he knew his duty. Whatever it took to see the clan kept safe, whatever it required to see that it continued to exist, that he would do. And that would not include having anything to do with a MacLeod witch.

But 'twas a pity all the same.

Chapter 5

Sunny woke, then wished she'd stayed asleep. She felt dreadful, as if every cell in her body had been put through a grinder. She groaned as she tried to make herself more comfortable, then opened her eyes gingerly to see where she was and what had happened to her.

Determining the second was easier. She had been taken to a lake and drowned. Well, obviously not completely drowned because she was alive, but the fact that she was still breathing air instead of water was probably an accident. She thought back further to the events that had led to her little unintended snorkeling trip.

She had woken at some point close to dawn after a night spent sleeping in the kitchen and found herself overpowered. She had used every trick Patrick had taught her, broken a nose or two, and left several other men on the ground, clutching their groins, but there had been just too many men too determined to see if she really was a witch to get away from them all.

It had never made sense to her, that whole business of dunking a woman to see if she was a witch. If a woman drowned, then she was innocent—but dead. If she floated, then she was a witch and they drowned her anyway—and she was still dead. Perhaps logic wasn't much of a requirement in the Middle Ages.

She supposed that someone had rescued her, finally, which was why she found herself in a bed instead of at the bottom of the loch. But who was that gallant soul?

And why was she naked?

She looked up at the ceiling. It was a nice ceiling, so it was a safe bet she wasn't in a villager's house. She turned her head and saw the fireplace set into the wall. That was the same fireplace she'd knelt in front of when she'd been trying to tend Breac mac Cameron. He was no longer there, so perhaps they had buried him already. There was a servant girl sleeping there now. Sunny looked at her for a moment or two, then realized they weren't alone. Someone shifted in a chair that sat to the left of the hearth.

She took a deep breath, then looked to see who it was.

Robert Francis Cameron mac Cameron was leaning back in that chair with his arms folded over his chest and his feet crossed at the ankles, watching her. He looked absolutely exhausted.

Too bad it took nothing away from his handsomeness.

She looked at his feet because looking at his face made her feel not only a little weak in the knees but extremely conspicuous lying in his bed, again, stark naked.

His feet were shod in rather rustic but imminently functional brown boots. They were very worn, though, as if he didn't have the luxury of running into Inverness to Marks & Spencer for a new pair. The haft of a knife stuck out of each of those boots. That was nothing she hadn't seen before in Patrick's family, nor were the bare knees that weren't nearly covered enough by a rustic looking plaid—a *very* rustic plaid, actually, though the Cameron's clothes were nicer than she would have expected. The bedchamber she was lying in was sturdy and well built, and the bed actually quite comfortable. Perhaps the Camerons were better off than most.

Then again, perhaps she just didn't have all that much experience with medieval lairds still living in their medieval surroundings.

She took a deep, steadying breath, then allowed herself the pleasure of looking at his face. She found herself rather glad, all things considered, to be lying down.

He was just stunning—and she wasn't unaccustomed to good-looking men. James MacLeod was very attractive. His cousin Ian just as easy on the eye. Patrick MacLeod made the word gorgeous hang its head in shame at the thought of applying itself to him. She'd stared at those faces for over a year and become accustomed to being in the presence of absolute male beauty.

So why was it she could hardly look at Cameron mac Cameron without having her mouth go dry?

His dark hair hung down to his shoulders, framing a face made up of features that were softened just enough to make them handsome and not sharp. His eyes were so blue, she could tell their color from across the room. And his mouth . . . well, it was just a marvel. She was half tempted to crawl out of bed and go over to touch it.

That mouth quirked up on one side. "Finished, lass?"

She met his amused gaze. "Fever," she said promptly. "I'm delirious."

"No doubt," he said with a smile. He yawned hugely, rubbed his hands over his face, then shook his head sharply. He got to his feet and stretched, then started across the room. "I think you're whole. I have business."

"Wait," she said, sitting up and clutching the sheet to her throat. "Where are you going?"

He stopped and looked down at her. "Out."

"Where are my clothes?"

"Burned."

She retrieved her jaw from where it had fallen. "Who took them off me?"

He leaned against the foot post of his bed and looked at her mildly. "I did."

"But—"

"I didn't look at you whilst I was at it."

"You didn't?" she asked in surprise.

"Well," he said, dragging the word out quite a while, "no more than a polite glance or two."

She felt unaccountably and uncomfortably hot. She would have put her hands to her cheeks, but that would have meant letting go of her sheet and that would have drawn attention to the fact that she was still completely without any clothes.

Cameron nodded toward a trunk in the corner. A dress lay draped over it. "That's for you."

"Oh," she said, feeling vastly relieved. "Thank you."

He pushed away from the post and started toward the door. He put his hand on it, then stopped and looked at her. "Are you whole, in truth?"

"I'll live," she managed. "I have you to thank for the rescue, don't I?"

"You do." He smiled and shrugged. "I don't believe in witches, as it happens."

"Yet you rode onto MacLeod land and fetched me."

"I do believe in healers." He studied her for a moment or two. "Are you a MacLeod?"

She pulled the covers up closer to her chin. "Are you fighting the MacLeods?"

"No more than usual, I suppose," he said with a smile.

She wasn't sure if that made her feel better or not. "I'm not actually a MacLeod by birth," she admitted. "My sister is wed to one and they accepted me because of it. The laird is pleased with my knowledge of herbs." She paused. "I'm sorry that knowledge didn't serve your brother."

"He was dead the moment the sword pierced him. Besides, there's nothing to be done about it now, is there?" He looked at her thoughtfully. "If you're not a MacLeod, what are you?"

"A Phillips, though I'm actually a MacKenzie by blood." She looked at him quickly. "Are you at war with MacKenzies?"

"The MacKenzies are too far away to trouble ourselves over, so I suppose you're safe." He leaned his shoulder against the door and folded his arms over his chest. "Does your sister call you Sunshine or does she have a pet name for you?"

"Sunny."

"Sunny," he repeated. He smiled at her for a moment or two, then straightened abruptly. He turned away and opened the door. "Take the clothes. I'm sure you'll want to get home today."

He walked out the door and slammed it shut behind him before she could say anything else.

Sunny put her hands to her cheeks and found that they were very warm indeed. Fever, no doubt, not the fact that she was blushing furiously. Or at least she had been a moment ago. Now, she was rather cold.

She surely hadn't expected that Robert Cameron would have wanted to keep her, but his abrupt departure wasn't exactly flattering. Well, she had no business looking twice at a medieval laird—no matter what he had done for her. He felt responsible for bringing her to his keep, no doubt, and hadn't wanted her death on his hands.

But now she was alive and she was finished in the past. There was no time like the present to get back to her future.

She considered the complete improbability of that thought, then pushed it aside. She would philosophize later, when she was sitting in front of Moraig's hearth with a cup of hot chocolate in her hands. She might even go so far as to borrow some marshmallows from Madelyn.

She managed to get her feet on the floor, but had to sit there for several minutes until her head stopped spinning. She finally got up and staggered toward the opposite side of the room. The girl lying before the fire leaped up and rushed over to her.

"Let me aid you, my lady," she said, taking Sunny by the arm.

Sunny was grateful for the help. She let the girl help her the rest of the way across the chamber, then sat on the trunk while the girl pulled the dress over her head. It was a little disconcerting to be without any sort of underwear, but there was nothing to be done about it. Besides, she wouldn't be there long enough for it to be a problem. She looked at the teenager.

"Thank you, ah . . ."

"Brianna, my lady."

"Thank you, Brianna," Sunny said gratefully. "I'm not very steady yet."

"The fever was hard upon you," Brianna said. "Laird Cameron was worried, though I dinna suppose he'll show it. He never left your side, my lady. Well," she amended, "he did, but only to bury his brothers."

Sunny closed her eyes briefly. She couldn't imagine having to bury her sister with her own two hands. It was no wonder those MacLeod men were tough as flint when this was the reality they had grown up with.

Once her head had cleared enough to allow her to get up, she thanked Brianna again for her help, then shuffled across the room. She shut the door behind her and made her way down the passageway. It took her an appalling amount of time to get down the stairs, but she managed them as well.

She had to rest at the bottom for quite some time. She looked out over the great hall, though she suddenly wished she hadn't. Men looked at her, then deliberately crossed themselves. That didn't surprise her, but it did alarm her. She couldn't manage another trip to the lake. She didn't have the strength to fight and she didn't dare hope that Cameron would be there to rescue her again. Obviously, the sooner she was out of Cameron Hall and off Cameron land, the better off she would be.

She gathered the tattered remains of her energy and walked to the front door, struggling not to betray her weakness. No one stopped her, no one called her anything untoward, no one was waiting outside to carry her where she didn't want to go. She pulled the door shut behind her, stumbled down the steps to the courtyard, then hurried across it as quickly as she could. She didn't expect to see Cameron and she didn't.

It was better that way.

She stopped outside the front gates, then took her bearings. She wasn't a particularly good navigator, but she knew where Cameron Hall was in relation to Moraig's little house. She shuffled through the village as quickly as possible, then turned south and east. She wasn't moving very well, but at least she was on her feet. It could have been worse.

The sun was high in the sky before she knew she wasn't going to be making it any farther that day. She sat down on a rock and wondered who would capture her first: Cameron's suspicious men or those even more suspicious MacLeods.

Neither alternative was good from where she was sitting.

She wanted to get up, but somehow, despite the potential danger, she simply couldn't. She slipped off her rock to the ground, leaned over, then lay down. The ground was cold but at least the grass wasn't wet. For once, she appreciated a bit of Scottish sunshine. Maybe all she needed was a little nap to help her shore up her strength for another push.

She thought she might have dozed. She was almost certain she had dreamed—of rain, of all things. Only this wasn't a fine Scottish mist, or a dry rain, it was a full-blown storm. She heard the thunder before she managed to get her eyes open to see what the clouds were going to unleash on her hapless self.

But the sky was blue.

Sunny realized that the rumbling was horse's hooves against the ground. She sat up with a start, but couldn't bring herself to run. It was just a lone horseman anyway. Perhaps he wouldn't trouble himself to finish her off and would simply continue on by.

She realized, as he came closer, that it was Cameron. He reined in his horse a handful of feet away from her.

"You haven't gotten far," he noted.

"I'm tired."

He held down his hand. She sighed and crawled unsteadily to her feet. She looked at his foot in the stirrup and wondered if she could possibly get hers all the way up there to help herself up behind him.

Nope, not happening. She looked up at him. "I can't."

He held down both his hands. "Try."

She took his hands and tried, but still couldn't manage. She could hardly keep herself upright, much less get herself onto his horse. He slid down to the ground with a curse, cupped his hands, then tossed her up into his saddle. He swung up behind her without any effort at all.

That was almost enough to make her want to lie down again.

He wrapped an arm around her and took the reins. "Let's get you home."

"I can get there," she protested. "Eventually."

He snorted. "Aye, perhaps in a fortnight or two. I'll see you there today instead."

She knew she should have objected a bit more, but she was just too tired to. Besides, Cameron could get her back to Moraig's, then get himself home without getting himself killed, couldn't he?

He'd certainly done it before.

"Thank you, Cameron," she said with a deep sigh.

"That is *my laird* to you, wench."

She smiled. "I already have a laird, thank you just the same."

He grunted, then pulled her back to rest against his chest. Sunny closed her eyes as he put his arms around her and held her upright as they rode. She was, she had to admit, enormously grateful for the help. She couldn't have walked for more than an hour or two already, yet it had almost done her in. If it hadn't been for the thoughts of a hot shower and a roaring fire, she might not have even managed to keep herself upright on Cameron's horse.

She looked at his hands holding the reins in front of her and studied the scars there. They were obviously things he'd gotten either training or in battle. She reached out and trailed her finger over them, wondering how old he'd been when he'd earned them, where he'd been, whom he'd been fighting.

Then she realized what she was doing. She pulled her hand away abruptly only to have him take it and put it back over his. He covered that hand with his other and squeezed gently.

Perhaps he was just as delirious from lack of sleep as she was.

They rode without haste south. It was late afternoon when they reached the forest to the north of Moraig's house. Cameron reined in his horse under a tree, then swung down. He looked around for a moment or two, then held up his arms for her. She put her hands on his shoulders and let him help her to the ground.

He set her gently on her feet, then looked down at her. "We'll walk from here."

"You shouldn't," she said seriously. "Really. I'll be fine on my own."

He snorted. "Woman, you can scarce keep yourself upright. I will see you back to your house."

"But what about your horse?"

"He'll wait."

"And if he doesn't?"

"I'll run home. I've done it before." He picked her up in his arms.

"Cameron!"

"You have no shoes."

"But—"

"Quiet, wench. I'm being gallant."

Well, if that was the case, who was she to argue? She surrendered and put her arms around his neck. She tried not to notice that she was approximately six inches from his face and his mouth was just as beautiful—in a manly sort of way, of course— up close as it was from far away. She pressed her face against his hair in self-defense. He might have shivered. She knew she had.

Why did he have to be 650 years older than she was and light- years out of her league?

They reached Moraig's hut—or what would be Moraig's hut eventually—sooner than she would have liked. Sunny wondered if Cameron was completely worn out from carrying her, but he set her down without grunting and didn't even stretch or complain. He merely put his arm around her shoulders and led her around the corner to the front door.

Sunny pulled up short, then forced herself to relax. It didn't look like her front door, but then again this was the medieval side of that time gate. She supposed she shouldn't have expected anything else.

She turned to Cameron. "Thank you for bringing me back," she said quietly.

"Thank you for coming with me in the first place."

She wanted to say something else, but what else was there to say? *Come with me? Don't let me go?* Neither was possible.

Before she could think up a clever response, he had pulled her into his arms. Sunny closed her eyes and put her arms around his waist and let him settle her close. It was madness to allow herself to enjoy it, but she couldn't help herself. He held her closely for several minutes, then kissed her hair and put her away from him.

"Go on, witch," he said gruffly. "Be off with ye."

Sunny took a deep breath, then turned and pushed open the door before she started to cry. She stepped over the threshold, then pulled up short.

There was nothing inside.

Not a single stick of anything.

She looked behind her, but Cameron was still there. He frowned. "Well?"

She wasn't panicked, no, not at all. She was probably just doing it wrong. Granted, she had no experience with time travel, but she remembered vividly being pulled from her time back to Cameron's. There had been something in the air. A tingle of something.

Or perhaps that had just been the touch of his hand.

She didn't feel the same thing at present, but she wasn't going to let that stop her. She took a deep breath, backed up, then stepped over Moraig's threshold again.

Nothing happened.

She backed up, tried again, only this time she closed her eyes and wished for a hot shower.

Nothing. Nada. Zip.

She went back outside and tried to look at it in a more pragmatic way. Much as she didn't want him to go, having Cameron near was distracting in the extreme. It made it very difficult to realize that what she should be wishing for was what lay on the other side of that door, not what was standing five feet behind her. She turned and looked at him.

"I think you should go."

He looked at her in consternation. "And leave you here alone?"

"I'm all right."

"I don't like it," he said slowly. He paused, then took a pair of steps closer to her. "I will do it, but I don't want to."

She realized that tears were running down her cheeks. It was because she was having trouble with the gate, not because she didn't want to leave him. She didn't know him. She was almost sure that if she *got* to know him, she wouldn't like him. He was bossy, aggressive, brusque, and—

One helluva kisser.

She threw her arms around his neck and held on. His mouth was a marvel, softer than she had imagined, more demanding than she'd expected, stealing her breath before she thought it was possible.

Just as quickly, she was holding on to nothing. He was standing again five paces away from her. Sunny wrapped her arms around herself.

"I'll be all right."

His look almost burned her to a crisp. "Very well," he growled, then he turned and strode away with a curse. He disappeared around the corner.

Sunny touched her mouth, then turned and faced Moraig's house again. She couldn't see it for her tears, but she knew it was in front of her. She knew she had to go through it because there was nothing for her in the past. Nothing at all.

She held out her hands and felt for the doorway, then crossed it before she could think better of it.

Chapter 6

Cameron stood under the eaves of a hut that was standing only because it was leaning against a sturdy tree and cursed silently. He shouldn't have held that bloody MacLeod witch. He certainly shouldn't have kissed her. What he should have done was left her in front of her house and walked away without a backward glance. 'Twas that damnable sense of honor his mother had instilled in him, no doubt, rearing its ugly head yet again. It just might be the death of him one day.

Unfortunately, he was too old to change now. He waved a fond farewell to his good sense and eased along the side of what was masquerading as a house to see what Sunny was about.

He didn't have to go far to discover it. She was cursing and weeping and stomping about so loudly, he almost bid her stop before she attracted every MacLeod ever spawned to her. It wouldn't have gone well for either of them. He was the Cameron and she was completely mad.

She was blethering on in Gaelic, then something that sounded a bit to his ears like French, then in perfect English. Well, perhaps her English wasn't perfect. She spoke her words strangely, though she was intelligible enough. He peeked around the corner and watched her as she continued to step back and forth over the threshold of the hut, growing increasingly frantic. Cameron pulled back and gave that some thought. She obviously expected to find something inside that wasn't there. He understood that, for as he'd looked over her shoulder he'd been equally surprised to find that the inside of the house was completely empty.

But the one he'd pulled her out of hadn't been.

He contemplated that for a bit longer before he realized that there was no more cursing coming from around the corner. He leapt forward in a panic only to find Sunny kneeling in front of the threshold, rocking herself and muttering in Gaelic things about gates through time, Xs on a map, and death to a certain MacLeod laird named James.

Well, the last he could certainly agree with.

He walked over to her and stopped next to her. "Sunny?"

She looked up at him quickly, her expression one of absolute anguish. "My sister calls me that."

He frowned. "Aye, so you said." Did she miss her sister so that his using that name would distress her so deeply? Or was it, the saints forbid, something of a more womanly nature that he couldn't immediately divine and wouldn't be happy to know about if he discovered it? He was not at his best when women wept.

But he was also nothing if not courageous, so he put his shoulders back and squatted down beside her.

"What is amiss here?" he said briskly. "Tell me of it and let's be about seeing to it."

She looked at him for several moments, her mouth working futilely—as if what she had to tell him was of such a monumental nature, she simply couldn't find words to express it.

Cameron did his damndest to ignore her mouth. He knew what it felt like under his and it took all his formidable amounts of self-control not to lean forward and taste it again.

He drew his hand over his eyes. By the saints, he was just as daft as the woman in front of him. There he was, less than half a league from Malcolm MacLeod's front door, and he was thinking less about his sword and more about Sunshine Phillips's mouth.

Madness, that.

He pulled her up to her feet and forced himself to concentrate on the problem at hand. "Why have the innards of your house disappeared? Did the MacLeods steal all your belongings whilst you were gone?"

She started to speak, then shook her head. "You wouldn't believe me if I told you."

"Of course I would," he said without hesitation.

"You wouldn't," she said just as firmly, "and even if I told you, you couldn't help me. I think the best thing you could do is get out of here before the MacLeods find you."

"I will *not* leave you here alone," he said sharply, "and I *can* help you. You forget who I am."

She smiled, though it wasn't an insulting smile. "I haven't forgotten who you are."

"Then be about answering my questions."

She looked at him for a very long moment or two, then nodded. "All right, I'll tell you. But let me see your hands first."

He blinked. "Why?"

"I want them comfortably away from anything with a hilt."

He held up his hands slowly.

She looked at them, looked at him, then took a deep breath. "Very well, here's the truth. This isn't just a doorway from the outside of this little house to the inside; it's a doorway through time."

He blinked. He heard the words, assumed they would thicken inside his poor head into something resembling a coherent thought at some point, then frowned when they didn't. Perhaps he'd missed something somewhere. "I don't think I heard you properly," he said.

She pointed toward the doorway. "On this side of that threshold is the year 1375. On the other side, through a gate you can't see, is the Future. The year 2005, to be exact."

She paused, no doubt to gauge his reaction. He had to admit, without hesitation, that he was too surprised to have any sort of useful one.

"That night when you came to fetch me, I was standing on the other side of the door over six hundred years from now," she continued. "I should be able to just walk over that threshold and get back to my time." She paused for quite a while. "Apparently, the gate isn't working."

He shut his mouth when he realized it had fallen open.

Bloody hell. How could a woman who was that beautiful, who smelled that good, who had such perfectly lovely teeth and bright eyes, be so thoroughly, completely, entirely, stark raving mad?

She must have seen his thoughts on his face because she backed up. Then she turned suddenly and bolted.

He caught her before she managed five paces. He wrapped one of his arms around her waist, the other around her shoulders, and pulled her back against him.

"Stop," he whispered against her ear. "Stop fighting me. Breathe in, Sunshine, and don't scream when you breathe out. I have no intention of hurting you."

"Your hand was on your sword."

"It wasn't."

"It *was*."

"I have bad habits," he said without hesitation, realizing that she had it aright. "That madness you spouted startled me, nothing more. I won't hurt you."

She didn't relax, but he understood that. The same thing happened to him when he knew someone was behind him, preparing to stab him. He rested his chin on her shoulder, hummed the most cheerful love song he could bring to mind, and kept her immobile.

"Breathe," he whispered. "In and out."

She did, though they were ragged breaths indeed. Finally, he felt her hands come up to rest over his arm. A sob escaped her, but she stifled it almost immediately. He was impressed. He wasn't accustomed to women who could do anything but shriek when they'd determined that giving vent to a womanly bout of weeping was the thing to do.

"A time gate," he said finally, turning the words over on his tongue. "From one century to another."

"Aye."

He had to work very hard to suppress a mighty snort of disbelief. It was simply the most ridiculous thing he'd ever heard. There were rumors, of course, of mysterious things happening on MacLeod soil, but this was beyond what foolishness even a giddy MacLeod could spew. Men were men and they lived and died in the years Fate had decreed for them.

Unless it was a MacLeod telling the tale, of course, and then anything was possible. Most of their long winter evenings were spent speculating on the fate of the laird James, who had apparently escaped death and gone on to some glorious paradise with his wife, Elizabeth. Cameron had always suspected the scatterbrained pair had left the keep for a bit of privacy, been assaulted by some plucky Fergusson, then been tossed by that same Fergusson into the loch where they had been resting comfortably on the bottom for the past sixty-four years.

He shouldn't have been surprised that Sunshine should have believed something that fit in with their tales so well, even if she were a MacKenzie by birth. Any MacLeod influence on a susceptible mind was obviously a bad one.

He closed his eyes and permitted himself a deep breath of a woman who smelled like flowers, then made his decision without hesitation. He would humor her for a bit, convince her afterward that she had been led astray, then he would carry her back to his keep where he would—

Wed Gilly, that's what he would do.

He suppressed a curse. He had never in his life regretted more his position in life than he did at that moment. If he'd been a simple clansman, he could have asked the lord for permission to use his threshold, taken Sunshine Phillips in hand, and handfasted with her. Surely he could have managed over the ensuing year and a day to convince her to stay with him. He might have even found a way to borrow the laird's priest for half an hour and wed her properly.

Unfortunately, he wasn't a simple clansman and he had a duty he couldn't shirk. He would have to be about the fulfilling of that duty very soon.

But perhaps not quite yet. Perhaps he could lay his duty aside for a bit longer and concentrate on the woman in his arms.

"Sunshine, are there any more of these gates you speak of?" he asked.

"There's one in the forest to the west of the keep."

Of course. He shouldn't have expected anything else. "Shall we attempt an assault on that one?"

She pulled away from him, then turned and looked at him in surprise. "You would help me?"

"Of course."

Tears streamed down her cheeks. She looked so grateful, *he* almost wept.

"Thank you," she whispered.

"Aye, well, I'm not one to deny a daft wench her little requests," he said gruffly, putting his arm around her shoulders. "We'll fetch my horse and ride so when we're attacked by scores of those pesky MacLeods, I'll nudge you off the back into their arms and be on my merry way. Though I'm not quite sure why I can't just take you to the keep."

"Because they won't know me," she said quietly.

He grunted, but said nothing else as he pulled her along with him. Daft wench. Beautiful, enchanting, *daft* wench.

And there he was, being swept into her madness.

He ignored the fact that her house hadn't been empty when he'd fetched her, or that her clothing had been like nothing he'd ever touched before, or that the way she'd stitched up his brother had been more expert than any healer he'd ever seen.

He picked her up in his arms at one point because, though she didn't complain, 'twas obvious that things were hurting her feet. She didn't protest. She merely put her arms around his neck and rested her cheek against his hair.

He quickened his pace. He had to get her out of his life before she drove *him* mad and his madness wasn't going to include any bloody time gates. It would include finding a secluded spot and bedding her repeatedly whilst he suggested to her that, no matter his station or hers, handfasting with him would be a good idea. He was damned sure he wouldn't last all the way home to find a priest if she blew in his ear much longer.

"I don't blame you for not believing me," she said at one point.

He latched on to the distraction gratefully. "I'm just sorry that a lass so lovely is obviously missing so many wits. But I'll take you where you want to go just the same, to prove you wrong. Then I'll take you home and lock you in my dungeon where you can't hurt yourself."

"How thoughtful of you."

"Altruistic to the last," he agreed.

She might have laughed, he supposed, but it was only a hint of one. He put her up on his horse, then swung up behind her. He knew very well where the MacLeod keep was, but he followed her directions just the same to test her. He was faintly surprised to find that she did indeed know her way about.

"Tell me again why we don't want to just ride up to Malcolm's front door?"

"Because he won't know me."

"Because you're not from the Year of Our Lord's Grace 1375."

"Exactly."

A chill went down his spine. He crossed himself surreptitiously, but he had to use her body since she was sitting in front of him, so he supposed it hadn't been all that subtle.

"Warding off evil, my laird?"

He grunted. "My laird, indeed. Finally, the wench accords me the respect due me and it takes an event of this import to wring it from her. I'll have you know, Sunshine, most fall to their knees and beg for mercy when I frown at them. You've shown me a distinct lack of respect."

She patted his arm around her waist. "You're not my laird."

But he would have gladly been so, he realized. He closed his eyes briefly and prayed for strength. He had to wed Gilly. He had to raise up his brother's children as his own, simply because if he didn't, Giric would and then the clan would go to hell. He wouldn't have been surprised to find Gilly's children disappearing on some long night and Giric returning home with blood on his hands. But even if he wasn't doomed to wed Gilly, he couldn't wed a MacLeod witch, no matter how tempting the thought suddenly was. His clan would never accept her, and he couldn't subject her to a lifetime of that sort of misery.

There came a point in the forest where Sunshine wanted to stop. He hopped down, then held up his arms for her. He held her away as he set her down, simply because he was so damned tempted to pull her against him and kiss her yet again. The farther away she was from him, the better for the remains of his self-control.

She looked at him for a moment, then leaned up and kissed his cheek.

"Thank you."

She was gone so quickly that his hands clutched nothing but air as he tried to reach for her. He settled instead for holding on to his horse's reins with one hand and loosening his sword in the sheath on his back with the other. No sense in not being prepared.

He watched Sunny go stand on several likely spots. He wasn't surprised to find that nothing happened.

The wench was beautiful, but completely muddled.

She shooed him away at one point. Cameron went, because she demanded it. He led his horse deeper into the shadows, put his hand on its withers, then waited. His horse was silent as the tomb. He was just as silent. Even Sunny was quiet, standing there for several minutes with her arms wrapped around herself.

And then came the sounds of a twig crunching under a boot and a soft curse. Cameron watched a very large man—Malcolm MacLeod's nephew Walter, as it happened—step out of the shadows and go stand directly behind Sunny.

"Lost, missy?" Walter asked politely.

She whirled around in surprise, then backed away. "I might be."

Walter rubbed his hands together purposefully. "Then let me help you find your way, lass, right into my bed—"

Cameron didn't dare wait to see if there were any more MacLeod clansmen loitering uselessly about with the same thing on their minds. He leapt out of the shadows and jerked Sunny out of the way, pulling his sword free of its scabbard with a hiss.

"Horse," he barked at her. He heard her run, then turned to

face his foe. "I've no quarrel with you," he said quietly. "Let us go and you'll live to see sunrise."

Walter snorted. "Are ye daft, man? The Cameron himself right here in my hands? I'm not about to let ye go. Or the wench. She's a pretty thing, isn't she?"

"Do you know her?" Cameron asked, because he couldn't help himself.

"I don't," Walter said with a grin, "but I'd surely like to. Now, my laird, come along quietly so I can get to that."

Cameron knocked Walter's sword out of his hands, then struck him in the face. Walter went sprawling. Cameron ran across the glade and pulled himself up behind Sunny.

"Go," he shouted.

His horse took off like a shot. Sunny lost the reins and almost fell off leaning forward to recapture them. Cameron leaned over quickly to catch *her*—and fortunately so as he heard something whiz over their heads. He bent over Sunny, pressing her against his horse's neck, until he decided they were out of range of any well-flung knives or rocks.

He resheathed his sword behind his head, then took the reins from Sunny. He wrapped his arm around her waist and rode like the wind, grateful for the speed and endurance of his mount. They easily could have fallen into MacLeod hands, but luck was thankfully on their side. Either that or the MacLeods weren't interested in coming after them.

He turned that over in his mind for quite a while. Walter hadn't known her—but he certainly should have, shouldn't he? A clan's healer was a very important person, one generally treated with respect.

Well, except on his land.

Aye, Walter should have known her, but he hadn't. She should have felt very comfortable and secure going to Malcolm's front door and knocking, but she didn't. She should have opened her door and found the house she'd left behind waiting for her.

But she hadn't.

He began to wonder if she were telling the truth.

He slowed once he was half an hour from his own village, just to give himself time to decide what to do. He couldn't keep her in his bedchamber; his clan would think he was bedding her. He supposed that if he had to look at her much longer, he would give into the impulse and do just that.

Unfortunately, even if he wasn't bedding her, the moment anyone thought he was, he would be branded a witch as well and both he and Sunny would meet their end in the loch. As Giric had so kindly pointed out, a man's skill with a blade only went so far when that man was hopelessly outnumbered.

Perhaps James and Elizabeth MacLeod had found themselves in those exact straits. Overpowered. Slain. Spoken of in hushed tones for years after their deaths.

He didn't want the same fate for either Sunny or himself. He had to protect her somehow. If he left her alone in the village, though, she wouldn't last a night before someone broke through her door and either ravished her or slit her throat.

Damn it, what to do now?

He considered it all the way to the village, then decided all he could do was see that she stayed as far away from the keep as possible. Giric had, over the past handful of years, been working quite diligently to turn his men against him one by one. It hadn't mattered so much in the past because he'd had his brothers behind him and the three of them had made a formidable group. But now that he was alone, the keep would be a dodgy place indeed.

Nay, 'twas best he keep Sunshine somewhere else. Even if he couldn't provide her with many comforts, he could at least keep her alive. He owed her that, because she had tried to save his brother and because he was the reason she found herself in his time.

He could scarce believe he was taking her seriously, but it had been that sort of se'nnight so far, apparently.

He stopped before a hut at the far eastern edge of the village. A stream ran not far away from the little house, and the woods were but a short way away. She would have water and fuel. Perhaps she could ask for no more than that.

He slid down to the ground, then held up his arms for her. Her expression was very grave as he set her on her feet. He pulled a knife from his boot and put it into her hands.

"Kill first," he said simply.

"And if it's you?"

"I'll knock."

"Well, you have before."

He smiled before he could stop himself, then sobered. He wanted to pull her into his arms and hold her safely there. He wanted to haul her against him and ravage her mouth until he lost track of where he ended and she began. He had the most ridiculous impulse to go down on one knee and beg her to be his.

Perhaps she *was* a witch and had bewitched him with sparkling green eyes and a hesitant smile.

He pushed past her inside the deserted hut before he lost what few wits remained him. He cursed silently. There was nothing there but a stool. Not even a bed to lie on.

He struck his knife against flint to spark the pile of wood in the middle of the floor. He could build her a bed and a chair, at least. That and a sturdy door with a bar across it.

He fed the small fire he'd started until he thought it actually might serve her, then took the two strides that separated him from the door. He stepped outside and looked at her.

"This is the best I can do," he offered quietly.

"Thank you. It's very generous. Whose was it?"

"My healer."

"She's not here anymore?"

"Dead."

She pursed her lips. "Unsurprising."

He smiled faintly and tapped his temple. "Gather your wits together, wench. This is a far sight more comfortable than my dungeon."

"I imagine so." She took a deep breath, let it out, then looked up at him. "What are you going to do now?"

"With you, or with my future?" he asked, stumbling a bit over the last word.

"Both."

He chewed on his words for a moment, then spewed them out as brusquely as he could. Any other way would leave him showing much more emotion than he cared to. "I will wed my brother's widow," he ground out, "raise his children as my own, and sire more children on her. I suppose that answers the first as well, doesn't it?"

She flinched, though she covered it quickly enough. She looked up at him and put on a smile that might have been convincing had it not been apparently so difficult for her to maintain. "Of course. It's your duty."

He cursed under his breath, then took off his plaid and wrapped it around her shoulders. "I'll find blankets for you tomorrow."

"You don't have to—"

"I must," he interrupted sharply. He took a deep breath. "And I wish to," he said in a gentler tone. "I'm sorry I cannot do more, Sunshine."

"I'll be fine."

It bothered him that she would make do with so little, yet accept it so readily. Unfortunately, there was nothing more he could do. His duty to his clan came first, before what he might have wanted, before what Sunshine might have been willing to have from him.

He stepped back. "Sleep well, Sunshine."

She nodded, then went inside and shut the door. He realized then that she hadn't eaten in days and he hadn't fed her that day. He was actually a bit surprised she was still on her feet. It said much about her stamina.

He swung up onto his horse and headed back toward the keep. He would fetch food and drink and bring it back to her.

But he would knock.

And after what he'd just said to her, and the way in which he'd said it, he wouldn't have blamed her at all if she didn't open to him.

Chapter 7

Sunny stood huddled near a fire in the middle of a dead Cameron healer's house, pulled Cameron's plaid more closely around her, and wondered what in the hell she was going to do now.

She wasn't having a good week. It was bad enough that she had been jerked out of her comfortable little cottage—replete with running water and a fridge—and deposited back in a time where her profession was a lethal one, worse that she had barely survived a drowning, and catastrophic that she had tried to get home and found it impossible.

Now, she had to have increasingly fond feelings for a man who was going to marry his sister-in-law?

She wished with a fervor that left her a little unnerved that she had asked any one of those damned MacLeod time travelers about their experiences. All it would have taken was a single conversation with Jamie to have cleared up quite a few things. Instead, she had just taken to heart the advice to stay on the right path and she wouldn't have to worry about anything.

And why not? She'd been happily oblivious in modern Scotland with her hot showers and endless rain. If she wanted to get up close and personal with a medieval expat, she went to dinner at her sister's, or down to Jamie's, or over to Ian's. She had wondered, now and again, what it would be like to visit a time that wasn't her own, but she had never, not even in her wildest nightmares suffered after the occasional indulgence in dark chocolate, imagined she would be the one doing the visiting, much less finding herself stuck.

With men who thought she was a witch and a laird who was going to marry his sister-in-law.

She took a deep breath and turned away from that thought. She just needed to look at the whole thing logically. If a gate had worked to get her into the past, a gate should work equally as well to get her back to the future. And even if Moraig's gate had somehow self-destructed on her way through it, the

super-duper, mother of all gates in the forest should have
worked for her. She knew several individuals who had used it
successfully—or unintentionally, in her sister's case. Madelyn
had found herself in medieval Scotland and captured by
Fergussons—yet another reason to dislike them—but Patrick
had rescued her and gotten them both back home—

She caught her breath. *Her sister had been in medieval Scotland.*

For a split second, she felt a rush of relief so strong, it almost
knocked her to her knees.

Just as quickly, though, she realized why it wouldn't work.
Madelyn had traveled back to *1382*.

She blew out her breath. 1382? She was going to wait seven
years for her sister to be in the same year as she found herself?

Not bloody likely.

No, she wouldn't wait for Madelyn because she wouldn't
have to. She would go try the gates again and this time one of
them would work. She spared a brief regret that she hadn't
taken more time to memorize all the gates on Jamie's map, but
she did have the little red *X*s between her house and Madelyn's
indelibly burned into her consciousness. Those were ones that
led to places she hadn't wanted to go. She'd had no desire to
wind up back in seventeenth-century Barbados drinking rum
with pirates, or in twelfth-century Spain enjoying the Inquisition,
or in fifteenth-century France enjoying all sorts of other de-
baucheries. At least she'd only landed in relatively friendly
Scotland. Things could have been worse.

She wanted to laugh, or make a joke, or stare the facts down
and force them to look away, but she couldn't. All she could do
was sink down beside the fire that Cameron had built with his
own hands and realize she was on the verge of losing it. She was
hungry, exhausted, and, quite frankly, terrified. The tears didn't
help, nor did the shuddering sobs that came at her from nowhere.
She put her hands over her mouth and did her best not to make
any noise.

Cameron's knife was solid and comforting in her hand, his
plaid was warm around her shoulders, but in spite of both of
those things, she had never in her life felt more alone.

And she would stay alone because she couldn't get home and
she couldn't imagine anyone would come and find her. How
could they, when they wouldn't have any idea where she'd gone?

She supposed they might somehow stumble on Moraig's gate—despite the fact that she'd lived there for a year without so much as a hint of anything untoward in that doorway—but even if they did, how would they know *when* she'd landed? She was the proverbial needle in history's haystack and it would take them months to even narrow down where she might have gone.

And even if they did find the right time, they wouldn't have the right place because she was living in Robert Francis Cameron mac Cameron's dead healer's house, two hours on horseback away from where she should have been.

Unfortunately, she couldn't go back and wait for them at Moraig's. The MacLeods would be just as unfriendly as Cameron's men had been and she would find herself summarily turned into castle call girl, if they didn't just kill her outright. At least on Cameron soil she might be able to count on Cameron coming and rescuing her now and then.

If Gilly allowed it.

A soft knock on the door almost sent her tumbling into the fire. She rose unsteadily to her feet, then crossed silently to the door. She put her hand on the wood, but said nothing.

"Sunshine?"

She closed her eyes briefly, then opened the door. Cameron stood there, dressed in another plaid, and carrying a leather bag in one hand and a rough linen drawstring bag in the other. He caught sight of what she realized had to be her tear-ravaged face and sighed deeply.

"I'm sorry, Sunshine," he said quietly.

She shook her head sharply. "I'm fine. I just lost it."

He looked at her with a frown. "Lost what?"

She smiled in spite of herself. "Control over my womanly emotions. I'm fine."

"Perhaps you're hungry," he offered. "I haven't fed you today." He held out his burdens. "The finest I could find."

"Thank you," she said, taking them and holding them close. "Do you want to come in and eat with me?"

"I dare not," he said slowly. "My villagers are suspicious enough as it is and I've no mind to fuel any speculations. I'll return tomorrow, though, to see how you fare."

She put on a smile, though she supposed it hadn't been all that successful. "You've been very kind to me. Thank you."

He blew his hair out of his eyes, then took a step backward.

"Bolt your door as best you can. You should sleep with that dagger in your hand."

"I will."

He motioned for her to shut the door.

She did, then flipped the perfectly inadequate latch over and pretended that it was locked. She put more wood on her fire, was silently grateful to whoever had chopped it and left it behind, then sat down with what Cameron had brought her.

The wine was dreadful, but she drank it anyway. He'd brought bread and cheese and very wrinkled apples. She ate some of everything and thought kind thoughts about him. She couldn't imagine he could keep up feeding her forever, but she would be grateful for it while it lasted.

She sat up until she couldn't sit anymore, then she lay down on the dirt floor and closed her eyes. It made her appreciate the luxury of Cameron's bed, though she didn't spare any regret for it. She could have just as easily been sleeping in the slime of his dungeon. At least she was marginally safe where she was.

Though she supposed, when she heard the faint scratching at her door an indeterminate amount of time later, that in the dungeon, her door would have had a lock.

The little piece of wood that had been her lock was finding itself lifted by means of a knife slid between the door and the door frame. Sunny sat up and clutched Cameron's knife in her hand. She wasn't one to succumb to fear easily, but she had no trouble admitting that she was absolutely terrified. She pushed herself to her feet and slipped over to the darkest corner of the little hut. At least that way she would stand a chance of attacking before she was attacked.

The door swung open. A man took a step inside, then flinched and grunted. He started to lean forward. Sunny pushed herself back against the wall and tried to make herself as thin as possible as he continued to fall. He landed face down at her feet.

An enormous sword quivered in his back.

It wasn't but a handful of seconds later that Cameron appeared at the doorway. He jerked the sword from the man's back, wiped it on the man's shirt, then resheathed it.

"Sorry about the floor," he said shortly, then he heaved the man up, hoisted him over his shoulder, and carried him from the hut.

Sunny put her hand over her mouth to keep her hysterics where they belonged—running rampant inside her—then stumbled across the room and looked out the door. Cameron was dumping the body in the street right in front of her house. He shot her a look.

"Deterrent," he said succinctly. "Shut your door."

Sunny opened her mouth to speak, but he had already melted into the shadows. She wanted to ask him if it wouldn't be easier to just let her stay in the keep, but maybe he had his reasons for that. Maybe he was going to train his clan to leave her alone, then he would leave her alone as well. She would live and die in medieval Scotland, in the rain, without a decent fire, all by herself.

She put her hand back over her mouth to keep herself quiet. She shut the door, put the inadequate lock back in place, then went to sit against the opposite wall.

She didn't sleep.

She left her hut the next morning at dawn. She hadn't been able to lie down, no matter what sort of deterrent Cameron might have left in front of her door. Perhaps she could talk Cameron out of a training sword and use it to jam against her door until she could fix some sort of way to bar the door with something heavier. She was going to have to sleep eventually and she wouldn't be able to do so in peace until she felt safe.

Well, as safe as she could feel, given her circumstances.

She looked around for a bathroom, but there wasn't a biffy in sight. She found a likely spot just inside the forest, made certain she was alone, then went about her business. She had a bit of a wash in the stream, then stood just outside her little house and looked around her. She saw no clansmen with murder on their minds, no villagers with bundles of wood in their arms, no laird come to tell her she was out of her mind. Well, she did see one villager, but once he saw her, he crossed himself and scurried inside his house. She sighed. Just what in the world was she going to do for the next thirty years in medieval Scotland?

Actually, it could be much longer than that. Her ancestors on both sides routinely lived happily and coherently into their nineties. She could be conceivably spending the next sixty years trying to get warm by a fire burning in the middle of her living room.

She closed her eyes and prayed for a miracle. She prayed for

Patrick MacLeod to come rescue her. She wished she'd at least left a note on the mirror of her bathroom, though she wasn't quite sure what she would have said. *Hey, Pat, there's this fabulous-looking guy standing at my doorway and I think he's Jamie's idea of a great blind date. I agree! Gotta run.*

Unfortunately, she could imagine all too well how that particular evening had gone in reality. Joshua had probably come to get her for supper only to find her gone. He would have called Patrick who would have called Jamie, then the pair of them would have come to Moraig's while Ian kept all the women and children safe in Jamie's keep. When they had seen no sign of foul play, they would have known what had happened. It happened to Jamie quite regularly, but he was very adept at getting himself out of whatever scrape he'd gotten into.

He also never went anywhere without a pair of dirks slipped down his boots under his jeans.

If she ever got home, she was going to sign up for Jamie's course on Portal Classification and Identification. Hell, even Madelyn had sat through that one. She, on the other hand, had been too busy sitting at Moraig MacLeod's feet, discussing the many uses for plantain, to have been bothered.

She took a deep breath and put it all aside. Maybe she had a task to accomplish in the past and she wouldn't be able to get home until she'd done that. Maybe she was supposed to train a new healer so Cameron could save a few of his men in the next battle. At the very least, she could replenish the very old herbs she'd used on his brother.

At least doing so at present would keep her from thinking about the look her sister would have worn when she realized what had happened.

She made certain Cameron's dagger was still residing in the makeshift belt she'd fashioned out of the hem of her dress, then walked around behind her house and looked over the meadow she could see on the other side of the stream. It was blooming with all sorts of springtime things and that was somehow almost encouraging.

She hiked up her skirts, waded across the shallow stream, then clambered up the opposite bank. She turned Cameron's plaid into an extra skirt and tied it around her waist so she could use a corner of it as an apron. She supposed she made quite a sight in her dress that had been too short but was now substantially shorter and the laird's plaid wrapped around her on top of that. But considering all the other strikes she had against her, she supposed no one would care how she was dressed.

She picked and plucked quite happily until she realized that she wasn't alone. The footfall behind her was so quiet, she wouldn't have noticed it if she hadn't seen the hint of a shadow coming up behind her. She waited until the last possible moment, then she kicked backward with all her strength, turned, and swept the man's feet out from under him. She had Cameron's dagger out of her belt and was bringing it down toward the man's eye before she realized just who she was about to stab.

Cameron held her wrist in a grip of iron and kept the knife a mere inch away from his eye. He was breathing raggedly. Then again, so was she.

He pushed her arm back another half foot, then looked up at her.

"Who in the hell *are* you?" he wheezed.

"I told you who I was," she managed.

"I think you broke something, you bloodthirsty wench. Who taught you to fight?"

She sat back on her heels, but he wouldn't release her wrist. "My brother-in-law."

He took a careful breath. "I forgot to knock."

"You did."

"You almost killed me."

"Oh, you're a little tougher than that, aren't you?" she said with a smile.

He grunted, then pried his knife from her fingers and plunged it into the ground next to him. "You can have that back when I'm sure you won't use it for any other untoward purposes." He breathed in with a wince. "I daresay you owe me some tending."

"What will your villagers think?"

"They'll think I have proper control over my witch."

She reached out and touched his side. "Did I really hurt you?" she asked.

He gasped. "By the saints, Sunshine, I daresay you did. I don't suppose you have anything handy to heal something this serious quickly so when we're attacked half an hour from now, I could actually wield my sword?"

"I had no idea it was you," she said apologetically. "That was meant to disable."

"I daresay." He pointed toward the stream. "I left wine cooling in the water and food on the bank. I think the least you can do is fetch it and leave me here to salvage some of my pride." He squinted at her. "Don't suppose you'd want to come be my garrison captain, would you?"

She found it in her to smile. "Tempting, but I'm not all that good with a broadsword."

"Lass, all you would have to do is use your feet. We'll discuss it later. Now, be a good witch and bring me something to at least dull the pain."

She opened her mouth to tell him he could go get his own wine, but realized that his eyes were twinkling. She wasn't sure how he could joke about anything when everything was so miserably serious, but maybe there was a lesson there. She scowled at him, had a brief laugh followed by a gasping curse as her reward, then jumped to her feet before she let down any more of her guard around him.

She found a sack full of food in the grass and a leather bag wedged between two rocks on the edge of the stream. She was surprised she hadn't noticed Cameron doing that, or heard him coming her way. In her defense, she'd been a little distracted.

She returned to find him still lying on his back, staring up at the sky, rubbing his side absently. He turned his head and looked at her.

He smiled.

Her first instinct was to run. She couldn't let herself get involved with him, not even the slightest bit. That path would only lead to heartbreak. Too bad he was the only thing that seemed solid and familiar in a world she hadn't asked for and wasn't quite all that sure how to navigate.

She set the food and drink down next to him. "You shouldn't be here, should you?"

He only looked at her gravely. "I cannot leave you alone, Sunshine. Or by yourself," he added, as if he meant two entirely different things.

"Surely you have other things to do," she said, a little desperately. "Train, perhaps. Sleep, definitely."

"Again, you forget who I am."

Unfortunately, she hadn't, and that was the problem.

She closed her eyes and backed away. "I'll go look for herbs to ease your pain." She turned and walked away before she had to look at him anymore. She would see if there was something to use for the damage she'd done to him, then pick a few herbs against the time when she might have a need for them. Who knew what the future might hold?

She only knew who couldn't possibly be in it and that man was lying thirty feet behind her.

Chapter 8

Cameron unbuckled his sword belt and rolled off his blade with a hearty groan. By the saints, the wench had done him a serious bit of damage. He pulled the blade from the sheath, then laid it near his face with the hilt in easy reach. Even if he couldn't lift it, he could put his hand on it and give any potential murderers a stern look of warning. Sunshine could expect no more of him than that. After all, 'twas her fault he winced every time he breathed.

Obviously, approaching her silently had been a very bad idea indeed.

He propped his head up on his hand and watched her as she wandered through the meadow, bending now and again to pluck up some weed or another. Those were, he suspected, either things to cure him or poison him with. He supposed he deserved nothing less. He had made a great hash of things already and he didn't seem to be improving it any. The list of things he'd already done that he shouldn't have was long enough to satisfy any scribe. He shouldn't have pulled her out of her house to start with. He shouldn't have left her unprotected that first night. He certainly shouldn't have cut her clothes off her himself.

And he most definitely shouldn't have kissed her in front of what had turned out to not be her house.

He should have turned away from that memory immediately, but he couldn't even muster up a halfhearted effort. He watched her continue to study his meadow with a practiced eye and all the while, he thought about how she felt in his arms and how she'd caught her breath when he'd kissed her.

As if he'd pleased her in some way.

He didn't suppose she would be amenable to any more of that sort of kissing—and he would be a damned fool to ask her. He was planning on wedding his brother's wife, and though he might have been many other things, an adulterer he was not.

But, by the saints, he couldn't look away from her.

He waited until she had come within twenty paces of him

before he cleared his throat loudly and patted the grass in front of him.

"Come and sit, lass."

She only looked for somewhere else to go.

"I'll just follow you," he added.

When he saw the expression on her face, he wished he'd kept his mouth shut. He closed his eyes briefly, then looked at her.

"Please, Sunshine."

She looked at him for several moments in silence before she sighed deeply, then walked toward him. She emptied her makeshift skirts in front of him, then sat down near his knees and started to sort her weeds. He watched her periodically taste something she'd picked, then either keep or throw away piles of the same stuff. He decided, after quite some time, that she would ignore him all day if he didn't do something about it.

"What sorts of things do you have there?" he asked politely.

"Plantain," she said, pointing to one pile, "dandelion greens, and pretty flowers. But I imagine you knew that already, didn't you?"

"I might have," he agreed. "I know the uses for the first, suspect the second would make a particularly bitter stew, and I've no idea what you intend to do with the third."

She took a handful of the blossoms and began to string them together. She deftly made a modest size circlet of them and reached out to place it on his head.

"They serve to make a crown," she said solemnly. "For Himself's fetching head."

He tried to muster up some sort of gruff reply to cover how her smile had smote him to the heart, but all he could do was look at her, helpless and speechless.

"Well," she said, with mock surprise, "we've reached some sort of historic event here, haven't we?"

He couldn't even curse her.

"Don't you have anything to say, Robert Francis?"

"Bloody hell," he managed. "And don't call me Francis."

She smiled. "What does everyone else call you? What did your last witch call you?"

"My laird," he said promptly, "but she said it with a fiendish sort of cackle that left the hair on the back of my neck standing up every time. My cousins call me Cameron, but then again so do my enemies. After this, I daresay you might call me anything you liked."

"I should make you crowns more often then," she mused. "It makes you quite tractable. Either that, or you had a particularly good night's sleep."

"With a tree root under my arse and bark digging into my back?" he grumbled. "Nay, not particularly, though I don't begrudge you my lack of comfort."

She was watching him in astonishment. "You slept in the forest?"

"How else was I to watch your door?" He shifted a bit so his knees were pressing against her back. She didn't lean back against him, but at least he was touching her and she wasn't bolting. She was still watching him with that same look of absolute surprise. "What is it?" he asked.

"You watched my door?"

"Of course," he said. "You are in my care. Whilst you are there, I will do all I can to keep you safe."

"Oh," she murmured. "I see. Thank you."

He couldn't imagine that she would have expected anything less; then again, she was a witch and was perhaps not accustomed to being looked after well.

All the more reason to do so himself.

"Any trouble this morning?" he asked.

She shook her head. "I think the warning sign you left in front of my door was actually quite useful, if not a little gruesome."

"That lad won't be mourned," he said dismissively. "He's given a pair of lassies trouble before, which is why I wasn't surprised to see him at your door last night. Perhaps my reaction was a little stronger than it might have been otherwise, but I can't say he didn't deserve it."

He felt a shiver go through her, but she said nothing more. For himself, he was content to lie on the mostly dry grass and watch Sunshine Phillips sort her weeds. It wasn't warm—it was spring after all—but it wasn't unpleasant. He finally, though, had to get off his side. He rolled onto his back, wincing as he did so.

"Did I really hurt you?" she asked.

"Do you think I'll actually admit as much?" He stretched uncomfortably. "You're dangerous."

"I didn't mean to be so violent. I'm a little on edge."

He understood that. He had been as well that morning after he'd returned from making a quick foray into his kitchen for food, then come back and found her house empty. When he'd finally realized she was in the meadow, he'd had to simply stand still and rest until his heart had stopped beating so strongly he feared it would beat out of his chest.

He sighed as deeply as he could manage. He had to do something about her—beyond just seeing to her needs and her safety. Either he had to get her back to where she belonged, or he had to have her for himself. Unfortunately, he suspected the latter would only worsen his preoccupation with her. And given that he couldn't have her, perhaps it was best to think about how to get her home.

But perhaps not quite yet. Perhaps he would spend the day with her and decide once and for all that she was not for him.

He didn't hold out much hope for that, actually.

He sighed as deeply as he dared, then closed his eyes. "Tell me if anyone comes."

"Who are you looking for?" she asked. "Gilly?"

He almost smiled. "Woman, you've a mouth on you that could stand to be tempered. Did your laird fail to teach you your place? Or when not to talk about women your new laird doesn't want to discuss?"

"You're not my new laird, and you're the one who said you wanted to marry her."

"I never said I *wanted* to marry her," he said, opening one eye and looking at her. "I said I was going to."

"Then why are you here?"

He closed his eyes and considered that for quite some time in silence. Why? Well, the list was quite long. Because Sunshine Phillips was lovely, canny, and apparently willing to put herself in danger to do her duty—as she had done when she'd come to tend to Breac. Because he had spent three days looking at her as she burned with fever, and somehow the vision of her face had haunted him ever since. Because she spoke to him with a tartness he enjoyed very much, as if he were just a man and not a laird, as if she actually enjoyed being in his company.

Why, indeed.

"Because," he said, finally, finding there were more reasons still, "I want to pull you down into my arms and kiss you until neither of us can think clearly. But since that seems ill-advised, I'll forbear. But I still can't leave you alone."

She was silent for so long, he finally had to open his eyes and look at her.

She was staring at him with an expression on her face that was such a mixture of apprehension and dreadful hope, it was all he could do not to do just as he'd threatened.

He lay there, watched her, and wondered how it was that a woman who was obviously daft as a duck had managed, in the space of less than a se'nnight, to overwhelm him so fully that his eyes burned at the thought of her smile, his heart burned at the thought of having her near him for the rest of his days, and the rest of him burned with the thought of her in his bed for years to come?

Bloody hell, how was he ever going to do without her?

He sat up with a groan, then reached out and took her hand. "I think you're a witch in truth, Sunshine Phillips."

"What does that have to do with either your future or mine?"

"Nothing," he said, lacing his fingers with hers, "except I will spend every day of my future wishing ours lay together."

"You can't be serious," she said in a low voice.

He looked down at her fingers intertwined with his, then met her eyes. "I find that I am," he said slowly.

"You don't know me—"

"I know enough."

Her eyes welled up with tears. "It's pointless to think about it, talk about it, even allow the slightest moment to imagine—"

He leaned forward and cut off her words with his mouth. It was an extraordinarily bad idea, but he couldn't stop himself. And once he was about the very pleasurable business of kissing her, he didn't *want* to stop himself. He wished his side didn't hurt so much, for he would have pulled her down into his arms and done quite a few other things besides kiss her.

And then he realized, as her breath began to come in gasps, that she was no practiced wench with a score of lovers to her credit.

He softened his kiss immediately, turning it to something far chaster than it had been but a moment before. It took a bit, but she finally relaxed in his arms. In time, he felt her hand steal up to rest on his shoulder.

By the saints, he was in trouble.

He kissed her mouth softly, her closed eyelids, her cheeks. He pulled away whilst he still had some hint of sense left in him, but he kept his hand under her hair, buried in it to keep her close.

A single tear trickled down her cheek. "Heaven help us," she whispered, not opening her eyes.

"Sunshine, I fear we're past any aid."

She looked at him then. "We can't do this."

He took a very deep breath, nodded, then smoothed his hand down her back before he stretched out next to her again. He stayed close enough, though. It was killing him to touch her, but he suspected it would be far worse not to. He dredged up something useful to say. "I'll list all my faults for you," he said lightly. "It will make you vastly relieved you never need have me."

She reached up and touched her mouth. He suspected 'twas unconsciously done for when she caught him watching her, she dropped her hand immediately.

"All right," she said, putting on a smile that didn't convince in the slightest. "You'd better make it a good list."

"It will take some effort," he said wryly, "but I'll try. First, I'm brusque. Demanding, as well. I have many sour and unpleasant humors. I've no patience for stupidity and I do not tolerate disloyalty." He paused, trying to see if any of that frightened her off.

She only watched him silently.

He pressed on. "I don't trust easily. I spend an unholy amount of time training with the sword, and I tend to kill first and wonder if I've made a mistake later." He paused. "Frightened yet?"

She shook her head. "Better dig deeper, I suppose."

He smiled in spite of himself. "I like a hot fire, a hot bath, and a willing wench in my bed. *Now* are you put off?"

"Do you have many willing wenches in your bed?" she asked, with a faint smile, "or do you frighten them off with your sour and unpleasant humors?"

"There have been a few," he muttered. "How many willing men have *you* had in your bed?"

Her face was suddenly quiet red. "I'm certainly not going to tell *you*."

He watched her blush furiously and a thought he'd never considered suddenly presented itself. He felt his mouth fall open. "Are you a *maid*?"

She was the single fastest wench he'd ever seen. It didn't help that the moment he tried to crawl to his feet to chase her, pain shot through him so suddenly it left him there on his knees. He heaved himself up and ran after her just the same. He caught her halfway to the stream and turned her around, but he didn't dare pull her into his arms, or kiss her again, or make any display of what he might or might not have felt for her. They were too close to the village for that. He simply held her by the arms to keep her from running any farther.

"I thought of another flaw," he said, latching on to the first thing that came to mind.

"What?" she said miserably.

"I'm too bloody nosy. I have been known to think too much and ask too many questions. My father found it a most undesirable trait in me. He was wont to tell me that I should have been a lady's maid in some fine house rather than a swordsman in his." He paused. "He called me a gel from time to time as well."

She smiled. "He didn't."

"He did," Cameron said honestly. "I think it might have been to inspire me to step out and train a bit more, but who knows? The man was completely without scruples."

"You seem to have quite a few."

"To my eternal shame." He wanted to pull her into his arms and let his heart be at peace, but knowing it would endanger her cooled his ardor abruptly. He released her, smoothed his hands down her arms, then took a step back. "We should go fetch your weeds, woman. I think I feel a wind coming up." He smiled his most unassuming smile at her. "Come with me?"

She took a deep breath, then nodded. He wished he'd had something charming to say, but charm was not his strong suit, despite whatever his mother had claimed about him. He could muster up a decent smile now and again for Cook to have an extra bit of something sweet, but nothing more than that. He had to at least say something at present, though. He opened his mouth and hoped for something useful to come out.

"What do you want from your life?" was apparently the best he could manage.

She looked at him in complete surprise.

He agreed. He had never in his life asked such a stupid question, not even in front of his father to inspire yet more lectures on the perils of asking too many questions. He looked at her in consternation.

"I am not given to introspection," he said weakly. "I don't know where the hell that came from."

"Flowers in your hair."

He reached up and found that his crown was still lying atop his head. "I daresay. And you needn't answer, if you'd rather not. 'Tis a very personal thing."

She shrugged. "I'll answer, though I'm afraid it won't be a very interesting answer. I would like a husband and children. A garden." She smiled briefly. "Rain on the roof."

"You are a proper Scottish lass, aren't you? Besides, those aren't dull things, Sunshine. They're worth having."

And given that he would never have them freely from anyone, they were precious indeed.

"And you?" she asked.

He shifted uncomfortably, but supposed she deserved an honest answer. He clasped his hands behind his back. "I want a woman who would love me if I weren't laird."

"Is there really all that much benefit to it?" she asked. "It seems to me that you're in front in the battle, the last to sleep when there's something amiss in the keep, and the first to wake when you're needed."

"It could be worse. I could be a kitchen lad and get just as little sleep but not eat nearly so well."

She smiled. "Would that be so bad?"

"Normally, I would say aye. Today, I think I might settle for it quite happily." He paused. "It would allow me quite a few freedoms I don't enjoy."

She stopped as he reached down to pick up his sword. "What does Gilly think about you and your lairdliness?"

He resheathed his sword with a smile. "Actually I have no idea what she thinks and couldn't care less. Why is it you speak of her so often?"

"You're going to marry her. I thought it was appropriate."

He supposed she had that aright. He groaned as he strapped his sword to his back, then cursed as he started to lean over. Sunny stopped him, then gathered up her herbs and their sustenance.

"Well?"

"Gilly would sooner stick a knife in my belly than give me a kind word," he said with a snort. "I'm quite sure she would much prefer to wed Giric. Then again, I suppose what she really would rather do is kill me *and* Giric, then take over the clan herself."

"Duty is a difficult thing sometimes," she offered. "Especially when it involves your heart."

"Sunshine, love, you've *no* idea. But since I cannot change mine, let us go back and make the best of it."

She nodded and started across the meadow with him. "Where are you off to now?" she asked.

She wore a smile that bothered him somehow. It was the single falsest smile he'd ever seen. He supposed that should have flattered him that she felt the need to wear it, but it didn't. He was too busy wishing it hadn't been necessary.

He took the crown off carefully, then put the flowers over her brow. "I need to go beat some respect into my men this afternoon, but I will come back later and bring you something else to eat."

"Cameron, you don't have to—"

"I *will* come back later and I *will* watch your door tonight."

She looked up at him. "You can't stay awake forever."

"When I can't stay awake any longer, I'll simply hand you my sword and trust you to guard me. You're up for that, aren't you?"

She nodded and wore that smile again.

He walked with her back across the meadow, then left her at her door with the food he'd brought.

"Be careful."

She nodded, but said nothing.

He understood. What was there to say?

He walked back through the village, made a point of chatting easily with the heads of households, then continued on up the way. The sooner his people grew accustomed to Sunny, the sooner they saw he was unaffected by her, the sooner they would believe she was just a woman and the safer she would be.

He supposed he could save his grief over the fact that he could not have her for the privacy of his own bedchamber.

He walked into the hall and looked over the men loitering uselessly about before the fire. Only a few of them looked up and acknowledged him and that sparked his anger. He walked over and put his hand on the back of Brice's chair.

"Well, lads," he drawled, "no work today? No steeds to be tended? No swords to be sharpened so you don't die on the end of a Fergusson or MacLeod blade? No time spent actually *training* with those swords so you remember how to use them?"

Brice stood. "Come on, lads. He has it aright."

"*Cameron* has it aright," Cameron growled. He swept them all with a look. "Must I take you out into the yard as a group and beat the remembrance of who is your laird into your thick heads?"

They all managed some sort of deference before they trooped out of the hall. Cameron watched them go, then realized who hadn't been there.

Giric.

He turned and walked over to the stairs. He took them two at a time until he reached the landing, then padded silently down the passageway. He put his ear to his own door, but heard nothing but Brianna singing happily. She was no doubt stitching or cleaning or going about something behind a safely locked door. Cameron continued on down the passageway and stopped in front of Breac's chamber.

The noises coming from within that chamber had very little to do with grief.

Cameron pushed the door open and looked at the occupants of his brother's bed. Gilly looked at him in consternation, Giric with a smirk. Cameron leaned against the door and waved them on.

"Finish, by all means."

"I have," Giric said, rolling from the bed and pulling a plaid around him. He folded his arms over his chest and looked at Cameron. "You wanted something?"

"My brother's wife," Cameron said placidly.

"You cannot have her," Giric said in a low, dangerous voice.

"Can't I?" Cameron said. "I believe I have a duty to my brother's memory." He looked at Giric coolly. "Or am I mistaken?"

Giric pushed past him. "Watch your back."

Cameron snorted. "I could best you half asleep."

Giric cursed him, which Cameron ignored. He looked at Gilly, who was sitting up, clutching a sheet to her throat.

"Get dressed," he suggested.

"I don't want to wed you," she spat.

Well, he certainly shared that sentiment, but it didn't particularly matter what he wanted.

She pointed to her son with a shaking hand. "He's not Breac's, he's Giric's."

Cameron had certainly never considered asking his brother about the state of his marriage bed, his own damnable curiosity aside, but unfortunately for Gilly's attempt at deceit, Aidan looked exactly as Sim had as a young lad—something Cameron could actually remember quite well. She was obviously quite desperate to avoid his bed if she was willing to lie to keep herself from it.

And if she was willing to claim she was bearing other men's children, perhaps he had less of a duty to Breac than he thought. Perhaps he might wed where he willed.

He wondered what sort of uproar it would cause if he wed with the MacLeod witch.

Probably better not to know.

He looked at Gilly. "I'll give you a se'nnight."

"I'll kill you first."

Cameron grunted at her, then turned and walked back down the passageway. He didn't doubt she would try, so perhaps he would be safer to camp out in the forest for a bit until she had accustomed herself to her fate.

Besides, that would put him closer to Sunshine.

That was certainly the most pleasant thought he'd entertained in the past quarter hour.

He went to join his men in a bit of training, but he supposed he wouldn't be at it long. His side ached abominably and he knew just where he could go for a few herbs.

Could he be blamed if his heart might be eased by the same woman?

Chapter 9

Sunny dragged her hand through her greasy hair and wished desperately for a bath. She'd been in the fourteenth century for two weeks, long enough to be getting a little desperate to be clean. She supposed her trip to the loch counted as something of a bath, but she wasn't all that eager to repeat that experience so she supposed she would just have to be dirty. Maybe she would turn into a proper medieval gal at some point, grimy and rather less than fresh-smelling. She had already been to the meadow that morning, picking things to dry for when they were needed, and she'd at least put her hands and feet into the stream. It wasn't perfect, but she supposed it would have to do.

She was making do with quite a few things, most notably her location in time. She'd thought about going back to Moraig's, but it had never seemed the right time to try again. She wasn't sure she could live the rest of her life in medieval Scotland, but for the moment, she was surviving. She had the rain, she had earth under her feet, and she had the sky pressing down on her like a comforting embrace. She could survive without hot showers for a bit longer.

Besides, medieval Scotland did have its advantages. No traffic, no cell phones, no pantyhose. Cameron wasn't exactly the simple man she'd wanted—and she wasn't going to have him anytime soon—but in time she might be able to tend a garden for him without his villagers and men wanting to drown her. It could have been much worse.

She rebraided her hair, tied the end with a few threads worked out of the fraying hem of her dress, then put her shoulders back. She did have Cameron's dagger stuck into the back of her belt, so she felt slightly better about her chances of surviving the rest of the afternoon. She opened the door, prepared for just about anything. The body was no longer in front of her doorway, but apparently just the memory of it had been enough to ensure her safety.

She'd seen Cameron every day, several times a day as it

happened, but he had never stayed with her again for longer than it took to have a brief conversation about the situation up at the hall. His answers had ranged from *as I expected* to *not good.* Yesterday the only answer she'd gotten was a tightening of his mouth and a shake of his head.

She wondered what he would do. She had ventured to suggest that perhaps she was the reason for his troubles. He had disagreed so strongly that she hadn't brought it up again.

She pulled her door shut behind her, looked around to see what she might face, then jumped a little in surprise. There, fifty feet away, standing under the eaves of the edge of the forest, was the laird of the clan Cameron.

She tried not to think about how pleasant it was to see him, or to know that he was watching over her. Over the past week, she'd learned that, if nothing else, the man was relentless—and stubborn. He'd ignored her comments that she didn't need to eat so much, snorted at her suggestion that he shouldn't be spending his nights under the eaves of the forest watching her, and glared at her when she said that perhaps she should just pack up a little hobo bag and try her luck with another clan.

Actually, he'd done more than glare about the last. It had been the only time he'd touched her in a solid week. He'd jerked her into his arms, wrapped those arms around her so tightly that she'd squeaked, then he'd whispered harshly into her ear.

If you leave me, it will kill me.

And then he'd proceeded to kiss her until she'd promised she wouldn't fight him any longer. He hadn't touched her since, but he'd given her so many smoldering looks, she'd half wondered why she hadn't caught fire.

The situation was untenable. He was a medieval laird and she was a twenty-first-century commoner. Even if he hadn't been planning to marry his sister-in-law, he couldn't have married her. There was no hope for them in the real world.

He lifted his hand and crooked his finger at her.

She closed her eyes briefly, took hold of the butterflies taking flight in her stomach, then ducked out from under the eaves of her house and ran across the muddy path to where he stood. He wrapped another plaid around her shoulders.

" 'Tis cold out," he said.

"It's spring."

"Aye," he said with a faint smile, "so I hear."

She pulled the plaid closer around her and looked at him. "What are you doing today?"

"Walking in the woods with you."

"Are you?" she asked in surprise. "Why?"

"Because, love, if I don't have an hour of privacy with you, I will go mad."

"But—"

He looked at her with an expression so serious, she decided it was better to just keep her protests to herself.

"All right," she said.

He put his arm around her shoulders and pulled her deeper into the woods with him. "I'm sorry I have no shoes for you, but the path is soft. 'Twill be safe enough, I imagine."

"Safe," she echoed, "or comfortable?"

He smiled grimly. "I meant to say comfortable."

She imagined not. She pulled the knife out of her makeshift belt and handed it to him. "You might want that."

He hesitated, then took it and stuck it in his boot. "I'll give it back to you tonight."

"I won't remind you that you don't have to keep watching over me," she began, "but I could point out that it might be easier for you if you would let me sleep in the keep."

He hesitated, then shook his head. "'Tis too dangerous, Sunny, and I'll tell you why as we walk."

Well, that promised to be more answer than she'd had up until then. She nodded and continued on with him. The path was, as he had promised, soft under her feet, untroubled by the rain that fell onto the treetops. If there was prickly spot, he lifted her over it, otherwise he simply walked beside her. He would stop every now and again, as if he listened.

"Cameron?"

He looked down at her. "What?"

"Why do you stop?"

"I like to know what's in the woods," he said simply. "Now, as for why you're safer in the village, the answer is complicated. 'Tis partly because if you sleep in my bedchamber, they will all think I'm bedding you and then I don't think it will go very well for either of us."

"Because I'm the MacLeod witch?" she asked.

He smiled briefly. "Aye, that is part of it. I also can't leave you *outside* my bedchamber, because—well, you've already seen what happens when I make the mistake of leaving you at their mercy. And if you want the entire truth, I'm not sure I trust any of them with either of us inside the keep anymore." He shot her a look. "Too many lads between us and the front door, aye?"

"Oh, Cameron," she said with a wince. "They're your kinsmen."

"You would assume that might mean something to them, but apparently it doesn't." He took a deep breath. "Why don't you take my mind off my traitorous kinsmen by telling me of your family. I assume they aren't lying awake at night, imagining up in their black hearts ways to kill you without making too much mess."

She managed a smile. "I don't know how you can make light of this."

He shrugged. "'Tis either that or weep and I never weep. So, 'tis your duty now to humor your laird's curiosity."

"And curiosity is your worst fault," she said. "Or is that your chivalry?"

"Chivalry," he said with a snort. "That's English rubbish, lass. We don't have it here in Scotland."

"Of course you do. It's called honor."

He smiled at her. "I suppose so. Now, get on with ye, gel, before I blush. Tell me of your parents first. And I see you're no longer denying that I am your laird."

"I'm humoring you."

"As you should."

She laughed at him. "You're relentless—and shameless. But I'll answer your nosy questions. My parents are scholars. They spend their days teaching languages to other scholars."

"Even your dam?"

She smiled at the surprise in his voice. If her mother had heard that, her hackles would have immediately risen and Cameron would have found himself skewered linguistically as a result. "Actually, yes," she said. "It's a different world where I come from."

He looked at her thoughtfully. "They sound quite learned. Even your mother."

"She would agree. They're probably too learned for the rest of us. I only have one sibling, my sister, Madelyn."

"The one brave enough to wed a MacLeod?"

She nodded. "Patrick loves her to distraction, so I can't fault him. He is a lovely man."

He walked next to her in silence for quite a while. "He'll be worried about you," he said finally.

"I imagine so."

He put his arm around her shoulders, then reached behind his back and caught her hand so he could draw it around his waist. Sunny took the moment and fixed it in her memory. She was walking in a beautiful forest, with a springtime shower falling softly through the trees, and a gallant, powerful man was holding on to her as if he truly wanted to.

Of course, she was without a home, hundreds of years out of her own time, and she had no shoes, but perhaps those were things she could continue to do without for the moment in trade.

Cameron finally stopped, looked around them for a moment, then pulled her over to sit with him on a fallen log. He took her hand in his, studied both sides of it for several minutes in silence, then looked at her.

"How old are you?" he asked.

"Thirty-three," she managed. "Why?"

He shrugged. "I'm curious why you're still a maid. Are the men you know merely blind, or blind and stupid as well?"

She shifted uncomfortably, but he only continued to watch her without a flicker of anything on his face that might have been construed as scorn or ridicule.

"I'm not going to evade answering this, am I?" she asked finally.

He shook his head slowly.

"Why does it matter to you?"

"Because I think it says quite a bit about you, and I'm curious as to what that is."

It took her a moment or two to decide what she could tell him that would make any sense.

Why hadn't she slept with anyone? Because she'd been a geek, that's why. High school had been a nightmare. It hadn't helped that she spoke a dozen languages, found plants more interesting than clothes, and vegetarian dishes tastier than hamburgers. If she hadn't had Madelyn, she wouldn't have had anyone to talk to.

Of course, that had changed once she'd gone to college and found like-minded friends, but even then she hadn't fit in precisely. She had a leather coat because she liked the feel of it, she delivered babies because she loved how the world shifted when a new life took its first breath, and she wore linen because it looked good right out of her suitcase. She wasn't extreme enough for the green crowd and she was too weird for the burger crowd. And somewhere along the way, she just hadn't found a man she wanted to get involved with.

Until she'd met the one next to her.

"Was it the herbs?" he prompted.

"Partly," she agreed. "And partly because I've always liked things that others didn't find particularly popular."

"Things like meadows of flowers and nosy, unpleasant Highland lairds?" he asked with a smile.

She smiled in return. "You aren't unpleasant, but I do like meadows of flowers. And aye, all that witchly sort of thing tended to leave men looking past me. But you don't have any of my problems, so why aren't there women fighting over themselves to get into your bed—which I imagine is the case no matter what you say."

"You would think it would be so, but you would be wrong." He shrugged. "I'm very choosy. And I don't like women who haven't the spine to stand up to me."

"That's a little difficult when you're the laird, isn't it?"

"You seem to have no problem with it."

"Shall I be fawning and deferential, then?" she asked lightly.

"The saints preserve us both if you tried," he said with a weary smile. He stared down at her hand in his for quite some time before he looked up again. "I am very unhappy with all this, Sunny. I would like to have you near me, but I'm not sure how to arrange that so it doesn't put you in peril."

She found that her eyes were stinging all of a sudden. She blinked furiously to keep the tears where they belonged. "Thank you."

"You're welcome, damn it." He dragged a hand through his hair, cursed, then slipped that hand under her hair and pulled her tightly against him. "I'm going to kiss you now—chastely, I hope—and good sense be damned."

She closed her eyes as his lips met hers. It was not the kiss he'd taken from her in front of Moraig's hut, or the one he'd given her in the meadow, or the one he'd all but branded her with the other day, but it was the same tingle she'd felt when he first touched her hand. Only this was a hundred times more intense.

She shivered as he pulled away. "Cameron—"

"Cam," he corrected.

"Cam?"

" 'Tis what my brother Sim calls—called—me . . ."

He went suddenly still. Sunny started to speak, but he squeezed her hand, hard, and she stopped. She watched him as he turned himself into some sort of bad-guy antenna. He sat perfectly still for a moment or two, then he looked at her.

"We aren't alone."

She felt panic slam into her. She would have jumped to her feet and bolted, but he shook his head just the slightest bit.

"Just carry on, love," he said quietly. "As if you noticed nothing amiss. Come here and let me distract you for a moment."

"Cam—"

He cut off her word with his mouth. Sunny wished she could have enjoyed it. In fact, she was almost tempted, but her heart was beating too quickly for it. She felt his hand come up and press against the back of her head. He put his lips against her ear.

"We're going to walk back at a leisurely pace. No harm will come to you."

"But—"

He kissed her again, then pulled back far enough to smile at her. "As usual, you've forgotten who I am."

"Never," she said promptly. "But I think that's part of the problem here, don't you? Whoever this is certainly doesn't have it in for me."

"You are the single mouthiest wench I've ever known," he said with another smile. "Have a little faith in me, Sunny. I'll get you back to the village in safety."

She could only nod and try not to throw up with fear. She let him pull her to her feet, went somewhat willingly into his arms as he held her close for a moment, then tried to keep breathing normally as he put his arm around her shoulders and pulled her back the way they had come.

"Not to worry," he said lightly.

She didn't believe him, but she wasn't going to argue. He actually didn't seem overly concerned, so perhaps it had been his imagination on overdrive. She was the first to admit she tended to do that when she heard a noise in the middle of the night. In fact, there for a while she'd been terrified every time she thought she saw something out of the corner of her eye at Moraig's.

Of course, that was before she'd realized she actually *had* been seeing things out of the corner of her eye—mainly ghosts and bogles—but perhaps that was something to think about another day.

"I'm cursed," he remarked at one point as they walked along the path without undue haste.

"Are you?" she asked. "How so?"

"You," he said, pursing his lips. "I finally find a woman I want and what is she? A bloody virgin. I should just bed you anyway and see if it satisfies me on the matter."

"Is *that* what you're thinking about right now?" she asked in astonishment.

"What else?"

"Aren't we being followed?"

He shrugged. "I'm always being followed. I'm just not usually with a woman I want, so now I'm being a bit more careful than usual. But even so, I'm permitting myself a few pleasant thoughts along the way."

She smiled as she walked with him the rest of the way back to the village in silence. *A woman I want.* She was tempted to just do what she wanted to and burst into tears, but she wasn't a weeper. She was more likely to take out her frustrations on her garden or stand on her head and let the tension drain out of her.

The fact that what she wanted to do at present was take Cameron's sword and go beat on someone with it was indication enough that perhaps she had spent just a few days too many in medieval Scotland.

Too bad that wasn't going to change anytime soon.

He stopped her at the edge of the village. "Want to be my mistress?" he asked suddenly.

"Thank you, but nay," she said, though she was appalled to find out she was very tempted.

He grunted. "I didn't expect you would, but I had to ask." He sighed, squeezed her shoulders, then slid his hand down her arm and linked his fingers with hers. "Well, that's behind us for the moment. I don't suppose you have anything on the fire, do you?"

"That's it?" she asked in surprise.

"It was only one lad, so I'm not going to fash myself over it." He shot her a smile. "Dandelion soup, or dare I hope for anything tastier?"

"Are you really eating with me?"

"After this morning? Aye, and the villagers be damned."

She suspected she should have argued, but she felt safer when he was two feet away, so she didn't. She let him enter her little house first, then made him sit on the stool.

She started the fire as Patrick had taught her, then set her soup to warm again. She had a pot—and a plate, a cup and a tallow candle, which she understood the scarcity of very well—thanks to Cameron's generosity. She set a plate of bread and cheese on the floor next to him, then sat at his feet with her legs curled underneath her. When she finally looked at him, she found him watching her gravely.

"What is it?" she asked.

"I am thinking about what I can't have and it bothers me," he said simply. "I can't have you in my bed, or in my hall, or in my heart, and I don't like it."

"Some things just aren't meant to be, apparently."

He pulled her closer, placed her crossed arms on his knees, then reached out and unbraided her hair. He dragged his fingers through it for quite some time in silence, then he met her eyes. "I want you to tell me it all again," he said quietly. "I've given it much thought as I've sat and watched your door this past se'nnight. I don't think I believe any of the babbling you did about time and gates, of course, but I'll hear it again anyway."

"You aren't going to throttle me, are you?" she asked with a half smile.

He took her face in his hands, bent and kissed her softly, then sat back with his hands on her arms. "Nothing worse than the occasional kiss."

She took a deep breath. "All right. Where do you want me to start?"

"At the beginning, again. You were in your house, no doubt brewing up something to secretly poison a MacLeod with, and you opened your door and found me there. What then?"

"There isn't much more to it than that. You pulled me back into your time through the gate on the threshold of my house. I actually wasn't all that surprised to find I was in the past because my laird in the twenty-first century, James MacLeod, was the one to tell me about time gates. He should know, given how many of them he's found." She paused. "He was, if you can believe this, laird of the clan MacLeod in 13—"

"11," Cameron finished for her. He didn't look terribly surprised. "The tale is he left the keep with his bride, Elizabeth, and found a way to Paradise." He paused. "I had always assumed he'd ended up in the bottom of his loch."

She shook her head. "He didn't. He went to the future. As did his brother Patrick and his cousin Ian—"

"Patrick," Cameron said, looking surprised then. "Your sister is wed to *that* Patrick MacLeod? *He's* the one who taught you to fight?"

She nodded silently.

Cameron studied her for a moment, looking as if he were trying to come to terms with something he'd begun to believe before but hadn't quite accepted. He started to speak a time or two, then shook his head. He looked at her, then shook his head again. He patted her arms, then eased out from underneath her, rose, and began to pace. Sunny took her soup off the fire, then watched him. He was far too large for such a tiny room and the energy he was expending cursing made the chamber seem even smaller.

He strode over to her suddenly, then pulled her up and made her sit down on the stool. He looked down at her.

"What in the hell am I going to do with you now?"

"What difference does any of this make?" she asked, puzzled.

"It makes a difference because I believe you. It wasn't that I didn't think *you* believed your tale before, but now . . . well, now you can't stay."

She swallowed, hard. "I can't get back, either, seemingly."

He looked at her, then took her by the arms and pulled her to her feet. He yanked her against him and wrapped his arms around her tightly.

"Damnation," he said curtly. "Damn it to hell."

"It doesn't matter," she managed. "You're marrying Gilly."

"When hell freezes over," he said, before he bent his head and kissed her.

Sunny threw her arms around his neck and held on. It wasn't, as he would have said, a chaste kiss. She'd never felt anything like it before, though she was the first to admit she didn't have all that much to judge him by. He was so far out of her experience, she could only put herself in his hands and trust she would emerge unscathed.

He must have felt her surrender because he groaned and muttered a curse against her lips. He gathered her even closer, but he held her gently and kissed her so sweetly, she felt her eyes begin to burn. He finally lifted his head and looked at her for a moment in silence, then he released her abruptly. He poured her soup on the fire, stomped out the remaining embers, then took her hand.

"Come."

"Cam—"

He flashed her a sudden smile. "Thank you. I like hearing that name again from someone I love."

Sunny was still reeling from that as he pulled her out of the hut.

She hardly had time to decide that maybe they should have paid a little more attention to what had been following them in the woods.

Chapter 10

Cameron heard the sound of a sword cutting through the air before it occurred to him that he was being attacked. He ducked, pulling Sunny down with him. He shoved her toward the protection of a wall behind them, then rose.

"Whoresons," he spat, pulling his sword from the sheath. "Let the wench go."

There was no response. Cameron didn't expect it from two of the lads, for he'd just slit both their throats with a single mighty swing, but the others certainly could have offered an opinion.

"Take one of the knives," he barked at Sunny.

He felt her pull one out of his boot. He drew the other quickly and threw himself into the fray. He called for aid, but no one came.

He was somehow not surprised.

Damnation, but he should have taken more care in the forest. Well, at least here there was some cover available. He tried to keep himself close enough to Sunny to protect her, but he was continually drawn forward. He had no idea how many were coming against him. There seemed to be an endless stream of lads eager to engage him.

And still no one came to help him.

He fought with sword and knife and curses. He felt more anger than he ever had in battle before. These lads weren't Fergussons come to avenge their dead. They were lads he didn't know, but he knew what they wanted, and he knew who'd hired them.

Giric would pay dearly.

By the time the sun had set, there was no one left standing and he was covered in blood. Very little of it was his own, fortunately. He dragged his sleeve across his face to rid himself of the sweat that dripped down into his eyes, then turned and felt terror slam into him.

A man stood pressed against Sunny. He could see one of her hands spasmodically clutching the wall.

He couldn't move. He could only stand there and shake.

Then the man began to fall backward. He landed in the mud at Cameron's feet with Cameron's knife sticking out of his gut. The front of Sunny's dress was covered in blood. Cameron met her eyes. They were wide with terror.

"Did he hurt you?" he asked weakly.

She shook her head in a jerky motion.

He bowed his head briefly, then took a deep breath and put the moment behind him. He pulled his knife free of the man's belly, shoved it back in his boot, replaced his other knife, then grabbed Sunny's hand and pulled her into a stumbling run with him. He didn't bother to resheath his sword. He had more business to do with it that night.

He ran with Sunny up to the keep and wasn't sure if he was surprised or not to find a handful of his kin milling about there. It wasn't possible that they hadn't heard his calls. He marked each of them, then continued on his way to the door. He would repay them later.

He walked into the great hall to find Giric lounging in a chair in front of the fire with his feet up on a stool. He looked up tranquilly.

"Been out in the wet, Cam?" he asked.

"I told you to not call me that," Cameron growled. "And this is blood, not rain, you whoreson." He left Sunny standing against the wall, then walked over to the hearth. He put his foot on the front of his cousin's chair and shoved, sending Giric flying backward onto his arse.

Giric scrambled to his feet, swearing. Cameron waited, bouncing on the balls of his feet, more than ready to take a few last frustrations out on his cousin. Giric drew his sword and Cameron felt the first crossing of their blades rattle his bones. A pity it would be no more interesting than that. His cousin was boastful, but he was not skilled. Cameron dragged the whole affair out far longer than he needed to only because he had several things to repay his cousin for. Even after what he'd just been through, he had more than enough energy to humiliate the man standing in front of him. The only reason he didn't kill the fool was because it had been Giric's suggestion to go fetch the MacLeod witch.

He beat on his cousin's sword until it fell from his fingers. He slid his own sword back across the floor to Sunny and continued his instruction with his fists.

By the time Giric was a bloody heap at his feet, his own fists were bloody and he was shaking with weariness. He looked at Gilly standing in the circle of torchlight.

"Enjoy him," he said, his chest heaving, "but you'd best brush up on your swordplay. You'll need someone to protect your bairns given that it won't be this fool here."

Gilly said nothing. She only walked across the hall and looked down at Giric lying there, senseless.

Cameron found that his men had gathered to watch the spectacle, as well. He swept them with a very cold look. They all bowed their heads, one by one, then turned and melted back into the shadows.

Cameron turned and walked over to Sunny. She leaned against the wall near the hearth with his sword resting point down on the floor in front of her. The sword was taller than she was and she had to lift her arms to hold on to the hilt. He took it from her, resheathed it in the scabbard on his back, then took her hand.

"I think we're due a bath," he said pleasantly.

"Together?" she squeaked.

He laughed. "Nay, lass. You'll go first."

She looked insultingly relieved. He smiled again and pulled her toward the kitchen.

"Cam, look at your arm."

His heart sighed a little at the sound of that name from her, but he supposed it didn't serve him to show it. He looked down at his left arm and saw the slice that ran from his elbow to his fingers. It was nothing he hadn't seen before, but it burned like hellfire so he supposed it would need to be seen to. "You can have at it—after I've had something to eat."

She nodded and walked with him into the kitchen. Cameron fetched Sunny a stool and put her near the fire, requested a tub of hot water be prepared, then went to look for some sort of cousin to help him in a little endeavor. He retrieved Brice and brought him back to sit at the cook's work table.

"Taste," he invited.

Brice looked up quickly. "What?"

"I'm hungry and I want to make certain Giric hasn't been adding his own spices to my stew. I can wait for a bit before I eat, just to make sure my supper hasn't killed you."

Brice blanched. Cameron drew the bloody knife from his boot and gestured with it toward the things on the table he thought

Brice should try. Brice was not an enthusiastic taster and he completely refused to drink any wine. Cameron put his hand on a cup and looked at his cousin purposefully.

"And if I help a bit of this to find its way to your gut?"

"I beg you, cousin, nay," Brice whispered.

"Is *all* the wine poisoned," Cameron asked, "or just what you and Giric have been trying to give me?"

Brice closed his eyes briefly and swallowed with difficulty. "There's a barrel with your name scratched near the base."

Cameron allowed his cousin to rise. "I won't tell Giric you told me," he said quietly, "but I imagine he'll find out. You'd best watch your back, hadn't you?"

Brice apparently couldn't find anything useful to say to that. He stumbled from the kitchen and disappeared into the gloom of the hall.

Cameron put him out of his mind and set to a quick meal with Sunny. When the tub was filled with moderately warm water, he looked at her.

"Here's your chance for a wash," he said.

She looked down at her dress, then at him. "What good will it do?"

"You wouldn't be bloody anymore. If we wash your dress tonight and set it by the fire upstairs, 'twill be mostly dry by tomorrow."

"And what am I going to wear in the meantime?" she asked uncomfortably.

"You could wear my plaids," he said. He pulled her up off her stool and bent his head to whisper in her ear. "Besides, I've already seen you without your clothes, lass."

"But you don't have to look now—and neither do the rest of your kitchen people, do they?"

He laughed at her. "I won't, though I should, just to show you who is laird." He turned his back on her, waved away the kitchen lads and shot his cook a warning look, then folded his arms over his chest. "Make haste, wench, before the water grows cold."

He felt her toss her dress over his shoulder, heard her get into the tub with a groan, splash a bit, then get out. She took his plaids off his other shoulder.

"Finished," she said a moment later.

He turned and looked at her, hastily wrapped in his plaids. He rearranged one to pull it up toward her neck. She looked so miserably uncomfortable that he left her alone.

A maid. Why wasn't he surprised?

He pulled his sword free of the scabbard and rested it against the side of the tub, then stripped. He looked, just to see if Sunny was watching, but she had turned her back to him. He tapped her smartly on the shoulder.

"Hold my gear," he invited.

She turned around, but her eyes were closed. He smiled as he put first his knives, then his clothes into her hands. He shucked off his boots, then sank down gratefully into still-warm water. He leaned his head back against the edge of the tub and sighed in pleasure.

"Let me know if anyone else wants to kill me," he said lazily. "I'll see to them after I'm finished here."

"I think you're safe for the moment," Sunny said, setting his things down on the table and pulling a stool up next to the tub. "Let me see your arm."

He could see the slice needed tending, though he couldn't say he was looking forward to it. He waited while Brianna was found and sent to fetch what was necessary, then closed his eyes whilst Sunny sewed him up. She was quick and deft, but it wasn't comfortable. When she was finished, he reached up and pulled her down where he could kiss her briefly.

"Thank you," he said with a smile.

"It could stand a poultice and a wrapping about it, but I don't suppose you care about the scar."

"Add it to the others," he said with a snort.

She turned herself around on her stool and faced the entrance to the great hall. "I'll keep watch if you want to relax."

"Sure you don't want to get back in with me?"

She shot him an uneasy glance over her shoulder, scowled at his grin, then turned away from him.

He left off provoking her and merely dragged his fingers through her hair, watching her shiver as he did so. He continued with his idle ministrations, but turned his attentions to their surroundings. He wouldn't have been the first Cameron to be murdered in his bath.

When the water was colder than he cared to endure any longer, he rose, then took a clean saffron shirt from Brianna and pulled it over his head. It came down almost to his knees, so perhaps that was concession enough to modesty. He took his plaid, filthy shirt, and Sunny's dress and dumped them into the tub. He swished them around, then pulled Sunny's dress out. It wasn't ever going to be the same, but it was better than it had been. Perhaps it could have a proper scrub when the kitchen felt a bit friendlier. He wrung everything out, handed it all to Brianna, then took his sword and Sunny's hand.

"Let's go up," he said.

"Are you sure I should come with you?" she asked.

He shot her a look. "Do you think I would trust you anywhere near any of these lads? I don't give a bloody damn what they think. I'll at least know you're safe."

She sighed, then nodded and continued on with him. He noted that Giric was still unconscious on the floor. Gilly was kneeling next to him, trying to get him to rouse. Cameron kept Sunny's hand in his and walked over to them.

"Dead?" he asked hopefully.

Gilly shot him a glare. "He's alive. Just senseless."

"So, little has changed," he said pleasantly. "Best of luck with him, sister."

He turned and walked away. He supposed he wouldn't have been surprised to find a knife in his back thanks to her at some point, but perhaps not that day. She would have her hands full enough with Giric's complaints when he awoke to keep her occupied for a bit.

He walked up the stairs with Sunny, looking at her every now and again to see how she fared. She clutched his plaid to her throat as if she expected someone to rip it off her at any moment. He supposed any sensible man would have been tempted, but he had more self-control than most. He led her into his bedchamber, bolted the door behind them, then went to find himself another plaid. He made himself far more modest than he would have otherwise, handed their gear to Brianna to set near the fire, then turned and looked at Sunny.

"You can go to bed, lass," he said with a smile. "I'll sleep on the floor."

"Thank you, Cam," she said quietly.

He walked across the floor to her because he just couldn't help himself. He put his hands on her arms.

"Say my name again," he commanded.

"Robert Francis—"

He shook his head. "Nay, not all that ridiculous business. The other."

She looked up at him gravely. "Thank you, Cam."

He bent his head and kissed her softly, because he just couldn't help himself. Then he kissed her again, far longer than he should have, but managed to stop himself before he reached for his plaids and pulled them off her. He lifted his head, took a deep breath, then turned her around and nudged her toward his bed.

"Get in alone, wench, whilst you can."

She walked to the bed, then hesitated. "Close your eyes—no, actually turn around and close your eyes."

He turned around with a heavy sigh, then waited until he heard her jump in and pull the sheet up before he came to sit down on the floor next to the bed. "You should sleep now, love," he said, leaning back against the wall. "I imagine all hell will break loose at some point in the next day or so and we'll both want to be rested for it."

She folded one of the plaids he'd given her into a pillow and rested her chin on it. "Are you worried?"

"Worried? Nay. A bit lost? Aye, I'll admit to that." He smiled, but he supposed it had been a bit on the bleak side. "I've always had kin about me, kin I trusted. My father was the most loyal man I've ever known. Breac would have died for me in an instant. He did, as it happened. He took the blade meant for me in that last battle. Even Sim, that giddy lad who was more inclined to drink than wield a sword, was always there at my elbow, always ready to turn and guard my back. But who is there now?"

"I don't know," she said gravely. "Who is there?"

"Not Giric, that is certain," he said grimly. "He would like to believe himself capable of holding this lot together, but even his sire didn't think him fit to be laird." He sighed and dragged his hands through his damp hair. "Nay, 'tis just me, trying to keep these unruly fools together in some fashion. And now 'tis just me alone."

She reached out and put her hand over his resting on his knees. "I'm sorry about your brothers, Cam. I'm especially sorry I couldn't do anything for Breac."

"You did what you could." He managed a weary smile. "And were it not for you and your fetching green eyes, I would have wed Gilly a se'nnight ago. You saved me from marrying a Fergusson, at least."

Her mouth fell open. "Gilly is a Fergusson? And your brother wed her?"

Cameron shrugged. "He thought it might bring peace. It didn't, did it?"

She swallowed. "It doesn't seem to have." She started to say something else, then blinked. "You aren't going to marry her?"

He reached out and trailed his fingers down her cheek. "Nay, Sunshine, I'm not."

She looked a little pale. "I'm afraid to ask what you *are* going to do."

"Sit here all night," he began with a smile, "and question a thousand times why I feel the need to hold to my damnable honor and not crawl in that bed with you. We could handfast, you know. I could take you downstairs, claim you on my threshold, then carry you back here and join you in that bed. Perfectly legal and acceptable and I wouldn't have to ride for a priest since mine was found floating in the cesspit earlier this week."

"Oh, Cameron, nay," she said in horror.

"Giric's doing," he said with a shrug. "But that other is something to consider." He paused. "You'd have a year and a day to decide if you wanted me, you know."

Her face was flaming. "I don't think I'd need that long."

He laughed in spite of himself, then leaned forward and kissed her. "Woman, if I didn't think there were three dozen lads below with my death on their minds, I would take you downstairs right now. I think if we survive the next few days, we'll turn our minds to something a bit more formal than that, even if I have to steal the MacLeod priest this time." He paused. "If you might be willing."

She took a deep breath. "I think I just might be."

He smiled, then sat back against the wall and reached for her hand. "Actually, I can't decide if it would be better to ask you to stay here with me or go ahead with you."

"Truly?" she asked in surprise.

"I'm thinking on it," he admitted. "What each would mean for the both of us."

She closed her eyes. He wondered, briefly, if the thought of it made her ill or not. Then she opened her eyes and looked at him.

Her eyes were full of tears.

"Oh, Cam," she whispered.

He had to blink a time or two as well. If she only knew how

much it pleased him to hear that name from her. He leaned forward and kissed her, not as thoroughly as he would have liked, but circumstances were what they were. He looked at her, her beautiful face so close to his, and found it in him to smile.

"What think you about that gate of yours? Will it work this time, do you think?"

"I wish I knew," she whispered.

"Well, we've nothing to lose." He had to chew on his next words for quite some time before he could spew them out. "Even if we've no promise of your gates working for us, we cannot remain here." He sighed deeply. "We'll think on it all later. You can tell me all about what there is for a medieval laird to do with himself hundreds of years out of his time. But for now, you should sleep. Tomorrow will be a difficult day, I imagine. I have an extra knife in my trunk. You'll keep it with you at all times, aye?"

She nodded, shivering.

He brought the blanket up to her ear and tucked her in securely, then sat back against the wall again. His sword was on the floor by his hand, his knives down his boots, yet still he didn't feel comfortable. There was something unwholesome about feeling as though the entire company of lads below was waiting for him to doze off so they could fall upon him and kill him.

He felt Sunny's hand twitch a time or two, then still. He closed his eyes as well, but it brought him no comfort.

A pair of hours passed, no more, before he woke with a start and realized he'd slept. He looked over at the fire and saw, with a sinking feeling, that Brianna wasn't there. He vaguely remembered her telling him she was going to see to a pressing need down the passageway. He'd nodded, then thought nothing more of it. He realized then that he should have.

He disentangled his fingers from Sunny's and rose silently. He walked across his chamber, then carefully opened the door.

Brianna was lying there on the floor in front of him.

He squatted and put his fingers to her throat.

He rose, shut the door soundlessly, then crossed back across the chamber. He put his hand on Sunny. She woke and looked up at him blearily. He bent down and put his mouth close to her ear.

"We need to leave now," he murmured. "Apparently, our battle is harder upon us that I supposed. We'll be fighting our way out, likely. I'll bring you your dress and a knife. Don't move until you must."

She shivered, once, then nodded.

He fetched her damp dress off the chair, found the knife in his trunk, then walked silently across the floor, avoiding the boards that made noise. He handed Sunny her dress, turned his back to her until she'd donned it, then pulled her out of bed and set her carefully on her feet. He wrapped one of his plaids about her hips, cinching it tightly. He pulled the other over her shoulders, then tied it under her arms and behind her back where it wouldn't get it her way but would still keep her warm. He put a knife in her hands, then leaned close again.

"Brianna's dead at the door. We might make it to the hall, but I imagine not any farther than that. Be silent as the tomb, love. Our lives depend on it."

She put her free hand over her mouth—no doubt to keep a gasp trapped there—and nodded. Cameron pulled her into his arms and held her there until she had caught her breath and was no longer gasping.

"Brave wench," he said quietly. "Stay behind me. Keep yourself against the wall if you can. I'll stand between you and the rest of them as we did in the village. Kill whoever comes near you, though. Don't hesitate, don't show any mercy, just kill. Those whoresons downstairs don't deserve compassion."

She nodded again, a jerky motion that showed him just how terrified she was.

"Put your feet after mine. The floor squeaks." He flashed her a quick smile. "Silent as the tomb, my love. I'll get you out safely."

She put one hand on his shoulder and nodded a final time. He led her over to the door, then opened it carefully. He stepped over Brianna, then led Sunny down the stairs. No one stopped them, which worried him. The hall was asleep as well. He made his way carefully but without hesitation to the front door. No one stirred and that unsettled him more than anything else. Surely they would not be let go so easily.

He lifted the wooden beam barring the door, then opened the door itself. It made a horrible squeak as he did so. He jerked Sunny out of the door with him, then pulled it shut behind him.

"Run," he said.

She bolted with him for the stables. He didn't bother with a saddle. He flung Sunny up onto his horse's back, grabbed a handful of mane, then swung up behind her. He drew his sword from the sheath as his mount leaped forward.

They were waiting for him at the gate.

"We'll run through them," he said.

Sunny had his extra knife in her hand. She flung it as he ran his horse right into Giric. He cut down three of his own cousins, and kicked another in the face that tried to bring down his horse, but he didn't stop.

"You all right?" he shouted.

"Fine," she said breathlessly.

Cameron pushed his mount into a gallop and the brave beast leaped forward as if he knew he had to fly.

But it wasn't over.

His cousins, his bloody *kinsmen* were behind them within minutes. He could do nothing but continue on and hope that good would triumph over evil in the end. There was no possible way for him to turn and fight them all. He resheathed his sword, then wrapped one arm around Sunny and held on.

He supposed that their best hope was to make for the MacLeod witch's house. Perhaps the gate hadn't worked the time before because Sunny had been destined to stay with him. Things were different now. It would work.

He would accept nothing else.

Two grueling, relentless, endless hours later he was hurtling through the MacLeod forest. Unfortunately, Giric was right behind him, shouting at him. At least his cousin was the only one with the spine to continue to follow him. The rest had fallen back an hour ago. The odds were, for a change, in his favor.

Cameron tightened his arm around Sunny. "I'm going to leap off soon and engage him. Ride on, then dismount and run for the house when you can."

She nodded.

He squeezed her, hard. "Brave gel."

She put her hand behind her and touched the back of his head. He slipped off his horse and ducked under the hooves of Giric's mount. He rolled up to his feet, then ran after his cousin.

"Fight me, you coward!" he shouted.

Giric whirled his horse around, but the ground was too soft. Giric leapt off his horse as it went down. Cameron ran up, punched his cousin as hard as he could in the face, then left him lying there in a stupor. Giric's horse struggled to its feet, then bolted. Cameron turned and sprinted after Sunny.

He caught her as she was sliding down off his horse. He took her hand and ran with her toward the witch's house.

He heard crashing in the underbrush behind him. He whirled around and saved himself having his head cleaved in twain by nothing but luck. He shoved Giric back.

"Take the clan," Cameron spat. "You've left it full of nothing but liars and bastards. Take it and leave us be."

"Never," Giric growled.

Cameron shoved Sunny along behind him as he backed up toward the house. He fought Giric ferociously, beat him back, then turned and ran with Sunny.

"Go," he said, pushing her ahead of him.

The house loomed up in front of him. Cameron pushed the door open, then shoved Sunny inside.

He felt something slam into his back. He realized that it was a knife. At almost the same time, he heard Sunny cry out. He whirled around in time to see Giric bend over and pick up a rock. He watched, feeling a little detached, as that very sharp rock came down toward his head.

The pain was blinding.

He fell backward, then spun at the last moment. If he landed on whatever was sticking into his back, he would kill himself. At least if he fell on his chest, he might survive.

He pitched forward.

Damnation, he had wanted to die as the laird of his own clan, with Sunshine Phillips at his side, with a cluster of children standing by his bed, children who were grateful for the legacy he'd left them. He didn't want to die now and leave Sunny behind, alone.

He didn't remember hitting the floor.

Chapter 11

Sunny woke to a crushing pain in her head. She lay perfectly still, trying to figure out where she was and what had happened to her. She didn't hear anything untoward. No swords ringing. No enemies yelling. No angry Cameron clansmen shouting curses. It was, she had to admit, eerily silent.

Was she dead?

She felt the floor under her fingers and found it to be very cold indeed. She still had fingers to feel with, so she supposed it was a safe bet she was still alive. She just didn't know where she was—or with whom. She closed her eyes and listened, but all she could hear was her own ragged breathing. She held her breath and listened a bit longer, but to her dismay, heard nothing. Had Cameron been hurt?

Was *he* dead?

She thought back to the last thing she remembered. Cameron had turned to fight his cousin, backed her up to Moraig's house, then pushed her inside. She remembered a blinding pain in the back of her head, as if she'd been hit with a rock.

She felt around her. She found a rock, a very sharp one, but nothing else. There was also something wet on the floor next to her head. Was it blood?

Before she could come to any decision on that, she heard a noise. It sounded like someone outside the door. She fumbled for a weapon, but came up with nothing. She didn't have Cameron's knife any longer. She had flung it at one of his clansmen and watched him stumble away, clutching his throat.

Was it Cameron at her door? But he shouldn't have been at the door; he should have been right beside her. She reached for the rock, just in case it was someone she might have to do damage to. She might be able to protect them both until she could figure out what was going on.

The door at her feet opened. She tried to get up, but she couldn't. The lights went on and she screamed in pain.

"Sunny!"

She clutched her head, then forced herself to squint at what was in front of her.

Patrick MacLeod stood there, looking at her in astonishment.

Patrick MacLeod, not Robert Francis Cameron mac Cameron.

Sunny pressed her hands against her head and looked around her. She was in Moraig's house, Moraig's twenty-first-century house that was now her house, with her coat on the peg by the door and her pictures on the anything-but-straight walls and her additions and subtractions to Moraig's collection of furniture.

But she was alone.

She started to hyperventilate. She felt strong arms go around her, then heard Patrick's voice.

"She's here, love. Nay, I don't think I should move her. Her head is bleeding. Call Jamie for me, will you? He'll call Ian."

Of course. Those MacLeod lads had a calling tree that would have been the envy of any ladies' aid society.

"Nay, love, don't worry about bringing anything. Sunny will have everything here I need."

Sunny heard him set his phone down.

"Sunny, you're bleeding," he said, sounding very worried.

Sunny shielded her eyes from the light with one hand and peered at him.

"Where's Cam?"

"Who?"

She pushed him away and struggled to her feet. "Help me up," she begged. "Please. I have to get to the threshold."

"'Tis a bad idea, lass," he said. "Let me at least look at that bump. And do you realize you're babbling in Gaelic?"

"Just help me up, damn you," she said fiercely. "Either that or get out of my way."

He stood and pulled her up. She swayed as the room spun violently. Patrick put his arms around her and held on to her until she managed to stand without help. She turned away and looked around her house. The light hurt her eyes, but she forced herself to look at the floor, her bed, the kitchen.

There was nothing except a misshapen circle of blood and a sharp rock. She was still alone. Well, except for Patrick.

"Did you"—she had to think about the word for a minute— "drive?"

"Nay, sister, I walked," he said, sounding puzzled. "Why?"

"I need light for the outside," she said, holding out her hand.

He pulled his flashlight out of his jacket pocket, turned it on, and handed it to her. "Sunny, where have you been?"

"Not here," she said. She pulled him along with her so she could use him as a crutch. She shined the light all around her threshold, looking for boot prints, or blood, or something to indicate that Cameron had been there as well.

There was nothing.

She pulled Patrick outside with her. She looked all around the house.

There was still nothing.

She went back inside, feeling increasingly frantic. She looked all over, but still the only sign of anything out of the ordinary was the pool of blood she'd been lying in and the bloody rock lying next to it. Nothing else. No evidence that anyone had come back to the future with her.

The flashlight fell from her fingers because she simply didn't have the strength to hold it. She felt Patrick pull her into his arms. She clutched the edges of his coat and gasped for breath she couldn't seem to catch. He hadn't made it. Cameron hadn't come with her through the gate.

In time, she heard others come into her house, but they were like ghosts floating on the edge of her vision. She thought she might have sobbed in Madelyn's arms. She was fairly certain Patrick had helped her throw up.

Eventually, she found herself in her own bed, dressed in her damp dress and wrapped in two of Cameron's plaids, alone except for Patrick who sat on a stool next to her bed, watching her with the gravest expression she'd ever seen him wear.

"I'm going to stay with you tonight," he said quietly, "but I'll be waking you every half hour. Tomorrow we'll go into Inverness for tests. That is quite a serious bump you have on the back of your head."

Sunny closed her eyes to keep the tears where they belonged. The Gaelic Patrick was speaking, complete with his medieval accent, was incredibly soothing. "Thank you," she managed.

He brushed the hair back from her face gently. "Want to talk about it?"

"No."

"Sunny, you were gone for over a fortnight."

"Apparently so," she croaked.

He sighed. "Very well, I suppose you'll tell me the rest when it suits you." He paused. "We've worried. Jamie especially."

"I missed his dinner."

"He'll want a full report, you know."

"I'll tell him to stuff it."

Patrick laughed softly. "He's your laird, gel. Show some respect."

She couldn't agree. Her laird was lost somewhere in 1375, probably dying from Giric's sword across his throat or knife buried in his back. For all she knew, Cameron was a ghost and she would find him standing in front of her fire the next day—only she wouldn't be able to touch him.

"Want the loo again?" Patrick asked quickly.

"No," she managed. "No, I'm all right. Thank you."

He squeezed her hand. "Of course. I'll be here when you need me."

She nodded and closed her eyes. She couldn't talk anymore, couldn't think anymore, couldn't bring herself to face the harsh reality of what had happened.

Cameron hadn't made it.

She wasn't sure she would survive it.

Ten days later, she knew she could put off the unavoidable no longer. She would have to go see Jamie, tell him something reasonable about her activities over her missing two weeks, then find the strength to ignore the look of extreme skepticism he would give her when she lied about whether or not she had used one of his gates.

Then again, perhaps he wouldn't ask her anything yet. Even Patrick hadn't asked her anything past inquiring about her headache. Maybe she looked as bad as she felt.

Sleeping hadn't helped much. She had been in bed for a solid week, lying in her filthy dress, wrapped in Cameron mac Cameron's two marginally clean plaids, and wondering when it was that he was going to show up at her door. She'd spent two more days sitting in a chair in front of a cheery fire, waiting.

But he hadn't come.

She'd eventually given up hoping he would. If he was going to find his way to her, he would have done it by then. But he hadn't and he wouldn't—not even as a ghost, apparently.

The only bright spots were that the cut on the back of her head had healed enough that she could wash her hair and a test done in Inverness had revealed that while she had a very good bump, she also had a very hard head. She'd been told to go back to bed and rest, which she'd happily done. It was easier to deal with life when she was sleeping away most of it.

She shuffled to the bathroom and looked at herself in the mirror. Actually, it was less of a look and more the occasional peek when the stars cleared long enough for her to see herself, but she wasn't going to quibble.

She didn't think she looked much different, though she was thinner. Patrick had tried to force all kinds of liquid things down her, things made of fruits and vegetables she usually liked quite well. It had been an effort to drink and she'd done it only because she'd known she had to.

She leaned on the counter and looked at herself. Did she look as if she'd traveled through time, fallen in love, then lost that love? Did her hands look as if they had tried to heal, succeeded at killing, touched the face of a man she cherished?

She wasn't sure she wanted to know.

She brushed her teeth, then had to sit down and rest. Well, one thing was for sure: she didn't dare drive to Jamie's. At least if she passed out while she was walking, she wouldn't run off the road and kill anyone.

She sat again for a few more minutes, then got to her feet and tottered out of her house. She shut the door behind her, then stumbled along the path that led to Jamie's upper meadow. She stopped and looked down its length.

She almost went back to bed.

But she'd promised to show up, so show up she would. At least the path led downhill. It could have been worse.

What should have been a half-hour walk took her almost two. By the time she got through Jamie's gates, she wasn't at all convinced that she wouldn't pass out before she managed to get to the front door.

She walked up the way, then leaned for quite some time against a dusty Range Rover she didn't recognize. She made it to the steps, then had to rest against the wood a bit more. When she thought she could manage it, she lifted her hand and knocked.

The door opened suddenly and she pitched forward. Strong arms caught her and put her back on her feet. She peered up at Zachary Smith, Elizabeth's youngest brother.

"You've grown," she managed.

"You're loopy," he said with a smile. He shut the door behind her, then put his arm around her shoulders. "Sunny, you should have called. I would have come and gotten you."

"I didn't know you were home. Is that your car out front?"

"Nah, too pricey for me," Zachary said with a smile. "It belongs to some guy Jamie's doing business with. And that, it happens, is the reason I'm home. Jamie and this very rich new friend of his are thinking about putting up a leisure centre in the village and they want me to design it."

"Nice," Sunny wheezed. "Yoga classes for me to teach?"

"Yeah," Zachary said with a grin. "Let's put Tavish Fergusson out of business."

Tavish Fergusson. She hadn't thought about him in a month. Or the village, for that matter. She had been, for all intents and purposes, on another planet. Somehow, though, life had continued on in the world she'd left behind.

It was very strange.

"Sunny?"

"Sure," she said quickly. "Whatever you said." She put her arm around his waist. "Help me find a chair, Zach. I don't feel very good all of a sudden."

"You should have called," he chided again.

"I don't have a phone."

"I'll have Jamie get you one. You call me the next time you need to go anywhere."

She nodded and closed her eyes briefly. "All right, I will. Thank you."

He helped her down into a chair, then left her in peace. She leaned her head against the chair's back and closed her eyes. Tears leaked out from under her eyelids and she didn't have the energy to wipe them away. What did it matter, anyway? Her heart was shattered and she looked like hell. Maybe it would come to the point where people would just leave her alone to crawl into her bed, curl up in the fetal position, and cry herself to death.

She knew it wasn't doing her any good to continue to speculate about Cameron's fate, but she couldn't help herself. She had come to the conclusion, in those moments when she could actually think clearly, that Giric had killed him.

If only she'd known that's how it would have finished, she would have pulled him into the house with her faster, or put herself between him and his cousin, or told him to ride harder or leave sooner. Any one thing might have meant the difference between his being dead and his being with her. Just one thing . . .

"Sunny?"

She opened her eyes and found Zachary standing in front of her with a glass.

"Juice?" he offered.

She accepted it, drank some, then handed it back to him. "Thanks," she said hoarsely.

"I'm always happy to be of service to a beautiful woman."

"Nice line."

"In your case it isn't a line, but I'm practicing anyway. You never know when I'll answer a knock at the door and find a beautiful woman there waiting just for me."

Well, she knew what that felt like, but she couldn't say as much. Just the thought of it was about to kill her.

"Oh, here they come," Zachary said. "Want to meet the other half of the money? Once he sees you, he'll be begging to give us more so we can build that yoga studio."

Sunny would have snorted, but that would have taken energy she didn't have. She let Zachary pull her to her feet and lead her across the great hall. She heard Jamie coming down the stairs as she neared them. He was speaking animatedly, so she knew the deal must be a good one.

A man was following him down. She first saw polished black shoes, then dark trouser pants, then a matching suit coat that stretched over shoulders that had surely been made just for a girl to put her head on and be at peace. He was wearing a discreet burgundy tie in a plaid pattern that reminded her a bit of Cameron's plaids that were folded under her pillow.

Then she saw his face.

"Sunny," Zachary exclaimed.

Sunny realized belatedly that she had shoved him so hard that he'd gone sprawling. Her glass shattered against the stone of Jamie's great hall floor, but she didn't care. All she could do was look up at the man who had finished coming down the stairs and was standing five feet away from her. She could hardly believe her eyes.

It was Cameron.

"Sunshine," Jamie said, sounding pleased. He crossed the pair of steps toward her, then offered her his arm.

With a cry of relief, she ignored Jamie and threw herself into Cameron's arms. He was *alive*. She couldn't believe it, but the proof of it was standing right in front . . . of . . . her . . .

Stiff with surprise.

Sunny pulled back and looked up at him.

He was looking at her as if he'd never seen her before.

"Sunshine," Jamie said in consternation. "Sunny?"

Sunny looked up into Cameron's beautiful, beloved face and couldn't understand why he wasn't glad to see her. She couldn't understand why his arms weren't coming around her and crushing her to him.

Why the hell was he in a suit?

She wanted to say his name, but she found that her mouth wouldn't form words. It wouldn't have done her any good if she'd been able to, since she didn't have any breath for speaking them. She put her hands on his face and looked up into his vivid blue eyes.

Eyes that were wide with surprise, but not recognition.

"Sunshine?"

Jamie's voice pulled her back to herself. She realized quite suddenly and with a sickening feeling that Cameron wasn't as happy to see her as she was him.

She released him abruptly and stumbled backward. She backed into Jamie and felt his hands on her shoulders. She shook her head, because she just couldn't believe what was happening to her. She shook her head again, but it didn't change anything. She took another step backward, but Jamie was in her way.

"Let me introduce Robert Cameron," he said, his voice rumbling in his chest and rattling her back. "I rang him last week to see if he would be interested in putting his tuppence together with mine to build something in the village."

"Robert Cameron," Sunny echoed. She looked at Cameron and felt tears begin to stream down her cheeks. It was him. It had to be him. He looked older, somehow. More polished. Cleaner. But she would have known him anywhere.

"Actually, 'tis Lord Robert, if we're to be perfectly correct,"

Jamie continued. "He's laird of the clan Cameron. You've no doubt seen his hall up the way." He paused. "Perhaps you've seen him before."

Sunny was afraid to open her mouth for fear of what would come out. Perhaps she'd seen him before? She shook her head again, but it only made her dizzy.

"She's had a bit of a concussion," Jamie announced to no one in particular.

Sunny looked at Cameron to find him watching her with a guardedly pleasant expression—and no sign at all of recognizing her.

Why not?

She thought, quite seriously, that her heart would break, slice its way out of her chest as it did so, and shatter into innumerable pieces right there on the floor in front of them all.

"Mac? Mac, where are you?"

Sunny looked up the stairs and saw a woman gliding down them. She was absolutely gorgeous, dressed like a model, with all the grace and poise of a prima ballerina.

"Mac," she said, slipping her hand possessively into the crook of Cameron's arm, "you rushed off without me, darling."

"This is Lord Robert's fiancée, Penelope Ainsworth," Jamie said.

Sunny looked from Penelope to Cameron and back to Penelope. His fiancée? She wanted to tell Jamie that he was mistaken, that Cameron didn't have a blonde fiancée, he had her, but the words wouldn't come out. All she could do was stand there and gape.

Penelope looked down her nose. "Oh, I believe we've met before, haven't we, dear? You ran into me in the village last month. You'd had a bit too much to drink that evening, hadn't you?"

Sunny blinked, then felt her mouth fall open even farther. It was that rude Englishwoman who had plowed into her and then stepped on her hand. But that would mean that the man who had picked up both her and her purse had been . . .

Cameron.

She put her hands to her head because it hurt so badly, she thought she might throw up.

"This is my sister-in-law, Sunshine Phillips," Jamie said stiffly, "and she doesn't touch liquor."

"Are you sure about that?" Penelope Ainsworth asked doubtfully. "Perhaps she has habits you aren't familiar with."

Jamie made a noise of displeasure that sounded a bit like a growl. Sunny would have wondered why he seemed to be so bent on defending her, but she was distracted by the sight of Cameron extending his hand to her. She took it without thinking.

The jolt that went though her almost knocked her flat.

She looked up at him quickly to see if he felt it as well. He was pulling his hand away and frowning thoughtfully at it, as if it had done something he didn't quite approve of.

"A pleasure, Miss Phillips," he said, turning that frown on her.

Yet still he gave absolutely no sign of having recognized her.

She felt the room begin to spin in earnest. She was falling and couldn't do anything to stop it. She would break open the freshly healed wound and bleed all over Jamie's floor. She supposed that might be an improvement over the events of the past five minutes.

Cameron didn't know her.

It was worse than having him dead.

She fell into the blackness in front of her without fighting it.

Chapter 12

Cameron caught the dark-haired woman before she touched the ground. He lifted her up into his arms and felt more astonished than he had in years. It wasn't that he wasn't accustomed to beautiful women throwing themselves at him, for they did so with regularity. Nay, that wasn't what surprised him.

It was that he recognized this one.

It took him a moment to decide why. He supposed, as he thought on it a bit longer, that it was simply that she was the one Penelope had run into and sent sprawling—a month ago, was it, almost? He remembered picking Miss Phillips up, picking up her purse, then having an earful all the way to supper in Inverness about his damnable chivalry being damned inconvenient.

Penelope's words, not his.

"Hand her over, Mac," Penelope demanded, interrupting his thoughts. "Surely her friends here can take care of her."

Cameron looked at her evenly. "Penelope, I'll see her set down, then I'll meet you in the car. Why don't you go out and wait for me?"

She rolled her eyes, sighed gustily, then stalked across the hall floor to throw open the front door and leave it open behind her. Zachary Smith, Jamie's brother-in-law, walked over and shut it quietly. Cameron turned back to James MacLeod.

"This is your sister-in-law?" he asked.

James smiled wickedly. "And my witch."

Cameron smiled in spite of himself. "An interesting thing to have on staff, wouldn't you say?"

"'Tis tradition," James said with something of a purr. "We hold to it rather firmly here on my land. There has always been a witch in that little hut to the north."

I know, Cameron almost said, but he stopped himself in time. There had been witches there for as long as he could remember. In fact, he'd known one of them, Moraig MacLeod, but he didn't think anything good would come of saying as much.

"Sunny's a fine healer," James continued. "She came to visit last year and I asked her to stay here instead of returning to America."

"She's a Yank?" Cameron asked in surprise.

"Surprisingly enough," James said mildly. "We seem to wed them in droves. Sunny's very keen on all that business of yoga and natural cures. We should build her a shop in the centre. Give that damned Tavish Fergusson a reason to look for somewhere else to sell his wares."

Cameron pursed his lips. He never allowed a chance to vex a Fergusson pass him by. "Absolutely," he agreed. "Now, where can I take her? Back to her house?"

"Too far," James said. "Let's have her upstairs in the guest chamber."

Cameron followed James upstairs and listened to him babble on in Gaelic about the leisure center. As he followed him, he couldn't help but wonder about him. He didn't have anything to do with MacLeods, in keeping with tradition, but he'd listened to the gossip down at the pub often enough. The lads there said James MacLeod was a throwback to earlier times. In fact, there were those who said he *was* from earlier times. It was utter rubbish, of course. Men did not travel from one century to another.

'Twas easy enough to explain away James's oddities. His command of Gaelic was nothing more than a Highlander properly keeping his native language alive. He had the physique of a man who worked out hours a day because he likely worked out hours a day. He had a perfectly restored medieval keep with all the medieval trappings because he no doubt had a fondness for history. The souls in that keep treated him with lairdly deference because they loved him.

Cameron certainly had no experience with that himself.

James opened a bedchamber door, turned on the light, then stood back. "Here you go. Just lay her down here and we'll see to her. My brother was on his way over anyway. He'll look at her."

"Your brother Patrick?" Cameron asked.

"Aye. Do you know him?"

"We share a mechanic in Inverness," Cameron said slowly. "I've passed him a time or two going in opposite directions." He considered. "He's part of that stunt-training school your cousin runs, isn't he?"

"Stunt-training," James echoed slowly. "Aye, you could call it that, I suppose. And aye, he is part of Ian's school. He teaches the lads how to survive in the Highlands with only their hands, their wits, and a sharp knife at their disposal."

"Interesting skills to have."

James smiled a rather enigmatic smile. "Aye, they are, aren't they? Patrick also has a fondness for using sharp blades that Ian indulges often—an affinity I share, as it happens." He blinked owlishly. "You wouldn't have anything to do with swords, would you, Robert?"

"Rapiers," Cameron said, shifting uncomfortably, "when I can manage them."

James only lifted one eyebrow briefly. "I daresay," he murmured. "Well, you'd best put Sunshine down and be on your way. Your fiancée is waiting for you, isn't she?"

Cameron found, strangely enough, that he didn't particularly want to put Sunshine Phillips down. He looked down at her and felt something shoot through him, the same sort of tingle that had run up his arm each of the two times previous that he'd touched her.

Decidedly odd.

He shifted her in his arms and realized that there was very little to her. James had said she'd had a head wound, but perhaps she had been ill as well. Perhaps looks were deceiving; she had certainly thrown herself at him downstairs with a great amount of energy. Energy and relief, truth be told.

As if she'd known him.

But that was impossible. He'd never seen her before, except by the dim light of Tavish Fergusson's shop lights.

"Lord Robert?"

Cameron looked at James, then pulled himself back to what he was supposed to be doing. He forced himself to walk across the chamber. He laid Sunshine Phillips gently on the bed, then stood there for a moment. Perhaps the bump she had on her head had rendered her momentarily witless and she'd mistaken him for another.

"What happened to Sunny?"

Cameron looked around and saw that he and James had been joined by a man who could only be Patrick MacLeod, given his resemblance to his elder brother. Tough, powerful men, the both of them. Cameron liked that about them, actually, almost enough to forgive them the unfortunate burden of their last name.

He moved aside as Patrick came to sit on the edge of the bed.

Patrick put his hand on Sunshine's forehead, then looked up. Cameron supposed the look he received wasn't particularly unfriendly, but it was quite piercing.

"Lord Cameron," Patrick said slowly. "Here for a bit of business, are you?"

"'Tis just Cameron," Cameron said absently, "and aye, I am." He paused. "She fainted."

"She had a severe concussion," Patrick said, taking her hand and expertly checking her pulse. He shot his brother a look. "'Twas too soon to summon her, you fool."

"*You* told me she was well enough to come," James retorted.

"I never said that. I *only* said she was well enough to rise from her bed. She's too bloody stubborn to take my advice and stay home for another fortnight. You shouldn't have sent for her. And here she is, damned fortunate she didn't crack her head open yet again!"

James looked like he would have cheerfully throttled his brother and Patrick looked prepared to return the favor. Cameron cleared his throat.

"The fault is partly mine," he offered. "I think she thought she recognized me somehow and that set her off. I'm sure I've never seen her before. Well," he amended, "that isn't precisely true. I saw her a pair of fortnights ago. Penelope knocked her over in the village and I picked her up." He looked at Sunny in consternation. "Perhaps 'tis the bump on her head."

"Perhaps," Patrick agreed, "but I wouldn't worry about it. I appreciate your concern, but I'll tend her now."

Cameron nodded and knew he was being dismissed. He left the chamber reluctantly, then walked down the stairs with James. He stopped at the bottom and looked at the other man.

"Let me think on it a bit longer," he said slowly. "I'll be in touch soon, aye?"

James smiled, looking perfectly content to wait. "Of course."

Cameron looked at him for another moment or two, then shook his head. James MacLeod, a laird from several centuries ago? What rot. James MacLeod had created a little kingdom for himself, complete with a witch to brew him potions, and that was all there was to it. He would readily admit, though, that James's witch was one of the most beautiful women he'd ever seen. Beautiful and fragile and unaccountably familiar.

Very odd.

He pulled himself back to the present, nodded again to James, nodded to James's brother-in-law Zachary, then made his way out of the hall before he indulged in any more ridiculous speculation on things that were impossible or women he didn't know.

He shut himself reluctantly into his Range Rover and started it up, steeling himself for an onslaught of recriminations he knew lay in store for him. He didn't have to wait long.

"She was beautiful," Penelope said flatly, "but they always are, aren't they, Mac? I'm tired of women throwing themselves at you. *Literally*, in this case."

"I can't help what others do," he said, rather reasonably to his mind.

"Of course you can. You bring it on yourself." She tossed her head and huffed a bit. "Perhaps you could see your way clear to rein in all that bloody chivalry on occasion."

In Scotland, we call it honor, he almost said. It was something his father had said—nay, that wasn't right. He supposed someone had said it to him at one point, but he had no idea who. It suited him, though, so he'd taken the saying as his own. But as Penelope wouldn't understand it, he kept it to himself.

He nodded shortly, just to appease her, then drove through James's gates and down the way to the village. It would have been faster if he'd just been able to cut across James's lands and up through his, but since that wasn't possible except on horseback, he simply made his way west, then turned north and started up the very long track that led to his hall.

"I don't know how you bear it here," Penelope muttered. "There is nothing for miles but wilderness."

Cameron didn't bother to argue, because she had it aright. There were no exclusive shops, no expensive restaurants, no places to go to see and be seen.

But there was quiet and endless meadows of Highland wildflowers and still lochs that reflected mountain and sky back on a calm day. There was fishing and hunting and riding. He had thousands of acres that belonged to him alone, just as James MacLeod did. His land to roam over as he pleased.

He decided, not for the first time, that he was spending far too much time in London for his own good.

Penelope was halfway out of the car before he managed to get it parked in his garage at home. "I'm going to go make sure all the invitations were sent out," she said shortly, then she slammed the door shut and stalked off to the house.

Cameron sat back against the seat and watched her go. She was, he had to admit, absolutely stunning. She had platinum blond hair, cut up to her chin. It seemed to stay in place no matter how many times she tossed her head in irritation. The rest of her was just as perfect as her hair. It was truly a pity that all her redeeming qualities ended with her looks.

He could hardly believe he was engaged to her.

But since that was a situation he didn't have the stomach to face at the moment, he supposed the best thing to do was go search out something very strong to drink.

He took the keys out of the ignition and got wearily out of the car. He walked into his hall and paused to appreciate its medieval splendor. It had been preserved quite well and he'd spent a great deal of his own sterling to see it restored over the past few years. It was an impressive place, and he wasn't displeased to find himself master of it.

Penelope was standing in the middle of his hall, talking on the phone. She looked at him narrowly, then turned her back on him and walked away.

Cameron sighed and walked to the sideboard to pour himself a very tall whisky. He then made his way up the steps that led from the medieval part of the hall to the wing where bedrooms had been built in the sixteenth century, then redone in the eighteenth. He walked into his, shut the door behind him, and came to a halt.

Was Sunshine Phillips conscious now?

He didn't want to think about her, but he couldn't seem to stop himself. In desperation, he began to pace about his chamber, trying to find some way to distract himself.

He came to a stop in front of a door. It was a locked door that opened to reveal a closet of sorts for which only he had the key. There were things inside there that he hadn't looked at in years. And why would he? He was Robert Cameron, the adopted heir of old Alistair Cameron. His life had begun eight years ago when he had woken in hospital with a dozen tubes sticking out of him and Alistair Cameron leaning over him with a toothy, calculating smile. Anything that might have come before was nothing more than a bad dream brought on by not nearly enough whisky.

He looked at the closet, then looked down at the glass in his hand.

He cursed, walked into his bathroom, and poured the liquor down the sink drain. Obviously he was going to be as incapable of drinking himself into a proper stupor today as he was every other day. He set the glass on the sink, then fished his mobile phone out of his pocket and dialed. The phone rang only once on the other end before a voice answered.

"John Bagley."

"Any free time today?"

The man on the other end laughed. "For you, Cameron, always."

"I'll be there within the hour," Cameron said grimly. "I may need the rest of the afternoon."

"Done."

Cameron hung up and shrugged out of his suit coat. He walked across his room, stripping off the rest of his business gear as he did so. He hung things up in his closet out of habit, then found shorts and a T-shirt. He put trainers on his feet, grabbed the rapier that was propped up in the corner and his keys, then walked swiftly out of his room. He ran down the stairs and made it almost all the way across the hall before he was caught.

"And just where are you going?"

He took a deep breath and turned to face Penelope. "Out."

She frowned at him. "What are you doing with that sword? And why is it you can't engage in some sort of civilized exercise?"

"Civilized?" he asked, because he couldn't help himself. "Any hints on what that might be?"

"Polo. The odd hour at the gym."

He did spend the odd hour at the gym, both in the basement of his keep and in a very expensive studio in London. But polo? He couldn't imagine anything more torturous.

Cameron decided there was no point in responding. He merely made her a low bow, and left his house whilst he still could. He made it to the village without being pulled over by any overzealous traffic patrolmen, drove into the car park of a very ugly building, and sat back for a moment after he'd turned the car off. It was strange, actually, how many places there were within a thirty-league radius of his hall where a lad could pick up a sword and have a little exercise with it.

He wondered what sort of blade Ian MacLeod used in his stunt school—if that's what it could be called. Cameron considered James's reaction to his term for it.

Very odd, indeed.

He got out, locked his car behind him, then made his way inside before he could think about that anymore. John was waiting for him, dressed in fencing garb and holding on to his mask. Cameron tossed his keys in the corner with his sunglasses, then stretched his hands over his head. John looked at him.

"Gear?"

"I'm wearing it."

"Someday I'm going to poke your eye out," John said pleasantly. "Don't blame me for it when it happens."

"You will never manage that," Cameron said seriously.

And he meant it. He had, as it happened, grown to manhood with a sword in his hands. A six-foot broadsword. He didn't allow himself to think about it often, but it was the truth.

He wondered what sorts of rumors went round the pub about him when he wasn't there.

Suddenly, unbidden, the vision came to him of a woman with dark curling hair, enchanting green eyes, and a face a man could look at for the whole of his life and count himself fortunate indeed. He had to stand there for a minute and catch his breath. Would he feel that shiver go through him every time he touched her, or had it been just an aberration?

Would he ever be able to pass a single day again without thinking of her?

"Cameron?"

"I'm fine," Cameron said promptly.

"Never said you weren't," John said cheerfully. "Distracted, though. Is Penelope planning another dinner party soon? It seems as though you just had one up here a couple of weeks ago."

Cameron looked at him narrowly. "You know too much about my private life."

John only grinned. "You natter on when you fight, you know. It's pitiful, really."

Cameron lifted his rapier. "I hope you're well rested."

John put on his mask. "I had a nap whilst I waited for you."

Cameron spared a final moment to wonder why in the world it was Sunshine Phillips who had thrown herself into his arms with a cry of . . . what had it been? Gladness?

Relief?

He shook his head sharply. It had been the blow to her head that had rendered her witless. He could certainly understand that.

She wasn't fully herself and she had mistaken him for someone else.

That man was a lucky one.

He forced himself to put aside thoughts of a woman he shouldn't be thinking about and instead concentrated on his swordplay.

He didn't hold out any hope that it would be nearly distraction enough.

Chapter 13

S unny knelt in the damp dirt and pulled weeds. Weeding Moraig MacLeod's garden patch had been her job from almost the moment she'd arrived in Scotland. She had tended the garden while Moraig had sat in the sun and talked about life and death and all the lovely things that were to be found in the woods thereabouts if a girl looked hard enough. Sunny had never once considered that Moraig might have been talking about a man, much less the laird of the clan Cameron.

Who was, apparently, quite alive in the twenty-first century.

She wanted to stop thinking about him, but she couldn't. She'd been thinking about him since she'd woken up in Jamie's guestroom three days ago with Patrick sitting on the edge of the bed and Jamie peering over Patrick's shoulder at her. Fainting wasn't her usual response to things that shocked her, but maybe the bump on her head had been more serious than she'd wanted to admit. Or maybe what she'd seen had just been too much to handle in a conscious state.

She suspected the latter.

She had escaped the keep with Patrick before Jamie had had the chance to ask her any questions. She'd promised him she would come to dinner when she felt better. Perhaps he would spend so much time buried in his texts on head wounds that he wouldn't notice when she didn't show up for, oh, a year or so.

Patrick, very wisely to her mind, hadn't asked her a single question on the way home.

Madelyn had brought Hope and kept her company for the subsequent two days while she'd lain in bed and tried to catch her breath. She'd spent most of the time trying to convince herself she hadn't seen what she'd seen.

She hadn't been successful. Whatever the facts might have been, the one most impossible to dispute had been that she'd seen Robert Francis Cameron mac Cameron and he hadn't known her from Adam.

When she hadn't been obsessing over that, she'd been

puzzling over his age. He was older. He had also been wearing a suit. Not only that, he was apparently again lord of Cameron Hall. How had he managed to hop over almost seven centuries, acquire all sorts of modern polish, land on his feet as laird of the same clan, and forget about her all in one fell swoop?

She'd been tempted to drive up to Cameron Hall—or be driven, in her case—and find out just what had happened to him. She would have, but she didn't think she could take seeing that blank expression on his face again. She also wasn't sure she would get past his flawless model fiancée to ask him anything.

"Sunny?"

She jumped in surprise, then put her hand to her chest when she realized it was just Zachary standing at the edge of the garden. "You scared me."

"I called," he offered. "You didn't answer the phone Jamie gave you."

"I turned it off. I don't like cell phones."

"Careful, Sunny," he said with a smile. "You're starting to sound like Patrick." He walked over and looked appraisingly at her work. "The garden looks good. The house looks good, too. Nice addition on the back there."

"You would know," she said, sitting back on her heels and dragging her forearm across her face, "since you designed it. I have the most luxurious bathroom a witch could wish for. Now, did you just come to make sure I didn't damage the grout, or did you have another reason?"

He laughed. "Take it easy on me, Sunny; I'm just the messenger today. Young Ian has the flu and Elizabeth wondered if you could do anything for him."

Sunny crawled unsteadily to her feet. "Do I have time for a wash?"

"The poor kid's puking his guts out," Zachary said, "so I'd say no. No one cares about a little mud anyway."

"All right." She wiped her grubby hands on her jeans, grabbed her bag from where it lived just inside the door, then collapsed gratefully into the front seat of Zachary's modest little Ford. Walking to Jamie's would have been beyond her, no matter how awful his son was feeling. She closed her eyes and thought she might just have a little nap while she could.

"Sunny?"

"What?" she asked, not opening her eyes.

"Where did you go?"

She forced herself to take a handful of deep, even breaths. She'd known the question would come eventually—she just hadn't expected Zachary to be the one doing the asking. No one else had dared. Maybe they all thought she was so fragile, they would push her right over the edge into someplace they couldn't rescue her from. Either Zachary thought she was tougher than that, or he was too curious for his own good. She suspected a bit of both.

"Nowhere interesting," she said, when she thought she could say it convincingly.

"Would that nowhere interesting have anything to do with you throwing yourself at Robert Cameron the other day?"

"I was delirious," she said without hesitation.

"But, Sunny," he said slowly, "you were perfectly lucid when you saw him."

She looked at him and found he was studying her far too closely for her peace of mind. "Watch the road, kid."

He smiled briefly. "Nice try. Want to give me an answer this time?"

She had to take another deep breath. "I thought I recognized him, but I was wrong. Please, Zachary, just don't ask me anything else."

He turned at the fork in the road and started toward Jamie's. "I won't push you. Just remember that I'm good at keeping secrets."

"Which is why you're Jamie's time-travel research companion of choice."

He laughed. "Probably. It also helps that I'm self-employed. I don't make much money, but my hours are flexible."

She managed a smile, but she supposed it hadn't been a very good one. Zachary said nothing more and she didn't volunteer anything. She was very grateful when they reached Jamie's front door, though, as she walked through it, she wondered why. Zachary might have backed off when she wanted him to; Jamie wouldn't be so accommodating. If he thought it was in the best interest of her mental health for her to unload a few details, he would be ruthless about encouraging her to cough them up.

"Is young Ian upstairs?" she asked Zachary. Maybe she could make a quick dash upstairs and avoid the inquisition entirely.

"In the bathroom, probably."

"I'll go find him," she said, taking her bag back from him. "Thanks for the ride."

"My pleasure."

She let her eyes adjust to the light, then started across the great hall. She realized, as she was halfway to the stairs, that the place wasn't empty. Jamie was sitting in front of the hearth talking to someone. He looked up, smiled, and motioned for her to come over. She supposed Ian would last a few more minutes, so she nodded and walked over to stand next to his chair.

Then she realized who was facing him.

Her bag slipped from her fingers and landed on the floor. The sound of glass breaking was very loud in the silence of the hall.

Cameron rose immediately. He took her by the arm and drew her over to his chair.

"Sit," he commanded.

She sat before she thought better of it. Too much time spent being bossed around by him in a different century, apparently. She watched him fish through her bag and pull out things that were salvageable. Within moments, Zachary appeared with a rag. He didn't say anything, he just looked at Cameron periodically as he tidied up the floor.

Zachary stood finally. "Come on, Sunny. Let's go make that tea for Ian."

Sunny pushed herself to her feet, but found Cameron in her way. She didn't want to look, but she couldn't help it. He was wearing jeans and some species of long-sleeved shirt. If she hadn't known better, she would have thought him nothing more than an average, albeit exceptionally handsome, Highlander.

Only she knew better.

"Come back when you're finished if you please, Sunshine," Jamie said. "Our good Lord Robert has decided that he will take on half the financial responsibility for the new leisure center in the village and we'll want your input."

Before she had to come up with a decent way to refuse, Zachary had taken her by the hand and pulled her out of harm's way. She sighed in relief when the kitchen door closed behind them both.

"Thank you," she said.

"Interesting," he noted.

"Shut up," she suggested.

He laughed and dumped the towels with the broken glass into the garbage. "Come on, Sunny. It's killing me not to know."

"Die a little longer," she said grimly. She certainly was.

He leaned back against the counter and folded his arms over his chest. "You know, Sunshine, we don't like it when our women get hurt."

"Are you a MacLeod these days?" she asked with a snort.

He shot her an even look. "I knelt and pledged Jamie my fealty just as you did, my little Colonist friend. And I'll repeat what I said: we MacLeods don't like our women being hurt. He who does the hurting will find himself regretting it."

"I'm not being hurt."

He pursed his lips, but turned away just the same to make tea out of what she handed him. He kept his back to her while it steeped, then poured it into a thermos. "I won't say anything," he conceded, turning around and handing it to her, "but I will keep my eyes open. And he *will* pay if he hurts you."

She escaped from the kitchen before she had to respond, then made for the stairs without looking at anything in the hall besides the stone under her feet. She would have run up the stairs, but she wasn't up to that, so she contented herself with merely climbing them as quickly as possible.

And then she found she had more to concentrate on than her heart lying broken downstairs on Jamie's floor. Young Ian, Jamie's eldest son, was indeed very sick. She found him in Elizabeth's master bathroom, sitting on the floor and looking very green.

"Poor lad," Sunny said, sinking down next to him. "Is it bad?"

"Horrible," he managed. He looked at her bleakly. "I don't suppose you have anything tasty in that flask, Sunny, do you?"

She smiled and reached out to feel his forehead. "You know I don't. But if you drink all this, maybe your mom will find you something sweet a little later."

Ian nodded gamely. He drank as much tea as he was bidden, threw up once more, then sat back and stroked his chin in a gesture so reminiscent of his father, Sunny almost laughed.

"I might feel better," he conceded.

"Give it another hour," Sunny said, suppressing a smile. "If you still feel dodgy, drink the rest." She looked at Elizabeth. "I left a bag of red raspberry leaf downstairs for you. If he can stay just on tea today, he'll get over this faster."

Elizabeth reached for her hand and squeezed it. "Thanks so much, Sunny. I don't know what we'd do without you."

"Oh, Patrick could just have easily come and done the same thing," Sunny said deprecatingly.

Elizabeth snorted. "I love him to death, but he has no bedside manner. He would just tell Ian to take it like a man, then go downstairs and see what was in my fridge before he went home to decimate his own. We much prefer you."

"I'm always happy to be useful," Sunny said, feeling pleased. "I'll check on Ian tomorrow." She stood, then leaned over and ruffled Ian's hair. "Drink your tea, lad."

He nodded gratefully. Sunny exchanged another smile with Elizabeth, left the bedroom, then slowed when she remembered that her way home lay through the great hall below.

She supposed it wouldn't be wise to just jump out the window and hope to land in a soft part of the garden.

She took a deep breath and made her way downstairs. If Jamie was going to be doing business with Cameron, she was going to have to deal with seeing him. Besides, she was probably just blowing the whole thing out of proportion. She'd only known the man for two weeks. It wasn't possible to fall in love with someone that quickly.

Was it?

She told herself it wasn't and stopped at the bottom step to peer out into the great hall to see if someone she couldn't possibly be in love with was still loitering there.

Jamie and Cameron were sitting at the lord's table, looking over papers. She eyed the front door and started to sidle that way.

"Ah, Sunshine," Jamie said loudly. "Come and give us your opinion."

Damn, caught. She took a deep breath, then turned and pasted on her best false smile. She walked over to the table and hoped for nothing but a quick look, but apparently it was not to be. The moment she approached, Cameron stood up and held out his chair for her.

She couldn't meet his eyes as she sat down. If she'd had to look at him again and have him not see *her*, she would lose it. She forced herself to listen to Jamie. He was talking, she thought, about the building they were putting together in the village and what it would mean to the villagers. Activities for teenagers. Socializing for seniors. A pool, workout facilities, a yoga studio for yoga classes. He continued to talk, but she couldn't hear him. She couldn't stop watching Cameron's hands as they fiddled with a pen. She had felt those hands on her face, in her hair, on her arms. He had held her close with them, kept her safe with them.

She could see, as he stretched out his left hand to reach for a piece of paper, the scar that went along the back of that hand and disappeared under his sleeve. It went, she was certain, almost up to his elbow. She knew that because she'd been the one to sew it up.

"Sunny?"

She dragged herself back to the present and looked at Jamie. "What?"

"The leisure centre, Sunshine," Jamie said. "What do you think?"

She thought that if she had to sit next to the man she loved—and yes, it was possible to love someone in just over two weeks—she would simply throw back her head and howl. She shoved her chair back and stood up.

"Great," she said. "Gotta go."

She didn't hear anything else he said to her. It was all noise, all confusion, all terrible pain that clutched her throat and wouldn't let her go.

She bolted for the hall door, jerked it open, then slammed it shut behind her.

She ran all the way home.

She pushed her way into Moraig's, then fell to her knees, gasping desperately for breath.

She finally had to stretch out on the floor. The stone was cool against her cheek and that was helpful until she remembered that the last time she'd lain on her floor, she'd woken to find herself alone. She couldn't bring herself to move, though, so she lay there, weeping, until she realized that someone was knocking. It was probably Zachary coming to find out if she'd really lost it or had just been pretending.

She managed to get to her feet, though she had a hard time staying there. She put her hand against the wall and leaned heavily against it as she struggled to get herself to the door.

She brushed away her tears. Putting on a good face would help her deflect any unwanted questions. She opened the door, then found that all her good intentions weren't worth very much when faced with reality.

It was Cameron.

He was so desperately handsome, so terribly familiar, so completely and utterly remote, she started to cry again. He looked at her in surprise.

"Does your head pain you?" he asked.

"I'm fine," she croaked.

He frowned thoughtfully, but didn't argue. Instead, he held her bag out toward her, then froze. He looked in surprise at the threshold, then pulled his hand back. It was less than steady. "You forgot your gear," he said. He started to hand it to her again, but apparently couldn't manage it.

"What's wrong?" she asked.

He took a step backward. "There is something about your threshold . . . something that . . ." He started to speak again, then shook his head. He took a deep breath and held her bag out to her. "I thought you might need this."

Of course. He wouldn't have come to see her without a reason. She reached out and took her bag from him, then held it to her chest.

"Thank you," she managed.

He hesitated. "Is there anything I can do for you?"

She closed her eyes. *Yes, take me in your arms and never let me go.*

But she'd tried that recently and the result hadn't been very good.

"I'm tired," she said. "I need to go lie down."

"Of course—"

She shut the door in his face before he could say anything else, before she had to look at him any longer, before she started sobbing so loudly it frightened him. She turned and leaned back against the sturdy wood, then slipped down until she was sitting on the floor.

She couldn't do this. She couldn't run into him again. She simply could not bear one more time having him look at her as if she were just another woman in his way.

She reached up and locked her door, then crawled across the floor to her bed. She pulled Cameron's plaids out from under her pillow, wrapped herself in them one after another, then lay down on top of her covers.

She closed her eyes and ignored the tears that burned her cheeks. All she had wanted was a reason to stay in Scotland.

What she had gotten was a reason to get out of it as quickly as possible.

Chapter 14

Cameron scored a final point on John, put the hilt of his sword to his chin, then dropped his sword point down and called peace. He mopped his sweaty brow with the hem of his shirt, then took a deep breath. He'd been down at John's studio for most of the day, looking for a distraction. Actually, he'd been at John's for an unwholesome amount of time over the past two days, looking for the same thing. He couldn't say he'd been completely successful at finding it.

John took off his mask and tucked it under his arm. "When are you going to tell me where it was you learned to use a sword?"

Cameron suppressed the urge to shift uncomfortably. He'd been dodging that question for years, but perhaps it had been just a matter of time before John grew weary of the evasion. He shrugged. "I just picked it up here and there."

"Rubbish," John said seriously. "You walked into my studio seven and a half years ago—"

"Crawled in," Cameron corrected.

"Crawled in," John conceded. "You crawled in all those years ago, never asked me to teach you anything, never asked for aught but someone to beat on. Don't you think by now you can trust me with the truth?"

Cameron rested his rapier against his shoulder. It was none of John's business, of course, but perhaps politeness demanded that he give some sort of answer. "My father taught me," he conceded. "There, that is some truth."

John studied him. "But the weapon wasn't a rapier, was it? I know that's what you settled for when you first came here, but I imagine it was only because that was all you could lift. It isn't your weapon of choice, is it?"

Cameron shot him a look of irritation. "Is there any other kind of sword?"

"We're in Scotland. I've seen—and used—all kinds. Something else I think is odd," he continued without hesitation, "is how similarly you and Ian MacLeod fight—especially given that you just said you didn't learn your swordplay from him."

Cameron forced himself to snort dismissively. "A pint down at the pub, mate, will answer all your questions. Thank you for the workout. I needed it today."

"I have a couple of Claymores in the back," John continued relentlessly. "If you're interested."

Cameron forced himself to maintain a neutral expression. "When you think I'm equal to the challenge, you let me know and I'll think about it."

John only stood there, watching him silently.

Cameron nodded briskly, grabbed his keys and sunglasses, and strode as casually as he could to his car.

He didn't like those sorts of speculations.

He tossed his rapier onto the passenger seat, rolled down the window, and made his way home. He checked his watch and swore. He was running very late.

Trying to distract oneself from a woman one didn't know and shouldn't want took time.

He probably should have put his foot down on the gas, but he found himself, not for the first time in the past two months, not overly anxious to return home whilst Penelope was there.

Being engaged to a woman one *did* know and didn't want did that.

He sighed and hung his arm out the window as he drove. Even though he didn't particularly want Penelope, he had a very compelling reason to stay engaged to her, so perhaps it didn't matter whether or not he loved her. It was a certainty she didn't love him.

But since thinking on *that* gave him a sharp pain between his eyes, he decided that for the safety of all those he might encounter on the road, he just wouldn't. He wasn't being cowardly by avoiding those thoughts, he was being practical.

He was a Scot, after all.

Forty-five virtuous minutes later, he pulled into his garage, shut off his Range Rover, and got out. He walked into the house, but kept his shirt on instead of stripping it off as he so desperately wanted to do. Taking off his shirt outside the privacy of his own bedchamber was unthinkable. Penelope had looked at him with revulsion the first and only time he'd done so in front of her, so he'd stopped—at least whilst she was gracing his hall with her enchanting self.

"You're late."

Cameron looked up to find her standing in the middle of his great hall with her arms folded over her chest, tapping her foot impatiently.

"Sorry," he said. "I'm running a little behind today."

"A little?" she echoed incredulously. "Mac, we have *guests* arriving in an hour!"

He took a deep breath and walked away. "I'll be ready."

"I want to go back to London tomorrow," she said curtly. "I want you to come with me."

"If you like," he said over his shoulder.

"I insist on it. And don't be so stubborn about being prompt next time."

Cameron jogged up the stairs, walked into his bedchamber and slammed the door behind him. Stubborn, his arse. What Penelope wanted was a man she could control, which he most certainly was not. He could hardly believe he'd allowed himself to be maneuvered into a place where the only honorable thing to do had been to agree to marry her.

Duty was a bloody inconvenient thing.

He shot his locked closet a dark look, dropped his gear on a chair, then went to the bathroom.

He shaved, though he had to force himself to be careful. It was his own face, after all, and it didn't serve him to take out his frustrations there. He turned on the shower and stood under its spray for far longer than he should have. He rested his hands against the wall and let the water run down his back. It was hard to avoid looking at the scars that were spread over his body or to skirt the memory of how he'd gotten them. His chest bore many. His left forearm sported a long slash that hadn't healed very well. He honestly couldn't remember how he'd gotten that one.

He actually couldn't remember quite a few things, truth be told.

But one thing he could remember with perfect clarity was the other dinner party he'd endured with Penelope in Scotland. Her friends were snobs, every last one of them, interested only in money and how much of it he had. He couldn't bear it again.

Ten minutes later he was bounding down the stairs, dressed in jeans and a denim shirt, fully prepared to lie through his teeth.

"What are you wearing?" Penelope demanded in astonishment. "Go back up and change!"

Cameron grabbed his favorite leather jacket off the hook near the front door. "I've a meeting I just learned about," he said as convincingly as possible. "I might lose the castle if I don't at least make an appearance. You'll be fine without me, darling."

Penelope spluttered in fury. Cameron slipped out the front door whilst she was otherwise occupied and ran around the keep to his garage. She didn't chase after him. Perhaps the thought of not having Cameron Hall to potentially sell after she'd killed him off with too many London brunches had made her decide he wasn't worth following.

He jumped in his Range Rover and bolted down the road to the village before she could rethink that—though perhaps there was little danger of it. Penelope would think he was making money, she would have a marginally satisfactory dinner with things and people imported at great cost from somewhere besides the village, and he would be off doing what he wanted to do. Everyone won.

He drove through the village and continued on. He turned up the way that led to Jamie's keep, then came to a fork in the road. The left led to the MacLeod keep. The right led somewhere else. He took the right without hesitation.

After all, he had no intention of seeing James MacLeod that evening.

He wondered, briefly, if he might be making an enormous mistake by presenting himself at Sunshine Phillips's door. It was obvious she couldn't stand the sight of him. Either she was fainting or she was running away—or she was slamming doors in his face. It wasn't promising.

But there was something about her, something that tugged at him in a way he hadn't felt in years.

Eight years, to be exact.

He suppressed a shiver, then continued on. He passed Patrick MacLeod's keep on the right, which he'd seen the day before on his way to deliver Sunshine's bag to her. The castle was a rather lovely place, actually, but he wasn't interested in a visit there.

But apparently he was quite interested in a visit to the morgue, for he almost ran Sunshine over before he realized she was walking down the far side of the road toward him and he had drifted quite a bit to the left. He hit the brakes so hard, he sent his Range Rover skidding sideways. Sunshine dove out of his line of sight.

He threw open the door and leapt out, praying he hadn't hit her.

"Mistress Phillips?" he said anxiously, hurrying around the front of his car to look for her in the grass. "Are you hurt?"

She sat there for a moment, breathing hard, then scrambled to her feet. She swayed for a moment, avoided the hands he extended to help her, then brushed herself off with brisk strokes.

Then she turned and walked away from him.

He looked after her in surprise. By the saints, what was it with that irascible wench? Was it his looks? His dress? The fact that he'd almost run her over not a handful of moments ago?

Was it that he was engaged?

He supposed the last would be enough to put her off, but he wasn't one to give up at the first sign of a good skirmish. He followed her back across the road, then caught her by the elbow.

"I wasn't trying to run you over."

She stopped, then looked down pointedly at his hand on her arm. "Excuse me," she said stiffly.

He supposed he should have taken that personally, but he wasn't so thin-skinned—and she was so damned familiar, it almost knocked him flat. He released her, but continued to walk beside her.

"Where are you going?"

"My sister's for supper," she said shortly.

"Is there any extra?"

"No."

He clasped his hands behind his back. "Might I come along and see for myself?"

"No. There's a pub in the village. Go eat there."

"The food's terrible."

She put her head down and quickened her pace. "Not my problem."

"It might very well be your problem when I show up at your door afterward, begging for some potion for indigestion only you can fashion for me."

She stopped abruptly, then turned and looked up at him. Her expression wasn't welcoming. She looked rather devastated, actually, as if she had suffered a loss so great that even thinking on it was too much to bear. He would have reached out to comfort her, but he feared to touch her. She looked so fragile, he thought she might shatter if he touched amiss.

But instead of backing away from him, which he half expected, she took a step closer to him. "And just what sort of potion, my laird," she whispered hoarsely, "would you want the MacLeod witch to make for you?"

Cameron took a deep breath, hoping to clear his head enough to find something useful to say, and breathed in her scent without thinking.

She smelled like wildflowers.

The pain that slammed into him without warning was blinding in its intensity. He realized, quite suddenly, that he was on the verge of passing out. He stumbled back a pace and doubled over.

He stood there with his hands on his thighs, desperately sucking in air, and wondered what in the hell was happening to him. How was it a fresh-faced, potion-brewing Yank who smelled like meadow wildflowers on a warm summer's day could affect him so?

"Lord Cameron?"

"Headache," he ground out. "Nothing more."

"Are you really ill," she asked in a much kinder tone than she'd used before, "or just angling for dinner?"

He would have shaken his head, but he didn't think he could manage it. It was all he could do to close his eyes and pray he wouldn't sick up his lunch on her feet.

She sighed deeply, then took his keys out of his hand. He heard his car door slam shut and the alarm be set. The next thing he knew, Sunshine had ducked under one of his arms and drawn it over her shoulders. Her other arm went around his waist.

"Can you make it to Patrick's? I don't think I can carry you."

"I'll manage." He straightened, felt the world spin wildly, then forced himself to remain upright. He was appalled to realize how hard he was leaning on her. He dredged up reserves of strength he didn't often use and steadied himself. "Forgive me. I'm not usually so feeble."

"You probably need to eat. I'll make you some tea so you can go do that."

He supposed he couldn't hope for anything else. He stumbled along with her and found himself, eventually, standing in front of Benmore Castle. He closed his eyes and bowed his head as Sunshine knocked. The door soon opened.

"Sunny," a woman's voice said happily. "And . . . a friend?"

"Cameron mac Cameron," Sunshine said. "He's got a headache and I promised him I'd get him something for it here. He is *not* staying for supper."

Cameron would have smiled, but he was too busy keeping himself on his feet. He had the impression of a woman who looked a great deal like Sunshine Phillips peering at him with great interest before she backed up and welcomed him into the hall. He followed Sunshine as best he could, then found himself pushed down into a chair. His keys were slapped into his hand and he was summarily abandoned.

He wasn't unhappy for the chance to simply close his eyes and let the pain in his head recede. It helped to sit. He put his keys into his pocket, then rested his head against the back of the chair and listened to the sounds of family wash over him. They were good, homey sounds of supper being prepared and sweet women happily discussing in dulcet tones the pleasant things that interested them.

"Hell no, I am *not* going back in there! *You* take it to him."

"Sunny, what in the world is your problem? I think he's a perfectly lovely looking man. Are you out of your *mind*?"

"I don't care what you think, I'm not out of my mind, and he's *engaged*!"

"Oh," came the answer, drawn out quite a long time. "Why is he here with you, then?"

"He's not here *with* me, he's just here. Now, please just take him his tea so he can be on his way."

"If you're sure—"

"Maddy!"

Cameron waited until he heard light footsteps stop in front of him, then he opened his eyes. He had to look twice to realize that it wasn't Sunshine he was staring at. He managed a smile.

"You must be Patrick's wife."

"Madelyn," she agreed. She handed him a mug. "Dinner will be ready soon."

"He's *not* staying for dinner!" came the call from the kitchen.

Madelyn smiled politely. "I think my sister's afraid we don't have enough placemats. I'll go look and see if that's the case or not. Can I get you anything else in the meantime?"

"Tea is lovely, thank you," he said politely. "I'm sure it will help."

"Sunny's concoctions always do."

"Anything by the MacLeod witch would," he said, intending it as a jest, but he found quite suddenly that those words could not be spoken so lightly.

"Lord Cameron?"

He looked up at Madelyn MacLeod and forced a smile. "Just a headache. Not to worry."

She looked at him closely for a moment, then frowned thoughtfully to herself and walked away.

Cameron finished Sunny's tea without any more company. He actually began to feel quite at ease sitting in a well-appointed hall with a roaring fire in front of him. The pounding behind his eyes began to fade and he had to agree that Sunshine Phillips did indeed make good brews.

He closed his eyes again and attempted another bit of eavesdropping. It was made easier, several moments later, by the arrival of the lord of the manor into his kitchen.

"Who?" Patrick MacLeod said, sounding very surprised.

Cameron wondered if any of them knew how to whisper.

"Lord Robert Cameron."

That wasn't Sunshine. She wouldn't have said his name that way.

"The Cameron? Really. Why?"

"Who knows? He almost ran over me."

That was Sunshine. He suspected, to his surprise, that he would have recognized her voice in a crowd.

"Well," Patrick said, sounding amused, "all the more reason to have him in for supper."

"I don't want him to stay for supper—damn it, Patrick, stop!"

Cameron heard the tread of a heavier foot and opened his eyes in time to see Patrick MacLeod sit down in the chair across from his.

"Welcome," Patrick said with a smile.

"Thank you." Cameron held up his mug. "Your sister-in-law was kind enough to offer me a bit of tea."

"She's altruistic—especially after she's almost been run over."

"I didn't run over her."

"I said *almost*."

Cameron managed a smile. "I'll concede almost."

Patrick propped one of his ankles up on the opposite knee. "Why are you here?"

"No small talk?" Cameron asked.

"I'm not good at it. I like my speech plain and my answers unadorned."

Cameron studied the mug in his hands for several moments in silence. "I'm not sure," he said quietly. "I just had to see her." He looked up. "Sunshine, I mean."

Saying it sounded completely daft, but he couldn't deny the words. Perhaps it was nothing more than seeing a beautiful woman and having his imagination run wild. Perhaps it was but a very pedestrian case of cold feet—and the saints only knew he had reason enough for that.

"Well, you're honest, at least," Patrick said, rising. "Take off your coat, man, and stay a bit."

"That easily?" Cameron asked lightly.

Patrick shot him a look. "Highland hospitality. I should think *you* would know all about that."

Cameron nodded, because he did. There had been a point in his past when he had allowed quite a few souls to sleep in the comfort of his hall regardless of whether or not it had been wise. Highland weather was unpredictable; the comfort of a roaring fire was not to be taken lightly. The sight of a beautiful woman to enjoy whilst sitting in front of that fire made it all the more desirable.

He left his coat hanging on the back of the chair, then picked up his mug and followed Patrick into his kitchen.

He had to pause for a moment at the entrance and admire the three beauties there. Madelyn was lovely, with her dark curling hair falling down her back and her muddy green eyes full of good humor. The fairness of her face made her beautiful, but the happiness she wore—perhaps unconsciously—made her exceptional. She planted a kiss on the head of the second beautiful female there, a small one who was sitting in a high chair, banging toys onto an empty tray.

And then there was Sunshine Phillips.

She carried things over to the table, things he didn't normally eat like salad and steamed vegetables. He supposed it didn't matter what she intended to feed him; he wouldn't be paying much heed to it.

She was, he had to admit, the loveliest witch he'd ever seen.

At the moment, though, she looked as if she was on the verge of either weeping or reaching for some sort of blade to end her agony. It wouldn't have surprised him if she'd used that blade on him. He took the seat Patrick offered him because he feared that Sunshine would find a way to keep him out of it if she could.

Besides, sitting brought him closer to the object of his scrutiny. He pointedly ignored the fact that he shouldn't be looking. Sunshine was not his—and, given how she was pretending he wasn't there, she likely wouldn't have wanted to be his even if he were free.

He was surprised to find how much that bothered him.

A quick grace was said, interrupting his cheerless thoughts, then Patrick passed the potatoes. Cameron accepted a bit of everything, accepted another cup of tea from Madelyn, and watched Sunshine take nothing that wasn't green. An herbalist to the core, apparently.

An herbalist who was, again, making a point of ignoring him.

She was perfectly willing to speak to Patrick and Madelyn. At one point, she even took baby Hope out of her chair and paced with her so Madelyn could finish her supper in peace. But nary a glance did she cast his way.

He could see that Patrick noticed, for the man shot his sister-in-law a pair of quizzical looks. He got back far worse than he dealt out. Cameron was gratified to find that he wasn't the only one she was apparently irritated with. Madelyn didn't do anything but carefully step around her sister verbally and give her husband the occasional look that said very clearly that he should just keep his mouth shut.

Interesting.

Cameron again ignored the fact that he shouldn't have been there, shouldn't have even been looking at a woman who wasn't his, shouldn't have felt so at peace. He turned his attention back to his meal and kept it there.

'Twas safer that way.

Chapter 15

Sunny sat at her sister's dinner table and wished she had the guts to take her knife, lean over the table, and plunge it into her brother-in-law's black heart. She glared at him but had only a bland look as her reward. She sent him another look of retribution, then watched as he turned to Cameron and put on his most disarming smile.

"So, Cameron," he drawled, toying with his fork, "what really brings you to my humble table tonight? Besides seeking forgiveness for *almost* running over my sister."

"Isn't she your sister-in-law?" Cameron asked.

"I have no sisters of my own," Patrick said with a shrug. "That makes me, as you might imagine, especially protective of Sunshine."

Sunny wanted to kill him. But since doing so would make her sister unhappy, she settled for shooting him another murderous look, then burying curses in a triple shot of wheatgrass.

"What are you drinking, Mistress Sunshine?"

Sunny realized it was Cameron talking to her. She held out her cup without looking at him. It was better that way. If she didn't have to look at him, she didn't have to acknowledge him. And if she didn't acknowledge him, she didn't have to face the fact that while he might be looking at her, he wasn't seeing her.

"Good heavens," he gasped, setting the cup back down in front of her. "How do you drink that swill?"

"It's good for you," she muttered. She downed the rest, then looked around to see if it were possible that the torture of supper might be over. Patrick was leaning back on two legs of his chair and had reverted to the native tongue. A perfect opportunity to clear the table.

She rose, then shook her head at Madelyn. "Sit," she said in French.

"Why?" Madelyn asked.

"Because I need something to do," Sunny said in a low voice. And she did. She took all the plates to the sink, then came back for the cups and glasses. She reached for Cameron's last of all, because her worst fault was procrastinating things that were difficult. She took his glass only to have him put his hand around hers.

"Leave it, if you will," he said.

In French.

She suppressed a grimace. She would definitely have to be more careful about which languages she chose to ignore him in. She would also have to learn to ignore the tingle that ran up her arm every time they touched. Yet another reason to avoid him as often as possible.

She released his glass and pulled her hand away, then quickly went back to the sink and started to do the dishes. Gaelic flowed freely at the table behind her, as it usually did after supper. It should have been comforting. Unfortunately, listening to Cameron speak it, with the medieval accent he seemed not to have lost, was about to do her in.

He cleared his throat suddenly. "Perhaps we should speak in English," he said in that tongue, "in deference to Mistress Sunshine."

"Don't fash yourself," Patrick said. "Sunny and Madelyn both speak Gaelic like natives."

Cameron expressed surprise that she and Madelyn would know his tongue, and Patrick told him the Phillips girls were full of surprises. Madelyn laughed and the conversation continued on first to talk of village affairs, then a discussion of the new leisure center.

Sunny wondered if she could make the dishes last all night.

At one point, as she was scrubbing flecks of nonexistent crust off a baking dish, Madelyn came over to her and put her arm around her shoulders.

"You okay?" she whispered.

"Not that you care," Sunny groused.

"Of course, I care. I just couldn't send the poor man back out into the night when he looked so green. I will send you there, though, if you don't stop trying to scrub through my pan."

Sunny stopped, then took a deep breath and rinsed the pan. "I'm finished."

Madelyn kissed her cheek. "Details later."

"There are no details, counselor."

"Sunny, I'm not stupid. There are things you aren't telling me.

Things you should be telling me. Things you would feel better about if you told me."

"Please, Maddy," Sunny whispered, "not tonight."

Madelyn assessed her ruthlessly for another minute or two in silence, then nodded slowly. "All right. Not tonight. But soon."

Sunny closed her eyes briefly, nodded, then put the pan aside. She cleaned the counters, then looked around for something else to do. She made tea, but that didn't take as long as she needed it to. Far too soon, her sister was standing next to her again, cutting slices of cake.

"Go and sit," Madelyn said, elbowing her aside.

Sunny sighed, then carried tea things over to the table and poured four cups.

Cameron took one, then sniffed. "Mint," he said. "Lovely, thank you."

Sunny nodded, but she couldn't look at him. She was strung so tightly she feared the least little thing would have snapped her in two. She was desperately tempted to just bolt from the kitchen and run all the way home. All that stopped her was the fear that if she did, Cameron would follow her there, and then she would be alone with him.

And that would have been a thousand times worse.

So she sat and listened to him chat comfortably with her sister and brother-in-law and wondered what in the hell he was doing there.

"Give us all your details," Patrick said at one point. "'Tis a rare thing to have a Cameron at my table."

Sunny found that if she turned her head just so, she could see Cameron out of the corner of her eye. It was torture, plain and simple, but she couldn't seem to help herself. She turned a bit more, then let herself look her fill.

He was beautiful. No, not beautiful. Stunning. His face was as it had been in medieval Scotland, yet something had been added. Little lines of age at the corners of his eyes that added strength and character. His hair was just as dark as it had been, still on the longish side, and he still raked it back from his face with his fingers impatiently when it got in his eyes.

And his eyes were still that bright blue, intense, full of good humor.

She watched him a bit longer and decided there was something else there, as well. It was the same sadness she'd seen in his eyes when he'd talked about leaving his clan behind, only this was more pronounced. What had he lost?

And why the hell hadn't he recognized her the moment he'd seen her?

"Cameron Antiquities is just for sport, really," he was saying with a small, modest smile. " 'Tis just me and a lad or two I trust looking for things that can't be found and buying them from souls who don't want to sell them. It doesn't keep the lights on at home, of course, but I like old things."

"How old are *you*?" Madelyn asked.

Sunny kicked her sister under the table. Madelyn glared at her briefly, then smiled at Cameron.

"Well?" she prompted.

"Thirty-five," he said easily. "How old are *you*?"

"Careful," Patrick said with an amused smile, "my wife is a lawyer. If you start this with her, you'll finish bloodied."

Cameron smiled at Madelyn. "I'm not afraid, though I reserve the right to refuse to answer anything that makes me look an arse."

Sunny suspected that Madelyn was giving him her standard answer that she wouldn't hurt him as long as he cooperated, but she couldn't hear the exact words her sister was using. The blood was pounding in her ears so loudly, she couldn't hear much of anything at all.

Thirty-five? When had Robert Francis Cameron mac Cameron become thirty-five years old?

Had he been in the future *that* long?

Maybe that fortnight he'd spent with her in the past had been so unremarkable that it he'd actually forgotten it. Or maybe he was truly in love with that blonde shrew who thought nothing of stepping on drunks—or innocent herbalists just trying to get away from lousy former employers.

"I didn't mean to almost run over her," Cameron was saying. "I was escaping a society dinner and I fear I was distracted."

"And you thought Sunny would feed you?"

Sunny jumped up. "I hear Hope. I'll go check on her."

She bolted from the kitchen before she had to listen to his answer. She didn't want to know why he'd come or what he was escaping or what he thought of her.

She went into Patrick's library and hoped Cameron would soon become so irritated by Madelyn's questions that he would go home. Until that happy event occurred, she was perfectly content to hide.

Unfortunately, there was no fire burning in the library hearth and the stark coldness of it chilled her even more than what she had faced in the kitchen. It wouldn't have surprised her to have turned around and seen any number of ghosts sitting in the chairs there. She'd seen them before. She suspected she would see them again. But maybe they thought she was unsettled enough without them adding any of their otherworldly selves to the mix.

Cameron was thirty-five. She could hardly believe it.

She stood there with that number spinning through her head until she heard footsteps stop a few paces behind her. Not enough time had passed for Madelyn to have taken pity on her and thrown Cameron out. It was probably just Patrick coming to tell her to get a hold of herself and come be polite. She supposed he had a point. She could manage that, at least. She took a deep breath, then turned, ready to acquiesce. But it wasn't Patrick standing there.

It was Cameron.

He was leaning against the door frame, watching her. "Your tea is growing cold," he said quietly.

"I'm not thirsty," she managed.

He frowned. "Have I done something to offend you, Mistress Sunshine?"

She felt as if someone had just punched her in the stomach, making it almost impossible to catch her breath.

How could he not know what he'd done?

"Of course not," she managed. She bit her lip, hard. It was all that saved her from bursting into tears.

She was really not a weeper—the past two weeks aside. She generally ran away from her problems, or tried to bury them in the dirt, or scrub them off her dishes. Unfortunately, it was too dark to just run out the door, and Madelyn's dishes were already finished. All she could do was stand half a room away from a man who had repeatedly kissed the socks off her almost seven hundred years ago, and try to keep herself from shattering.

And then it occurred to her, with a terrible sense of finality, that he wasn't pretending not to know her. That look of utter bafflement on his face wasn't feigned.

He honestly didn't remember her.

Something had obviously happened, something dreadful,

something that had wiped out anything he knew about his past—
or at least the part of his past that included her. That realization
was so terrible, she had to put her hand over her mouth to keep
from making noises that would have frightened him.

He strode across the room and took her by the shoulders. "Are
you going to faint?" he asked sharply.

She shook her head, then she pulled away from him. If he actually pulled her into his arms, she *would* make those terrifying
noises.

"I'm fine."

"You don't look it. Why don't you come and sit by the fire?"

She didn't want to, but she knew if she said no, he would pick
her up and just carry her to where he wanted to put her. Despite
the polished exterior, she supposed he hadn't changed all that
much. So she nodded and let him walk her back to the great hall.
Patrick had built up the fire and was pulling four chairs closer to
it. Cameron saw her seated in the chair closest to the hearth, then
sat down next to her.

She heard them talking around her, but she couldn't make
sense of anything anyone said. She stared down at Cameron's
feet so she wouldn't be tempted to look at his face. She supposed
he might have bought his boots in Edinburgh this time around.
They were scuffed, though, which led her to believe that whatever else he did, he still walked over his land. His knees might
have been covered with jeans, but he still rubbed them absently
now and again, just as she'd watched him do in his own time. She
supposed if he'd had a knife to hand, he would have been finger-
ing it as well.

She looked up reluctantly past a denim shirt stretched across
shoulders she had put her arms around a dozen times, up to his
face. She had to blink several times to manage to actually see it.

She realized she was shivering only because Cameron had
taken a black leather coat off the back of his chair and was putting it over her.

"I'm all right," she said quickly.

He shot her a look that said he had no intention of listening to
her protests. She'd seen that look before, more than once.

It almost killed her to see it now.

He tucked his coat up under her chin, then sat down again.
Sunny closed her eyes. It smelled like him, like heather and wind
over Scottish meadows. It was just more than she could handle.

She pulled her knees up into the chair with her, bowed her head, and wept. She didn't care what anyone else thought. She absolutely could not stand another moment of the torment.

She felt Cameron's hand come to rest gently on her head. "Let me take you home, Sunshine," he said quietly. "Head wounds aren't anything to toy with."

"How would you know?" Madelyn asked promptly.

Cameron paused. "I had one once," he said finally, "and it took me months to feel myself again."

"Did you indeed?" Patrick asked, sounding far too interested for his own good. "How long ago was that?"

"Eight years," he said, sounding as if he were very reluctant to divulge even that much. "I was in hospital for a month. I would have been there longer if Alistair and Moraig hadn't fetched me out."

Sunny lifted her head and looked at him blearily. "Moraig MacLeod? You knew her?"

"Aye," he said. "I assume you did as well, given that you're living in her house."

Sunny couldn't speak. *I'll leave ye my house after I'm gone,* Moraig had said to her once. *You'll be wanting it—for reasons ye don't yet understand.*

Sunny felt a cold chill run down her spine. It wasn't possible that Moraig had known Cameron—well, of course it was possible. She'd obviously pulled him out of the hospital. But it wasn't possible that Moraig would have known about *her* having known Cameron. She'd certainly never said anything about it.

Sunny shoved aside any more speculation. Perhaps old Alistair Cameron had needed help getting Cameron out of the hospital and asked Moraig to come along. Perhaps Moraig had left her house to her because she'd loved her.

Perhaps coming to Scotland had been a terrible mistake.

She felt Cameron's arm go around her shoulders.

"Let me take you home," he said. "I'll go fetch my car—"

"No," she said, leaping to her feet and swaying violently. She steadied herself, then shoved his coat at him. "I'm staying here tonight."

"Are you—" Madelyn began in surprise.

Sunny shot her a look that had her biting off the rest of what she'd no doubt intended to say. Patrick was looking at her calculatingly, but he said nothing.

"As you wish," Cameron said slowly. He put his coat on just as slowly. "I suppose I should be off anyway. Any later and it won't go well for me."

Patrick held out his hand. "A pleasure, Cameron. Come back again."

"I would like that," Cameron said, shaking Patrick's hand. "I'll be in London for the next little while, but perhaps the next time I'm home." He took Madelyn's hand and bent over it. "Thank you for the hospitality, my lady."

Madelyn only smiled. "It was a pleasure to meet you, Lord Robert. Do come back."

Sunny slunk over to hide behind Patrick and hoped Cameron wouldn't feel the need to tell her good-bye as well. She realized all too quickly that he had shifted so he could see her.

"Good night, Mistress Sunshine."

She nodded briskly, but said nothing.

Patrick put his hand on Cameron's shoulder and walked him to the door. Cameron thanked Patrick again for the meal and the pleasant conversation. Sunny turned and looked at the fire until she heard Patrick shut the door and bolt it.

"Well," he said brightly, "that was an interesting visit."

"Wasn't it though," Sunny muttered. She looked at Madelyn. "Thanks for the place to crash. See you guys in the morning."

"Oh, nay," Patrick said, striding over and blocking her way. "You'll not escape so easily, sister. After I made the effort to be polite to a neighboring clansman I would have slain without hesitation in another lifetime, I think I'm entitled to a few answers."

"I don't have any answers."

"I imagine you do," Patrick said easily. "I'm curious, Sunshine, why Robert Cameron has lived up the hill for years and 'tis only tonight that he decides to grace us with his admittedly charming self."

"Why don't you go ask him?" Sunny stalled, eyeing the hallway and wondering if it would be rude to just run toward it before they could catch her.

"I just might."

She caught her breath as she realized what she was goading him to do. "Please, Patrick," she said quickly, "please don't say anything to him."

"Then spew out a few answers, Sunshine. I find it very odd

that you returned home almost three weeks ago from points unknown and undisclosed wearing a pair of Cameron plaids."

"Highlanders didn't have set tartan patterns in the Middle Ages, which you know."

"True, but I saw enough Cameron plaids in my day to be very familiar with the colors they favored."

"What are you tonight, a lawyer?" Sunny said, with an attempt at lightness.

Patrick only looked at her calculatingly.

Madelyn exchanged a look with her husband, then stepped in front of him. She put her arms around Sunny and hugged her tightly. "Go to bed, sister. Everything will look better in the morning. I have Pop-Tarts."

"Tempting," Sunny said, though she didn't think she could stomach one. She paused, then looked at her brother-in-law. "Thank you for being kind to him."

"It wasn't an effort," Patrick said with a shrug. "Not much of one, at least. I only had to suppress the impulse to reach for my sword half a dozen times instead of a score."

Sunny nodded then escaped while Madelyn was teasing her husband about his warped view of reality and finding herself reminded that she loved him in spite of it. Sunny had to shut the guest-room door quickly, so she didn't have to hear any more. Usually, their happiness made her smile, but not that night.

She pulled a clean pair of Madelyn's old pajamas out of the drawer, changed into them, then went to bed without even brushing her teeth. She hadn't eaten all that much anyway.

She wished she'd had Cameron's plaid to wrap around her. It helped her sleep. As it was, all she had was a pair of Madelyn's ducky print pajamas. Not the same at all.

Well, he wasn't stupid and he hadn't been lost. He hadn't been coming to see Patrick; he'd been coming to see her. A man who was engaged to another woman had come to see her. A man who didn't remember that he'd loved her centuries ago had come to see her.

All the more reason to get out of Scotland before he came to see her again.

She would go home—

She stopped immediately. No, not home. Home was a crooked little house in the Highlands full of herbs and magic and a fire that kept her warm year-round. Home was a brief walk through

silent woods from her sister's house. Home was being part of a
clan full of souls who loved her because of who she was and what
she could do.

Home was also, apparently, thirty miles as the crow flew from
a man she loved but who didn't have a clue why he should love
her back.

She knew that if she'd had any sense at all, she would have
gone home right then, thrown things into a suitcase, and driven
herself to the airport to wait for the first flight to London so she
could hop a plane back to Seattle and spare herself any more
heartache. It would demonstrate a distinct lack of sense to remain
in Scotland and make a little foray into James MacLeod's library
and see if he had anything on how to help the man you loved
regain the memories of you he seemed to have lost.

If she pushed him, would he remember?

Would it do her any good if he did?

Those were questions she could hardly ask herself, much less
try to answer. There were times, she supposed, when the best
course of action was to wait and see which way the wind was
blowing before doing something drastic. It worked with healing,
sometimes; it worked with a laboring mother, most of the time. It
might work with untenable situations she couldn't rectify herself.

Yes, maybe for once, she would stay when she wanted to run.
Just for a bit longer. Just to see which way the wind would blow.

She hoped she could bear the direction when she discovered it.

Chapter 16

Cameron stood in his office and looked across to Hyde Park in the distance. It was a spectacular view full of cars and buses and the swarm of humanity that made up modern-day London. It was nothing he could have begun to imagine in his youth, much less ever supposed he might be a part of so easily.

Then again, how could he possibly have dreamed that at thirty-five he would be running a company worth billions of pounds, dressing in suits, and flying in a private jet instead of just fighting to keep himself alive with his bare hands alone? His father never would have in his most fantastical moments of wishing for glory and honor for the clan Cameron imagined such a thing.

Yet there he stood, with the weight of all that on his shoulders, watching the traffic in front of him from the comfort of a luxuriously appointed office that had been decorated specifically to put souls at ease so they would hand him vast sums of their money to invest as he saw fit. He was very fortunate, he knew it, and he was very grateful for it. It gave him something useful to do, though it kept him away from Scotland more often than he liked. That hadn't bothered him before.

It bothered him now.

He wasn't sure he wanted to think about why.

So, instead, he contemplated where he was and how he'd come to be there. Alistair Cameron had built Cameron Ltd. thirty years ago, then left it to Cameron six years ago upon his death, trusting that Cameron wouldn't run it into the ground. He supposed Alistair would have been pleased with the fact that he'd doubled the numbers in his personal Swiss bank accounts and expanded by an equal amount the number of pies Cameron Ltd. had its fingers dipping into. For himself, he was merely grateful for the trust of an old man who had given him a chance at a new life. It was certainly more than he could have hoped for eight years ago when he'd woken in hospital without a clue where he was or how he'd gotten there.

He dragged his hands through his hair and turned away

abruptly from those thoughts. He'd given far too much thought to his past recently and it had left him indulging in maudlin sentimentalizing. It wasn't something he did often, but he hadn't been able to stop the impulse. Then again, it was a bit difficult to ignore the past when it had so much to do with his current straits.

Fortunately, or perhaps not, it wasn't his past that troubled him at present—it was Alistair's. And thanks to a friendship made by Alistair during that past, Cameron found himself at the center of the bitter inner workings of a family that wasn't his.

He pushed himself to his feet, walked around his desk, and began to pace from one end of his office to the other. Though he would have liked to have laid the blame on Alistair for his troubles, he couldn't. Though Rodney Ainsworth and Alistair Cameron had been friends from their youth and carried on that friendship over years of business associations, it was Cameron who had kept up the relationship after Alistair had died. He'd done it partly because it seemed fitting and partly because he genuinely liked Rodney.

It was through his visits with Rodney at Ainsworth Hall that he'd come to know Rodney's children, Nathan and Penelope. Well, perhaps *know* was too generous a word for it, especially where Penelope was concerned. He'd only seen her on those rare occasions when she had deigned to grace her father's hall with her presence between jaunts to this trendy locale and that exclusive resort. She'd behaved herself enough to lead him to believe she was as well mannered and gracious as she was lovely.

He'd seen quite a bit more of Nathan and recognized him for what he was: completely reprehensible and without a shred of honor to call his own. Nathan was aggressively disagreeable and never pretended to be anything else. Cameron had, on one level, respected that. At least with Nathan, he'd known what to expect. Penelope's true character had come as a complete, and very unpleasant, surprise.

He paused in front of the window again. None of it would have made any difference except for a pair of things he'd felt duty bound to see to because Rodney had asked it of him.

The first had been promising Rodney on his deathbed that he would do as the man wished and take care of Penelope.

The second had come after Rodney had drawn his last and Cameron had gone to look for Nathan and Penelope only to find them rummaging through their father's desk for his will. The absolute silence that had filled that room when Nathan had read that he, Cameron, was to be the executor of the will instead of Nathan himself had been almost frightening.

Nathan had stood there in a towering rage until he'd gotten himself under control, then nodded shortly and left, leaving the will lying on the floor behind him. Penelope had only smiled, complimented her late father on his good sense, then gone off ostensibly to grieve.

Cameron had then poured himself a very tall whisky from Rodney's decanter, looked at it longingly for a bit then poured it down the sink before he rendered himself quite unfit to fight off the attack he'd been quite certain Nathan would mount the moment he could.

He hadn't realized it was Penelope he needed to have guarded against until he was sitting at a jeweler's first thing the next morning, paying a ridiculous sum for an enormously gaudy diamond ring to put on her finger.

He'd gone along with the idea at the time because he'd supposed Fate—and Rodney—had been taking a hand in his life and forcing him to wed. He'd needed a wife who could move in his social circles with ease and he'd long since given up on finding someone to love. He had hoped that in time he might become fond of Penelope.

It had taken approximately two hours after the ring was on Penelope's finger for him to realize how impossible that would be. She'd shrieked at his chauffeur for some imagined slight and Cameron had wondered if it would be impolite to change his mind.

Before he'd decided how best to go about that—and by that point he'd been perfectly willing to write off that excessive bit of business on her finger—he'd found himself spending a night lying on the floor of his hotel loo, resting between bouts of heaving. When he'd finally managed to get himself to his feet and look in the mirror, he'd been appalled to find his face the same color that Rodney's had been for that last week of what had been a very rapid and unexplained decline.

Poison?

He'd wondered. He'd wondered about it quite a bit, actually. First that unpleasant night, then finding himself mugged on a handful of occasions during his predawn runs through the city, then having his offices broken into and his hotel room ransacked.

All that had taken place in just the first month after Rodney's death.

Cameron Antiquities hadn't escaped assault either. It had begun with the theft of a piece of lace Cameron had tracked down for a regular client. The lace had turned up somewhere else and it had cost him a bloody great deal to buy again and put in the right hands—far more than he'd made on the original bargain. Added to that was an obscure little trust that had begun to quietly buy up shares of his investment firm.

At first he'd suspected Nathan was behind it all, but Nathan hadn't been at that dinner party where Penelope had pressed wine on him all evening—that evening that had ended with him becoming so ill. He hadn't been eager to suspect her of treachery, but he'd been the first to admit he didn't know her past superficials and what he had come to know did not recommend her. And she had been, he realized upon further reflection, just as angry about the terms of her father's will as her brother had been. She'd just been quieter about it. He could readily imagine her having hired someone to assault him, and he could easily envision her wanting to put her greedy hands on the profits from his business.

Then again, he had no problem suspecting Nathan of all that as well.

All of which left him where he was, still engaged to a woman he didn't love, still keeping her brother in his sights, still wondering which one of them was plotting against him in secret. For all he knew, they were in league together. It certainly wouldn't have been the first time he'd found himself outnumbered and hemmed in on all sides.

He wasn't one to call for aid prematurely, but he wasn't home where he knew the landscape for leagues around his hall. He was in London trying to protect more than just his own sweet neck. He sighed deeply and pulled his mobile out of his pocket to dial his attorney. Time to find out how the reinforcements were doing. He was put through immediately, which never ceased to amaze him.

"Ah, more billable hours," came the voice on the other end.

"My pleasure," Cameron said sourly. "How lovely to think I can help you continue to make payments on that little hovel you have around the corner."

"One does what one must, you know, to keep the old ball and chain happy."

Cameron suppressed a snort. Geoffrey Segrave had just spent fifteen million pounds on a stunning row house not far from Hyde Park to please his wife, one of the most lovely, decent women Cameron had ever met, a woman who had protested vociferously that she would have been much happier with something simpler.

Suddenly, the impression came to him that Sunshine Phillips would have said the same thing.

Sunshine. Just the thought of her name made him smile. Thinking of her was like taking a deep breath after a terrible battle, or finding a meadow full of wildflowers where he'd expected rocks and thorns.

"Cameron? Cameron, old man, you're paying for this. Did you call for a chat or something important?"

Cameron dragged his thoughts away from a woman he could not have and forced himself to think about why he had his mobile in his hand. "I called to find out how your digging was coming," he said. "You were checking on that trust that seems to be buying up so much of my company of late?"

"Yes, I remember," Geoffrey said dryly. "And it's going rather well actually. The layers are rather deep so we haven't found the original creators, but I can tell you who has his name on the papers for the front company."

"Nathan Ainsworth?"

Geoffrey laughed. "That came as an enormous surprise, apparently. We'll need a bit more time to work on the other tiers, but we'll have those for you as quickly as possible. I'm wondering, though, if you couldn't just make me a list of whom you've irritated lately to cut out some of my legwork."

Cameron pursed his lips. "I don't know if I could stomach that sort of list today."

"Then have a bit more patience, Cameron, and we'll find you what you need. You're still buying up shares of Ainsworth Associates, aren't you?"

"Through various entities," Cameron agreed. "Rather cheaply, as it happens. Nathan's doing a brilliant job of seeing his father's company devalued."

"No doubt." Geoffrey paused. "I wonder, given whom you're doing business with here, if you might be interested in a few less savoury details. If you are, I think I might have a man you should meet. He's almost as nosy as you are. Do you know Alexander Smith?"

Cameron made a noise of distaste before he could stop himself. "I faced him over a conference table in Manhattan several years ago and the experience was not pleasant. I didn't realize he was plying his vile trade over here."

"Has been for years," Geoffrey said, "though he's less of a lawyer now and more of a private investigator. Given that you're able to pay his exorbitant fee, he could likely be convinced to take on your troubles. Are you interested in a bit of a go with him, then?"

Cameron chewed on his words for a moment or two. "Is he discreet?"

"Painfully."

"All right," Cameron agreed. "Ask him to see what he can find out about the trust. Perhaps he could also take a look at Rodney's will and see if there's something there that we've missed." He cleared his throat. "Be ginger about sorting all this, though, Geoffrey. I don't want to tip any hands." He paused. "And realize how much trust I'm placing in you."

"Robert, my friend, I'm never under any illusions about that."

Cameron smiled. "Give my love to Ginny. She's too good for you, you know."

"I'm charging you extra for that comment," Geoffrey said with a snort. "Have a lovely party tonight."

"How did you know?"

"Penelope put it in the paper, of course. For being such a private man, you certainly have quite a bit of your personal life splashed all over the society pages, don't you?"

"Thank you for reminding me."

"My pleasure," Geoffrey said pleasantly. "I'll let you know when I've reached our new friend. And Cameron? Don't drink the wine."

Cameron hung up on him with a curse. There were too many people who knew too bloody much about his life.

At least the past eight years of it.

He threw himself down into a chair with a deep sigh. He wouldn't have trusted anyone with tales of what had gone on before then. It was difficult enough for him to trust anyone with details of his present life. He still had to suppress the urge to go around behind the backs of the lads he kept closest to him to make certain they weren't betraying him.

Old habits died hard.

The phone on the desk rang before he could think about that more than was good for him. He sighed, then reached for it.

"Aye?"

"Hello," Penelope said shortly. "It is *hello*, my lord Robert."

He suppressed a sigh. "Hello, Penelope."

"You haven't left your office yet? We're not eating until nine, but I want you here early to greet our guests."

"Of course," he said, wondering if he might have time to order takeaway before he left the city. He had no intention of eating anything at Penelope's table that night.

"Tell George to hurry."

The phone went dead in his hand. He spared Rodney Ainsworth an unkind thought, then set to the rest of his afternoon.

He finally gathered up his papers, shoved them into a briefcase, and left his office. It was tempting to just go back to his hotel and hope the evening took care of itself without his presence, but he knew he couldn't. He had to keep up appearances with both Penelope and her brother. It wasn't wise to allow enemies free rein out of sight.

He'd learned that well enough in the past.

He walked out of the building to find George waiting for him downstairs. George was his driver in London, a discreet, wry man who thought nothing of Cameron's hours, the fact that he stayed in a hotel because he couldn't bring himself to purchase a flat, or his disgust for proper society. George also put up with Penelope making him ferry her everywhere on those rare occasions when Cameron was in Scotland.

"My lord," George said with a small bow, opening the back door.

Cameron got in, leaned his head back against the headrest, and trusted that George would get him where he needed to go with a minimum of fuss.

He would have given much to have been in his Range Rover, bumping over the road to Patrick MacLeod's house. Now, that was the sort of dinner party he would have looked forward to. He might have even forgiven Madelyn MacLeod her ruthless, persistent, and damned prying questions. She had become a MacLeod in truth, protecting her sister with a ferocity that even a MacLeod by birth would have had to appreciate.

He hadn't answered anything about his activities over the past several years, and not just because he never discussed his past with anyone. It had never set well with him to be the recipient of Alistair Cameron's charity—not that Alistair's charity had lasted overlong. Once Cameron had been able to get out of bed, Alistair had put him to work. Schooling, business, hobnobbing with society in London—the expectations had been brutal and unrelenting, but Cameron had agreed without hesitation to everything because he'd known the only way to survive in the future was to master the intricacies of it.

He'd asked Alistair several times why he'd bothered with it all—the education, the contacts, the change of his will that had sent Alistair's distant cousins into a frenzy. Alistair had answered only once.

Once laird of the clan Cameron, my boy, always laird of the clan Cameron.

That had been answer enough. Cameron had never asked again and instead been grateful for an old man who'd accepted the vagaries of his first twenty-seven years with a shrug. And he himself had happily accepted all Alistair's worldly possessions and his business upon his death. He'd been busy and very successful. Why, then, had his life seemed so damned empty?

He tried to fill it in a variety of ways. Discreet women. Travels to far-flung locales. Hunting down that which couldn't be bought and haggling over its price. He'd never gambled, never gotten drunk, never slept about casually. Somehow, though, nothing had satisfied. When his life had begun eight years ago in that hospital in Inverness, something inside him had died.

And then he'd seen Sunshine Phillips.

And his world had ground to a halt.

He hadn't wanted to admit it at first. He'd tried to convince himself that when she'd thrown herself into his arms, he'd been surprised because he'd thought her mad. The true surprise had been that when he'd had her in his arms, something in his heart had sighed with relief.

"George, how long before we're there, do you suppose?" he asked reluctantly.

"Perhaps half an hour, my lord, no more."

Cameron cursed silently. Not nearly long enough to put off the torture. He was dreading the thought of spending the evening in uncomfortable shoes, avoiding food that would have been too rich for his belly even if he'd been assured of its purity, and enduring the stares of disbelieving servants who would come to refill his wineglass only to find there was no need. He would be forced to make polite conversation with spoiled, minor nobles who didn't have an original thought in their poor heads, listen with rapt attention to everything Penelope said, and avoid killing her brother.

He almost had George turn around.

What he wanted was to be in Scotland with his feet up in front of his Aga, enjoying a proper bit of stew. He wanted to be in the village, stretching himself to keep John at bay and make it look easy. He wanted to be in Patrick MacLeod's great hall, watching Sunshine Phillips by the light of the fire.

Damn it, anyway.

"George," he announced suddenly, "I'm leaving at midnight. Be ready to go."

George looked in the rearview mirror. "Another party?"

"A date with my club." Perhaps he could drink himself into a stupor and stop thinking about things he shouldn't.

"Do you have a club, my lord?"

Cameron glared at him.

"Nothing good happens after midnight, my lord."

By the saints, he knew that. But he was facing a miserable evening, he was trapped in a hell not of his own making, and where he wanted to be was exactly where he shouldn't go.

Another thought occurred to him suddenly. If he had a hangover dire enough, perhaps Sunshine Phillips wouldn't slam the door in his face when he came begging for a cure. He hadn't seen her in a week; perhaps she would have forgotten her loathing of him in that time.

There was only one way to find out.

Cameron woke to the sound of a gunshot.

He sat bolt upright, then found hot pokers plunged straight into his eyes. He fell backward with a cry and dragged covers over his head.

The sheet was ripped away. "Get up, you fool."

He pulled his pillow over his face. It was Penelope. The gunshot noise had been her snapping the drapes open and the pain in his eyes was the bloody sun itself. Damn it, when would the concierge stop letting her into his room? She was *not* what he wanted to wake up to first thing in the morning—especially when he wasn't quite sure where he was or how he'd gotten there. He lifted his pillow slightly and was vastly relieved to find that he was alone in his bed.

He really shouldn't drink.

Penelope jerked his pillow out of his hands. "Sit up and be a man."

He threw his arm over his eyes to try to save himself the pain of sunlight stabbing into his brain like very large swords.

"I'm indisposed," he mumbled.

"You're still wearing your shoes," she said in disgust. "What were you thinking?"

And just how the hell was he supposed to tell her that?

Apparently an answer was not what she wanted. "Go shower," she commanded. "I'll wait for you downstairs."

That was enough to sober him abruptly. "You'll wait?" He sat up and peered at her. "Why?"

Her mouth fell open. "You didn't forget brunch with Lord and Lady Huntingdon."

He couldn't muster up a decent reply. He was, quite obviously, not at his best. Brunch. Who had thought up that stupid, bloody, inconvenient word?

She glared at him. "I can't believe you would sink this low. The Huntingdons, Mac! I'll never be able to show my face again at *any* party in town if you don't show up—*sober*—and be charming."

"I'm not drunk."

"You've a bloody hangover!"

He rubbed his hands over his face. "Hell."

She stalked across the room. "I'll have coffee sent up."

Cameron dragged himself out of bed, then realized that he was not only wearing his shoes but the rest of his clothes as well. Only his suit coat was missing and he found it hanging on the back of a chair across the room. He vowed to cut George's pay as soon as was convenient.

He showered and dressed, threw his clothes in a suitcase, then fetched his papers out of the safe. He staggered downstairs in twenty minutes, which seemed to mollify Penelope somewhat. He escorted her out to the waiting car, then opened the door for her. He shut the door so she wouldn't hear anything he said, then handed George his suitcase and his briefcase.

"I don't care about the clothes," he said pointedly.

George nodded. "I understand."

"I'm demoting you," Cameron grumbled. "Couldn't you have at least taken off my shoes?"

"I tried, but you wouldn't let me," George said. "You said the path through the MacLeod forest hurt your feet."

Cameron gaped at him. "I said *what*?"

"Apparently you have tender feet."

Cameron, ride for the MacLeod witch.

The words came out of nowhere and slammed into him with the force of a dozen fists. He put his hands on the car and leaned against it heavily as he struggled to remember who had said that.

Giric. Giric who had been standing with him as Breac lay dying at his feet. Giric who had suggested that he fetch the MacLeod witch because there wasn't anyone else within a hundred leagues who could save his brother. He remembered getting on his horse, but he didn't remember anything after that.

He had difficulty catching his breath. Had he actually gone to the MacLeod forest? Was it there that he had somehow fallen into the twentieth century?

The thought was astonishing.

He breathed raggedly. The pain that screamed through his head was almost enough to bring him to his knees—and it wasn't the pain of a hangover.

"My lord?"

"I was sloshed last night," Cameron managed.

"Completely, my lord."

He heard George shut his things in the trunk, then felt his chauffeur's hand on his arm.

"Lord Robert?"

"I'm fine," Cameron said, through gritted teeth. "Just a headache."

"If you say so, my lord. Here, I've opened the door for you."

Cameron felt his way down into the backseat.

Cameron, ride for the MacLeod witch.

He had to roll down the window and gulp in several deep breaths of unpleasant London air until he felt slightly better. By the saints, where was that coming from? The words echoed in his head, drowning out even Penelope's blethering on about the various fine qualities of the Huntingdons and their even more numerous antiquities. He knew he should have been paying attention at least to the latter, but he couldn't. All he could do was breathe and hope he didn't start to weep soon. What he endured presently was far worse than the headache he'd had in Patrick MacLeod's front courtyard. At least then he'd had Sunshine Phillips to help him with her soft hands and marvelous brews.

Perhaps if he could get himself all the way to her front door and look pathetic enough, she might actually help him again.

Perhaps he would hurry back to Scotland after what he was certain would be an endless brunch, have a little ride south, and see if anyone was home at Mistress Phillips's house. A simple knock on her door, a cup of tea at her hearth, a little conversation. How much damage could that possibly do?

He was surprised by how just the thought of seeing her again made the pain in his head—and his heart—ease.

He was very surprised, indeed.

Chapter 17

Sunny walked quietly through the forest to the north of her house, grateful for the trees that kept the rain off her head and even more grateful that she could touch the back of that head and not feel a lump anymore. Sleep, tea, and green things had wrought a remarkable bit of healing in her.

And a week without a sighting of Robert Cameron himself had almost left her feeling that her heart might heal as well.

After she'd gotten over the shock of having spent the evening near him at Madelyn's, she'd allowed herself to wonder about him in a detached sort of way. She'd wondered if that bump on the head had wiped out all his memories, or just his memories of her. She'd wondered if his stunning fiancée had any idea when he'd been born or if she merely thought of him as a successful businessman who happened to own a castle in Scotland.

She likely would have believed the latter herself if she hadn't known better. She had used Patrick's computer to its best advantage one morning and found out all sorts of details about the modern Cameron, his business, and his very public engagement to Penelope Ainsworth less than two months ago. It had been very odd reading about his life in the future, a life that she hadn't been a part of in any way, a life he'd been conducting just up the way while she'd sat in Moraig's house, busily sniffing herbs and being completely clueless that she would fall in love with that same very public man in a completely different century.

She'd let the wind blow for a week and decided that it wasn't going to blow any stray Cameron lairds back her way, so perhaps it was time to let it all go. He would marry the gorgeous Lady Penelope and she would continue to look for a decent guy to date. Nothing had changed. In time, maybe she would even manage to stop sleeping with his plaids wrapped around her.

And if she managed that, she could still bring herself to call Scotland home. She would still be able to roam over Scottish soil, still have the mountains and trees, still have the rain. She wanted that very much.

She paused at the edge of Moraig's forest and looked up the meadow that stretched in front of her, then pulled her hand-drawn Jamie map out of her pocket and looked for any potential problems. Either the ground in front of her was safe, or Jamie felt some small bit of hesitation about investigating the quirks of Cameron soil because the land north was remarkably free of Xs. She felt no compunction at all about her own ramblings, though, mostly because she knew the laird in question wasn't home. She knew this because Patrick knew John Bagley, who apparently lived to fence with Cameron, and John had said Cameron was currently trapped in London, no doubt escorting his beloved to party after party and happily living a socialite's life she was happy not to be a part of.

She stuffed Jamie's map back in her jacket pocket, then started across the meadow. She walked for a very long time, finding that the longer she walked, the better she felt. She would get over him. In fact, she felt fairly confident that she *was* over him.

After all, it wasn't as if she knew him very well. She didn't, for instance, know what his favorite color was, or what his favorite food was, or what sort of music he liked. She couldn't have said whether or not he would hog the remote, squeeze the toothpaste from the top instead of the bottom, or leave his dirty dishes on the floor for her to pick up the next day.

She pointedly ignored the fact that she knew exactly how he looked when he was watching over her, or teasing her, or wanting her. She knew how he looked with a crown of wildflowers on his head, how his hand felt around hers, how his muscles worked when he was fighting with a six-foot broadsword so she would live another day to wonder what his favorite color was.

He'd wanted her to call him Cam, because he wanted to hear that name from someone he loved.

She closed her eyes briefly. She couldn't go back down that road again. He had his life; she had hers. They were obviously not destined to be together. The sooner she came to grips with that, the better off she would be.

And for the moment, maybe the best thing she could do was get herself back to Moraig's. She pulled her coat closer around herself and shivered suddenly. The sky above her was black and a bitter wind had come out of nowhere. It had been stupid to come out so late in the afternoon. She looked around her and realized that she hadn't been paying attention to where she was. She was in the middle of a very long meadow, but she couldn't see any of the mountains that should have flanked the ground she stood on thanks to the mist.

She wondered, with a substantial bit of alarm, if she'd just blundered into the past again.

The whinny of a horse right behind her startled her so much that she screamed as she whirled around to face the sound. A chestnut horse skidded to a halt five feet from her. She put her hand over her heart, then looked up to see who was trying to run over her.

It was Cameron.

She was so surprised to see him that she couldn't do anything but stare up at him in astonishment. Well, at least he was in jeans this time. She wasn't sure that that wasn't worse, actually. He might have been dressed in modern clothes and alive in a modern year, but he was as inaccessible as if he'd been hundreds of years in the past.

He pulled up close to her. "Give me your hand, Mistress Sunshine."

She put her hand into his before she realized what she was doing, then shivered at the tingles that went through her just from touching him. She would have pulled away, but he wouldn't release her.

"Let me take you home," he said.

"I don't need you to," she protested.

"Don't be daft, woman. You can't walk back in this storm."

She had to admit that he had a point. If she walked back home—assuming she could actually find home—she would arrive half frozen. Riding with him was the lesser of two evils. She wanted to ask him why he was there just when she needed him, but she couldn't bring herself to. Perhaps he'd just been out riding and she had been in his way. It had been chance.

Just like his coming to look for a healer for his brother almost 650 years ago and finding her instead.

"Sunshine."

She looked up and met his eyes. He was looking at her and actually seeing her with some sort of recognition, though she supposed it was nothing more than the look a man might give a damsel in distress he was trying to rescue, a look that said she really should comply with his heroic attempts before they both caught their deaths out in the wet.

She took a deep, fortifying breath, then nodded. She put her foot on his, then let him pull her up so she could swing around behind him.

He pulled her arms around his waist. "Hold on."

She supposed she didn't have any choice when the alternative was falling off his horse. She didn't want to, though. It reminded her far too much of the last time she'd ridden with him. Only then he'd had a six-foot Claymore strapped to his back and she'd been terrified they wouldn't live to see dawn, much less the future. Now, he merely rode easily over his land and then Jamie's, apparently not overly worried that an angry MacLeod clansman might plunge a sword into his chest for daring to come on MacLeod lands.

Times had changed.

He stopped in front of her house, then swung his leg over the saddle and jumped down lithely to the ground. He turned and held up his arms for her.

She closed her eyes briefly against the absolute familiarity of what he'd just done, then put her hands on his shoulders. He caught her around the waist, then carefully set her on her feet. She pulled away from him immediately and wondered if she had the guts to simply tell him to get lost while she still could.

Then she made the mistake of looking up at his face. He looked terrible.

"What happened to you?" she asked in surprise.

"Hangover," he said, rubbing his forehead gingerly.

"What in the world were you doing out riding, then?" she asked in surprise.

He smiled faintly. "I wanted to see if you might have something to ease me. As you did before."

It took her a moment to realize what he'd said. "You rode down here to see *me*?"

"Actually, I flew home to Scotland to see you."

She backed away before she realized what she was doing. She would have turned and bolted for her door, but he caught her by the arm before she could.

"Please, Sunshine," he said, giving her a pained smile. "Please. If you have any pity in you at all, please put aside whatever it is you have against me and make me something that doesn't include raw eggs."

She didn't dare look in his eyes, so she stared at his chin. "You could have stopped at Boots, you know."

"I didn't want to stop at Boots."

She wanted to tell him to go look in his own medicine cabinet, but she couldn't bring herself to get the words out.

"Besides," he said, rubbing her arm where he'd held it, "surely you aren't going to send me away without at least allowing me to dry off a bit by your fire, are you?"

Actually, sending him right back off into the storm seemed like the best idea she'd heard all day. Unfortunately, Cameron didn't look as if he would make it to her fire, much less all the way back home.

Damn it anyway, she hated that Florence Nightingale side of herself.

"I'll make you something," she said heavily. "You'd better drink it fast, though, so you can get home before it's completely dark."

Apparently that was all the invitation he needed. He gave her a quick smile, one that was unfortunately close to dozens he'd given her centuries ago, then turned to see to his horse. Sunny took a deep breath, then walked toward her door.

"Wait."

She stopped on her threshold and looked at him. "Why?"

"So I might go first. To make certain your house is safe."

She wanted to tell him that she had no reason not to feel safe, especially if she was on the inside and he and his charming smiles were loitering on the outside, but she couldn't manage it. She watched him take off his horse's gear and send the beast off with a friendly slap on the rump. She sighed and stepped aside so he could open her door and go inside.

She realized that he'd come to an abrupt halt halfway across her threshold because she ran into his back. He reached behind to steady her.

He held on to her arm quite tightly, actually.

She eased past him, then turned on her lights so she could see his face. He looked like he'd just seen a ghost.

She glanced at the chairs in front of her fire to make sure that wasn't the case, then looked back up at him. "What is it?"

"There's something about your threshold—" He shuddered violently, once. "I don't like it."

"But surely you've been here before," she said. "Didn't you come to visit Moraig?"

"Nay. Alistair always sent a car to bring her up to Cameron Hall." He took a deep breath, but it did nothing to improve his color. "I feel as though I've been here before, but that's impossible—"

Well, it wasn't, but she didn't bother to say as much. He had looked bad before; now he looked like he just might pass out if she didn't get him into a chair. She drew his arm over her shoulders just as she had on the way to Patrick's, then put her arm around his waist and forcibly pulled him into her house. She led him over to one of the comfortable chairs in front of the fire, then pushed him unresisting down into it.

"I need to see to your fire," he said faintly.

"What you need to do is to put your head between your knees before you pass out," she said. "I can make my own fire. I can even see to your horse. Jamie keeps my little stall stocked with hay and oats and Patrick was here this morning so I'm sure there's still water out . . . um . . . there—"

She shut her mouth when she realized she was babbling.

She was nervous, that was it. She had wished so fervently during those first days that Cameron would somehow find his way into her house and take up his place before her fire. Now, there he was, yet it was so far from how she'd pictured it that it was all she could do not to burst into tears.

Running was a better alternative.

She would see to his horse, then escape to Patrick's house. Cameron could dry off in front of her fire and be on his way before she returned . . . say, in a day or two. His headache would pass without any help from her.

She left Cameron to his own devices and went outside. She lured his horse to the little stall with a handful of oats, rubbed him dry, and made sure he had enough food to satisfy him for a bit. She hesitated, then went back around the house to get Cameron's saddle. There was no sense in letting it get ruined in the rain. She heaved it up, then shrieked when it left her hands. Fortunately—or unfortunately, perhaps—it was only Cameron holding on to it from the other side.

"Go sit by the hearth, woman," he rasped. "I'll be right behind you."

She wanted to protest, but he looked even worse than he had ten minutes earlier. She watched him walk off very unsteadily into the deepening gloom and realized with a start that he'd been speaking Gaelic. That she couldn't remember how long he'd been doing so, or whether or not she'd answered him in the same language was probably a good reflection of her state of mind.

She was insane.

She took a deep breath. All right, so maybe it wouldn't kill her to make him some tea and let him sit for an hour. She would make nice, find out once and for all that he did not know her and had no desire to make her acquaintance, then be on her way to healing her broken heart for good this time.

In Seattle, if she had any sense.

She went back inside and kept herself busy first tending her fire, then making a killer batch of hangover cure.

Cameron came in and shut the door behind him. She heard him take off his boots and set them by the door, no doubt next to hers. She heard him take off his coat and hang it on a hook. It seemed so perfectly normal, so I'm-home-honey-what's-for-supper-ish, so much as it might have been had things been different.

His footsteps came to a halt behind her. "Let me take your coat, Sunshine."

She allowed it, then picked up a mug of something unpleasant for him and something tasty for her and carried them both into her little great room. She handed him his, then sat down on Moraig's stool in front of the hearth. Cameron sniffed what she'd given him, considered, then took a deep breath and drank.

It took a handful of minutes, but she finally saw the lines of tension and pain begin to fade from his face. Silence enveloped them both, silence that should have been full of knowing that she had him and modern sutures both in the same century, but wasn't. She tried to be content with what she had, but that didn't work, either.

He had to go if it meant pushing him out her front door herself.

She took his mug out of his hand and escaped to her kitchen before she had to pretend to be comfortable with his silence any longer. She poured him the last of what she'd made for him, then washed up. He could finish that, then he could go. Not even Moraig would have faulted her for wanting to kick him out, not considering the extenuating circumstances. She picked up his cup and turned toward her great room, expecting to see him sitting in front of the hearth.

Instead, he was leaning against the wall, four feet away from her, watching her.

She almost dropped the mug. He leapt forward and caught it, then took it and leaned back against the wall again.

"Why are you so nervous?"

"I'm not," she lied. "I'm just worried that you won't make it home before dark, so you'd better drink the rest of this in a hurry."

He smiled faintly. "Are you throwing me out now?"

"Absolutely."

His smile deepened. "Aren't you even going to offer to feed me first?"

"Do you *want* me to feed you?" she asked in surprise.

"Actually, I don't think I dare eat," he admitted uneasily. "I was forced to endure brunch—and a London brunch, no less—this morning. I'm still trying to keep it down."

"Am I supposed to feel sorry for you?" she asked, more sharply than she had intended.

He didn't respond. His smile faded, then he applied himself to his tea. He finished, then handed the cup to her slowly. "What did I do to make you dislike me so?"

She shifted uncomfortably. "I don't dislike you."

"Then why are you so angry with me?"

"I'm not angry with you."

"Then why is it, Mistress Sunshine, that you run each time I get close to you?"

Because looking into his bright blue eyes and seeing no true recognition there was killing her. Because having him standing four feet away from her and knowing exactly how she would feel if she crossed those same four feet and flung herself into his arms was killing her. Because looking at his mouth that was still so beautiful and knowing what miracles it was able to work on hers was simply *killing* her.

She grasped for the first thing that came to mind. "Why do you care?" she asked desperately.

He considered, then seemed to choose his words very carefully. "I'm not certain I have the answer that question deserves."

"Thank you so very much for making the effort anyway," she said tartly. She said it that way because it was easier to be angry than hurt—and she had no reason to be hurt. The man was missing several critical memories and couldn't be blamed for what that did to her.

But he could be blamed for standing in her house when he should have been standing somewhere else. She turned away and washed his mug. That would give him time to get his boots and coat and get the hell out.

She heard him walk away. That was promising. She set the cup on the drain board and closed her eyes as she heard her front door open. She let out a shaky breath, then turned around as the door closed again.

Cameron was, unfortunately, on the wrong side of it.

He leaned back against the wood and looked at her. "The storm is terrible. Definitely too wet to go out."

She felt her mouth fall open. "What?"

He walked over and leaned against the little counter that separated Moraig's kitchen from the great room. "My horse is quite happily installed in your shed and I think I would be just as happily installed here on your floor." He looked at her with a very small smile. "I wouldn't even need a pillow."

"But you can't stay here," she said in astonishment.

"I wasn't suggesting anything unseemly," he said easily. "Just a bit of Highland hospitality."

"Ha," she said with a snort. She was tempted to remind him of all the times that had gone awry for the hosts, but she refrained. "I think I've already done my duty for the day."

He smiled. "But surely you don't want me retching all the way home, do you?"

"Why would you do that?"

He shot her a look. "I have a fair idea of what you put in that tea, woman. I should think you would feel slightly guilty about denying me access to your loo."

She closed her eyes briefly, knowing she was being backed into a corner and not really sure how she was going to get herself out of it. Worse still, she didn't know that she wanted to get herself out of it.

It was madness. Her plans to question him had vanished, her determination to boot him out her front door had evaporated, and now she was seriously considering letting him spend the night in her house. The only thing that made it seem marginally reasonable was that he would probably be spending most of that night in her bathroom, puking his guts out.

He reached over the counter and took her hand. "If you had a blanket for me, I would be most grateful."

"You are completely without scruples."

"But not without honor."

Sunny sighed deeply, then trudged off to fetch him an extra blanket and pillow. She rolled her eyes and searched a bit more for a camping mattress she knew was loitering in the back of her ridiculously large closet. She made sure his plaids were safely tucked in the drawer where she had taken to keeping them during the day, took the other gear out to him, then retreated back into her bathroom and changed into sweats.

She looked in the mirror as she brushed her teeth. It was no wonder he only wanted tea and some floor space. She looked like hell.

She went back into her little great room, ignored the man standing there, and started to bank the fire. Cameron caught her hand, then took the fire iron away from her.

"Leave it. I'll see to it later, when the storm passes," he said hoarsely.

She looked up at him quickly. He was pale again and his forehead was damp with sweat. "You don't look good."

"I feel worse."

She pointed to her bathroom. "Throw up in there."

He put his hand over his belly protectively. "I think I just might."

She watched him go and shut the door behind him, considered, then rolled her eyes. She spread out the mattress for him, then spread out the blanket and pillow. She took an extra throw off the back of one of the chairs and settled it for him. Then she tucked herself in bed and prayed for sleep.

She was, unfortunately for her peace of mind, still awake when Cameron came out of the bathroom. He hesitated, then sat down and stretched out with a groan.

"Brunch?" she asked.

"A fond memory."

She turned on her side and watched him by the light of the fire, waiting for him to sleep.

Perilous.

And, quite suddenly, futile. He rolled to his feet with a groan and strode back into her bathroom.

Perhaps she'd been a little too generous with a particular herb or two.

He came out quite a bit later, cursing her. Sunny reached for a book on flora and fauna in the Hebrides. She already knew most of what was in it, but it was thick and very dryly written. She'd used it several times over the past month to help her sleep. She turned on a flashlight and prepared to let it help her again. Perhaps if she read it aloud, it would drown out Cameron's curses.

She realized, with a start, that he had moved his bed. Next to hers, as it happened.

"What are you doing?" she squeaked.

" 'Twas too hot by the fire," he said. He sat up, stripped off his shirt and his socks, then lay back down. "Damn you, woman, you used too much lobelia in that tea."

"Which means you'll feel better all that much sooner."

"The path to that happy place is, I suspect, going to be very long and thorny."

She smiled in spite of herself. "You never said *how* you wanted to feel better, just that you did."

"I'll be more specific the next time."

Sunny couldn't help but hope for the sake of her poor heart that there wouldn't be a next time. She tried to concentrate on her book, but it was, as she'd conceded before, dull as dust.

And Cameron had apparently found a new batch of unkind things to say about her. He started muttering in French, moved to Latin, and had just warmed up in Italian when she decided she'd had enough. She rolled over to tell him so.

Her book fell from her fingers and landed on his face.

He yelped, then sat up and glared at her. "Why in the hell did I think it would be a good idea to spend the night on your floor?"

"I never asked you to!" she shot back.

He looked at her with his mouth open, then shut his mouth. "Ach, hell," he said with a sigh, setting the book aside. "Sunshine—"

"I'm all right," she said brightly. "It's all right."

"Nay, that was uncalled for. I apologize." He reached out and put his hand over hers. "I didn't mean what I said. I'm very grateful for your kindness to me, especially when I didn't give you much choice about it."

"Oh, I don't know," she managed. "I could have thrown you out bodily, I'm sure."

He smiled and pulled his hand away. "I'm sure you could have and I appreciate your restraint. Why don't you lie down, love, and be at peace. I'll watch over you."

"From the bathroom," she muttered under her breath. She lay back down, though, because she thought that that way she might be able to pull the covers up over her head and avoid having to look at him anymore. She closed her eyes as she felt his hand on her hair, smoothing it back from her face.

"From the loo, if necessary," he agreed. "You have offered me much more hospitality than I deserved and I am grateful for it." He paused. "And I'm very grateful for a place in front of your fire."

She looked at him, mute.

He tugged her covers up to her ear, touched her face again, then lay down. He was silent for quite some time. "Thank you for the refuge, Sunshine."

She couldn't answer. She waited until she heard his breathing deepen before she rolled over and took many, many deep breaths to keep from weeping. She didn't want to be his refuge.

She wanted to be what she had been to him.

She wanted to push him, to see if he could remember more than just what he felt on Moraig's threshold, to see if he could remember everything he'd forgotten. She wanted to push him so hard that he demanded that she stop. She wanted to back him into a corner where he had no choice but to either admit to her that he knew who and what he'd been, or acknowledge that he had no clue about anything that had happened before he'd been clunked on the head.

She wanted with equal fervor to run away from him as fast and as far away as she could get. She was so torn between the two, she was surprised she didn't make a horrible rending sound right there next to him.

Push him, or push him away.

Maybe he would be gone by the time she got up in the morning and she wouldn't have to make that decision.

She didn't hold out much hope for it.

Chapter 18

C *ameron* resurrected Sunny's fire as quietly as possible, then rubbed his arms as he made his way to the kitchen to start water for tea. It was spring, or so the calendar said, but he wasn't believing it at present. Then again, he'd faced twenty-eight springs with far less clothing and much skimpier rations, so he had no reason to complain.

Actually, he had no reason to complain about anything, especially since he was no longer heaving his guts up. He felt wonderful, though he suspected Sunshine had brewed her tea stronger than necessary to get him to that point. Perhaps he could add *murderous herbal rage* to all the reactions she seemed to have to him.

At least she'd allowed him to stay. Either he'd looked truly pitiful, or she'd simply wanted to watch what happened to him each time he walked over her threshold. It gave him the same sort of headache he'd been having for various reasons over the past se'nnight. Sunshine's threshold, Patrick MacLeod's courtyard, words from the past . . .

Cameron, ride for the MacLeod witch.

Odd, how he hadn't thought about those words or that battle in years. He also hadn't thought about the gaps in his memory that seemed to follow that battle. It was as if he'd gone for a ride, then fallen off his horse and woken in hospital in a century that was most definitely not his own. Magic? He'd been convinced of it at the time.

He wasn't so sure he wasn't convinced of it still.

He took a deep breath, pushed aside his unproductive thoughts, then caught the kettle before it whistled. He poured boiling water over red raspberry leaf, then waited for it to steep in the French press. After a few more minutes of studying the view from the window, he poured two cups of tea and walked over to where he could enjoy a different view.

He sat down and applied himself to a cup of something he was quite certain wouldn't make him retch. And whilst he drank, he looked his fill. Sunshine was the picture of peace. How lovely to have a life where one knew that the day that followed waking would be just as agreeable as the day that had passed.

He envied her.

She took a deep breath suddenly, sighed, then opened her eyes. She looked up at the ceiling for a moment, then sat up and looked at him.

"You stayed."

He pointed to the darkening circle beneath his left eye. "I was wounded at your hearth. Poisoned, as well."

"I think you deserved both."

He smiled. "Likely so." He held out a cup. "Too early for tea?"

"Is it ever too early?"

"Never, especially when the tea is liberally laced with whisky."

"I wouldn't recommend that," she said, taking the cup from him. "Look where it got you last time."

Aye, looking at you first thing in the morning. He could honestly say it had been well worth the price.

"Did you shower?" she asked. "I didn't hear you."

"I didn't, but I did cut my face to pieces with your razor, then nosed about in your loo and nicked a new toothbrush. I'll let you have one of mine in return when you come to my house."

She froze. Then she very carefully got up and stepped past him. She set her mug on the mantel, then continued on into the bathroom. He heard the distinct sound of the door locking.

Cameron bowed his head. His first thought was that he had grossly overestimated his appeal. Hard on the heels of that came the realization that Sunny's hesitation likely had less to do with him and more to do with his situation.

Of his being engaged to another woman, that was.

He rubbed his hands over his face. If he'd had any sense at all, he would have agreed with her, left a note of thanks on her counter, then ridden decisively back to Cameron Hall to return to the unwholesome bit of business that was his life. Nay, if he'd had any sense, he never would have plunged himself into an intoxicated stupor to have an excuse to seek her out, nor would he have spent the whole of the past week trying to avoid thinking about her. Actually it had been more than a week; it had been from the moment he'd had his arms full of her in James MacLeod's great hall. He'd spent the ensuing days either thinking about her or trying not to think about her. Now he was supposed to walk away when he was actually sitting in front of her fire?

Impossible.

He finished his tea, made Sunny's bed for her, rolled up the camping mattress and folded the blankets, then sat in the chair near the fire and watched the bathroom door.

He heard the shower running. Soon after it stopped, he heard the sound of a blow-dryer briefly. Then there was silence for so long, he wondered if she had ducked out of the bathroom window to escape him. He wouldn't have been surprised.

But before he could decide if he should knock or not, the door opened and a fresh-scrubbed Sunshine Phillips came out. It was the single most appealing sight he'd ever seen in his life.

He pushed himself to his feet and walked past her into her kitchen before he did something monumentally stupid, such as haul her into his arms and kiss her.

"I'll make you breakfast," he said.

She hovered at the edge of her kitchen. "Do I dare eat it?"

"I promise to leave out the lobelia," he said. He opened her fridge and looked inside. No butter, no eggs, no milk, and no sausage. Bread that looked like it might have been ground in a medieval mill hemmed in on all sides by lots of green things. "There's not a damn thing in here to eat," he said in surprise. He looked at her. "What do you live on?"

"Salads. It keeps my chi balanced."

He shut the fridge. "You're not one of those nutters who runs about trying to save the rest of us from our bangers and mash, are you?"

"I don't care what *you* eat," she said archly. "I'm just particular about what *I* eat."

"Lass, there's nothing wrong with porritch. I guarantee you, the oats never saw it coming."

She looked at him for a moment in surprise, then she smiled.

He was very grateful he had the counter to lean against. He was certain it was the first true smile he'd had from her. It made him want another.

Her smile faded all too quickly. It was followed by a look that somehow said she was coming to some sort of decision about him. He didn't move, lest he startle her into making one he wouldn't like.

She put her hands in her pockets. "We could go beg a meal from Patrick," she said slowly. "You might find something more to your taste there." She looked at him, then. "Unless you have plans for the morning."

Cameron hadn't survived thirty-five winters because he was dense, nor because he was unable to read his opponents. Sunny was pushing him in the direction she wanted him to go; he would have staked his hall on it. He found that he didn't care why. If it meant another hour or two in her company, he would gladly pay whatever price she intended to exact from him.

"I don't have plans for the day," he said. Unless those plans included thinking a great many things he shouldn't be, actually. Wondering how he might have her company for more than just the day, for another. Best not to think on that, probably.

"Let's go," he said without hesitation. He walked over to her hearth and banked her fire. He looked around the house to make certain it was put to bed properly, then took her jacket off the hook by the door and held it out for her.

She hesitated only slightly before she allowed him to help her. He shrugged into his own jacket, put his boots on, then opened the door for her. He was almost able to ignore the cold chill that ran through him as he followed her over the threshold.

He walked around the house with her, made certain his mount had food and water enough for a bit, then followed her along a thin, worn track.

"Stay on the path," she said at one point, looking over her shoulder at him.

"I have on boots," he said with a smile. "The nettles won't vex me."

"I'm not talking about nettles."

He snorted. "Are you now going to tell me some sort of MacLeod fireside tale about ghosts and bogles? Fairies? Other otherworldly happenings?"

"There's something spooky about MacLeod soil," she said seriously.

There always has been, he almost added, but decided voicing that would just give credence to the foolishness. But he did trade places with her just the same. "Let me go first. If something untoward happens, I'll be the one it happens to first."

"Very gallant, my lord."

He smiled at her over his shoulder. "My worst fault."

She smiled, a hesitant smile that left him wondering if he hadn't lost his wits along with everything he'd eaten the day before. What in the hell was he doing, flirting with a woman he couldn't have?

He was mad.

But she was like the first breath of true summer sunshine after an endlessly cold winter and a damp and nasty spring. He had the same feeling wash over him that he'd had whilst standing in his office, that feeling of pleasure at just the thought of her name. It was, the saints pity him, all he could do not to just stand and lift his face to the light.

He did look back periodically to see if she was still following him, then finally reached back and took her hand. She didn't pull away—which surprised him—but he wasn't going to argue. He enjoyed the feel of her fingers linked with his for a good quarter hour until he found himself within sight of Patrick MacLeod's courtyard. Sunshine pulled her hand away from his and tucked it firmly into her pocket. He would have protested, but he supposed she was right. He was even more convinced of that when he caught sight of the good lord of Benmore's glare.

He stopped a handful of paces away from Sunny's brother-in-law and wished acutely for a sword.

Patrick glared at him for a moment, then he must have caught sight of Cameron's blackening eye because he laughed.

"I was going to ask you what in the hell you were doing with my sister at this unearthly hour, but I can see the time has been well used—" He shut his mouth abruptly and turned a fierce frown on Sunny. "Did you punch him?"

"I dropped a book on him."

"Dropped a book?" he echoed. "Don't you mean 'threw a book'?"

Sunny sighed gustily. "Semantics, Pat. I wasn't defending my virtue. He was a perfect gentleman. It was just that when we were going to bed and I leaned over him—"

"You *what!*"

Cameron watched as Sunshine had the gall to laugh, then duck under Patrick's arm and escape into the safety of the hall. He wouldn't have been at all surprised if Patrick had challenged him to a duel with swords—if that was how he settled things, which Cameron suspected just might be the case.

"Would you care to offer an explanation?" Patrick asked frostily.

Cameron kept his hands in plain sight. "I slept on her floor, not her bed, but—"

"But, my arse," Patrick snarled. "What do you think you're doing with her, you bloody fool? And if you tell me again you're not sure, you'll regret it."

Cameron would have likely drawn his sword in response to Patrick's tone if he'd been in his youth, but he was less hotheaded than he had been then—that, and Patrick MacLeod was well within his rights to demand answers. He supposed the least he could do was offer the most honest ones he could.

"I drank myself into a stupor over her the night before last, then came home yesterday afternoon to see if she would make me a tea to undo it. There is your answer."

"You're engaged!"

"Trust me," he said grimly. "I'm unpleasantly aware of that fact."

Patrick folded his arms over his chest. "Let me see if I can pit my poor wits against this tangle of yours. You're engaged to one woman, yet you feel comfortable coming back home and bleating after another? Another who happens to be my sister? Are you completely without honor, or just completely without sense?"

Cameron dragged his hand through his hair. "A little of both, perhaps."

"You're not on Cameron soil here, laddie," Patrick continued in a low, dangerous tone of voice, "no matter how nicely we played together the other night. If you hurt Sunny, I will slice you open from heart to belly, pull your entrails out and strangle you with them, then make it all look like a terrible accident. And if you think I can't—or won't—you'd best think again."

Cameron hadn't truly expected anything else and he had no doubts Patrick would make good on the threat if pushed. "Warning noted." He paused. "It might ease you to know that she doesn't like me."

Patrick looked again at his black eye, snorted, then stepped back into the hall. "She still has sense, then. Come and eat."

Cameron did while the offer was still good.

And as he sat at the table and soon tucked happily into things he hadn't seen in Sunshine's icebox, he thought about Patrick MacLeod. He thought about those tales that went round the pub about James MacLeod. He thought about rumors from his youth, rumors about James, the laird of the clan MacLeod who had cheated death and taken his wife to Paradise. That laird's cousin, Ian, had disappeared several years later under equally mysterious circumstances. And his brother Patrick had gone missing years earlier than either of them.

Perhaps the tales of magic on MacLeod soil weren't so far off after all.

He turned his mind back to his meal, partly because Patrick MacLeod was an excellent chef and partly because he didn't want to think any more about things that made him uncomfortable. He finally sat back with a cup of coffee and sighed in pleasure.

"Thank you," he said, with feeling.

"Haven't you eaten well lately?" Patrick asked.

"I've been in London, so draw your own conclusions. I will admit, though, that I'm hungrier than usual, given that I spent most of the night in your sister's loo."

Patrick raised his eyebrows at Sunny. "In truth?"

"He had a hangover from too much whisky and brunch," Sunshine said. "I couldn't not offer my assistance with a little lobelia tea. You would think that the laird of clan Cameron would know a little more about the taste of herbs than that, but apparently not."

"I knew exactly what I was drinking, which you well know," Cameron said mildly. "I was being polite by not complaining. I was also very under the weather."

Sunny studied him for a moment, then turned to Patrick. "He doesn't have anything to do today."

"What do you want me to do about that?" Patrick asked with a snort. "Babysit him for you?"

"Perhaps he'd like a tour of Ian's," Sunshine suggested. "You know, now that he's feeling so chipper."

Patrick shot her a look that was gone too quickly for Cameron to identify. Before he could begin to speculate, Patrick had turned to him.

"Feel up to a little swordplay, Cameron?"

Cameron felt his mouth fall open. "Swordplay?"

"I know how much time you spend at Bagley's," Patrick said. "Surely you could manage a few minutes crossing blades with me. I'm certain I'm nowhere near your equal."

He said the last with a smirk, which led Cameron to believe that Patrick MacLeod had no illusions about his own skill.

Cameron looked at Sunshine. She was watching him carefully, as if she simply waited for him to come to some sort of decision. So that's what she'd been about, but why? Why would she suggest a morning at Ian MacLeod's? Why would she care if he said aye or not?

Something slithered down his spine. He wouldn't have called it unease, but perhaps it couldn't be termed anything else. It wasn't possible that she knew anything about his past, was it? The thought that he might have been born in a century far removed from hers was so laughable that he hardly entertained the thought anymore himself. His life had begun eight years ago. Anything else was business he'd happily left in the past.

Including swordplay with anything but rapiers.

"Go fetch different clothes," Patrick said abruptly.

Cameron pulled himself back to the present. "I wish I could," he said with feigned regret, "but I didn't bring my car. It would take me so long to ride home and back that it wouldn't be worth it for you to wait."

Patrick pulled keys out of his pocket and slid them across the table. "Take mine and hurry."

Cameron looked at Sunny. She was still watching him with that look that said she was just waiting for him to show what he was made of. Heaven help them both if she ever found out.

"You aren't afraid, are you?" she asked.

He tried to loosen his jaw, but it seemed to be set quite firmly. "Are you baiting me?" he asked carefully.

She only smiled and reached for his plate. "I don't think you really want to know. Best hurry and get your stuff before Patrick thinks you're chickening out."

He looked at Patrick, but the man was only waiting, watching him dispassionately. Cameron reached out slowly and took Patrick's keys.

"It would take me an hour home and an hour back even with a car," he said slowly. "I have shoes at John's, but no clothes."

"I'll loan you clothes," Patrick said with a hint of a smile. "Make haste, lad. We'll be waiting."

That's what he was afraid of. He looked at Sunny, but she was very busy with breakfast dishes and he supposed forcing a good-bye out of her wouldn't endear him to Patrick MacLeod. He thanked the lord of Benmore for breakfast, then left before anything else unsettling happened to him.

He drove Patrick's car to the village, managed to get his shoes out of John's storage room without answering any questions, then returned back the way he had come.

He parked Patrick's car where he'd found it, then noticed Patrick and Sunny standing on the front stoop, waiting for him. Patrick had a sword resting against his shoulder like an old-fashioned Colonial rifle.

A six-foot bloody Claymore, if anyone was curious.

Sunny didn't look as if she thought it out of the ordinary. Then again, she consorted with MacLeods on a regular basis, so perhaps it didn't seem strange to her. Cameron walked over and tossed Patrick his keys.

"Thanks for the loan."

"There are clothes in the loo," Patrick said. "Hurry."

Cameron changed, then returned outside to find only Patrick waiting for him. Sunny was already well on her way down the path leading toward the woods to the east. Cameron cleared his throat.

"Where's your wife?"

"Practicing her fiddle."

Cameron blinked in surprise. "I thought that was a recording I heard inside. She's very good."

"She is," Patrick agreed. "I think she should make a career out of it, but she's content enough to mother our wee one and spend the occasional afternoon with Angus McKinnon down at the pub, wowing the lads."

"I've never heard her there and I think I regret it." He considered. "As for the other, I can't say I blame her. There are many who would give much to be home."

Patrick shot him a sharp look, but said nothing.

"What of you?" Cameron continued, looking for something to concentrate on besides the sight of a woman he couldn't have walking fifty paces in front of him. "How do you feed your family?"

"I teach wilderness survival as part of Ian's school. And swordplay, when it suits me. I dug up a chest of doubloons in my garden last year and sell those when the mood strikes." He shot Cameron a look. "I'm also writing a book on medieval Scottish warfare."

Cameron stumbled before he could stop himself. "Are you," he managed. "Have a publisher yet?"

"Aye, if you can believe it. Between that and spending as much of my time as possible simply looking at my wife and contemplating how fortunate I am to have her, I'm fairly busy."

Cameron watched Sunshine walking in front of him. "I can understand that."

"Sunny's beautiful as well, though, isn't she?"

"Stunning," Cameron agreed.

Patrick leaned in close. "Well, she's not yours, so you'd best not look too hard, had you?"

Cameron thought Patrick might have that aright.

But he looked anyway, because he couldn't help himself, and continued to look until he found himself standing in Ian MacLeod's backyard. Well, it wasn't precisely a backyard; it looked more like a training field. There was space enough near the house with children's toys and places for adults to relax, but Sunny didn't stop there. Cameron followed her and Patrick to where Ian MacLeod was waiting for them in that training field.

Ian pulled Sunny over and put his arm around her shoulders. "So, this is the soft-handed woman Pat said you were bringing," he drawled loudly. "What sewing circle did you drag him away from?"

Sunny smiled dryly. "Cameron Hall, which you knew, where he is laird, which you also knew. Have a little respect for your betters, Ian."

Ian only laughed. "Lord Robert and I have met before and he knows I'm merely provoking him to get his blood going."

"He'll need it," Patrick said shortly. "Ian, give him a sword."

Cameron judged by the look on Patrick MacLeod's face that he would need all the heat in his blood he could muster. Patrick had also just tossed away the scabbard to his sword as if he'd done it thousands of times—which Cameron quite suddenly had no doubt he had. He took a deep breath, then turned to look at Sunny. He saw something in her face that he'd never expected.

Hope.

Something inside him shifted, something so elemental that he couldn't quite catch his balance for a moment. He had to stop himself from reaching out and yanking her against him. But he couldn't stop himself from walking over and putting his hand gently on her shoulder.

"What is it, love?" he asked quietly.

"Nothing," she said quickly. "Nothing. Go have a good time."

He put his arms around her before he thought better of it. Ian said nothing, Patrick didn't fling a sword into his back, the world didn't end.

But something inside him wrenched its way out of its moorings, shifted, then settled in a place he'd never expected.

Sunny hugged him suddenly, tightly, then pulled out of his arms and backed away. "You'd better go before Pat comes to get you."

He was too winded to speak. He looked at her again and saw that despite her lighthearted words, she still wore that same look on her face, as if she hoped for something so dreadful she didn't dare voice it.

He wondered what it was. He also wondered why in the hell he had allowed himself to be backed into any of this. He could have invented half a dozen excuses to avoid finding himself facing men who he was quite sure knew which end of the sword to point away from themselves. He supposed he could still walk away. After all, he'd been studiously ignoring his past for eight years now, a past where he might or might not have grown to manhood with a sword in his hands. A medieval sword. Given to him by his very medieval father.

He wondered what Sunny would think when she saw what he could do.

Before he could think any longer on any of it, Ian chucked a sword at him. He caught it without thinking. And once it was in his hands, there really wasn't any point in leaving it sheathed, was there? And once the blade was bared, there was even less point in not using it for its intended purpose, was there?

Patrick attacked him suddenly and with a ferocity that left him stumbling backward.

Briefly.

Eight years fell away as if they'd never passed. He held that heavy sword in his hands and wielded it as if he'd done nothing the day before besides train with a sword from dawn till dusk. He fought back now out of habit, fought hard, fought with every canny trick he'd ever learned.

He felt as if he had stepped back in time hundreds of years. He would have enjoyed that, but he was too busy. Patrick MacLeod was a spectacular swordsman and just as ruthless as every other MacLeod clansman Cameron had ever fought. Cameron had to stretch himself far beyond what he normally did to keep up with him. It felt marvelous.

An hour passed, perhaps longer, before he managed to look

over to see what expression Sunshine was wearing. At that point, he wouldn't have been surprised by anything. Surprise, horror, disgust; he was prepared for any of the three.

He wasn't prepared to see tears streaming down her face.

Only a lifetime of knowing when he was about to have his head chopped off saved him from it at present. He threw up his sword and listened to Patrick's screech down the length of it. He looked at Patrick in shock.

"You almost killed me."

"Best pay attention then, hadn't you?"

Cameron felt his eyes narrow. "You'll regret that."

Patrick snorted. "I doubt it. But I don't doubt that you and I are going to have serious speech together very soon. I'll make a list of pointed questions for you."

"Can you manage that and fight at the same time?"

Patrick laughed out loud, then suddenly slapped Cameron's sword so hard, he almost dropped it.

But he wasn't William mac Cameron's son for nothing, and he had grown to manhood with a sword that he'd made a point of keeping in his hands, not on the grass at his feet, so he kept his sword where it belonged. He shot Sunny another look, saw that her expression hadn't changed, then had no more time to wonder about it. MacLeods were MacLeods no matter the century, apparently, and demanded his full attention.

He would, however, be turning that attention to their witch just as soon as he was free to do so. He wondered why she had pushed him into this so ruthlessly. He wondered why she seemed to wish for an outcome he couldn't divine.

He wondered if he would be able to bear the answer when he learned it.

Chapter 19

Sunny stood next to Ian MacLeod on the edge of his training yard and wondered if she had just lost her mind. She'd woken up that morning to the sight of Cameron sitting near her bed and felt her heart leap a little. She'd decided on the spot that orchestrating a little trip to Ian's would be a great idea. Now, she had a different idea.

She was insane. Still.

She managed a decent look—then wished she hadn't bothered. Cameron was . . . well, he was himself. He was wearing shorts, a T-shirt, and tennis shoes instead of a plaid and worn boots, but those were the only indications that he wasn't happily back in 1375. He was just as skilled, just as lethal, just as beautiful. He was all muscle and intensity, wielding his sword as if no time at all had passed for him. And he still pushed his hair out of his eyes with a curse as he had done in the past.

"That lad there didn't learn his swordplay in this century."

Sunny realized she'd forgotten that Ian was standing next to her. She focused on him with an effort. "What makes you think that?"

"Because he's not thinking about what he's doing." He studied Cameron for another moment or two. "Watch him as he fights. This is no choreographed dance for him. He's either reacting without hesitation to Pat's assault, or he's on the attack, moving to exploit Pat's weaknesses. His sword is just an extension of himself." He looked at her and smiled. "That's the difference between someone who grew up using a sword to keep himself alive and one who learned the skill for less pressing reasons."

"You do know what you're doing, don't you?"

Ian grinned. "Unbelievable, isn't it?"

"I know you know how to fight, Ian," she said wryly. "I just never thought about the theory behind it."

"Well, that's why they pay me the big bucks," he drawled with a very good American accent. "Turning those Hollywood stunt lads into the real thing."

"Which they never can be."

"Some manage it," he conceded. "But those men live and breathe swordplay for years. Occasionally I find one who truly has a gift for it." He nodded toward the field. "But your wee friend fights this well because he spent his youth with a sword in his hands and used it to keep himself alive."

"You think?" she said, her mouth very dry all of the sudden.

He shot her a look. "Sunny, I'm no fool. I can't give you a precise date, but I'd put him pre-fifteenth century, at least. I don't suppose you'd be able to shed any light on it, would you?"

"Me?" she asked hoarsely. "Why would I?"

"Because you're standing here not realizing that tears are running down your cheeks—which is something I'm doing my gentlemanly best not to notice."

She dragged her sleeve across her face. "You have an overactive imagination, Ian."

"Well, I'm not imagining what I'm seeing out there. Robert Cameron is very, very good. Even Pat's having to work a bit, isn't he?"

She turned back to the field and had to admit that Ian was right. She supposed it was nothing to her brother-in-law, but if she'd had to face Cameron over blades, she would have surrendered without hesitation.

Then again, he was fighting Patrick MacLeod, and that should have at least given him pause. He did pause, at one point, and look at her.

"Water," he demanded, his chest heaving.

Ian looked at her in surprise. "Are you going to humor him?"

"Maybe he'll take off his shirt," she said, before she thought better of it.

Ian looked at her and laughed. "Sunny, are you lusting after that lad there?"

She turned and walked away before she had to answer. She imagined Ian would waste no time in telling Cameron what she'd said, which was reason enough to hurry back to the house before she had to be privy to it.

She walked into Ian's kitchen but didn't even have the distraction of Ian's very pregnant wife, Jane, to keep her from having to go back out onto the field before she was ready to. She filled a pitcher with water, collected four cups, then walked back out into the garden.

She refilled Cameron's cup three times before he nodded his thanks.

"And what of her payment?" Ian asked mildly.

Cameron blinked in surprise. "Surely she wasn't serious."

Sunny hadn't been, really, but now she found that she couldn't help but push his buttons just a bit more. "I might have been," she said. "I might be still."

"I have a scar or two—"

"And I don't?" Patrick interrupted. He stripped off his shirt and hung it over Sunny's shoulder. "Give the gel her due and come on. I'm not finished with you yet."

Cameron balked. Sunny wondered why. He certainly hadn't had any trouble stripping in front of her to take a bath in medieval Scotland. Then again, he'd had the body of a medieval laird in that day and scars had been just a part of the package. Perhaps he thought that if she saw him now, she would be shocked.

"You took off your shirt last night," she reminded him.

"He *what*?" Patrick thundered.

"It was dark, though," she said regretfully.

Patrick strode back onto the field. "Cameron, get your sorry arse out here. I've a few lessons in *deportment* to teach you."

Cameron yanked his shirt off over his head. He took a step closer to her and laid it very carefully over her shoulder.

"I will repay you for this, believe me," he said in a low voice.

She imagined he would, unfortunately, She also decided that asking him to take off his shirt had been a very bad idea indeed. In fact, the whole morning had been a very bad idea. She'd hoped he would clunk himself on the head with his sword and find a few memories floating to the top of the soup as a result. Instead, he'd displayed his medieval self—his now shirtless medieval self—without any flashes of memory that should have either brought him to his knees or sent him into her arms.

And she was very much worse for the wear.

"Penelope Ainsworth is a shrew," Ian said idly. "He's a fool if he weds her."

"Does no one have a secret up here?" she muttered.

"Not when you're the laird of the hall up the way and the lads down at the pub thought you were daft to even look for a woman south of the border."

"He obviously loves her or he wouldn't have asked her to marry him."

"Then why is he watching you when he should be attending to his swordplay? And why did he spend the night on your floor?"

"He needed something for a headache and the storm kept him at my house," she said. "I pushed him into this here."

"To see what he was?" Ian asked. "Or to force him to see it?"

She sighed. "A bit of both, actually."

"I think, cousin, that there is a great deal more to this tale than you're telling me. But since I am the least nosy of my relations, I won't press you for the details. I will tell you, though, that I would kill him for you if you wanted me to. And if he hurts you any more, I'll kill him with or without your permission."

"Very medieval of you, Ian."

He winked. "You can't expect anything else, can you?"

She certainly couldn't.

She supposed, quite a while later, that Patrick would have carried on for the rest of the day if it hadn't been for Ian demanding his turn. Patrick relinquished his place finally, though he heaped abuse on Cameron's head as he walked away. Ian strode out, fresh as a daisy.

"Let us see, my lad, how you fare against a real swordsman," he said brightly.

Patrick cursed his cousin, but Ian only laughed. Sunny handed Patrick the pitcher of water. He drank straight from it, then up-ended the rest of it over his head. He shook himself off like a dog, sending water scattering everywhere—including on her.

She used the least damp part of his shirt to dry her face off, then handed it to him. He pulled it down over his head, then went to look for the scabbard for his sword. He resheathed his blade thoughtfully, then came to stand next to her.

"Well," he said finally, "I know *what* he is. Now I want to know who he is." He looked at her. "Are you going to tell me or shall I guess?"

She looked at him for a moment, then turned and walked away. She sat down on a bench that was hardly ever used by those possessing a sword. Fortunately, she wasn't one of those lads, and she'd had enough for the day.

Patrick sat down next to her. "You know, Sunshine," he continued relentlessly, "the first thing out of your mouth when you returned from your little jaunt was not *Patrick, how lovely to see you,* it was *Where's Cam?* I'm assuming Cam is short for Cameron. Odd, isn't it, that we now have a Cameron clansman standing fifty paces in front of us, one who can't seem to stay away from you, one I can personally guarantee was not born in the twentieth century."

"Are you sure?"

He shot her a look of faint disgust.

"All right, you're sure," she said with a sigh. "Now that you're sure, what is it you want?"

"I want you not to hurt," he said seriously. "I want to know what happened to you, where you went, who you fell in love with."

"Who I—" she spluttered.

"I recognize the symptoms, if not the disease."

She wanted to continue with her denials, but knew there was little point. Patrick had watched her weep for over a week after she'd come home—and he was no fool. She supposed he'd guessed most of it anyway. "Maddy will kill me if I tell you things I haven't told her," she said with a sigh.

"Trust me, Sunny, nothing you tell me can possibly equal the unrestrained speculation your sister has engaged in for the past month."

She imagined that was true. It was also true that Patrick was an absolute vault when it came to keeping secrets. She'd watched Jamie try to pry things out of him without any success. No matter the pressure, Patrick never budged. Whatever she told him in confidence would go no further, not even to her sister.

"All right," she said, surrendering. "What do you want to know?"

"Who is Cam?" he asked, without hesitation.

She nodded out at the field. "Him."

He didn't look at all surprised. "And you met him in the past?"

"Yes."

"Why doesn't he know you here?"

She looked out at Cameron fighting Ian with an energy that belied the hours he'd spent already with Patrick, then turned back to her brother-in-law. "It seems there are times when a pair of people use the same gate and don't wind up at the same destination time wise. This is especially inconvenient when one of the pair has his skull half bashed in and loses all memories of the woman he said he loved."

Patrick closed his eyes briefly. "Ach, Sunny, I'm sorry." He smiled at her, pained. "Did you think a little swordplay might jog his memory?"

"I hoped so, but it doesn't look to have helped, does it?" She stared at Cameron. "Do you like him?"

"He's a Cameron and I've fed him twice. What does that tell you?"

"It tells me that you're a prince," she said honestly. "I'm so happy my sister found you."

"Thank you, Mistress Lobelia," he said dryly.

She smiled, then felt her smile fade. "Please let me come tell Maddy the rest. You can tell her what I've told you here, if you like, but let me give her the details."

"She's guessed this much already, actually. And you should know that she was torn this morning between telling me to beat him senseless and begging me to leave something left of him for you to have."

"He's engaged."

"Death, Sunshine, is the only thing that is final."

"Are you telling me you're leaving your marriage vows up for negotiation?" she asked.

He looked so shocked that she smiled.

"Answer enough," she said. "And just so you know, that's the kind of man I want. One who looks horrified at the thought of leaving me. But until I find one, I'll thank you for being kind to that one out there."

Patrick shrugged. "Anything for family. Even being civil to a Cameron," he added with a wink before he turned back to watch the carnage.

Sunny watched as well until the morning turned into afternoon. She'd fetched water several times, as well as a snack or two. It was well into the afternoon before Cameron cried peace. She watched Ian clasp hands with Cameron before they came off the field. They were both absolutely drenched in sweat. She tried not to think anything of Cameron coming over to stand next to her rather than Patrick. She ignored the way he touched her arm when he asked very politely for a drink. She didn't dare look at him, standing so close to her in just Patrick's shorts, as she handed him his shirt.

Ian clapped him on the shoulder. "Come back whenever you like," he said with a grin. "I won't even charge you for my time."

"Good of you," Cameron said easily.

Ian only laughed, kissed Sunny on both cheeks, then leaned in close. "I like him," he said loudly.

She wanted to tell him to be quiet, but he escaped before she could. He collected his other sword from Cameron, then walked back off to his house, humming pleasantly.

Patrick watched Cameron for a moment in silence, then looked at her. "You can bring that lad there to supper, I suppose. Perhaps he'll tell us where he learned that fairly passable swordplay of his. I'm sure we'd both find the answer enlightening. Don't dawdle, you two."

He took his sword in hand and jogged off toward his house. Sunny watched him go, then looked up at Cameron. He was watching her warily, as if he waited for some sort of reaction he wouldn't particularly care for.

"Well?" he asked, finally. "What did you think?"

She started to tell him that she'd been very impressed, then realized that it didn't matter if she'd been impressed or not. The facts were still the same as they had been that morning.

He was not free.

"I'm with Patrick in wondering where you learned that kind of swordplay," she said finally, "but I don't suppose you'll tell me."

"When I know how you'll react," he began slowly, "then I'll tell you."

"Before or after you're wed?"

He sighed lightly. "Why do you keep bringing that up?"

"Why aren't you with her?"

He looked at her so seriously, she wished she hadn't asked. In fact, not having the answer to that was probably the best thing she'd done all day.

"I don't want to know," she said briskly, walking away. "Have a nice dinner at Patrick's."

"You'll be there, won't you?"

"No. I'm going home."

"Why?"

"I'm tired," she said. She wasn't, but it was easier to tell him that than the truth, which was that in spite of all her fine resolutions she loved him as much as she always had, but having him in the future didn't matter one bloody bit because he was just as out of her reach as he would have been if he'd been stuck 650 years in the past.

Time traveling sucked.

She would tell Jamie that the next time she saw him.

"I'll see you home safely—"

"I don't need your help."

He made a noise of impatience. "Why won't you allow me to take care of you?"

"Because you already have a woman you should be taking care of." She walked faster, but his legs were longer than hers so it didn't do her any good. "Go do that."

"She doesn't like me."

She almost stopped and gaped at him, but managed to suppress the impulse. "She's an idiot, then."

"Thank you," he said, sounding as if he were smiling. "Now, give in gracefully, Sunshine, and let me make you dinner."

"Go make your fiancée dinner."

"She doesn't like my cooking any more than she likes me."

She shot him a look. "I'm not going to be your refuge, my lord."

He looked at her in surprise, but she didn't see any other expression he might have worn past that because she turned her face away and stomped off. And like clockwork, it started to rain.

She knew she shouldn't have been surprised.

In time, she trudged past Patrick and Madelyn's rock wall. Madelyn was standing just outside the front door, waiting for them.

"Still coming for dinner?" she called.

"No," Sunny said loudly. "I'm going home."

"Cameron, are you—"

Sunny pushed her damp hair back from her face and glared at her sister. Madelyn held up her hands in surrender.

"Never mind," she said. "Want your clothes though, Cameron?"

Sunny heard Cameron start across the courtyard and wondered if she could possibly outrun him and get her door locked before he caught up. She decided abruptly that it was worth a try.

He was, she found, very fast indeed.

By the time she reached her house, she was gasping for breath, soaked, and furious. She couldn't decide when it was that she'd become so angry, nor could she decide whom she was most angry at: Cameron, Penelope, or the damned time gate that had thrown everything into such disarray.

Then again, that gate had given her a brief slice of eternity with the man who had pulled her back to a walk a hundred paces ago and was now crowding under the eaves of her house with her, so perhaps she didn't have as much to complain about as she thought.

Cameron wouldn't let her open the door. He did it himself, shivered as he crossed the threshold, then turned on the lights. He looked in her bathroom, glanced in the kitchen, then came back to the front door.

"All safe."

"No one comes here," she said, struggling to catch her breath.

"There's always a first time," he said, drawing her inside. "Come and sit, lass."

She didn't bother to fight him any longer. She couldn't throw him out bodily and she suspected he was determined to at least feed her before he left of his own volition. She let him lead her over to the hearth, then collapsed rather gratefully in a chair and watched while he made her a fire. She watched him a bit more as he walked into her kitchen and started poking around in her fridge.

She decided right then that time travel didn't just suck, it was the most horrible, gut-wrenching, monstrous thing ever discovered on MacLeod soil. Never mind that Madelyn, Elizabeth, and Jane had had it work out well for them.

She didn't like being the exception.

She wanted to look away from Cameron, but she just couldn't. She wished desperately that he could have been there in truth, not just on clandestine loan.

He puttered, he hummed, he whistled, he even stopped for a moment and looked off into space as if he tried to remember a melody before he nodded to himself and sang as he chopped.

She wondered if her eyes would ever stop burning.

He finished, came out with a plate in his hand, then stopped in surprise when he saw her. "My singing?" he asked.

She shook her head and wiped her eyes. "It was lovely."

"Then you're weeping because you *liked* it?" he asked, obviously baffled.

"I'm tired."

"You continue to say that, but I'm starting not to believe it." He put a plate of an amazingly lovely salad on her lap and handed her a fork. "Eat. You'll feel better after you do."

"This looks wonderful," she said. "Thank you."

"My pleasure." He fetched his own plate, then drew up a wooden chair next to hers and sat down. "Can't guarantee the dressing, though. You don't have anything with fat in there."

"Bad for my—"

"Chi," he finished. "So you said before." He slid her a side-ways look. "Don't you ever long for an enormous order of fish and chips, woman?"

She took a deep breath. "Now and again."

"Do you indulge?"

"Now and again."

He smiled and set to his salad.

Sunny ate what she could, but it was difficult to eat when all she wanted to do was blubber.

Cameron finished, watched her for a minute, then finally took her plate away and put it in the fridge for her. He quickly cleaned the kitchen, then came back to her and held down his hands.

She looked up in surprise. "What?"

"I'm putting you to bed."

She let him pull her to her feet. "But, Cam—"

He looked at her as if she'd slapped him. "What did you call me?"

"Cameron," she amended. Good grief, she was really going to get herself in trouble if he didn't go soon. She pulled away. "I can get myself to bed."

"I know you *can*," he said patiently. "I'm being gallant. Now, go get your nightclothes on, woman, and allow me to tuck you in."

She so desperately wanted to throw her arms around him and cry until she couldn't cry anymore.

Why had she ever thought her life was terrible that night Tavish Fergusson had fired her? It would have been so much bet-ter if she'd never seen Cameron mac Cameron, never felt his arms around her, never had him lift her face so he could kiss it. He was so much what he had been. Chivalrous. Protective. Demanding.

It was killing her.

He turned her toward the bathroom. "Go change."

She did, because she was apparently incapable of arguing with him. Either that, or she was simply too numb. She changed into a pair of MacLeod plaid flannel pajamas that she'd poached from her sister's closet before Christmas, dragged a pick through her hair, then went back out to the great room. Cameron looked at her gravely, then slipped past her into her bathroom with his clothes. A handful of minutes later, he emerged, dressed, with Patrick's clothes in his hands.

"Let me go saddle my horse, then I'll see to you."

"I'll be okay," she said quickly. "I have to lock my door before I can go to bed anyway."

He considered, then nodded and pulled his coat off the hook. He set the clothes down by the door, pulled his coat on, then paused and looked at her.

Sunny couldn't meet his eyes. She looked at the spot under his collarbone, which was about where her nose came to. She felt him tuck some of her hair behind one of her ears.

"Sunshine . . ."

"I don't want to be the other woman, Cameron."

He sighed deeply. "I know." He said nothing more for quite a while. He simply tucked hair behind her ears, strand by strand, as if he couldn't bring himself to do it faster. "Sleep well, love."

She nodded, but couldn't say anything. It was all she could do to keep from weeping.

He dropped his arm, picked up his gear, then turned to let himself out the door. It closed softly behind him. Sunny bolted it, turned, and slid down to the floor. She looked, dry-eyed, into the middle of her house, Moraig's house, that was now so empty and cold she could hardly stand it.

She wrapped her arms around herself in an effort to get warm. It was useless. She just couldn't fathom what Cameron wanted from her, why he continued to seek her out, what she was going to do if she had to see him again. He was not free and she didn't want to be his refuge or a dalliance. Where did that leave them?

Maybe he would go back to London and she would be able to regroup. It was surely the only hope for what was left of her heart.

She locked her door, fetched Cameron's plaids out of her drawer and wrapped them around herself, then went to bed.

She was too devastated to even weep.

*C*hapter 20

I*t* was well before dawn when Cameron walked to his stables. He'd dreamt of battle and bloodshed and all sorts of activities where a sword was useful, activities that certainly did not find themselves in the current century, activities that had led to a terrible night's sleep.

He wasn't sure if he should blame Sunshine Phillips for it, or thank her.

He'd come home after the day spent in Ian MacLeod's lists and looked in his locked closet for the first time in eight years. It had been a little startling, truth be told, to see nothing but a Claymore, three dirks, a saffron shirt, and a handwoven plaid—all that he had to show for his twenty-eight years of living in fourteenth-century Scotland.

He wondered what those MacLeods had locked up in their closets.

He couldn't imagine their wives didn't know exactly who and what their husbands were. There was the problem of wondering how Jamie, Patrick, and Ian had come to the future, but he was certain there was an answer to that as well. Perhaps knowing it would help him determine how he'd done it—since he couldn't remember a bloody thing about it himself. But he could remember with perfect clarity the last thing Sunshine had said to him.

I don't want to be the other woman.

He dragged his hand through his hair and cursed. He didn't want her to be that, either, but he wasn't precisely sure what he was going to do about it. He was trapped by his situation in London every bit as fully as he'd ever been trapped by his duty in medieval Scotland. He cursed quite heartily, but it didn't ease him any. Why couldn't he have met her sooner? It wouldn't have needed to have been that much sooner, perhaps. A pair of months.

Though the thought of her having been drawn into any of the madness that surrounded Nathan and Penelope Ainsworth sent cold chills down his spine.

He pushed aside that thought. He was in Scotland, he was safe for the day, and he could perhaps take another few hours and do what his heart begged him to. He opened the stable door, quickly saddled two horses, then walked them out into a fine, spring mist. He swung up onto his mount, then cantered south without hesitation. He would spend the day with Sunshine Phillips and see what was left of them both at the end of it.

There was already light streaming out from her kitchen window when he got there. He dismounted and left his beasts behind her house, then walked quietly to the front door. He prepared himself for the unpleasant sensation that would assault him when he crossed Sunny's threshold.

He wasn't prepared, however, for what happened to him when she answered his knock.

A déjà vu slammed into him so hard, he felt as if he'd been run over by a horse. He clutched at the door frame to keep himself from falling to his knees.

He had come to this house, knocked, and seen a woman open to him. A woman with long, curling hair, a black blouse, and a swirling black skirt.

"Cameron? Cameron, are you all right?"

He had to take a step back. He wanted to speak, but he simply couldn't. He put his hand over his eyes and thought he just might be ill. Again, damn it anyway.

Sunny pushed him back several more steps. "Lean over," she said firmly. "Breathe."

He bent over with his hands on his thighs and did as she suggested. He stood there, hunched over, and struggled to keep his porritch down where it belonged. He felt her hands, one on his shoulder, the other smoothing over his hair as if she tried to comfort him. What the door had left of him, she finished off with that touch alone.

By the saints, had he actually managed to fetch the MacLeod witch as he'd set out to do almost seven hundred years ago?

Just thinking on it gave him a splitting headache, so he stopped and merely concentrated on breathing. He straightened, when he thought he could manage it with any success, and found Sunny looking at him with surprise.

"What are you doing here?" she asked faintly.

"I came to see if you would come riding with me," he said hoarsely, struggling to make it sound like a casual invitation.

Actually, he was struggling to make it sound like anything but a pathetic plea.

She looked at him for a moment, then turned away. "I can't."

He caught her hand. "Sunshine, please." He had to take another handful of deep breaths before he thought he could speak with any steadiness. "A platonic ride to Cameron Hall, then breakfast. Nothing more."

She bowed her head for a moment or two, then turned slowly and looked up at him. "Are you having breakfast for three?"

"Nay," he said quietly, "just you and me."

She pulled her hand from his and backed away. "It's a really bad idea—"

"Can you be bribed?" he said before he thought better of it.

She looked up at him in surprise. "What do you mean?"

"I mean I'll give you what you want if you'll give me what I want—and what I want is for you to ride home with me." He paused. "You could make your price steep."

She looked terribly indecisive. She looked at him for another moment or two in silence, then shrugged, though she didn't look particularly casual. "I suppose you could answer a few personal questions."

"Not *that* steep," he said, and he smiled, though he supposed it had been a rather sick smile indeed. He didn't care for personal questions. He had more than his share of secrets and he never put himself in a position where those secrets needed to be divulged. It was proof enough of how desperate he was for her company that he was even considering it.

"Go inside and fetch your coat, woman, and come home with me," he said, before she could change her mind.

"All right," she said slowly, though she didn't sound overly enthusiastic about it. She looked at him once more, then turned and went into her house.

He was tempted to wait by her doorway, to make certain she didn't run to Patrick's, but decided for the sake of his poor head that it was safest if he just went to wait with the horses. He put his hand on his gelding's neck and bowed his head, trying to take enough deep breaths to soothe the pain that still screamed through his head.

"Cameron?" Sunny called a moment or two later.

He closed his eyes. Penelope never called him that unless she attached a *Lord* to the front and unless she was talking to him in front of someone else. She called him *Mac*, which he'd had various people call him over the years and never loathed until she'd taken it up.

"Cameron?"

"I'm here," he managed.

Sunny came around the corner with a jacket in her hands and stopped next to the horse he'd brought for her. She hesitated. "Won't your staff wonder why you're having breakfast with someone who isn't your fiancée?"

"They'll all be thrilled to see a proper Scot at the breakfast table."

"I'm not a Scot."

He frowned. "I thought you were a MacKenzie."

Her mouth fell open. *"What?"*

He rubbed his fingers between his eyes, then managed to focus on her. "What, what?"

She looked at him as if she'd just seen a ghost. "How on earth did you know that?"

He opened his mouth to tell her she'd told him, then realized he couldn't remember when she had. He started to speak several times, then finally shrugged. "I have no idea. Are you?"

"I'm a MacKenzie through my mother," she said, her voice nothing more than a whisper.

"A good guess," he said. He decided that no good would come of delving too deeply into it, so he would leave it at that. There were, as he could personally attest, strange things that happened on MacLeod soil. The sooner they were back at his hall, the better off they both would be. He boosted Sunny up into her saddle, then swung up onto his own horse's back. He urged his horse forward, then looked over his shoulder. "Will Patrick and Madelyn wonder where you've gone?"

"I left a note in the bathroom. It's standard procedure."

He nodded, then headed north out of the woods. Once they reached the meadow, he simply watched Sunny watch the countryside gravely, as if she found something about it that touched her too deeply for banter.

He understood. He felt that way when he looked at her.

Two hours later, he was dismounting in his own stables. He walked around to help her down, but he wasn't fast enough. He took her reins from her and handed the horses off to a new stable lad. The man looked at Sunny with a frown of disapproval on his face. Cameron stepped between them, cursing silently. He needed to spend more time in Scotland and see who was being hired to tend his horseflesh. He put his hand on the small of Sunny's back.

"Allons-y," he murmured in French.

She shot him a look that said very clearly that she thought he was an idiot, then she jerked open the door and walked out of the stables without waiting for him.

He followed immediately, pulling the door shut behind him. "Sunshine—"

"I need your phone. Patrick will come get me."

He followed her, then caught her before she could push her way inside. He pulled the door shut, then put his hands on her shoulders and turned her to him.

Her look of irritation melted into something entirely different. She looked for the first time since he'd seen her in front of Patrick's hall that evening when he'd almost run over her as if she would shatter if he wasn't careful with her. He took off his jacket, wrapped it around her, then pulled her wet hair out from under it. He leaned his shoulder against the door under the porch some enterprising soul had put up in the nineteenth century and put his arms around her.

"Sunny, please stay," he whispered. "Please."

She was stiff for a moment or two, then she let out a shuddering breath. He drew her close and she didn't fight him. He smoothed his hand over her hair for several minutes until she finally sighed deeply, put her arms around his waist, and rested her cheek against his chest.

"I shouldn't stay."

"The man in the stables is a recent addition and one I'm not happy about," he said quickly. "He glares at me as well, so don't take it personally. Besides, you can't go until you've exacted your price from me, can you? Here I am, at your mercy. I can't believe you aren't going to twist the knife whilst you can."

She relaxed just the slightest bit more. "For a minute or two, I guess. Since you're at my mercy."

He smiled. "Agreed."

"Patrick says Alistair made you his heir eight years ago," she began without hesitation. "What were you doing before then?"

He shut his mouth only because he realized it was hanging open. By the saints, that was the last thing he'd expected to have her ask him.

"Reneging?"

He tightened his arms around her. "I'm just catching my breath. You go for the jugular."

"I'm curious. It's what makes me a good herbalist."

"'Tis what drives you to find lobelia wherever you are, no doubt," he muttered. He took a deep, fortifying breath, then gave his normal dodge a go. "I am, of course, um . . . kin of Alistair's. I found myself rather . . . abruptly in his company."

"How?"

"My memory fails me on that," he said honestly.

"What's the last thing you do remember?"

He wanted to ask her why she was so curious, but since she was standing willingly in his arms, he thought it might be best not to encourage any thoughts of flight. "I remember going out riding," he said slowly. "The next thing I remember is waking in hospital. Everything in between is gone."

Except that memory of pulling someone out of Moraig's house. He wondered who that someone was.

Could it have been Sunny?

"Cameron, you're trembling."

"'Tis cold out," he said without hesitation, because it sounded less daft than the truth—that he suspected he'd knocked on the MacLeod witch's door and Sunny had opened it. But that was impossible.

Wasn't it?

"It's spring and I imagine you'll survive," she said firmly. "Now, how exactly are you related to Alistair?"

"Thinking to challenge the will?" he managed.

He'd been jesting, but saw when she lifted her head to look at him that she was deadly serious. He reached up with one hand and dragged his fingers through her damp hair, lifting it away from her forehead and tucking strands of it behind her ears.

"Why do you want to know?" he asked with as much of a smile as he could muster.

"Because I want to know everything about you," she whispered. "I want to know who your father was, your brothers, your mother. I want to know what your life was like from dawn to dusk. I want to know why my doorway makes you so ill."

He opened his mouth to give her some bland bit of something that would deflect the question yet leave her still in his arms and him with his privacy intact. Instead, words he hadn't intended to say came out before he could stop them.

"Perhaps," he heard himself saying, " 'tis the knowledge that every time I step over it, I'm leaving you behind."

She stared at him in shock for a moment, then tears sprang to her eyes so suddenly, it was as if someone had slapped her. He tried to speak, to apologize, to soothe her, but he was so far from what was comfortable and sensible, all he could do was pull her against him and hold her tightly.

She wept. Just the sound of it tore at his heart. Her weeping was rough and so unrelenting, he half thought she would be ill.

"Sunshine," he said helplessly, but he realized that she couldn't hear him. He feared that she truly would come undone if he didn't do something. He fumbled for the doorknob, swept her up into his arms, and carried her into the house.

Madame Gies met him halfway across the hall, wearing a look of surprise. He had told her that morning he was bringing a guest home for breakfast, a guest he could guarantee wouldn't send everything back as Penelope did. He supposed she hadn't been expecting that breakfast guest to be one who had fallen apart before he'd even gotten her to the table.

"Take her upstairs immediately," Madame Gies said without hesitation. "I will see her put in the bath." She shot him a stern look. "You shouldn't have had her out in the rain."

He suspected the rain had nothing to do with Sunny's present condition, but he didn't bother to say as much. He merely followed his chef and chief terrorizer of the other staff upstairs and into one of the guest chambers. He set Sunny on her feet, then found himself summarily ejected from the room.

"But—"

The door was shut in his face.

He knocked, but there was no answer, and the door had been locked. He frowned, then decided that perhaps he would do well to change quickly so he could be of use if Madame Gies ever opened the door again. He found dry clothes for Sunny, sent them along with one of his young serving maids, then changed his own gear and retreated to his solar. He built a fire, then started to pace.

Perhaps 'tis the knowledge that every time I step over it, I'm leaving you behind.

He realized that those words were closer to the truth than he had intended to go. He wasn't sure when it had happened, but he realized with a shocking bit of clarity, that what he felt for Sunny went far past where it should have gone for his having known her such a short time. It was madness. He'd only seen her for the first time . . . how many weeks ago was it? Four? Five? He could count on one hand the number of times he'd been with her since that first unexpected encounter.

Then how was it he had longed for her so fiercely every moment of every day since?

He considered that for quite some time, but found no useful answer. Soon enough, he heard voices coming down the passageway. One belonged to Madame Gies. It took him a moment to realize that the other was Sunny speaking in perfectly unaccented French. They exchanged kisses on the cheek, Madame Gies promised Sunny a delicate tea to warm her insides and breakfast suitable for her particular tastes, then she hastened off to deliver on her promises.

Sunny turned and looked at him.

She was wearing his only pair of flannel pajamas. The sleeves and trouser legs were rolled up and her hair was wrapped in a towel. She was so utterly fetching, he couldn't help but laugh.

She glared at him. "I couldn't find anything else."

"I had those left for you," he said, walking over to her.

"Was there nothing else here in my size?" she asked plaintively.

"I suppose you could have had something of Madame Gies's, but you're quite a bit taller than she is."

"Doesn't Penelope leave things here?"

"She never would," he said without hesitation, "even if she were here often, which she's not. She's been here twice and complained constantly during both stays."

"How long have you been engaged to her?"

"Almost two months."

She looked a little winded. "So recently," she managed.

He wanted to flatter himself that he knew what she was getting at—and he shared her sentiments exactly. He'd paid for Penelope's ring, then seen Sunny in front of Tavish's store a fortnight later. If only he'd had the good sense to put the engagement off—

If only he could break it off now.

"You would think she would have left something in your room to remind you of her," she continued pointedly. "Since she's not here very much."

"She's never slept in my bedchamber," he said automatically, then shut his mouth and found himself growing rather red in the face. He could hardly believe he'd said anything at all, but apparently the spewing of secrets hadn't ended at his front door.

Her mouth fell open. "You've *never* slept with her?"

He shifted. "I think I would like to, as you would say in the Colonies, plead the Fifth."

"You're Scottish, you don't have the Fifth," she said promptly. "Why haven't you slept with her?"

The list of reasons was rather short, actually, and mostly had to do with a distinct lack of love. He wasn't sure, though, that he could say as much to Sunny and not have her wonder what in the hell he was doing remaining engaged to the woman. He searched for the least revealing but most pertinent reason he could name at the moment.

"She has other lovers," he said slowly.

"And you don't care to be added to her list?"

He lifted his eyebrow briefly. "Actually, nay. I don't."

She studied him for another moment or two, then moved past him. "Good for you. I'll stay for breakfast."

"What sort of admission must I make to convince you to stay for luncheon?" he asked, before he could stop himself.

"You probably don't want to know and you probably shouldn't push your luck. Here, I'll go peer into your nooks and crannies and make you uncomfortable with all sorts of other personal questions. That'll be distraction enough, won't it?"

He smiled. "Aye, I imagine it will be."

She looked at him over her shoulder. "She's out of her mind, by the way," she said, then turned away and made herself comfortable in his solar.

He had to lean against the door frame just to keep himself upright. He smiled, because he couldn't help himself, partly because of what she'd said and partly because she looked so completely at ease in his favorite chamber.

Unlike Penelope, who never would have tolerated nightclothes and bare feet, much less a morning without shopping, society, or paparazzi.

He watched Sunny wander through his private sanctuary, touching things that interested her, pausing before pictures, putting her hand on the cold stone of the wall, and wasn't surprised to find how much he wished she could have been there for more than just the morning.

"This is a great addition," she said finally. "It wasn't here in the Middle Ages, was it?"

He blinked. "Actually, nay, it wasn't. It was done first in the sixteenth century, then expanded during the eighteenth. I made a few changes several years ago as well."

"Of course," she said, looking supremely uncomfortable. "I should have realized that."

"Have you seen drawings?" he asked carefully.

"Um, sure," she said, nodding vigorously. "Lots of them. Oh, look over there. What a great hearth."

He watched her walk over to stand in front of the fire. He wanted to think on what she'd said, but just the sight of her was so distracting he found he couldn't. He merely stood and watched her as she watched his fire.

In time, he took a tray full of delicacies from Madame Gies and set them down on the coffee table. Sunny left the older woman beaming from compliments on her superb cooking. Madame Gies gave him a look that told him quite clearly that he was a fool to let Sunny get away, then left them alone. Sunny knelt down next to the coffee table and began to fill up a plate for him.

"Your French is perfect," he said quietly.

"My parents are linguists," she said with a shrug, "and I spent a year at a Swiss boarding school where French was *de rigueur.* Then I spent another year in Paris after med school."

"Your parents must have been pleased with that, if languages are their life's work."

"Actually, they were furious," she admitted. "I'd finished medical school, but bailed before taking a surgical residency so I could go to Paris to learn to cook—to their eternal disgust."

"Why didn't you want to be a physician?"

She shrugged. "I couldn't see myself spending all my time in a hospital, cutting people open. I'd rather be outside."

He could believe that. "So, what else have you done to drive your poor parents mad?"

"I'm thirty-three, Cam," she said, handing him his plate. "I've done it all."

He blinked in surprise at the sound of that name, then had to set his plate down so he could leap up and catch Sunny before she bolted from his solar. By the saints, she was fast. He barely managed to stop her at the door.

"Don't run."

She was trembling badly. "I meant to say *Cameron*."

He put his hands on her shoulders and turned her around slowly. "I don't mind," he said slowly. He very carefully took her hand and tugged. "Come back to the fire, lass, and eat. You'll never live it down if you don't make substantial inroads into what Madame Gies has brought you."

Sunny nodded though she looked ready to run again at the slightest provocation. He saw her seated, then sat and concentrated on his meal, giving her time to relax and himself time to digest what she'd called him.

It had been so long since he'd heard that name from anyone, just the sound of it was startling. But she couldn't have meant anything by it. It had just been an aberration.

Unbidden, that vision of a woman standing in Moraig MacLeod's house in a long, flowing black skirt came back to him.

That was just the beginning of the things that puzzled him. How had Sunny known about the state of his hall in any century but the current? There were no bloody drawings of his hall over the years that he knew of save the ones in his private library. How had she known he'd had siblings? As far as anyone knew, he'd been the only surviving child of a distant cousin of Alistair's who had died with his wife in a fire thirty-five years ago.

How had she known to call him Cam?

He felt a cup be pressed into his hands.

"Drink. You look pale."

He felt pale. He drank what she'd given him, then looked at her. She was studiously avoiding him, dividing her time between pretending to eat and eyeing the exit. He wanted to ask her if she had . . . if she had what? Known him in another time?

It sounded completely barking. She would look at him as if he'd lost all sense, then bolt for good. He rubbed his hands over his face, reached for some vestige of common sense, then looked about him for something to do. He saw a stool near the hearth, hooked it with his foot, then beckoned to Sunny.

"I'll do your hair for you."

She closed her eyes briefly, then sighed deeply and walked over on her knees to sit on the stool. She held up a comb.

He unwrapped the towel from her hair, set it aside, then began his work. It was perhaps the single most pleasant thing he'd done in years. It gave him something to do besides think, and it afforded him the opportunity to have Sunshine Phillips within arms' reach without giving her reason to flee. He dragged the affair out as long as he could, then simply sat there and dragged his fingers idly through her hair, marveling at the fat curls. She shivered, more than once. So did he.

He finally crossed his arms over her shoulders and pulled her back against him. He rested his chin on the top of her head and closed his eyes. By the saints, he was lost. Completely and totally lost.

What in the hell was he going to do now?

He would sort the rest of his life later. For now, there was only one thing to do. He took a deep breath, then slowly turned her around until she was facing him. She looked up at him with absolutely enormous eyes.

"Cameron—"

He shook his head, then slipped one of his hands under her hair and put the other against her cheek. She didn't move, didn't pull away, didn't do aught besides stare up at him with a desperate sort of longing. It was something akin to that look of hope she'd worn at Ian MacLeod's, only this time he understood it perfectly because he felt the same way.

He smiled faintly, then closed his eyes as he bent his head to kiss her—

The phone rang suddenly at his elbow.

It startled him so badly, he almost fell over onto her. He sat back and cursed. "Don't move."

She shook her head, as if she'd just woken from a dream. Cameron cursed again under his breath, then reached for the receiver on the table next to him.

"Aye?" he demanded.

"That is hello, Mac. *Hello.*"

He sighed heavily. "Hello, Penelope."

Sunny stood and walked to the door. He put his hand over the phone. "Wait—"

She looked at him, shook her head, then walked out his door.

"Mac? Mac, you aren't paying attention to me!"

"What do you need, Penelope?" he asked wearily.

"I'm reminding you about the charity event we're hosting

tomorrow. You're supposed to be down here tonight, remember? Today is Monday, Mac, or hadn't you noticed?"

He had noticed, because he'd had to rearrange several things very early that morning in order to have what he'd hoped would extend into an entire day of leisure with Sunny.

"Think about who's coming," Penelope urged.

He honestly couldn't remember and, better still, he didn't give a damn. "I'll be there," he said, vowing it would be the very last time he went.

Well, perhaps not the last time. He supposed he would be attending quite a few more things just to keep both Nathan and Penelope Ainsworth close.

"Mac, are you *listening* to me?"

"Of course," he said automatically. "I'll be there tomorrow."

"Tonight," Penelope insisted. "I said tonight."

"I can't. I have business."

"Finish it early."

The phone went dead. He clicked it off with a curse, then ran from the solar. He paused in the passageway, then heard the front door slam. He ran down the passageway, took the stairs three at a time, then sprinted across his great hall. He hauled the door open just in time to see the passenger door of a black Range Rover close.

The gravel was miserably uncomfortable on his bare feet, but he ran across it just the same. He rounded the boot of the car and pulled open the door.

"You're wearing my pajamas," was the first thing that came out of his mouth.

The look Patrick MacLeod shot him from the driver's seat was simply murderous. Cameron looked at him.

"How did you come here so quickly?"

"I saw the note in Sunny's bathroom and thought she might need a rescue," Patrick said coldly. "I can see that was indeed the case."

Cameron reached out and put his hand on Sunny's arm. "Please don't go," he said quietly. When she continued to ignore him, he looked for a way to at least distract her until he could convince her to stay. "Why did you call me Cam?"

"Because it's what Sim called you," she whispered. She looked at him then. "Because you once wanted to hear that name again from someone you loved."

He felt as if she'd slugged him in the gut. He doubled over and was glad to be there. It made it easier to breathe.

Patrick reached over her. "Back away, mate."

Cameron did, certain that Patrick would simply shut him in the door otherwise. He stood back and flinched as Sunny's brother-in-law gunned the engine and sent gravel scattering backward. It almost put his eye out. He managed to look up far enough to watch the Range Rover fly down the road away from him.

Because it's what Sim called you. I want to know about your brothers. I'm a MacKenzie through my mother. Because you once wanted to hear that name again from someone you loved.

Her words echoed in his head so loudly, he thought he might be ill. He remained outside his front door in the rain until he thought he could straighten successfully. He heaved himself up, then turned and walked unsteadily back into the hall. Madame Gies accosted him before he was halfway to the stairs.

"Her clothes are dry now."

"I'll take them to her in a bit," he managed.

He made it to his bedchamber, then fell onto the bed only because he'd run into it and had no choice. His head was pounding mercilessly. He wished, absently, for a bit of Sunny's vilest brew.

Cameron, ride for the MacLeod witch.

By all the saints above, had he *known* her in the past?

By the time his headache had passed well enough that he could sit up, a good part of the morning had passed as well. He heaved himself up to his feet and went to look for his keys.

He had a few questions for that glorious MacLeod witch and he had no intention of waiting any longer to have answers.

He drove to her house because it was quicker than riding, then staggered out of his car and over to her door. He was so ill, he wasn't even troubled by her threshold. He knocked.

The door was opened by Patrick MacLeod, who didn't even bother with a friendly hello before he punched Cameron full in the face. Cameron whirled around and went sprawling—all along the bonnet of his quarter-million-pound-sterling Mercedes. He got to his feet only to have Patrick's iron fists connect with his gut several more times.

"Bloody hell, man," Cameron gasped, holding up his hands to hold him off, "that's enough!"

"Enough would be you fertilizing my garden," Patrick snarled.

Well, at least Patrick's fists were now down by his sides. Clenched there was better than clenched and coming toward his face. Cameron put his hand on the wall of Moraig's house just to keep himself upright and waited until he thought he could speak without losing his breakfast.

"I want to see Sunny," he wheezed.

"She's not here."

"Where did she go?"

"Inverness, so she could catch a flight to London. She's headed back to the States."

Cameron wondered if he was seeing stars because of Patrick's tender ministrations, or because of the tidings. "The States?" he echoed in disbelief. "Why?"

"Why do you think, you bloody fool?"

Cameron felt his way over to his car and looked down. The top button of his jeans had left a scratch from one side clear across to the other, damn it anyway. He sat down, took a few more bracing breaths, then looked up at Patrick. "I don't suppose you'd call her and stop her, would you?"

"I don't suppose I would."

Cameron took another deep breath, then winced at the pain in his side. "I don't suppose," he managed, "that it would make any difference to you if I told you I loved her."

"It doesn't make a damn bit of difference to me," Patrick said sharply. "At this point, I don't imagine it would make any difference to her, either. You've treated her abominably."

"I haven't meant to," Cameron said quietly. He put his hands on his knees and considered. It took a bit of digging to find words he thought might convince Patrick he wanted to help him. He looked at Sunny's brother-in-law. "I need your aid. Name your price."

Patrick folded his arms across his chest and leaned against the door frame. "Your birth date."

Cameron wasn't surprised by the question and he supposed Patrick wouldn't be surprised by the answer. "The twenty-fifth of November, 1346."

Patrick grunted. He pushed away from the door frame and reached into his back pocket. "That earns you what Jamie left for you. We'll discuss Sunny after you've read this."

Cameron stood up to take the letter, then felt something shudder in the air around him as his fingers touched it. He didn't believe in magic, as a general rule, but that moment, he felt quite certain he should rethink his position. He looked at Patrick, but Patrick only stood there with his arms folded over his chest, watching silently.

"Who's it from?" Cameron said uneasily.

"Moraig to Jamie."

Cameron unfolded the letter and began to read.

He had to read it three times before the words sank in. And once they did, he did the most sensible thing he'd done in a month.

He swayed into Sunny's doorway, hit his head on the threshold, and knocked himself unconscious. He surrendered to the blackness without hesitation.

It seemed fitting.

Chapter 21

Sunny dragged her suitcase along the sidewalk behind her and wished for a taxi—or maybe just for a suitcase that rolled. Perhaps she'd just been pulling it too vigorously over the past hour and the wheels had given up in self-defense. Shoving everything she owned into it haphazardly had left it a little heavier than it might have been otherwise, so maybe that had added to its stress. She didn't dare carry it, though; she had no desire to break her back along with her heart.

She stopped to rest. She was just not having a good day so far. Being in Cameron's arms first thing in the morning had been sublime. Wringing a few answers from him had been promising. Almost being kissed by him had been . . . well, she supposed she was lucky they'd been interrupted. She wasn't sure what would have been left of her otherwise.

She knew very well, however, what would have been left of Cameron if she hadn't been able to stop Patrick from turning around and going back up to Cameron Hall to kill him. All that fast talking she'd had to do had been a good way to keep herself busy until she'd gotten herself inside Moraig's to pack.

It was then that things had gone truly downhill.

She'd used the phone Jamie had given her to buy a plane ticket only to find that she had no money in her bank account. She had no money in her bank account because no money had been transferred from her stock account. There'd been no money there because her stockbroker had squandered her entire life savings. Not only had he done that, he'd gone the extra mile and left her owing the brokerage house money.

She supposed she should have checked her mail a time or two over the past couple of months instead of sitting inside her house and weeping over a man who had his breakfasts with other women interrupted by his fiancée.

Patrick had pleaded with her to stay and vowed that he and Jamie would take care of her, but she hadn't been able to accept his charity past allowing it to get her in the air. She would crash on her parents' couch and get a job. She would slip her father a few new Gaelic idioms and maybe that would earn her a respite from all the grad-school applications he and her mother would subtly tuck under her pillow every night.

Madelyn had said very little during the drive to the airport. Sunny hadn't expected anything less. Her sister had had her own reasons for leaving the Highlands once upon a time. But Madelyn had had her love come after her.

Sunny seriously doubted she would be so lucky.

She cursed until the urge to weep receded. At least if she was in America, she wouldn't have to see pictures of Cameron and his lovely bride—or just pictures of him crawling in and out of the back of his Rolls, exiting restaurants, flashing at paparazzi what she easily recognized as his polite smile.

At first, she'd thought that the only reason his picture had been in any weekly had been because he'd been escorting Penelope. Then, as she'd thumbed through a tabloid stuffed in the seat pocket in front of her on the way down, she'd decided that he had his picture in gossip rags because he was very photogenic. Well, that and the fact that he was a Scottish lord and the CEO of Cameron Ltd.

Actually, she suspected it was mostly because he was gorgeous and his photographs probably sold a lot of magazines to women who liked to look at him.

Maybe it was just as well she'd never be married to him. Sharing him with innumerable unknown females who lingered over photographs of him would have been just the beginning of the indignities. If she'd had to put on pantyhose, or make sure her slip wasn't showing, or have cameras shoved in her face all the time, she would have lost it. She was good with living things, as long as they were babies, yoga students, and things emerging from compost. Anything else was an unknown quantity, one she really had no desire to face. Yes, it was best she just head back to the States where she would be safe. She wasn't running away, of course; she was making a measured, deliberate change of course.

And the sooner that was done, the happier she would be. She took a firmer grip on her suitcase and continued to trudge up the street. She didn't care what happened north of Hadrian's wall. She had *had* it with Scotland. She wanted no more of those trilling *r*'s and soft *ch*'s and lilts and waterfalls of Gaelic—

Her suitcase suddenly left the pavement. She whirled around, ready to scream bloody murder.

She squeaked instead.

Robert Francis Cameron mac Cameron stood behind her, holding on to the handle of her suitcase and looking rather less groomed than usual. She was so surprised to see him, no, *stunned* to see him when she'd never thought to again, she could only stand there and gape.

He looked dreadful. His mouth was cut and his black eye was now purple. He had another bruise forming above the other eye, just under his hairline. He also looked very green, truth be told.

"What happened to you?" she asked without thinking.

"Your brother-in-law's fists."

"I'd hate to see what he looks like," she said with a low whistle.

"I didn't touch him," he said briefly, looking as if he would have liked to have done so—vigorously, and more than once. "I thought I had enough of your family angry with me without adding your sister to the list."

Well, he had that right. She looked down and found his hand covering hers, his scarred, strong, once-medieval-but-medieval-no-more hand. He was so close, she could feel his breath on her hair.

"What are you doing here?" she whispered.

He removed her fingers from her suitcase handle and took her by the elbow. "I'll tell you in a more private place, if you don't mind."

That was incentive to move. "Thanks, but no. I've been in a private place recently with you, and it didn't go so well for me."

"Sunshine, don't make me beg," he said quietly. "I guarantee I'll cause a scene if I go down on my knees here in the street. Please just come with me. I need to talk to you."

She wrapped her arms around herself and looked up at him, dry-eyed but in absolute anguish. "What in the world could you possibly want to talk to me about?"

He took a deep breath. "1375."

Things began to spin suddenly around her. She reached out and clutched his shirt to keep herself from falling. Maybe she shouldn't have indulged in any of Madame Gies's vegetarian omelet. She'd known she would pay for it, and apparently she'd been right.

"I don't feel very good—" she whispered.

She didn't remember hitting the sidewalk.

She woke to a very bumpy ride. She thought at first that she'd fallen asleep on the plane and they'd hit a patch of rough air. She didn't like to fly and she hated turbulence. It didn't make her sick; it made her terrified. She didn't care what sort of rational explanations she reminded herself of on the ground; when she was 39,000 feet up, she hated it when the plane bumped around.

She realized, though, that she wasn't on a plane, she was in a cab—and she wasn't alone. She sat up, but that made her see stars. Strong arms urged her back against an unreasonably comfortable shoulder. She gave in only because she thought she might throw up otherwise. She closed her eyes and willed her head to stop spinning.

"See if you can get me out of tomorrow, won't you?" Cameron was saying. "And I'll let you know about the other later. Thanks, Emily. Cheers."

Sunny heard him set his phone down on the seat, then felt his arms come around her.

"How are you?" he asked quietly.

"I feel terrible."

"I understand, believe me." He shifted, then caught his breath. "I think your brother-in-law broke something."

"He isn't happy with you."

"That, love, is an understatement."

Sunny was tempted to enjoy the absolute comfort of his arms for another minute or two, but she knew she would regret it if she did. She pushed away and leaned against the door, putting as much distance between them as possible.

"Where did you see Patrick?" she asked. "He promised me he wouldn't go back to your hall."

Cameron smiled briefly. "He didn't. I found him guarding your front door, actually, where he greeted me with his fists. He did me the favor of leaving me all my teeth, but I imagine that was an accident. He was very reluctant to give me any aid past directions to hell. I had to pay him to get your sister's mobile number so I could call her and find out the particulars of where you'd gone." His smile faded. "I had to see you."

"Well, you've seen me," she said, trying to sound brisk. She didn't think she'd succeeded in sounding anything other than shattered. "And now that you have, you can do me the favor of getting me to my hotel. I have a plane to catch tomorrow."

He shifted on the seat to face her. "Sunshine, if I were to ask you for one thing, would you give it to me?"

"Oh, not that again," she said. "Didn't we try this already today?"

"Let's try again. I promise to answer even more of your questions than I did this morning."

"You answered nothing this morning," she said with a snort. "You spent all your time hedging."

He smiled. "I'm a Cameron. 'Tis what we do."

"That's not a good excuse," she muttered. She glanced at him, but he didn't seem inclined to either apologize for not having been entirely frank earlier, or express any concern that he was driving her farther and farther away from where she should be going. In fact, all he was doing was watching her with a small smile, as if he actually saw *her* instead of a convenient herbalist, or Patrick's sister-in-law, or a crazy woman in James MacLeod's great hall. It was so close to how he'd looked at her in medieval Scotland that she had to look away before she started to cry.

"Well?" he prodded finally.

She wished she didn't feel like he was ripping her heart out of her chest with his bare hands. "What could you possibly want from me?" she managed, looking out the window at the buildings as they passed by.

"I'll tell you what I want—after you agree."

"And if I don't agree?"

"I think it would be in your best interest to do so."

She shot him a look. "Going to draw your sword soon, Cameron?"

He lifted one eyebrow. "Push me a bit further and see, Sunshine."

She almost smiled. She would have, if she hadn't hurt so badly. He sounded more like himself than he had in . . . well, in centuries. He also looked as if he was barely holding on to his lunch.

"Another headache?" she asked.

"Aye, that, too," he agreed, "but 'tis mostly that I knocked myself out on your doorway—and please don't ask me to explain how or why. The humiliation is still fresh. Your brother-in-law did me the favor of pouring ice-cold water from your stream on my face to rouse me, but he was averse to offering any other sort of aid."

"He has no bedside manner."

Cameron smiled. "Nay, he doesn't."

She reached up and smoothed her fingers over the darkening bruise showing from under his hair, then pulled her hand away when she realized what she was doing. He caught her hand, then held it with his.

She looked down at his hand, at those little stitches she had made in his flesh almost seven centuries ago with a needle that had been almost worse than nothing, and thought about when she'd done that bit of sewing. 1375. Exactly what he wanted to talk to her about.

"Sunny?"

She looked at him. "Are you going to nag me until I give in?"

"Tenacity is, I'll admit with all modesty, one of my more noteworthy virtues."

She had to fight the temptation to smile. The man was absolutely charming when he wanted to be. Charming, demanding, and ruthless. She supposed she could argue with him all day, but she wouldn't win.

And she had to admit that there was a tiny part of her—surrounded by her more considerable pockets of insanity, no doubt—that didn't want to win.

She sighed deeply. "All right. What do you want?"

"You, in London, for twenty-four hours."

She felt her mouth fall open. "Why?"

"Because we have several things to discuss, things about that date I gave you. I want ample time—and privacy—in which to do so."

"But we're speaking in Gaelic now," she said desperately.

"I want more privacy than this."

"My flight leaves tomorrow—"

"I'll change your ticket for you. I'll fly you to the States the next day first-class. I'll fly you to the States in my own bloody plane if you like, but I want an entire twenty-four hours before you go."

"But surely you have other things to do," she said in a last-ditch effort to save what was left of her heart.

"I'm cancelling them." He squeezed her hand. "You want answers; I want you. Stay with me and we'll both be satisfied."

The only thing staying with him for any length of time would do was leave her wanting more of him. She wanted to tell him no, but she couldn't get the word out. The man she loved was sitting next to her, willing to talk about something she was quite sure he hadn't discussed with anyone else . . . and he looked like Patrick had beaten the holy hell out of him.

"We'll regret it," she said miserably.

"I don't think so and I think that was an aye." He kept her hand in both his own and gingerly leaned his head back against the seat. "Thank you, Sunshine. Now, if you'll excuse me for five minutes, I have to close my eyes before my poor head cleaves itself in twain from the pounding. Prod me when we reach the Ritz."

"The *what*!" she exclaimed. "Cameron, I can't afford—"

"I can," he said, sounding supremely unconcerned, "so don't fash yourself."

"I am *not* going to stay there."

"They'll make you a spectacular salad," he murmured.

She glared at him, but his eyes were closed so he missed what she was sure had been an impressive expression of fury. The Ritz? She couldn't think of a place where she would have been more uncomfortable. She wasn't dressed to go to a nice pub, much less a hotel like that.

She fretted over that for quite a while, which only made her feel worse. She took to fussing with acupressure points on Cameron's hand to keep herself from stressing any more. That didn't help her any, but he began to breathe more easily.

At least one of them was.

The cab stopped before she could decide on a likely place to jump out and make a break for it. The door was opened for her and Cameron pushed her out onto the sidewalk before she could protest. She peered through the hotel doors and felt every single inch the country bumpkin who had fallen off a turnip truck approximately six minutes ago. Cameron paid the driver, then took her suitcase in hand and nodded toward the front door.

"Let's go."

She backed into him, hard. "No way."

"Don't make me throw you over my shoulder."

She looked up at him quickly. "You wouldn't."

"I would."

"You great, bloody barbarian—"

"Guilty as charged." He gave her a quick smile, then put his hand on her shoulder and gave her a nudge. "Walk on, gel."

Sunny wanted to balk, but she was too busy being shepherded—well, pushed, actually—inside a place she wouldn't have chosen even if she could have afforded it. She did her best not to gape at her surroundings, but she could hardly help herself. She felt horribly conspicuous in jeans and a wrinkled shirt. Then again, Cameron wasn't dressed any better than she was and he looked like he'd been brawling in the street outside. She was a little surprised they'd made it past the doorman.

A man at the desk looked up at them as they approached. "May I help you?" he asked, his tone suggesting that he doubted very much that he could.

"A reservation for Miss Phillips," Cameron said easily. "My assistant called half an hour ago."

Sunny tried to slip behind Cameron, but he caught her by the arm and held her to his side. She muttered uncomplimentary things about him in Gaelic under her breath, but he only winked at her.

The desk clerk asked Cameron for a credit card and ID, took them skeptically, then handed them off immediately to his supervisor. Sunny watched as that someone higher up the food chain took the card and checked the picture against Cameron himself.

A look of horror came over his face and he gave his desk clerk a glare. "That is Robert Cameron, the Earl of Assynt," he said in a low, pointed voice. He straightened and gave Cameron a welcoming smile. "We've never had the pleasure of your company here before, my lord."

"And you aren't having it now," Cameron said with an equally polite smile. "Miss Phillips will be your guest and I'm most eager to see that she's taken care of."

"Of course," was the response, delivered with just the right amount of enthusiasm. "I'm certain we do indeed have her suite prepared. A porter will—"

"Not be necessary," Cameron said. He signed the credit card slip when it was presented to him, held out his hand for the key, then picked up Sunny's suitcase. "After you, Miss Phillips."

Sunny went with him because it was the lesser of the two evils—the other being remaining behind at the reception desk. She waited until they were in the elevator before she turned on him.

"I'll ride to the top with you, then I'm turning around and going back down."

"Sunshine, you may *not* stay at that rat-infested slum you reserved for yourself."

"It's what I can afford, buster, and who the hell are you—"

"In charge of your care, that's who I am," he said firmly, "so allow me to see to it properly. You promised me twenty-four hours. You didn't put any stipulations on where it was to be spent."

She found, to her horror, that her eyes were starting to burn. She wrapped her arms around herself. "I hate these kinds of places. I don't like feeling small."

"I understand completely and I agree with you," he said seriously. "'Tis a safe place, though, Sunny, and I'm asking you to endure it for my sake. If someone is fool enough to look down his nose at you, just think of those endless meadows of flowers behind your house and that you have the right to enjoy them whilst he does not. That's what I do."

"I'm sure you do, Mr. High-and-Mighty Earl of Assynt," she groused, dragging her sleeve across her eyes and happily latching on to something else to discuss. "That's a little tidbit you didn't see fit to share with me."

"I didn't think you'd care."

"I couldn't care *less*," she said stiffly.

He actually laughed. "As I suspected." He smoothed his hand down the back of her hair. "Do this for me, Sunshine, that I might not worry about where you're sleeping."

At that point, she supposed she didn't have a choice, but she wasn't going to enjoy it. She dragged her feet as she followed him out of the lift, down the hallway, and into a suite that looked like something from a magazine.

Fruit and juice stood on the table, along with fresh flowers. She had a sniff, but it didn't make her feel any more comfortable. She walked over to the window and looked out. The view wasn't exactly spectacular, but she supposed that wasn't what Cameron was paying for.

She heard him cross the room and come to a stop behind her. She closed her eyes as he fussed with her hair, drawing it back over her shoulders and arranging it so it hung down her back. It occurred to her at that moment that she had made a grave tactical error. She should have left her suitcase in his hands and bolted for her hotel the moment she'd seen him. Why she'd thought she could make it through an entire twenty-four hours with him was beyond her—no matter what sorts of prying questions he'd promised to answer.

What she wanted to do was turn, go into his arms, and beg him to ditch his life and come live at Moraig's with her.

What she needed to do was push past him and run out the door.

Unfortunately, she couldn't bring herself to do either.

"I did manage to have a very brief conversation with Patrick earlier," he said slowly. "Actually, it wasn't much of a conversation. He merely cursed me, then gave me a letter to read."

Sunny dragged herself away from her unproductive thoughts. Conversation was good. It would take her mind off her miserable life. "A letter?" she echoed absently. "I didn't leave you a letter."

"'Twasn't from you," he said. "It was from Moraig to Jamie. Patrick thought I might find it . . . instructive."

His fingers trailing through her hair were tremendously distracting. She felt the tension start to drain from her, which was probably a very bad thing. She dug the heels of her hands into her eyes to try to stop them from burning. "What did Moraig have to say to Jamie? Was she telling him how to make a little potion to ward off hexes from any future witches?"

"Nay," he said quietly. "She told him what had happened to her one particularly stormy spring evening eight years ago."

Sunny heard the words, but it took a moment before they registered. And once they did, she felt her heart stop. Literally. It took her a moment before she could breathe again.

"Really," she said, though there wasn't much sound to her words.

"Aye," he said. "It seems that a half-dead Highland lad burst through her door and went sprawling at her feet. His skull was half crushed and there was a dirk sticking out of his back. He was conscious long enough to identify himself and to ask about what was apparently most important to him, which was the safety of a certain lass he'd been traveling with."

She swayed dangerously. Cameron kept his hands on her shoulders, which was handy as it was all that was keeping her upright.

"I imagine you can guess who the lad was."

She nodded.

"Care to know the name of the lass?"

By that point, she couldn't move, couldn't breathe, couldn't speak. She could only stand there and shake.

"Her name was Sunshine."

A sob escaped her before she could stop it. He turned her around and pulled her against him, wrapping his arms around her so tightly she could hardly catch her breath. She didn't care. She threw her arms around him in return and hung on. She knew she was making noises that should have frightened him—they were scaring the hell out of her—but he didn't seem to care. She wasn't entirely sure he hadn't made an unsettling noise or two of his own.

She fell apart completely, weeping until her breath was coming in gasps, and she thought she might be ill.

She knew she shouldn't have been surprised. After all, how many times had she caught Moraig simply looking at her with a grave smile, as if she'd known something Sunny didn't? Sunny had always thought it was just the wise, earth-mother sort of look she favored everyone with. Now, she knew better.

You'll want my house after I'm gone, lass.

Sunny had always assumed that was because Moraig had thought she would need a good place to dry her herbs. She had never once suspected it would be for a far more crucial reason.

And now Cameron knew. She wept a bit more for that reason alone. She wasn't the only one carrying his past, or his secret, or their past together. Even if he never remembered anything, at least someone else had proved to him that he'd known her.

The relief she felt was overwhelming.

She had no idea how much longer she stood there, fighting to get control of herself. Cameron had a seemingly inexhaustible supply of patience. He made a soothing noise or two, hummed snatches of things she didn't know, then finally just stroked her hair with one hand and held her close with the other.

She felt as if she'd come home.

Only it was a home she couldn't have.

She finally gulped in a decent breath. "I've ruined your shirt."

"Patrick ruined my shirt. I think you've just washed it for me."

She managed something that might have passed for a laugh if she hadn't been in such pain. She dragged her sleeve across her face and wished for a Kleenex. Cameron kept his arm around her and reached for one. She took it, then mopped up as best she could. He pulled her close again and pressed her head against his shoulder. He said nothing else, but Sunny felt him taking slow, even breaths. Maybe that was his way to keep from falling apart as she had.

"I want to know everything," he said finally. He fumbled for her tissues, used them on his own face, then leaned over to throw them away. He looked down at her, his eyes very red. "Everything."

She took a deep breath. "All right. Let me go wash my face first."

"But you'll return."

She closed her eyes briefly, then nodded.

He released her as reluctantly as she might have wished for. "Then I'll be waiting for you."

She walked away from him while she still could. Those were the words she wanted, but the timing was all wrong. And there was no way to make it right.

She escaped into the bedroom and shut the door behind her, then looked around until she spied the bathroom. Once that door was safely shut and locked, she walked over and sat down on the edge of the tub where she wouldn't have to look at herself in the mirror.

She could hardly believe what had just happened. Cameron *knew*. She'd waited so long, wanted it so desperately—now that she had it, she didn't know what to do.

She also wondered absently why it was Moraig hadn't volunteered any of that pertinent information. Then again, what could she have said? *Sunny, dearie, you're going to go back in time and fall in love with the medieval laird of clan Cameron and then you're going to lose him.* She would have run the other way because just thinking about it would have broken her heart.

A bit like what was happening to her anyway.

She splashed water on her face, then left the bathroom and went to flop down on the bed. She wasn't sure if this was better or worse, but she suspected it wasn't better. She never should have agreed to anything with Cameron, but apparently she had left all sense back in Scotland on Moraig MacLeod's threshold where she'd also left her heart. The thought of being with him for even twenty-four hours, being in his arms, watching him smile at her, heaven help her even having him pull her close and kiss her . . . it would just finish off what the past almost two months had left of her.

She forced herself to take the same deep, even sort of breaths Cameron had taken in the living room. It took quite a while before she felt herself begin to relax. After a bit of time spent in that marginally happy place, she began to look at things a little differently.

You want answers; I want you.

He'd said that, but maybe it applied just as much to her. She wanted him, if only for a single, glorious evening. It would give her memories enough to last her for years—because she was absolutely certain it would take years before she was over him.

Perhaps he needed memories of his past as much as she needed memories of him at present. And like it or not, she was the only person alive who could give him what he didn't have. It wasn't in her nature to deny someone aid when she could render it.

She took another handful of deep, steadying breaths. She could take the evening, spend it with the man who broke her heart a little every time she looked at him, and make her own set of memories of the Cameron who wore jeans and had a cell phone. And then she would get up early and go to the airport. She would walk away because she could not bear to be in the same country with him and know he was married to someone else.

She would give him the evening.

And then she would go.

Chapter 22

Cameron glanced at the bedroom door, but it was still shut. He felt, briefly, as if he were back in Moraig's house, sitting in front of the fire, waiting for Sunny to come out of the bathroom after he'd bedded down on her floor, and wondering what it was he'd done to make her run from him at every opportunity.

He understood, now.

He looked at his watch and was surprised to find that twenty minutes had gone by. It had given him time to talk to Emily, who had braved the maddening crowds at Harrods to buy Sunny an evening gown, make reservations for two at a very discreet French restaurant that never called the photographers to alert them he was dining there, and pace about the chamber a score of times before finding himself standing in front of an exquisite bouquet of flowers Emily must have requested.

He was half tempted to go see if Sunny had lain down and fallen asleep, but he forbore. Perhaps she was mulling over what he'd told her. The saints only knew he could stand to do the same.

He couldn't quite bring himself to, though. It was torment enough to think he'd fallen in love with her, hopelessly, unreasonably, impossibly in love with her during the past few weeks. It was made profoundly worse by the thought that he'd loved her before, forgotten her, then been perfectly capable of having her again well before he'd found himself thrown together with someone he didn't love.

If only Moraig had said something. If only James MacLeod, damn him to hell and back, had seen fit to give him that letter a year ago after Moraig's death instead of waiting until now.

In Jamie's defense—not that Cameron was particularly interested in defending him at present, but he was trying to be fair—perhaps he'd been waiting for Sunny to travel back in time before he made any sort of move. After all, it had been a sudden thing, Jamie's enthusiasm about the leisure centre and his absolute insistence that they have their meeting . . . when? Five weeks ago?

Almost a fortnight after Sunny had returned, just after she'd been able to rise from her bed and come to the keep.

He rubbed his hands over his face and blew out his breath. Perhaps Jamie had done the best he could. After all, it wasn't his fault that things had gone awry. It was no one's fault, but that didn't make it any easier.

Nor did deciding what to do now.

He'd had the drive to Inverness to accustom himself to the idea that he'd not only known Sunny, he'd apparently *loved* her in the past. He'd considered on the flight south what he might do with that knowledge, then decided that he would talk to her, apologize for the grief he'd caused her, then get her safely and with a minimum of fuss onto her flight back to the States. Until he solved his current problem, he wasn't free to ask anything of her. That had seemed a very reasonable, if not painful, way to carry on for the present.

Now, he wasn't so sure.

The bedroom door opened, interrupting his dismal thoughts. Sunny didn't look any less teary-eyed than she had twenty minutes earlier, but he supposed he didn't, either. He crossed the room to her, stopped, then held open his arms.

She hesitated only slightly before she walked into his embrace. He wrapped his arms around her and held her in silence.

He realized suddenly that Sunny was shaking. He had no plaid to wrap around her, so he merely drew her closer and tried to warm her with his body.

"Cold?" he asked.

"I think I'm in shock," she said, her teeth chattering.

He pulled back and realized she was serious. He swept her up in his arms before she could protest, carried her over to the couch, then set her down so he could call for a cup of herbal tea. He went and rummaged about in her bedchamber for an extra blanket, which he wrapped around her just before her tea arrived. He sat next to her and watched her as she drank.

Her hands were trembling badly.

He finally rescued her cup, set it on the coffee table, then pulled her close to him where he could put his arms around her.

"Better?" he asked.

She nodded. "A bit. Thank you."

He rested his cheek against her hair and wondered if she knew when she was speaking Gaelic and when she wasn't. Patrick had told him at one point that Sunny had spoken it all her life because her father had taught it to her. He supposed it had served her well in medieval Scotland. Just the thought of her having braved the dangers of that particular time period was enough to give *him* the chills.

"So," he said finally, "who first in this unprecedented spewing of secrets?"

"You," she said, her voice rough from weeping. "I know it makes you uncomfortable and that'll make me feel better."

He smiled against her hair. "You are a vile wench."

"Yet here you are."

"Aye," he agreed, "here I am."

She let out a deep, shuddering breath, then pulled her feet up onto the couch and hugged her knees. He slipped his arm around her shoulders and tugged the blanket up over her. She leaned her head against his arm and sighed.

"If it makes you feel any better," she said, "I will believe everything you tell me. And once you're through with all your secrets, I'll return the favor by telling you everything I know. They'll be things only you would believe."

He cleared his throat again before he gave vent to some sort of emotion that would have completely unmanned him in front of her. "Sunshine, you're killing me."

"And I've been in hell for quite a while myself, buster, so we're about even. Here, I'll help you get started. Your mother insisted you wear a handful of names, but gave your brothers only one each. Start from there."

He wasn't a lad given to excessive emotion that didn't involve being angry enough to use a sword or being terrified enough to run for his life, but he found, to his continued surprise, that Sunny continued to wring emotions from him that he'd hardly suspected he had. He muttered a few curses to make himself feel more himself, but it didn't help.

"I think I need a whisky," he said.

"That didn't work out so well for you the last time, did it? Just spill your guts, lad. You'll feel better after you do."

"And you would know, given how much gut-spilling lobelia you've no doubt dispensed over the years." He took a deep breath. "Very well. I'll begin at the beginning."

So he did. He told her of growing up as William mac Cameron's son, about his parents' rather tempestuous marriage and his own desire to avoid the same. He told her about the ridiculous adventures his brother Sim had convinced him to go on, about Breac's steadiness behind him at all times, about both his brothers' endless supply of wenches falling over them whilst he frightened any and all sensible maids off with his brusqueness and demanding nature alone.

By that time, she had stopped shaking and was watching him with a small, affectionate smile that had him wishing desperately that he did indeed dare order up something very strong. But as he knew where that would lead, he continued on with the tale of his father's murder and Giric's continual attempts to wrest the chieftainship away from him. He told her about the battle where Sim had died and Breac had been wounded, and how Giric had told him to ride for the MacLeod witch.

"And that is where my memories end," he said with a sigh.

"And mine begin," she said softly. "But I'm afraid you might not enjoy them very much."

"Will you hold my hand to make me feel better?"

She frowned at him. "Be serious."

"I *was* being serious."

She smiled, then reached up to her shoulder to hold his hand. "I sewed up the scar you have on this arm, you know."

He wondered when it was he would stop losing his breath around her. "Did you, indeed?"

"I did, indeed. I'll tell you about it later, if you want me to. For now, I'll start where you left off. What you don't remember is that you did succeed in fetching the MacLeod witch, only it wasn't the one from your day—who I actually don't think even existed—it was me. I knew fairly soon that you were definitely not a friend of Jamie's come in costume to get me for dinner, but by then it was too late. The moment you pulled me across my threshold, you had pulled me into the past. At that point, there was really no reason for me not to go with you and try to save your brother." She smiled briefly. "You were actually fairly persuasive."

"Was I charming?" he asked hesitantly.

"Well, let's see. First you tackled me and knocked the wind from me, then you refused to answer any of my questions about what year I found myself in, and finally you snarled what I wanted to know at me just before you threw me up onto the back of your horse and rode off with me."

He smiled. "Yet you're still speaking to me."

"You made up for it afterward. You were actually rather anxious to get home and I didn't blame you. I'm afraid there was nothing to be done, though." She paused. "Breac died under my hands. Well, our hands, actually. I held one hand and you the other as he passed on."

He wasn't surprised, but it was still difficult to hear. He looked at her fingers intertwined with his for quite a while before he trusted himself to meet her eyes and not weep.

"Thank you for trying."

Her eyes were swimming with tears. "He took the blade meant for you, or so you told me later, so you can take some comfort in that. I'm sorry you can't remember it, though."

"You'll have to remember it for both of us, then," he said quietly. He took a deep breath and dragged his free hand through his hair. Perhaps he would ask her for all the grim details later, when he thought he could hear them and not weep. For the moment, moving on was the best idea. "What happened then?"

"Your men tried to drown me, you apparently rescued me, then once I was conscious again you threw me out of your bed and told me to go home."

"Surely not," he interrupted, grateful for something less somber to discuss. "I can't imagine I was daft enough to cast you from my bed once I'd gotten you into it."

"Shocking, isn't it? From what I understand, you also did the honors of cutting my clothes from me yourself, though you promised you hadn't looked as you'd done so."

"I'm sure I lied," he said without hesitation.

She laughed a little. "I imagine you did."

He was so pleased to see her relaxed and smiling, he was almost happy for how he was being forced to wring it from her. The very thought that she had been in his past was overwhelming. That he couldn't remember a bloody thing about it was devastating in the extreme.

"You then watched over me while I was the very popular MacLeod witch in your village," she continued, "kept me fed, and reminded me at every opportunity that you were going to marry Gilly come hell or high water, but you'd be happy to bed me any time I was interested."

"I'm simply astonished you weren't willing to take me up on the offer," he said with mock surprise.

She smiled. "I'll bet you—" She frowned suddenly. "Why would you think I wouldn't?"

"Because as I was talking to your sister about where you'd

gone, I asked her for a few things you might like to talk about. She suggested we discuss your thoughts on abstinence before marriage—thoughts she said you'd apparently already given me in another time and place."

Sunny's face was suddenly quite red. "I'm going to kill her."

He smiled. "It's terrible having to tell the same man something like that twice, isn't it?"

"You know, you're about to find yourself out in the hall."

He laughed. "I'm teasing you, Sunshine—nay, don't pull away." He tugged on her. "Come you here and finish your tale. Tell me why I didn't have the good sense to keep you safe in the hall."

"Because you said it was too dangerous—and you were right. You were convinced Giric was trying to kill you. I actually watched you make your cousin Brice taste your food. He flatly refused to drink the wine."

He had to take a deep breath. "I always suspected that Giric had poisoned my father, so I suppose he was simply continuing on with what had worked before."

"I'm sorry," she said quietly.

Cameron shrugged. " 'Tis in the past. I was the only one who thought so, unfortunately. By the time he'd killed his own father the same way a handful of years later, he had already turned half the clan against me and it didn't matter what I had believed. The only reason I was able to hold that bloody group together was because Breac and Sim were behind me, guarding my back." He paused. "I suppose once they were gone, there was no reason to stay, was there?"

She looked at him solemnly. "That's exactly what you told me."

He sighed deeply. "Then how did we leave? I'm assuming we had time to actually make the decision to come to the future."

"We discussed it in your bedroom one night after you'd fought off about a dozen men single-handedly and kept me alive. I don't think you thought you had any choice but to leave. As it was, we had to cut our way out your front gates and even then Giric followed us all the way to Moraig's. You fought him in the forest near her house. You pushed me inside the door, something hit me on the back of the head—I think he threw a rock at me—and then I fainted. When I came to in Moraig's house, it was the right time but I was alone. The next time I saw you was in Jamie's hall." She paused. "That's why I threw myself at you, because I was so happy to see you alive."

He reached up and smoothed her hair back from her face. "And I was fool enough not to recognize you."

She was quiet for a moment or two. "I will admit it was one of the more difficult moments of my life."

He closed his eyes. It all made sense now, the look of relief she'd worn, as if she expected him to be just as glad to see her as she was him. "I'm sorry, Sunshine."

"It doesn't matter. This helps, though." She took a deep breath. "It's your turn again. What happened to you after you fell through Moraig's door? After you asked about me," she added softly.

"I fainted as well, apparently," he said, "then woke in hospital, wondering what in the hell had happened to me. Actually, I thought I was *in* hell, especially with Moraig and Alistair both peering down at me as I lay there strapped to the bed and pumped full of sedatives."

"That had to have been terrifying," she murmured.

"That's one way to describe it," he said dryly. He paused. "The rest is all rubbish. Learning to fit in, taking over Alistair's business, being damned grateful for it all."

She nodded, but said nothing. She merely traced his palm with her thumb absently, over and over again. Cameron put his hand on her feet, wincing at the chill of them. He pulled them into his lap and covered them with his free hand.

"I wish Moraig had said something," he said finally. "You would think she could have seen her way clear to remind me about what I'd said, wouldn't you?"

"To what end?" she asked. "Eight years ago I had just graduated from med school and was living in Paris, cooking all sorts of fleshy dishes that offended my vegetarian sensibilities. Can you imagine what would have happened if you had walked into my kitchen and told me that you'd known me 650 years in the past?"

"Would you have thrown a saucepan at me?" he asked.

"I probably would have thrown *myself* at you," she said, "but it would have completely messed up the fabric of time, as Jamie would say. Madelyn might not have met Patrick, then they wouldn't have had Hope . . ." She shook her head. "It wouldn't have worked." She looked up at him. "But I would have given you my phone number."

He smiled. "I would have used it. Repeatedly."

She met his gaze for a moment, then tried to disentangle her fingers from his. "I bet they have great room service here. Let me go find out."

He wrapped his arm around her knees and refused to let go of her hand. "Don't run, Sunshine."

"I'm a Phillips," she managed. "'Tis what we do."

He smiled in spite of himself. "Is that true?"

She attempted a smile, but failed. "No, it's just me who runs. In this case, I think it's a good idea because it doesn't matter what century we're in, the reality is I'm still the witch down in the village and you're still the laird up the way who's going to marry a woman he doesn't love."

He took a deep breath. "Is that how it was?"

"That, my laird, is how it was."

He sighed deeply, released her hand, then put his arms around her and drew her close. "Sunshine, I'm so sorry. I'm so bloody sorry."

She shook her head, then put her arm around his neck and held on to him as if she didn't particularly want to let him go. He closed his eyes and swore, silently. There were things she hadn't told him, he imagined, things about Gilly, things about his clan, things about her feelings for her. He didn't need to hear anything about the last because he could imagine quite well what he'd felt.

It was, he suspected, exactly what he felt at present.

He put his hand under her chin and lifted her face up. Her eyes were very red, but no tears spilled down her cheeks. He leaned forward and kissed her cheeks, one by one, then pulled back just far enough to look at her. She was wearing the same expression she had in his solar, the one full of miserable hope, as if she couldn't decide if she wanted him or wanted him gone.

He chose the former and bent his head—just in time to hear a knock on the door.

"Damn it," he said in disbelief. "What next?"

"Don't ask."

He sighed deeply and pulled away. "I imagine 'tis my assistant, Emily. She's brought you a gown and shoes that hopefully fit."

"Why?"

He paused. "I was hoping you would come to the theater with me tonight."

She blinked. "Are you asking me out on a *date*?"

"I think we might be a little past that, Sunny."

She scowled at him. "Call it what you want. You still have this unwholesome habit of pulling me into things I can't get out of easily."

"But you'll come with me anyway?"

"Do I have a choice?"

He took her face in his hands and looked at her seriously. "Aye, but please don't say nay. And don't think for a moment that I'm going to forget the precise point where we were interrupted. Twice today, as it happens."

She closed her eyes and swallowed convulsively. "Glad to know your short-term memory's okay."

"My short-term memory is perfect," he said as he rose and walked to the door. He supposed he had no right to kiss her, but he would—after he'd wooed her properly first.

Well, as much as he could whilst not being free to do so.

He opened the door to find Emily standing there, her arms full of bags and the porter behind her carrying more. She was, as usual, a whirlwind of grace, elegance, and organization. She swept into the chamber, dismissed the porter, then looked at Cameron in shock.

"What happened to you? Another mugging?"

"Another what?" Sunny said, climbing to her feet.

Cameron shot Emily a look of warning. "It was nothing." He walked back over to take Sunny's hand. "Emily, this is Sunshine. Sunshine, Emily."

Emily frowned at him as she shoved his clothes into his arms, then she turned to Sunny. Once she found out Sunny could speak her tongue, she swept her off into the bedroom in a cloud of sweet perfume and rapid-fire French.

Apparently, his aid was not necessary.

He showered and changed in the other bedroom's loo, then came back out and started to pace. Usually, he thought better that way. At the moment, he was doing his damnedest not to think. The *if only*s were going to do him in otherwise.

In time, the bedroom door opened. He turned around to see what sorts of tortures Emily might have put Sunny through.

He caught his breath in spite of himself. Emily had found an elegant gown in a blue that was the exact color of the loch near his house on the right sort of day. Emily had put Sunny's hair up somehow, yet left a few stray bits curling down her neck, and finished off any hope of his having any self-control with a simple strand of opera pearls and a pair of flimsy sandals that left Sunny's toes peeking out from under her gown. She was so utterly charming, so gloriously herself in spite of the trappings, he could hardly catch his breath.

He looked at Emily. "You chose well."

"It is the woman who makes the gown, *n'est-ce pas?*" Emily said with a smile. "Your lady is the goddess. I have only draped her as befits her beauty."

Sunny blushed. "Enough, Emily," she said, in her perfect French. "I appreciate the help, though I want it noted that I'm being dragged against my will to the theater. Think he'll feed me as well, or will I have to buy my own cookies during intermission?"

Emily laughed. "I only dress him, *cherie*; I cannot control his manners. You call me tomorrow, *oui*, and let me know if he's behaved himself." She kissed Sunny on both cheeks, gave Cameron a pointed look that spoke volumes about her approval of Sunshine, then left the room, pulling the door shut behind her.

Cameron held out his hand. "You look lovely. Ready to go?"

"This is crazy," she said breathlessly.

"A discreet dinner and a darkened theater where I might hold your hand in peace seems reasonable to me," he said with a shrug.

She hesitated, then put her hand into his. "We'll regret it."

He pulled her toward the door. "Sunshine, my love, I have never once regretted a single moment spent in your company. Tonight will be no different."

She didn't comment further, but she didn't pull her hand away, either.

It was a start.

Several hours later, he leaned back against the door of Sunny's hotel room and watched her come out of her bedchamber. He was well aware that he was on borrowed time, as the saying went, and he was fully prepared to take advantage of it—when he thought he could actually bring himself to do something besides simply stand there and admire the woman in front of him.

She was lovely, true, but that wasn't what stole his heart. It wasn't her grave smile, or the way she twisted her hands together as if she were nervous, or the way her bare toes still peeked out from beneath the bottom of that very expensive gown. It was that she would have rather been sitting in jeans in front of Moraig MacLeod's hearth, or puttering in her garden, or trying to throw him out her front door.

He knew all that because she'd muttered those things—and several more—not completely under her breath as they'd been sitting in a very exclusive French restaurant where she hadn't been able to find prices on the menu.

He supposed, looking back on it now, that he could just as easily have taken her to a pub and a film, but he hadn't wanted to. Foolish or not, he'd wanted to show her that he could actually feed her and clothe her and entertain her in lavish fashion. He'd wanted her to know that he could provide her luxuries far beyond what he would have been able to in medieval Scotland. He was quite sure she hadn't given a damn. After the past two months he'd had, it had been surprisingly refreshing.

For himself, he couldn't remember a more pleasant evening—even with the lengths he'd gone to make sure they remained mostly anonymous. And even though he'd only managed it in the dark of the theater, he realized he had never in his life enjoyed more the simple pleasure of holding a woman's hand.

A woman he loved.

And if she wasn't going to throw him out right away, perhaps he might dare what he hadn't risked before. He pushed away from the door and crossed over to stand in front of her. She held out her hands.

"Don't."

He stopped. "In truth?"

"If you kiss me, I won't survive it."

"Then I'll just hold you." He smiled down at her. "I've kept my hands to myself all night under enormous duress. Surely you'll want to reward such good behavior by a chaste embrace or two."

She sighed and walked into his arms as if she'd done it for years. He couldn't help but wish that had been the case. He wrapped his arms around her and closed his eyes. He wasn't quite sure how long they stood there without speaking; all he knew was he couldn't bring himself to let her go.

"Is something wrong?" she asked finally.

Was something wrong? He hardly knew where to begin to answer that. He'd gone from thinking he would just ask her a few pertinent questions to thinking he could actually let her get on a plane to now wondering if he could possibly keep her near him and keep her safe. Assuming she would even want to stay if he asked.

He had to take a deep breath. "Nay, Sunshine, nothing's wrong."

"Has your short-term memory gone, then?"

He laughed in spite of himself, then took her face in his hands and kissed her. It was only as he was making serious inroads into that that he realized it was not at all how he'd planned it. He'd wanted the first time he touched her lips to be monumental, thought-out, approached with an appropriate amount of solemnity and seriousness.

Instead, he found himself kissing her as easily as if he'd done it dozens of times before.

He couldn't help but smile as he lifted his head just enough to look at her. "Now, *this* I think I remember."

"You do not."

"We'll try again and I'll see." He slipped one hand around the back of her neck, the other around her waist, and decided that perhaps 'twas time that new memories were made.

He didn't kiss her nearly as long as he would have liked, forced himself to do so with as much gentlemanly politeness as he could manage, and ignored the fact that while her dress was remarkably modest for an evening gown it still left too much of her exposed for his peace of mind. And when he managed to think again, he thought he should pull away whilst he still could. He rested his forehead against hers.

"Sunny, if I don't walk out that door now, I won't be able to."

"Oh, I imagine you could," she said faintly. "You have impressive self-control."

"Let me rephrase that. If I don't walk out that door now, it will kill me to walk out that door later. Satisfied?"

She nodded. "Very. Go on and get out of here."

"In a minute," he said, pulling her close again. "Maybe two."

It was a marginally respectable number of minutes later when he forced himself to lift his head. "I'll be back in the morning," he promised.

"My flight leaves at one."

"That cuts into my time, woman. Fetch your passport number for me and I'll change your ticket before I go to bed."

"But—"

"Twenty-four hours, Sunshine. You agreed."

She started to balk again, then sighed. "All right. But you have to let go of me so I can."

He released her reluctantly and watched her dig her passport out of her bag. He waited whilst she wrote down for him what he wanted, listened to her swear at him while he checked the numbers against her passport to make sure she hadn't purposely given him the wrong ones, then went to gather up the clothes he'd left behind in her spare loo. He pulled her to the door with him, kissed her once more, very softly, then looked at her.

"Be here in the morning," he said seriously.

She wrapped her arms around herself and shivered. "We'll regret it."

"Did you regret tonight?"

She looked up at him, her green eyes clouded with more pain than he would have liked to see.

"It was a lovely evening." She took a deep breath and smiled. "Thank you for it."

She was back to those forced smiles she'd worn in Scotland. He hated that she had to resort to them, but he had no means to ease them.

Not yet.

He opened the door, walked out into the hallway, then turned to look at her. "Wait for me."

She nodded, then shut the door in his face.

Cameron took a deep breath, then found the stairs and ran down them. He walked swiftly out of the hotel and turned to hasten up the street. He would return at dawn, before she had time to bolt again. A day spent doing things she might enjoy; what harm was there in that?

He only managed half a block, though, before the chill evening air blew a bit of sense back into his fogged brain and he realized just what the harm would be. He didn't want to face the truth, but he had no choice. If he asked her to stay—if he allowed her to stay—he would be putting her in danger she hadn't asked for and didn't deserve.

He came to an abrupt halt. Apparently, he was doing the same thing he'd done when he pulled her back to 1375. Only this time, he knew what he would be asking of her.

He took a deep breath, then forced himself to walk on. One more day. He would memorize every look, every sigh, every touch of her hand on his and the feel of her mouth under his.

And he would hope to hell that some solution presented itself, because the mere thought of losing her was like a dirk in his heart.

He put his head down and continued on his way.

Chapter 23

Sunny stood in the bathroom and looked at herself in the mirror. She was pale. Time traveling did that to a person, apparently. Or perhaps it had been a lack of sleep. She had unpacked the night before only far enough to find pajamas and one of the plaids of Cameron's she had brought with her. She'd put herself to bed, but found that sleep would not come.

Closing her eyes had only made things worse. Every time she had, she'd been confronted with a vision of Cameron. She'd seen his head bowed at the theater, seen him simply stroking her hand as if he strove to memorize how it felt in his. She'd remembered the look on his face when she'd told him about Breac. She had been unable to forget how it felt to be in his arms with his *knowing* who she was and what she'd meant to him.

No wonder she had tossed and turned until dawn.

She'd gotten up, showered, dressed, then dithered. If she'd had any sense at all, she would have dragged herself and her faulty suitcase through the lobby and down the street to the nearest Tube station. But since she apparently had left any sense she'd once had behind in Scotland, she'd spent the past hour pacing and returning periodically to the bathroom to see if she looked any less devastated.

The phone rang, startling her. She took a deep breath, then went to find it. She put her hand on it for a moment or two before she picked up. "Hello?"

"Is this too early?"

She had to close her eyes. Even the sound of his voice on the phone was ruinous to her poor heart. "No, I'm awake."

"Are you ready to come be a plebeian with me?"

She swallowed. "Is it too late to beg off?"

"Aye. Get your fetching self downstairs, woman, and make sure you're wearing walking shoes. We're tourists today. And hurry up, Sunny. You're still on my clock."

"All right." She hung up before she dropped the phone. She

wanted to remind herself that she was an idiot to be going along with his plans, but she wasn't an idiot.

The simple truth was she had never before and would never again meet anyone like him. She could have easily gone to the airport in the middle of the night, but she hadn't. What she'd wanted deep down was another day to soak up what it would have been like to have had him in the twenty-first century.

It would probably be what kept her warm at night for years to come.

She tried to bring to mind Cameron's flaws that Emily had listed for her yesterday while she'd been doing her hair, but she couldn't. There just hadn't been very many except his propensity to work too much, his tendency to be prickly when people asked him questions that were too personal, and his complete inability to choose a decent fiancée. Emily had listed in great detail all his virtues, many of which Sunny had already known. She'd wanted to know why Emily had seemed to be so determined to sell Cameron, but she hadn't dared ask.

She also hadn't dared tell Emily that no selling was necessary because she'd already bought the product with all her heart and soul.

She left her suite and kept herself busy by thinking about the other things she'd learned from Emily. She'd found out, along with that enormous list of Cameron's virtues, that Emily was Madame Gies's granddaughter, she had known Cameron since he'd come home from the hospital, and she had worked for him for the past six years as his personal dogsbody. Oh, and she hadn't ever slept with him.

Sunny supposed she could have gone all day without having known that last bit. She'd pleaded with Emily not to give her a list of women Cameron *had* slept with. Emily had shrugged in a particularly Gallic way and informed her that the list would be very short and it would be very discreet. It would also contain no one who had touched his heart. Sunny supposed that was a good thing.

She got into the elevator with a couple who were dressed to the nines. After a first look of contempt, they didn't pay her any attention. Reason number 357 why she shouldn't ever become involved with Robert Cameron. She couldn't possibly function in his London world.

She turned her mind to thinking about Highland meadows and was surprised to find it actually helped.

She followed the couple out and across the foyer. She noticed that the woman gave Cameron a lingering look, which Cameron completely ignored. He was leaning back against the reception desk with his arms folded over his chest, watching *her*.

That helped as well.

He looked exactly as he had the morning when she'd seen him standing under the eaves of the forest, waiting for her. All that was lacking was the crooking of his finger. She took a deep breath to still butterflies that had no business being in her stomach, reminded herself that he was not hers, then continued on her way to him.

"Good morning, Sunshine," he said with a small smile. "Sleep well?"

"Terribly."

His smile faded. "I understand." He pushed away from the counter. "You can nap in my arms in some darkened corner. We'll ride about on one of those tour buses until we find an appropriate spot."

"Is this discreet?" she managed.

He took her arm and led her toward the door. "It will be if I can keep my mouth off yours."

She tried to muster up a stern look. "Stop that."

He only smiled again, a more sincere one this time, and pulled her through the door with him.

He bought them both fruit and water at a street stand, then paused with her in front of a tour bus stop. He seemed to be watching what was going on around them, so perhaps he was looking for photographers. Perhaps he was looking for Penelope. Perhaps no one cared about him and it was Penelope who alerted the photographers to every opportunity to snap her on Cameron's arm.

She didn't suppose she really wanted to think about any of it, actually.

"Here's our ride, lass. Let's go."

She pulled herself back to the task at hand, then climbed on the bus and continued on to the upper deck. She walked to a pair of seats in the very back, then collapsed onto the window seat. Cameron sat down next to her and plopped his backpack on her lap.

"Hold that. I want my hands free."

She looked at him in surprise. "Why?"

"To take pictures with," he said, unzipping his pack. He shot her a look from under his eyebrows. "You've a rather carnal mind, lass, for being a—"

"Shut up."

He laughed, then pulled the camera out and pointed it at her. "Smile, love."

She did her best. He pursed his lips, put his head close to hers and took a picture of them both. Then he leaned back against the seat and smiled at her.

"Thank you for staying."

"Thank you for asking me to," she said quietly. She watched him put his camera in his pocket, then unfold the map they'd been given and study it. "I wouldn't have figured you for a touristy sort of lad," she said in Gaelic. "Being a Scot and all."

He held the map up as a shield, then leaned over and kissed her, a soft kiss that had her closing her eyes in defense.

"Tourist maps can be very useful," he whispered conspiratorially.

"Stop kissing me," she managed.

"Are you in earnest?"

She wanted to tell him yes. She wanted to tell him to leave her alone, to walk out of her life and not look back. She knew there was nothing but heartache in front of her if she spent the day with him, touched him, kissed him. She would go back to Seattle and he would marry a shrew who didn't deserve him.

But she was apparently a glutton for punishment because she put her hands on his face, then leaned over and kissed him herself. "You're too damn accommodating," she murmured against his mouth. "What's happened to you?"

He caught his breath, then let it out slowly. "I'm trying to behave," he said evenly. "I am trying, if you can imagine it, to keep my hands off you. I thought that keeping you captive in your hotel chamber would have been an extraordinarily bad idea, so I am keeping you out in public and trying to be *damn* accommodating."

She shivered. "I see."

"So you do."

She started to pull away, but he caught her before she could and kissed her quite thoroughly. In fact, she was fairly certain they had missed a stop or two before he lifted his head and looked at her with stormy eyes. "Give me the day, Sunshine."

"You're adding hours."

"Don't think about that. The only thing that matters today is the fact that we have each other within arm's reach. We'll leave tomorrow to sort itself by itself."

She smiled, though it cost her a bit. "All right."

He dispensed with the map and merely kissed her again before she could protest.

Not that she tried very hard.

By the time he pulled away, she was more than a little breathless.

"Stop that," she managed. "Really, this time."

"Why?"

"Because I feel faint, that's why."

He smiled and pulled his arm out from behind her. He put on a pair of sunglasses, then reached for her hand and took it in both his own. Sunny looked at him for a moment, a medieval laird in a windbreaker and Ray-Bans, then put on her own sunglasses and looked at the scenery that was starting to go by.

She was appalled at how little of it she was able to pay attention to.

They crossed the bridge to the Tower of London late in the afternoon after a day spent seeing things she never had time for usually. She couldn't say she'd paid any attention to them. Her eyes had been too full of Cameron for that.

The day had taken its toll on her. She'd been perky and cheerful, but it had been difficult. She wasn't sure she could keep it up any longer. Not even the thought of looking through the Tower dungeon with a man of about that vintage helped.

There wasn't even as much hope for them as there might have been in 1375. At least in the past he'd had reason to flee what his life as lord of the manor demanded and run to the future with her. There was no *deus ex machina* to rescue them now from the reality of his wedding a month from then. Not unless he was willing to simply walk away from it—and given that he hadn't said a single thing all day that indicated he might be willing to do that, she suspected he wouldn't.

He took her hand. "Sunny?"

She found her fingers tangled with his, but it brought her no comfort. She tried to smile, but failed miserably. "Cameron, I can't do this anymore."

He released her hand and put his arm around her shoulders.

"All right. Let us find a bit of privacy and we'll discuss the future."

What future? she wanted to ask, but she couldn't bring herself to. She simply walked with him where he wanted to go. He sat down on a bench against the wall, then pulled her down next to him. Sunny looked at her hand between his hands that had kept her alive and pushed her back into the safety of her time, and wished she had the right to hold on to them forever. She closed her eyes and leaned her head against his shoulder.

She would never get over him. It didn't matter what sort of good advice she would get from well-meaning friends and relatives, she would never ever have another day pass that she didn't think about him.

She felt him kiss her hair, then rest his cheek against her head.

"For eight years, from the moment I woke in hospital, I've felt . . . empty," he said quietly. "I looked all over the world for something to ease that—in treasure halls of medieval fortresses, boardrooms of the rich and powerful, lands I never dreamed existed in my youth. And then I walked down the stairs of James MacLeod's ancestral home and found what I'd been looking for all along."

She lifted her head. "What was that?"

"You," he said simply. "I touched you and my life turned upside down—nay, 'twas even sooner than that. I touched you the first time in front of Tavish Fergusson's store. Do you remember?"

She nodded. "You helped me up after Penelope ran over me."

"Did you know me?"

"No. It wasn't until the next night that you pulled me back to your time."

"And yet I knew you somehow," he mused. "'Tis odd how time folds back on itself. Odd and cruel."

She looked down at their hands intertwined together. "Time gates are fickle, Cameron. Jamie would be the first to tell you that."

"I didn't know," he said roughly. "I didn't know, Sunny. If I had, I never would have . . ."

Sunny nodded, though it just about killed her to do so. What had she expected? For him to completely change his life because he'd started to recognize her? He needed a woman of wealth and rank who could help him socially—

"Sunny."

She looked at him, but couldn't see him. Her eyes were so full of tears, she couldn't see anything. She was really going to have to do serious work when she got back to Seattle. Yoga several hours a day. Lots of tea. Maybe even a parasite cleanse. She was definitely out of balance.

"Sunny, look at me."

"I can't see you," she said with a half sob.

He stood and pulled her up to her feet. He put his arm around her shoulders and led her over to the shelter of a building. "I have a compelling reason to stay engaged to her."

"I'm not asking you to dump her, Cameron. It's all right."

"It isn't." He cursed succinctly, then pulled her close and wrapped his arms around her. "It isn't, but I can't change things now."

Sunny stood in his arms and felt the beginning of the end start to settle in her heart. Hadn't she known it that morning? He would marry where he had to, for whatever reason he had to, and she would have to get on with her life.

She had to get out of the country before being there did her in—for good this time.

"Take me back to the hotel," she said, pulling out of his arms.

"Sunny, please don't go—"

"And just what will I stay for, Cameron? A man I can never have? Who will never share my bed? Never give me children? Never take me out in public without looking over his shoulder?"

He opened his mouth to speak, then shut it and dragged both his hands through his hair this time. "There are things I can't tell you, Sunshine—"

"If you're going to marry her, then you've told me everything I need to know." She took a step backward, then very carefully wiped the tears out from under her eyes. She wasn't all that sure her mascara was waterproof and even if it was, she wasn't sure it could handle what she was putting it through. "I didn't bring any money," she said flatly. "Can I borrow enough for the Tube?"

He closed his eyes briefly. "Sunshine—"

"Tube fare, my lord," she said briskly. "Either that or give me my bus ticket. It's a little far to walk."

He was silent for another very long moment, then he let out his breath slowly. "Let me see you back. We'll talk."

Her first instinct was to tell him no, but it occurred to her that it might be very good for her. It would remind her in very physical terms how completely out of her reach he was. She would memorize how it felt to stand next to him and know that she had no right to take his hand, or put her arms around him, or pull his head down and kiss him until he groaned.

But she had no intentions of talking to him again.

She walked with him back out of the Tower, stood silently as he hailed a cab, and wished she'd never agreed to the day. It had only made things several orders of magnitude worse. High school math coming in handy yet again. She shouldn't have been surprised.

It was a very uncomfortable cab ride. Sunny sat next to Cameron and was excruciatingly aware of every breath he took. But she couldn't touch him. If she had, she would have bawled like a baby.

He didn't move. He merely sat next to her silently, watching her.

The cab pulled up in front of the Ritz not nearly soon enough to suit her, but since she was on the verge of escaping her torment, she wasn't going to complain.

"Thank you," she said, reaching for her door.

He caught her by the arm. "Your ticket is flexible," he said. "You can cancel it almost up to the flight."

She looked at him to tell him that wouldn't be necessary, but the absolute misery on his face, a misery that so fully mirrored her own, stopped her from saying anything.

"I don't want you to go," he said a low voice. "I thought I could watch you walk away, but I was wrong. If you could just trust me—"

She was so desperately torn, she thought she might tear in two in truth this time. She closed her eyes.

"I can't."

She escaped out of the cab, shut the door, then ran inside the hotel. She ignored the desk manager who tried to see if she needed anything, ran past the elevator, and headed for the stairs. She ran up them, found her room, then flung herself inside it and slammed the door shut behind her.

She sank down to the floor and wept until she was ill.

The next morning, she sat on the floor in much the same place and looked at the things spread out in front of her.

Her suitcase stood to one side, packed to overflowing. She'd packed the blue dress and the shoes, just because she felt bad about leaving them behind. She was wearing the pearls under her T-shirt. She wasn't sure why. They felt good against her skin, they were small enough to be discreet, and she was sure that an opera strand that long and of that obvious quality had been ridiculously expensive.

It had nothing to do with making her feel like Cameron had draped himself around her.

She forced herself to consider the rest. There was another pile made up of shoe boxes full of shoes that hadn't fit. A note sat on top of them with the number Emily had given as hers so the porter could call and have her come pick them up.

Flowers sat in an exquisite vase on the table in front of her, flowers that had arrived approximately five minutes after she'd finished throwing up. She'd accepted them, put them down on the table, then forced herself to read the card.

I'm sorry. Cam.

An hour later, a small box had arrived with a wallet inside. Inside the wallet had been £2,500 in very useful £50 bills and a note that read, *Please don't use this for a cab to the airport.*

Half an hour later, another bag had arrived containing a sachet filled with lavender and a box of herbal tea that guaranteed a good night's sleep. There had been no card. She supposed by then, he'd given up. He hadn't called, though she couldn't blame him for not bothering. She wouldn't have answered.

The box she hadn't yet opened lay in front of her. It had come early that morning. She'd been looking at it for over an hour, unable to bring herself to open it and see what was inside.

Her curiosity finally overcame the absolute, bone-wearying misery she'd been fighting all night. She pulled off the enormous green bow, slid the ribbon off, then opened the lid and looked inside.

There, nestled in white tissue paper, lay a shocking-pink cell phone. Sunny picked it up and looked at it. It was so far from a color she would have chosen that she could hardly believe Cameron had sent it. She found the card and read it.

Sunshine,

This is a satellite phone that will work anywhere in the world. If you need me, call me from Seattle, or from

*anywhere else on the face of the earth, and I will drop
everything and come fetch you.*

*Love,
Cam*

P.S. Please stay. Please trust me and stay.

She put her face in her hands and wept.
I like hearing that name again from someone I love.
She rose finally partly to look for a Kleenex and partly be-
cause she had to move. She blew her nose, then paced from one
end of the suite to the other, into the bedroom and back out again.
He was going to marry Penelope Ainsworth. No matter what
he said, no matter how many times he asked her to stay, the real-
ity of that would slap her in the face each time she cared to look.
Even if she took him to her bed, she couldn't keep him there.
She looked at the card in her hands.
Please trust me and stay.
And just what in the hell was that supposed to mean? Trust
him that he would find time to see her on more than just the odd
day when he managed to get back to Scotland?
She walked over and picked up her suitcase. She put her hand
on the door, but couldn't open it.
If she got on that plane to Seattle, she would probably never
see him again. She supposed she could just go and see if he came
after her, but that seemed a little too juvenile even for her fragile
state of mind. She would walk out of his life and she would never
again have the sight of sunlight on his dark hair, never again see
the welcoming warmth of his smile, never again tremble at the
feel of his mouth on hers.
The thought of simply never seeing him again was so horren-
dous, it stole her breath.
She put her suitcase down because it was heavy. That led her
to thinking about when she'd first seen him the day before and
how terrible he'd looked—so terrible that even Emily had noticed.
What had Emily meant about "another" mugging?
She hadn't thought much of it at the time, but she wondered
about it now. Cameron had said he was in a situation he couldn't

get out of, but why not? If he didn't love Penelope, why didn't he just dump her? He said he had a compelling reason to stay engaged to her, but what in the world was it? With Gilly, it had been his duty to raise his brother's children. But in modern-day Britain surely he had no such duty.

The other thing that had never made sense was why the wedding was so soon. She would have thought that Penelope would have wanted to drag it out as long as possible so she could be photographed as often as possible. Did she need Cameron's money so desperately or was there more to it than that?

At the very least, she knew that Cameron was dealing with less-than-pleasant people. She'd seen pictures of Penelope's brother, Nathan, and his soulless eyes had scared her just from the photograph. If the people who were supposed to be welcoming Cameron into their family were that nasty, who knew what else he was facing?

It was no wonder he'd been grateful for the refuge.

She looked at what was spread out on the floor for quite some time, then sighed and dragged her hands through her hair. She shoved Cameron's note into her pocket, then put the cell in her jacket pocket. She put the pillow on the chair and the tea on the table. She took the wallet out of her pocket, looked at it, then put it back in.

Cab fare, indeed.

She stood in the middle of that luxurious suite, surrounded by gifts from a man who had begged her to stay in spite of everything, and felt more miserable than she had in her entire life. At least she had people she could trust. She suspected Cameron had no one. And for years, he hadn't even had anyone to share his deepest secret with. If she left, he wouldn't even have that anymore. No wonder he wanted her to stay.

Though she suspected he wanted her for more than just that.

She turned away from that thought, picked up her suitcase, then turned and left the luxury behind her before she could think better of her decision.

She had to go.

She just had to.

Chapter 24

Cameron sat in the salon of Penelope and Nathan's ancestral home and checked his watch for what had to have been the hundredth time that night. It brought him no more relief that time than it had the first ninety-nine. It was almost ten p.m. Given that Sunny's flight had left about four, she was now over Canada. He wondered if she was sleeping, or weeping, or counting herself well rid of him.

He supposed he wouldn't have blamed her for the last.

Letting her out of that taxi the day before had been the single most difficult thing he'd ever done. He'd wanted to follow her into the hotel, pull her into his arms, demand that she never again give him one of those bloody false smiles she'd worn too often the day before for his taste.

But he hadn't, because during that miserable ride in the taxi he'd been thinking about reality, and the reality was this was not a medieval battle where he knew what to expect, where he could see the lads who were coming directly at him and sense the ones sneaking up behind him. This was modern life where he was in a city with millions of other people, a city full of cars and conversations and life that was perpetually in motion. He could hardly guarantee his own safety, much less that of someone not by his side constantly. He wasn't sure he could guarantee Sunny's safety if she *had* been at his side.

Though it was killing him to know she'd gone.

He told himself it was for the best. The assault on both his businesses was just the opening salvo in what he was quite sure would become a very brutal war. It wasn't inconceivable to think that his business could be taken over by someone else and run into the ground. If that happened, his honor would demand that the fortune that was now his thanks to monies scrupulously saved by generations of Camerons would need to be used to settle those business debts. That would leave him with no choice but to give up his keep, a place that had been in Cameron hands since his grandfather's grandfather Aongus had laid the first stones all the way down to

Alistair Cameron who had been Breac's son's son dozens of generations removed. And that could not happen. He had to see both to his hall and to his investors who had placed so much trust in him. In a sense, his clan was now spread out all over the world and he couldn't turn his back on them.

Nor could he ignore the fact that until he determined who was trying to kill him and why, he didn't dare keep the woman he loved anywhere near him.

Though letting her go, knowing he hadn't given her the whole truth, knowing he'd allowed her to think he intended to wed Penelope Ainsworth . . .

He bowed his head and looked at the rather shabby carpet beneath his feet. The simple truth was, Sunny would be safer living anonymously in the States. She wouldn't be mugged in the Tube as Emily had been, twice. She would never receive threatening phone calls as members of his board of directors had many times. She would never find herself assaulted in a darkened alley as he himself had been, regularly.

He told himself that because it sounded reasonable. It was better than facing the fact that he'd hurt her—and for that he feared she would never forgive him.

He couldn't do anything about making it up to her until he'd walked that dreadful, perilous path in front of him and was sure that when he went to Seattle, he wouldn't be bringing murderers trailing along after him. He hadn't seen anyone following them the day before. None of his own lads who'd been following him had reported seeing anyone, so he'd known they were safe, but still—

"Have some wine, Mac," Penelope said suddenly. "And you should have eaten. It was horribly impolite not to, especially after all the trouble I went to to have the chef replaced before Father's death."

Cameron wrenched his thoughts back to what was in front of him. He looked at the glass in Penelope's hands, then looked at her. She was actually quite a lovely gel, that Penelope Ainsworth. A pity her insides didn't come close to matching her outsides. He wondered if perhaps it was because her mother had died so soon after her birth. Perhaps it was because she'd spent too much time away at boarding school. He had no answer for it; all he knew was that if he ever managed to sire any children, he would keep them close.

Unbidden, a vision came to him of sitting in his kitchen whilst

Sunny made their brood things that had green as their primary color. He would have instructed his children to of course finish off what their mother had given them, then he would have piled them all—Sunny included—into the car and headed to the village to raid the local chippy.

Life would have been good.

"*Wine*, Mac."

Cameron looked at the goblet again, then shook his head.

"I don't drink, Penelope."

"You drank last Friday," she whispered furiously. "I was the one to pull you out of your stupor, if you remember."

Was it only last Friday? Cameron could hardly believe that. So many things had happened since then, so many things so happily removed from his reality in the south.

"Nay," he said firmly.

Penelope pulled the glass away suddenly and muttered in displeasure. Cameron checked his watch again, sighed, then watched as one of Penelope's set rose and approached the piano. She called gaily for someone to come accompany her.

Cameron put his fingers over his eyes before he could stop himself. Was it not enough that he'd spent the morning fighting the urge to call Sunny and beg her to stay, the afternoon wrestling with accountants, then the remainder of daylight hours trying to get out to Windsor to meet Penelope's impossible deadline for yet another party? Now he was to endure off-key singing that was only marginally less annoying than fingernails on a chalkboard?

His phone buzzed suddenly in his pocket. He pulled it out with a grateful sigh. Perhaps it was George, peering in the window and sending him a rescue ring. He looked down at the number just to check, then almost dropped the phone in surprise.

He started to his rise, but Penelope caught him by the arm first.

"Calls at this hour, Mac?" she said sharply.

"I have business all over the world," he said without hesitation, because it was true.

She released him. Perhaps she thought it might curtail her spending if he didn't keep his empire from imploding. He left the salon quickly, then answered the call the moment he'd shut the door behind him.

"Aye?"

There was silence on the other end for quite some time. Then

came the sound of a voice he'd feared he would never hear again
and could hardly believe he was hearing at present.

"Are you busy?"

He closed his eyes briefly. "I won't be in five minutes," he said
unsteadily. "May I ring you back?"

"All right."

The phone went dead. He slipped it back in his pocket, rubbed
his hands over his face, then went to look for Penelope's butler.
The man was standing near the passageway that led to the
kitchen, obviously preparing for the drinks to go round. All the
more reason not to be there, lest he be forced to try to identify
one that wouldn't kill him.

"Hitchens, would you inform Lady Penelope that I've been
called away on urgent business?" Cameron asked. "Send my regrets and tell her I'll ring her in the morning."

"Of course, my lord," Hitchens said, looking as if he would
have liked nothing better than to have been escaping as well.

An ally in the enemy camp, perhaps. Cameron filed that away
for consideration in a less dodgy place, then continued on his
way to the kitchen, hoping to find George investigating the depths
of Penelope's pantry for suspicious substances. Unfortunately,
his chauffeur was only investigating the depths of his tea cup. He
did, however, look up when Cameron entered.

"Finished so soon?" he asked hopefully.

"Aye. Let's go," Cameron said briskly.

George rose without hesitation.

Cameron tried not to run for the front door. Sunny had called
him. It couldn't have been from a plane because it was her mobile
she was using and they wouldn't have allowed that on a commer-
cial flight. That meant that she wasn't 39,000 feet over Canada at
present. Perhaps she'd used his money and purchased a different
ticket with another carrier and was just calling him to let him
know she was home early and hoped he would rot happily in a
hell of his own making.

"Why in such a hurry?"

Cameron turned around before Nathan Ainsworth could stab
him in the back. He stuck his hands in his pockets and gave
Nathan a cool smile.

"Business, of course. It goes along with all that working I do
during the days, Nathan. You should try it with your father's company whilst there's still something left of it."

"I'm busy enough."

Cameron supposed he was, but not with things his father would have approved of.

"You won't walk away untouched, Robert," Nathan continued in a dull, dead sort of tone that matched his eyes perfectly. "My father may have favored you over me, but he wouldn't have if he'd known the things about you I know."

"Your father didn't favor me over you, Nathan. As for the rest—" Cameron shrugged negligently. "It's all out there for public consumption, isn't it?"

Nathan lifted one of his eyebrows briefly. "I suppose we'll see, won't we?" He turned and walked away. "Drive safely," he threw over his shoulder.

Cameron watched him until he'd disappeared back down the hallway. He spared a thought for what Penelope's brother might be alluding to, then decided that could be digested later as well. He looked at George. "We'd best check the brakes, hadn't we?"

"Derrick's been watching the car all night, my lord," George said cheerfully. "Shall I bring it around, then?"

"No need," Cameron said. "I'm in haste."

"As you will, my lord."

Three minutes later, he was pulling his door shut and his phone out of his pocket. He looked at George as he slid in under the wheel.

"Private conversation," Cameron said sternly.

"Of course, my lord."

Perhaps he should have been worried about his private business remaining private, but George was, as Alistair had said more than once, a vault. Cameron might have been discreet about what he said in front of the man, but he was confident what he'd said had never gone any further. He took a deep breath, blew it out, then dialed Sunny's number.

She picked up on the third ring. "Hello?"

"Where are you?" he asked without preamble. He had to know.

She was silent for a long minute. "Where you dropped me off."

He let out the breath he realized he'd been holding all day. He actually had to put his hand over his eyes then rub his face to keep from making some unwholesome sound of relief. He ignored the hard reality that he should have been terrified that she was still in London and not on her way to Seattle where she would have been safe. The saints pity him for a fool, but he wouldn't send her away if she was willing to stay.

"I asked them to extend my reservation," she said hesitantly. "They were kind enough to do so."

"Exactly what you should have done, of course," he said without hesitation. He paused. "What are you doing presently?"

"Getting ready to watch a TV program on medieval Highland wooing practices."

He would have smiled, but he was too winded. "That should be interesting."

She was silent for so long, he wondered if she'd hung up on him. He even went so far as to check his phone to see if they were still connected.

"You might have an opinion on it," she said finally. "Maybe you'd better come watch it with me. Can you?"

He lost the rest of his breath. "Of course. I'm on my way back to town now."

She was silent for another minute. "I won't sleep with you, Robert Francis."

He smiled at the name. "I didn't think you would. And don't call me Francis."

"I could call you worse."

"You could indeed," he agreed.

"Hurry," she said, then she hung up.

Cameron leaned his head back against the headrest and shook. By the saints, it was worse than battle. He didn't know what had convinced her to stay, but he imagined it hadn't been anything he'd sent her. Perhaps she wanted him to come to her hotel so she could slide a dirk between his ribs to repay him for the pain he'd caused her. Perhaps she'd only stayed so she could tear into him in person—though she could have done that over the phone from anywhere.

He decided that it was probably best to simply not think at all for the next little while. She would say what she had to say to him, he would fall to his knees and beg her to stay, then he would figure out how in the hell he was going to keep her safe.

The one thing he was certain of was that he could never, ever let her go again. Not now. He wouldn't survive it.

"The Ritz, please, George," he said, when he thought he could speak calmly.

"How bourgeois of you, my lord."

Cameron grunted, then leaned his head back against the seat and closed his eyes. He allowed himself the pleasure of trusting that he would get to his destination safely and as quickly as the posted speed would allow.

In time, George pulled up in front of the Ritz and stopped. "Shall I wait?"

Cameron unbuckled his seat belt and leaned up. "I'll walk back. Go home and put your feet up. In fact, take tomorrow off as well. I'll manage on my own."

George turned and looked at him with a smile. "Himself is feeling magnanimous tonight. Dare I assume it isn't only because he escaped the party early?"

Cameron pursed his lips. "I was about to suggest that you should take the week off—"

"*Very* magnanimous."

Cameron smiled at him, then slowly sobered. "Thank you for your discretion, George, and your loyalty. I appreciate both."

George chewed on his words for a moment or two, then turned and faced forward with his hands on the wheel. "My lord, I watch you turn backflips for that harridan in Windsor who spends your money and dishonors you. I'm not sure why you're here at the Ritz, but the thought of what awaits you here has cheered you and that cheers me. As does a week off," he added, shooting Cameron a smile over his shoulder.

Cameron clapped a hand on his shoulder. "Enjoy. I'll make sure Penelope knows not to call you."

"Yet more sunshine coming my way."

Cameron thought he couldn't lose his breath again, but apparently he was wrong. "I'm due for some as well, I think."

"I daresay you are, my lord."

Cameron got out, shut the door behind him, then looked about him for anything unusual. Seeing nothing, he put his head down and walked quickly into the hotel. He introduced himself to the night manager, who was happy to call upstairs and see if Miss Phillips might still be awake. The man asked no questions and Cameron volunteered no answers. He was remarkably relieved when he was informed that Miss Phillips was indeed still receiving callers and he could certainly go up.

Cameron rode up in the lift, then walked down the hallway and stopped in front of her door. He stood there for a moment, then knocked softly.

The door opened soon after. Sunny was dressed in jeans and a T-shirt with her feet bare. She wasn't wearing a jacket or holding on to her suitcase, which led him to believe that she didn't plan on running out the door anytime soon. She was wearing the strand of pearls he'd bought her tucked into her shirt.

And she looked as if she'd been weeping since he'd last seen her.

She made room for him to come inside, shut the door, then stepped back away from him. She wouldn't meet his eyes; she merely stood there and shook.

He put his hands in his pockets. "Thank you for calling me, Sunshine. I—"

He never saw her move. One moment, she was standing in front of him, the next she had thrown herself at him and had flung her arms around his neck. She held on to him as if time itself threatened to drag her away.

He had to take a step backward to keep his balance, then he steadied them both, wrapped his arms around her, and clutched her to him with equal fervor. He buried his face in her hair and picked her up off her feet where he could hold her even more tightly. Sobs racked her body, forcing tears to his eyes in spite of his best attempts to stop them.

"Ach, Sunny," he whispered against her ear. "Sunshine, my love, I'm so sorry."

"Don't let me go," she said, her voice catching.

"By the saints, Sunshine, I never will," he said fiercely. And he wouldn't, damn those Ainsworths to hell. Whatever he had to do to keep her near him—*safely*—he would. He buried his face in her hair. "Today almost destroyed me."

"Me, too."

He continued to hold her tightly against him as she fought to catch her breath. He was just so bloody grateful to have her in his arms, he couldn't do anything but keep her there.

A great while later, he let her slide back to her feet. He smoothed his hand over her hair, he rubbed his hands soothingly over her back, he murmured thanks in her ear so many times, he feared the words would lose their meaning.

But she didn't loosen her death grip on his neck.

And he didn't release her.

It took him quite a while longer to decide that perhaps he should carry her over to a chair, but before he could, she pushed out of his arms.

"I'm done," she said with a gulp, backing away from him. "I'm done weeping over you, you bloody awful man. I will never, *ever* cry over you again. I'm finished."

He almost managed a smile. Almost. "I hope I never give you reason to again."

She wrapped her arms around herself and looked at him, tears still streaming down her face. "Do you want to know why I'm here?"

He found himself quite suddenly very reluctant to hear it, lest it be something less than he dared hope for. He put his hands in his pockets. "I'm not sure. Do I?"

"You might."

"Please be gentle."

She didn't smile. "I'm here because once upon a time you protected me with your own life," she began in a low voice. "Once upon a time you would have handfasted with me if there hadn't been three dozen of your murderous kinsmen cluttering up your threshold. You were willing to give up everything that you were comfortable with to stay with me." She was silent for several very long moments, then she met his gaze. "It seemed as if I should be willing to do the same for you."

He had a very difficult time swallowing. He could only stare at her, speechless.

She blinked rapidly, looked up at the ceiling, then surrendered and dragged her arm across her eyes. "I told you once that I *wouldn't* be your refuge, but I changed my mind because, despite what you said yesterday, I think that's exactly what you need."

"My refuge," he echoed, finding that he could hardly say the word.

She nodded. "That's what I'm offering you. Me, as your refuge. If you want me."

His heart was so full of so many things he couldn't begin to identify, he could hardly think clearly. What he did know was that he had gravely underestimated the woman in front of him. She brewed an exceptional cup of tea, had lovely, healing hands, and a smile that left him daydreaming of summer meadows. But underneath all that sweetness was a woman of such courage that any medieval laird with two wits to rub together would have fallen to his knees in gratitude to have called her his.

Which he would do, after he had held her in his arms long

enough to satisfy himself. He took a deep breath, then reached out and pulled her back into his arms.

She flung her arms around his neck and held on as he clutched her to him. Her tears were hot against his neck. He supposed his were drenching her hair in equal measure. He didn't care. That she should be willing to put her own comfort aside for his—

It was the single most humbling moment of his life.

He wasn't sure how long he stood there, holding her close to him, trying to master his emotions. He realized, finally, that Sunny was running her fingers through his hair, making soothing noises, holding on to him whilst he came undone in her embrace. He lifted his head and looked down at her.

"Aren't we a pair?"

She reached up and brushed the tears from his cheeks. "I'm fine. You're pretty much a mess, though."

He smiled in spite of himself. "Aye, my love, I most certainly am that."

She looked at him gravely. "How is this going to work, Cam?"

He mopped his face briefly with his cuff, then wrapped both his arms around her. "After I've found a way to be worthy of you, I'll give you an answer to that."

She hugged him tightly. "Be serious."

"I am being serious, Sunny." He paused. "Can you trust me?"

"I always have."

He had to chew on his next words for quite a while before he was able to spew them out. "Can you wait for me?"

"You waited eight years for me."

"By the saints, I hope it won't take that long," he said, with feeling. He continued to stand with her for several minutes in silence, stroking her back absently, dragging his fingers through her hair. "The road will not be pleasant. It may take us places we don't particularly care to go. And it may be longer than either of us cares for."

"Will you be at the end of it?"

He could only hope to survive that long. "Aye."

She looked up at him. "Then I'll walk it."

He had to blink several times. "Damned flowers," he managed. "I'm allergic, know you."

She smiled and pulled out of his arms, then took his hand. "Let's go distract ourselves by watching this show. I'm sure you'll want to make an angry phone call first thing." She tugged him toward the couch. "You do remember that I'm not staying to be your mistress, don't you?"

"You never want to be my mistress," he said, trying to match her light tone. He wasn't sure he'd succeeded, but she didn't seem to notice. He dropped down next to her on the sofa. "Refusals spanning centuries, Sunshine. 'Tis a wonder I don't begin to doubt my appeal."

She snorted. "You don't doubt it and you know that I *have* seriously considered it more than once. But I don't want to be your mistress, or your girlfriend, or whatever else might fit in with those." She paused. "I'm not really sure what you want me to be, all my flowery words aside."

Safe was almost out of his mouth before he could stop it. Safe and completely lacking in any knowledge about what he faced. If she knew nothing, she was of no use to anyone who might want to strike at him.

Though if those who wished him ill had any idea how much he loved her, they would have used her without hesitation.

"What I want you to be is simply what you are," he said finally. "The only light I have in my life."

She dragged her sleeve across her eyes. "All right, stop it. Eat something and then go home so I can bawl in peace."

He realized then that the coffee table was laden with everything from fruit to what have been mistaken for bangers and mash. "Thank you," he said with feeling.

"I thought you might not have eaten today."

"I can't remember," he admitted. "An altogether very forgettable day. Well, except for the last forty-five minutes. I could relive that bit a time or two quite happily."

She leaned back against the couch. "Maybe I should have done something earlier, so you could have enjoyed more of your day. I called Emily—"

"You called Emily?" he interrupted in surprise. "Didn't you want to talk to me—ach," he said with a wince. "Of course you didn't want to talk to me."

"Actually, I *did* want to talk to you, but Emily said you were with accountants, which would make you very cranky and I didn't want you to be cranky when I called you. Of course, it took a while before I even wanted to talk to you at all." She paused. "I think it was the pink phone that did it."

He smiled. "I thought you wouldn't lose it in your veg,

whereas you might lose a green one. But let's revisit that moment where you came to the conclusion that if you got on that plane, I would never again take a decent breath."

"Really?" she asked quietly.

He nodded and reached for hand. "Aye, really."

"Well," she began slowly, "I'll admit it was not a good morning. I dithered here for hours, then went downstairs and paced for another half an hour in front of the concierge. I think I frightened him. Finally, I just asked him to take my suitcase back upstairs, then I went to console myself at Harrods's chocolate counter."

"Chocolate?" he echoed in surprise. "You?"

"A reflection of the day I was having," she said with a wry smile. "I sobbed into truffles for a while, then called Emily and asked if she wanted to join me. That's when I found out what you were doing and learned that after you would be made excessively grumpy by the accountants, you would head off to a garden party that you would loathe. Emily imagined that you would be texting her by ten to give you a ring so you could escape." She smiled. "So I called instead."

"I have never been so happy to see a familiar number," he said seriously.

She shifted on the couch to face him. "I wasn't sure if you would have the privacy to even answer your phone, but I thought I'd take a chance. You haven't exactly been forthcoming about details, you know."

He suppressed the urge to squirm. "Aye, I know."

"I think there's quite a bit you're not telling me, but since you didn't tell me anything in medieval Scotland, either, I figured I couldn't expect anything else."

He realized he was gaping at her when she put her finger under his chin and shut his mouth. "Indeed."

"Indeed," she agreed. "So, I'm prepared to trust you. I will admit, though, that I'm still not at all sure how this is going to work—"

He bent his head and cut off the rest of her words with a kiss. He wasn't, either, and he didn't have a decent answer for her. If the roles had been reversed and she had been the one engaged to someone else, he wasn't sure what he would have done. Bloodied the whoreson who thought to claim her, no doubt.

He closed his eyes and kissed her as desperately as he dared.

He was tempted to sweep her up into his arms, carry her to her bed, and never let her out of it. But he supposed it was neither the time nor the place—and he knew that Patrick MacLeod would repay him very painfully if he did, so he forbore.

But he kissed her much longer than he likely should have.

"Robert Francis?" she said quite a while later.

"Aye?"

"Your supper is now very cold."

He smiled. "Do you mind?"

She shook her head. "Not really."

"Neither do I. And don't call me Francis."

She smiled and leaned her head back against the couch again. She reached up and trailed her fingers down his cheek. "I don't think it bothers you all that much."

"Lass, from you I would put up with quite a bit."

She gave him another affectionate smile. "Go home, Cam. I'll see you when I see you."

"You'll see me tomorrow," he said firmly.

"I'll be here—if I can stomach the thought of how much this room is costing you. But I can't stay here forever." Her smile faded. "You could get me a cheaper room, you know."

"Nay," he said seriously, "I cannot. Sunshine, I would like to believe that at some point in that past I can't remember, I promised I would take care of you. Allow me, if you would, to provide you with comforts I never could have in medieval Scotland."

"You just want another shot at the room service."

He smiled. "Actually, I was hoping for a sleepover. Interested?"

"Yes," she said simply. "When you're free. But since I don't know when—or even if—that will ever happen, maybe it's better we don't think about it." She squeezed his hands, then rose and pulled him up with her. "Go toddle on off to your own bed, my laird."

He wanted to tell her that he would most certainly be free if he had anything to say about it, and sooner rather than later, but he didn't. The less she knew, the safer she would be. Sunny waited for him to put on his shoes and jacket, then put his tie around his neck and knotted it loosely for him. She smiled, then her smile faltered.

"I don't know what to do next."

"Say, 'I'll see you in the morning for a delightful breakfast,

Cam,' tell me you love me, then push me out the door," he said, without thinking.

Then he realized what he'd said.

So, apparently, did she.

Her eyes filled with tears. He groaned and reached out to pull her against him.

"You said you wouldn't weep anymore."

"Then stop blindsiding me with those sorts of things," she managed.

He held her close for several moments, then pulled back, took her face in his hands, and kissed her softly. "I love you," he said, looking into her very green eyes. "I'll see you tomorrow."

She nodded, tears streaming down her face. He ran his hand over her hair, kissed her again because he couldn't help himself, then opened the door and stepped out into the hallway.

"Cam?"

He turned just outside her threshold. "Aye?"

"I'll see you for breakfast." She paused. "And I love you."

He had to blink a time or two before he could see her. "Thank you, Sunshine."

She nodded, smiled tremulously, then shut the door.

He waited until he'd heard her bolt the door, then he took a deep, cleansing breath and walked down the hallway. There were things he needed to put in place first thing in the morning, and yet others to give thought to. In the world outside Sunshine Phillips's door, nothing had changed.

But he had. He wasn't sure how it had happened, but he felt more himself than he had in eight years. It had begun that morning at Ian MacLeod's, when he'd held a broadsword in his hands. It had finished a moment ago when he'd held the woman he loved in his arms, the woman who knew his most intimate secrets, and heard her say that she loved him in return.

He pointedly ignored the thrill of unease that ran through him. He'd had much to lose before, but his heart would have remained intact. If something happened to Sunny, it would finish him as nothing else would have. He wished quite acutely that he was fighting something he could have settled with a sword.

But since he wasn't, he would make do. He and Sunny would make do.

And hope it would be enough.

Chapter 25

Sunny woke to the sound of bagpipes.

She thought for a moment that she'd fallen through a dodgy patch back to the Middle Ages, then she realized she was lying in bed in an horrendously expensive suite being paid for by a man who had wept over her the night before, and it was just her cell phone singing to her. She peered at the numbers on the clock, then groped for her phone and answered it.

"Do you have any idea what time it is?" she said sleepily.

"'Tis seven o'clock, Sunshine. Half the day is gone."

"Didn't you just leave a few minutes ago?"

He laughed. "I think so, but come let me in anyway. And hurry, before they throw me out for picking your lock."

She wasn't about to ask any questions about things she didn't think she would want to know. She hung up on him, borrowed the Ritz's robe to put over her nightgown, then stumbled out into the sitting room and over to the door. She opened it and looked at a disgustingly perky Cameron mac Cameron.

"Restrain your enthusiasm, please," she grumbled.

He kissed the end of her nose, then bounced into her suite. "Breakfast?"

"At this hour?" she asked incredulously.

He shut the door, then picked her up off her feet and swung her around. He let her slide back to the ground and held her tightly.

"Thank you," he whispered intensely. "Thank you for staying."

She only had to blink a couple of times to stop her eyes from burning. She steadfastly refused to think about anything but the fact that the man she loved was holding on to her as if he never wanted to let her go. He loved her. It was enough.

She smiled up at him as she pulled out of his embrace. "Thank you for wanting me to stay. Now, go order the saturated fat that you've probably been dreaming about all night and let me go to the bathroom."

He walked over to the phone. "What would you like?"

She smiled on her way to her bedroom. "Just you. But I'll settle for juice."

"I'll get you juice and work on the other."

She nodded, consciously chose not to think about when that other might happen, then retreated to the bathroom to at least brush her teeth. There was no hope for the rest of her, so she settled for dragging her fingers through her hair before she walked back out toward the living room. She had to stop in the doorway of her bedroom and just admire the view.

Cameron was dressed in a beautiful dark gray suit, with a crisp white shirt and patterned tie. He had taken off his shoes and his suit coat and was reading a newspaper spread out on her coffee table while chatting on his phone about some sort of business that seemed to please him. She watched him for quite a while and felt something in her heart give way. He was so much as he had been before. Intense. Restless. Full of good humor.

And watching her as he continued a conversation that she couldn't hear anymore.

He smiled.

She smiled back, because she couldn't help herself. She could hardly believe where she was or whom she was with. She couldn't believe what she'd willing volunteered for either, but perhaps that was something better left for contemplating in the middle of the night when she could cry if she needed to. Cameron had been willing to give up peace, comfort, and safety to brave the journey to the future with her. Surely she could give up a little bit of her own comfort and pride to be his refuge while he dealt with whatever he was facing.

Especially given that she was in part responsible for his finding himself with a life he hadn't asked for.

He rose and held out his hand. She crossed over to him and let him pull her against him. She closed her eyes and rested her head against his shoulder as he finished his conversation, then hung up. He tossed his phone onto the couch, then put his arms around her.

"I missed you."

"You were just here."

"I wish I'd never left," he said honestly. "But since I had to, I wanted to return early to satisfy my heart—and to catch you still warm from sleep without your hair combed."

"You've seen me without my hair combed before. And quite recently, if memory serves."

"Aye, but I didn't dare hold you then," he said seriously. "And I wouldn't have dared kiss you."

"You probably don't dare now, either, since that's your breakfast at the door."

"Is there no DO NOT DISTURB sign anywhere in this place?" he asked with a half laugh.

"It could be worse; it could be people with swords."

"The saints preserve us, love," he said with a shiver. "I'll take breakfast any day over that, I daresay."

She sat down on the couch and watched him as he retrieved his breakfast from the porter and brought it back over to set it on the coffee table. He sat down, then looked at her.

"Will you mind if I eat? I think better when I'm not hungry."

"Of course I don't mind," she said with a smile. "I'll just watch."

"Are you afraid this will ruin your chi?"

"Ruin doesn't quite describe it," she said, waving him on to a breakfast that should have clogged his arteries just by being in the same room with him.

She watched him for a moment or two, then couldn't help but touch. It was like having a treasure she'd dreamed about but never thought to have sitting right next to her. The temptation to make sure it was real was too strong to resist. She rubbed his back for a bit, then reached up and threaded her fingers through his dark hair that was still disreputably long. He shivered, more than once. She understood completely.

Sunny was tempted to ask him how in the world he thought they would survive the limbo they were in but decided there was just no point. He was probably making it up as he went, just as she was.

She sighed silently. She could find ways to keep herself occupied by herself for the foreseeable future. There were worse places to be enjoying an unexpected vacation from life than in a hotel where the suite rate would have bankrupted her in less than a week. If that vacation included the odd hour and unhealthy breakfast shared with an utterly gorgeous man who wasn't quite hers, who was she to argue?

She took a deep breath and put on her best smile. "What are you doing today?" she asked. "A little cattle raiding? A skirmish with a neighboring business?"

"You, my love, have a unique perspective," he said with a smile. "And we don't take over companies; we invest." He paused. "Well, I suppose there might be a little raiding involved now and again."

"Old habits die hard?"

He smiled. "Aye. As far as today goes, when I can drag myself away from you this morning, I'm going to be assaulted by some nutter from Artane Enterprises who wants me to pour money into a group that restores run-down historical buildings. I'll likely spend most of my time keeping his hands out of my company's coffers—without a sword at my disposal."

"That sounds a little like Jamie and the leisure center."

"Aye, it does, though 'tis my own money with Jamie—and he's going to beggar me if I don't get some sort of control over his plans. I think it may be that yoga studio that pushes me hopelessly into the red."

She gaped at him, then realized he was teasing her. "You're not funny."

He smiled. "I just like to watch you scowl at me. As for this business this morning, I thought that perhaps Zachary Smith might like to be involved."

"Zachary doesn't have any money."

"But he does have talent," he said, "and that counts for a great deal. And he has a good eye for old things, which will suit those Artane lads. Perhaps Zachary will persuade them that there are worthwhile structures north of the border as well."

"One could hope," she agreed. "So, what are you doing after you survive that part of your day?"

He didn't answer right away. "I have a social thing," he said finally.

It took her a moment or two to realize what he meant.

"Oh," she managed. She wondered why in the hell she'd thought it wouldn't be all that bad to stay; she realized then just how much she'd underestimated the difficulty. It shouldn't have surprised her, or bothered her, but there was something about sitting with the man on her couch and knowing that he would be sitting with someone else later that was particularly dreadful. Especially when it was the man she loved.

She didn't like being the other woman.

Patrick didn't like her being that, either. She had talked to Madelyn last night before she'd called Cameron. Madelyn had made all the right comments in all the right places. Patrick on the extension had been stone silent. She had told them she would call them when she was ready to come back to Scotland and assured Madelyn that she was happy.

He'd best be careful with you, had been Patrick's only comment.

She could have sworn she'd heard the sound of him sharpening his sword in the background.

"Sunshine, come here," Cameron said, tugging on her hand.

She let him pull her to her feet, then down onto his lap. She curled her feet up under her robe and put her head on his shoulder.

"I'm all right."

He tipped her face up and looked at her solemnly. "Please trust me."

"Please distract me."

He smiled faintly, then sought her mouth with his. She was fully prepared to have him kiss her socks off, but he didn't. What he did was almost worse.

His kisses were like sunlight on a meadow, sweet, tender. She felt tears well up in her eyes and spill down her cheeks, and she couldn't stop them. She wanted him in her arms, in her heart, in her life every hour of every day until she got him out of her system—in sixty or seventy years.

After all, those Phillips women did live extraordinarily long lives.

She felt his fingers on her cheeks, heard him make a sound of distress low in his throat, then escaped his mouth and put her arms around his neck.

"I can do this," she said, gulping in a fortifying breath. "I'm sorry. It's probably just hormones."

"Sunny, trust me, if the roles were reversed, I would be taking a blade to you by now."

She laughed miserably. "I have more patience than you do."

"Aye, you do." He rubbed her arm in silence for a moment or two, then spoke. "I have a crushing schedule the next fortnight here in London, but things will be easier after that."

She supposed it wouldn't be particularly prudent to point out to him that his schedule was going to lighten up because he was going to be getting ready for his wedding.

"Would you meet me every day?" he asked. "It would have to be very discreet. Maybe out of the way places, or touristy places." He paused. "We might have to arrive in disguise."

"Because you can't be seen with me?" she whispered.

"Because you can't be seen with *me*."

She lifted her head and looked at him in surprise. "Cameron, what *are* you doing?"

"Nothing immoral, illegal, or debauched," he said. He hesitated, then sighed. "Just business with dangerous people, Sunny, and I'll tell you no more than that. That was likely too much." He started to say more, but his phone rang. He reached over to pick it up off the table. "If you don't know what I'm doing, you aren't useful to anyone but me—and I mean that, Sunshine." He looked at the number and smiled briefly. "This, however, may be a step in the right direction. Hang on and let me see."

Sunny started to crawl off his lap, but he tightened his arm around her and shook his head, so she stayed. She put her head down on his shoulder and closed her eyes, taking an unreasonable and probably fairly hazardous amount of pleasure at just being in his arms. It was easier to block out her surroundings when she wasn't looking at them and it was easier to imagine that Cameron was hers alone when she wasn't concentrating on whatever he was discussing on the phone. She simply enjoyed the feel of his arm around her and the fact that—at least for the moment—she had him, hot showers, and no one coming after them with swords.

It could have been much worse.

"I imagine I'm interested in whatever he's had time to come up with," Cameron said. "When can he meet me?" He paused. "Actually, I might be able to come to him. Let me find out."

Sunny watched him put his thumb over the microphone of his cell phone and she lifted her head to look at him. "What?"

"What would you think if we made a quick trip to Paris tomorrow?" he asked. "If we took an early train, we could make the market, then be back before midnight."

She smiled. "Fresh flowers and herbs. Yes, definitely."

He smiled. "I thought you'd approve." He put his phone back to his ear. "Tell him I'd be happy to trudge across the Channel to come to him. Did he give you any hints, or is he saving all the dirt for me?" He laughed. "Of course I'm not going to tell you after the fact and nay, I don't owe you a bloody thing. Aye, and you can bill me double for that. Thanks, Geoff. Cheers."

He hung up, set his phone aside, and wrapped his arms around her. Sunny smiled.

"Your attorney?"

"How could you tell?"

"It sounded expensive."

"Aye, he's damned expensive, but well worth his price." He leaned his back against the couch and looked at her carefully. "He's hired an investigator of sorts to ferret out a few details for me."

"Are you going to let me listen in?"

He hesitated. "I'm thinking about it. At the very least, we can spend the morning somewhere you love. I'll even sniff flowers with you. Who knows but that we might find a treasure or two in some musty old bookshop."

"Shall we go in disguise there as well?" she asked lightly.

"Aye, Sunny," he said quietly. "We should."

She looked into his bright blue eyes, but saw no hint of levity there. Well, whatever the truth might have been, Cameron at least thought it was serious business. She reached up and touched his face. "All right," she said. "Emily and I will find something this morning."

"Emily?" he asked in surprise.

"She's coming shopping with me."

"And when was it she planned on telling me this?" he demanded with mock severity. "After she couldn't be bothered to show up for work?"

"Actually, I think she was just going to call in sick and leave you in the lurch. And we decided yesterday when I was still not particularly interested in making your life easy. I don't imagine I'll spend very much of your money, though. I can't shell out fifty bucks for a dress that I'm not sick to my stomach afterward."

He trailed his fingers through her hair with a half smile on his face. "Sunny, I think you can afford a dress or two without needing a little lie-down after the fact. And I'll happily fetch my own tea if it means you'll have an enjoyable morning. But you'll be cautious, aye?"

"Cameron, it's London."

"Exactly." He paused. "You know, I think I could throw de Piaget out by about two. What would you say to an exhibit of medieval swords at the Victoria and Albert?"

"Perfect," she said. "We'll see if you recognize anything."

He smiled as he slipped his hand under her hair, then leaned forward and kissed her softly. "I'll recognize you, which is the most important thing. And the sooner I go at present, the sooner I'll be able to leave. Though I would rather pass the morning with you, truth be told."

She stood. "You'd better not, or you won't be able to pay for this ridiculously expensive room." She ignored the knowledge that when they left the museum, he would be going off to spend the evening with someone else. Whatever else she might have been, Penelope Ainsworth was at least not his refuge.

That was something.

He collected his phone, chucked his newspaper in the trash can, then put his arm around her shoulders and walked with her to the door. "Please be *careful* this morning."

"I'm an adult, Cam," she said with a dry smile, "I think I can manage a simple shopping trip. Emily will protect me if someone looks feisty."

He started to say something, then shook his head. He simply shot her a meaningful look and slipped out the door. "Meet me at three."

"I'll be there."

He smiled. "Thank you."

"Cameron, you can stop thanking me."

He shook his head. "Can't." He leaned in and kissed her. "I should, however, stop kissing you or I'll come back inside and never leave. I'll see you at three."

She nodded and watched him pull the door shut. She could hear his final *be careful* through the wood. She rolled her eyes and headed for the shower. Too many years in medieval Scotland had obviously made him paranoid—though having lived through a couple of weeks of it, she supposed she could see why. But she was a modern girl who had grown up near a big city. She could handle herself.

Three hours later, as she lay sprawled on the pavement in an innocent-looking side street and listened to someone run off with her purse, she wondered if she should have taken Cameron a little more seriously.

She had met Emily for breakfast, then spent two hours making more of a dent in Cameron's money than she was comfortable with. Emily had suggested a break, which she'd happily agreed to, and they'd chosen the first alley they'd come to to use as a shortcut. It hadn't looked like a likely place to get mugged or she wouldn't have taken it.

She started to crawl back up to her feet, then had help. Hands were on her arms and she was lifted and steadied. She was torn between shaking off those hands and watching another twenty-something guy brush past her and run after the guy running away with her purse.

"What did you lose?" asked the man holding on to her.

Sunny looked blankly at him. He was almost as handsome as Cameron, and that was saying something. He was probably pushing thirty, built like a Highlander, with eyes almost as green as Patrick's, though not nearly as dark. He was dressed in normal business gear, suit and tie, nondescript and unremarkable. The only thing that seemed unusual was the earbud he wore and the cord that disappeared down into his shirt. She frowned.

"There wasn't anything in my purse," she said, "but who are you and why do you care?"

Emily put her arm around Sunny's shoulder. "It's Derrick, one of Cameron's lads. We should let him help us."

Cameron had lads? She remembered thinking that she might be a little uncomfortable with this incarnation of himself. She now realized she was seriously uncomfortable with it. At least in Scotland, all she had to worry about was getting run over by his horse.

What in the *hell* was he doing?

She found herself being helped out of the alley, down the street, and into a chair at a cafe before she could truly give that the consideration it deserved. She looked up at Derrick as he stood at the table, scanning the street in both directions and talking quietly into his cord.

"No, there wasn't anything in it of value to her. Follow him, though, and see where he goes. I'll call Himself."

Sunny found a glass of water in her hands.

"Drink," Emily suggested.

Sunny did, because she thought it might make her a little less nauseated. The familiarity of her situation was hard to take. She had been plunked down again in the middle of something that she hadn't asked for, something that had apparently been going on long before she'd arrived and would probably continue in spite of her presence in its midst. She had honestly wondered, as she'd thought about Cameron's insistence they go to Paris in disguise, if he'd lived one too many years in medieval Scotland and was now having delusions of grandeur in the future where he imagined that there were people so out to get him that he needed to hide them both—and keep her in the dark about his activities.

She suspected she'd just had a big taste of his reality.

She had just finished her tenth silent repeat of *don't run, you're his refuge* when she was distracted by her phone. She answered it absently. "Yes?"

"Are you all right?" Cameron asked tightly.

She was surprised at how comforting just the sound of his voice was. "I'm fine," she said. "Really."

She could hear him blow out his breath. "I want you to go back to the hotel—"

"No," she said firmly. "Cam, I'm sure it was nothing. Just an opportunist."

"I don't like it," he said, sounding as if he didn't like it *at all.* "You'll take Derrick with you for the rest of the morning."

She hesitated. "Do you trust him?" She realized as the words came out of her mouth that she was starting to sound as paranoid as he did.

"He wouldn't be standing five feet from you if I didn't."

She had to have another drink of water. "All right, but we're leaving him outside when we hit the lingerie shops."

Cameron laughed a bit. "Have a little pity on the lad, love. He'll watch over you well. And don't forget we have a date at three."

"I won't."

"Be careful, Sunshine."

"I will be," she said, meaning it this time. "I'll see you later."

"I'll be waiting."

She hung up, let out the breath she'd been holding, then looked up at Derrick. "He wants you to come with us."

He was smiling faintly. "Aye."

"Do you mind?"

"Of course not, especially if I'm left outside any shops where the merchandise might make me blush."

Emily laughed at him. "He's thrilled at the thought of escorting two lovely women everywhere for the rest of the morning—especially if food is involved."

"Too true," he said, sitting down. "Let's eat, ladies. I'm starving."

Sunny looked at her hands and found that several of her nails were ripped and there was gravel embedded in her palms. She could feel the blood dripping down her knees as well. She wondered if it would soak through her jeans or merely slip down her shins and pool in her shoes.

"You know, Sunshine, I have a charge card Cameron pays off every month for me," Emily said, leaning in close. Her eyes twinkled. "Let's hurry and eat, then we'll see what we can do to it, *oui?*"

Sunny nodded. All the stress over spending even more of Cameron's money would be a good distraction.

She curled her fingers into her palms so she wouldn't have to see what had just happened to her.

Four hours later she stood on a Tube platform and waited for her train. She looked up at the clock and suppressed a curse. She was late and she hadn't meant to be. It had taken her longer to repair the damage to her hands than she'd expected.

She got on the train when it came and found herself looking around, just to see if there was someone who might be watching her with evil intent. She didn't find anyone, but she hadn't noticed anyone that morning, either.

Life, she decided firmly, had been much simpler when all she'd had to worry about had been keeping the fire going in Moraig's hearth.

"What do you think of Manchester's chances this year?" said a voice close to her ear.

She looked up with a jerk at the man standing next to her, then realized with a start that it was Derrick. He was wearing a Manchester football jersey, an earring, a moustache, and really dorky glasses. She wouldn't have recognized him if she hadn't known the color of his eyes.

She bowed her head and let out a shuddering breath. The relief that coursed through her was so great, she almost had to sit down. It took a moment or two before she could speak. "I don't think very good," she said in her best working gal's accent. "Not that I follow it much, what?"

His eyes widened briefly, then he grinned at her. "Want to discuss it over a pint, ducks?"

"Sure," she said, because she wasn't sure she wasn't supposed to say that.

Derrick went on about the chances of his favorite football club and Sunny did her best to pay attention. When the train stopped, he put her in front of him and kept his hand on her back as they got off. He slung his arm around her shoulders and walked with her up the stairs.

"Let's take the street instead of the other train to the V and A," he murmured. "Crowds are good."

She ran up the stairs with him and walked quickly down the street. "Do you have an overactive imagination, or something else?"

He only smiled and switched sides with her so he was walking closest to the street. "Three lads against you and me in a relatively deserted Tube station isn't something Cameron would be happy about, so here we are, out in the open. By the way, you're late."

"I know," she said, feeling a little breathless. "Let's run."

He obliged her. Sunny ran with him all the way to the V and A, went inside, then had to lean over and catch her breath. Three lads chasing her? She didn't want to know any more, but she suspected she needed to. She straightened in time to watch Derrick pay for her entrance. He handed her a map.

"You're on your own now, pet," he said with a smile.

"Aren't you coming with me?"

"I imagine Cameron can stretch himself to keep you safe for a bit," he said dryly. "I've work to do outside."

She didn't ask what it was, but she imagined it involved three lads she didn't know. "Well, thank you for getting me here. I've never had a bodyguard before." She paused. "Are you my body-guard?"

"I most certainly am," he said with a grave smile. "Now, be on your way, gel. Himself's paged me five times in the past ten minutes. I'm going to have to answer soon or he'll sack me."

She imagined Cameron wouldn't be firing the man in front of her anytime soon, but she wasn't going to argue. "Don't answer," she said. "I'll hurry."

He nodded, then walked back out the front door. She took a grip on her rampaging imagination, then ran through exhibits and hallways until she found what she was looking for.

Cameron was leaning over a case with his hands clasped behind his back. He was wearing his Highland laird uniform of boots, jeans, and black jacket. He straightened, looked at the enormous silver watch on his wrist, then sighed.

She pulled her phone out of her pocket and dialed his. She saw him reach for his immediately, then start in surprise when he looked at the number. Obviously, he wasn't expecting it to be her.

"Where are you?" he asked without preamble.

"Lusting after you from about twenty feet away."

He turned in surprise. The relief on his face was actually quite difficult to watch. He stifled it quickly enough, though, then jammed his hands and his phone in his pockets and walked over to her.

"You're late."

"I was picking gravel out of my hands."

He took her hands in his and turned them over. He closed his eyes briefly, then pulled her into his arms. Sunny put her arms around his waist under his jacket and held on tightly. Her teeth chattered and she thought she might just burst into tears. Catching her breath was a lost cause. All she could do was hold on to him and shake.

"I should have put you on that plane to Seattle myself," he said grimly.

"You don't mean that."

"I think it would have been safer for you," he said, "but I fear 'tis too late now. I was a damned fool to take you out on the bus, apparently, and even stupider for allowing you to go out with Emily."

"I didn't give you much choice about the second."

He grunted. "You've forgotten the extent of my powers of persuasion, obviously." He sighed and rested his forehead against hers. "I'll find us somewhere safe for the rest of the day so you'll have the chance to let me remind you about them."

"Don't you have a date tonight?"

He shot her a dark look. "I have dates—if we're not past that—with you. I have social obligations elsewhere. Tonight I have something that I will get out of as quickly as possible. Then we'll go hide for the rest of the day." He drew her over to a corner and pulled his phone out of his pocket.

She listened to him inform Penelope that something had come up and he wouldn't be in Windsor that night. It wasn't difficult to gauge Penelope's reaction. She probably could have heard it from across the room. Cameron's patience was admirable, which she told him after he hung up and stuck his finger gingerly in his ear.

"Two more," he said, then made a quick call to invite them

both to someone's house for dinner and a cozy evening in the den. He called Derrick, told him they were on their way, then hung up and put his phone back in his pocket. "Let's be off. We'll try the back door."

"Will they let us out the back door?"

"I imagine they will, when I make a sudden and quite substantial contribution to a museum guard's pocket."

"Do you bribe guards often?"

He started to answer, then looked at her and laughed. "Sunny, I find myself doing quite a few things in your company that I don't normally do—and nay, I've never bribed a guard before. We'll see if it works."

She found as they were led to and shown out a door she wasn't sure was used very often that it worked quite well. She stood in the shadows of that door for a handful of minutes before Cameron pulled her across the sidewalk and over to a sleek black Mercedes that merely slowed down on the street in front of them. Sunny jumped into the moving car when Cameron opened the door, hoping he would follow her and she wouldn't find herself driven off to somewhere she wouldn't like.

She began to understand why Cameron looked over his shoulder so much.

"Yours?" she asked as he pulled the door shut and the car continued on.

"Aye." He nodded to the man driving. "That's Rufus. Rufus, this is Sunshine."

"Aye, she most certainly is, my lord," Rufus said, looking at her with a smile in the rearview mirror. "Where to?"

"Geoff Segrave's, if you please. His home, not his office."

Sunny looked at Cameron. "This feels unpleasantly familiar somehow," she managed in Gaelic. "All this business of people running around trying to kill you."

"Only the scenery has changed," he agreed.

"You don't have a sword."

"Nay, but I do have a fairly sharp pocketknife."

She smiled at his dry tone, then jumped when the front passenger door opened at the next stoplight and a dark-haired man hopped in. The doors were summarily locked and he turned around. The glasses and moustache were gone. Derrick smiled at her, then looked at Cameron and his smile turned grim.

"Three on the Tube. Oliver's still on the lead lad. The second was waiting for me when I went back outside, but he dashed into a car. I'll track the plate number if you'll hand me my laptop. Number three is gone, but I recognized him. Peter's behind us, watching who's watching us."

Cameron pulled a very small laptop out from under the driver's seat and handed it to Derrick, who turned it on and bent over it.

Sunny felt a little faint. Cameron took her hand and looked at her.

"Surviving?" he asked quietly.

"I'm beginning to think you have terrible secrets."

"Terrible, but not endless." He paused. "Thank you for the refuge, Sunny."

"I think you're providing one for me just as often."

He shot her a smile, then turned her hand over and simply traced the parts of her palm that were still intact.

She forced herself to breathe normally. She didn't run, not anymore. After all, it couldn't be any worse than medieval Scotland, could it?

She wasn't sure she wanted the answer to that.

Chapter 26

Cameron stood on a platform at Waterloo and looked at his watch. The train was pulling out in twenty minutes and he still hadn't seen Sunny. It couldn't have been because she'd gotten lost. Derrick's task had been to be fifteen feet away from her at all times and get her safely and anonymously to the station. He would have called if something had gone awry. Cameron hadn't wanted to leave her at the hotel the night before, but sleeping on her couch hadn't seemed wise. If nothing else, he had to keep up the appearance of his normal routine.

He hoped it was worth the trouble.

Perhaps Sunny was late because she was weary. They'd been at the Segraves' well into the wee hours. He hadn't intended to stay so long, but Sunny and Virginia had taken an immediate liking to each other and he'd had the very great pleasure of spending an evening with people he enjoyed. The temptation to linger had been irresistible.

But now he was where he was and Sunny was late, which led him to speculate on all sorts of things he shouldn't. Perhaps it was just his own discomfort that troubled him, discomfort that had everything to do with the disguise Emily had left for him at his hotel. Obviously, giving her free rein with his wardrobe had been a grave tactical error.

He was dressed in head-to-toe black with what of his hair he could get behind his head in a ponytail. If he hadn't had sunglasses to hide behind, he would have been drawing attention to himself with a string of vile curses. At least he had a change of clothes in his backpack.

"Sexy," purred a blond, artistic-looking lad who walked past him and winked.

Cameron blinked, then cursed. Derrick's chameleon-like abilities were nothing short of unsettling at times. "Where is Sunny?" he demanded.

Derrick only smiled blandly and continued on. "Behind me."

Cameron looked at the long line of people walking his way

and couldn't see her. He saw a few older couples, several families, a very handsome redhead, and a jaw-droppingly beautiful brunette with legs that went on forever. He wasn't one to look where he shouldn't, but he had to admit that that last lass was certainly worth admiring—

He felt his mouth fall open.

It was Sunny.

She caught sight of him and stumbled. Cameron would have leaped forward to catch her, but he couldn't move. All he could do was stand there and gape until she stopped a foot away from him.

"You're going to catch flies in there if you're not careful," she said solemnly.

"Bloody hell," he wheezed.

She smiled. "Am I late?"

"I don't know," he managed. He'd never seen her with her hair straight. He reached out and smoothed his hand down it before he could stop himself. "How'd you do that?"

"I ironed it." She leaned in close. "I'm in disguise." She tried to tug her black miniskirt down, but it was hopeless. "Too much?"

"Too little—of the skirt, that is." He took a deep breath. "I think I might have to find a place to sit down soon."

"Derrick said I looked hot. What do you think?"

He scowled at her. "I think I'm going to put his eyes out at my earliest opportunity." He looked at her mouth. "Will I spoil that fiery red lipstick of yours if I kiss you senseless right here and now?"

She smiled at him. "You don't dare."

"I most certainly will dare—after you go to the loo and I find the rest of that rot in your purse and throw it out the window."

"You sound like yourself today," she said with another smile.

He took her backpack from her, then put his hands on her shoulders and turned her toward the train door. "Don't I usually sound like myself?"

"Now and again."

He put his arm around her waist and pulled her back against him. "Sunny, my love," he whispered in her ear, "if my medieval lairdly self had seen you in a skirt that short, I would have thought you a demon and immediately tossed you in my dungeon."

She put her hand over his. "And then?"

"I would have locked myself in there with you. I'll leave the rest to your imagination. Now, move it, wench, before I spend the entire train journey thinking about where in Paris I might find a place to serve the same purpose."

She smiled at him over her shoulder and walked ahead of him. He put his hand on the small of her back as they entered the train, glared at every man who looked her over from foot to head—for that was the direction every male on the train with a pulse seemed to take—and finally managed to get her into her seat without doing any damage to anyone.

He found, unsurprisingly, that they were facing an older British couple who looked at Sunny's skirt—or lack thereof—with horror. He stowed his and Sunny's gear in the racks, then eased himself down next to her only to face even more intense looks of disapproval.

The ponytail obviously had to go.

He pulled it out, raked his fingers through his hair, then decided that ignoring the couple facing him was the best thing he could do. He turned to Sunny.

"All right," he said quietly in French, "I think I might manage coherent conversation now. What took you so long?"

"Apart from the fact that Derrick snuck me out through the kitchen like I was a celebrity escaping the press, I'm just not very good at high heels," she admitted. "I asked Derrick to page you, but he thought you should just stress a bit longer."

"One day he will go too far."

"He said you'd say that."

He muttered a curse under his breath, then sighed as he caught another disapproving glance from their unwanted chaperons. "I had intended to kiss you all the way to France, but I can see that's out."

"I have an idea, if you would get me my purse. I don't think I dare stand up again in this skirt."

He pulled her purse down for her, waited until she'd found what she wanted, then put it back for her. He sat to find her watching him with a small, affectionate smile.

"What?" he asked, smiling in return.

"I'm just happy to be with you," she said, looking happy indeed. She hesitated. "Are we safely anonymous?"

"Derrick would have paged me by now were we otherwise."

"Then we can speak freely, or is French not discreet enough? Should we choose something else?"

He was extraordinarily glad for all the trouble he'd taken to learn more than just modern English. "Spoken like the daughter of linguists. French will suit, I think, because I like to listen to you speak it. We'll dabble in other things later, if you like."

"I might." She tore up strips of paper, then handed him half the stack. "Let's write down a few get-to-know-you questions. You can consider them questions for the you that wears suits." She paused. "I'm not sure I know much about your favorite things, in either lifetime."

"You're my favorite thing," he said seriously.

She closed her eyes briefly, then wrote something down and slid it his way.

I love you. Now stop the mushy stuff before I cry and ruin my mascara.

He smiled, then waited until she'd finished with her pen before he wrote down his own set of questions. He supposed he couldn't be blamed if they were evenly divided between where her favorite darkened corners were in Paris so he could pull her into them and kiss her, and what sorts of things she liked well enough about Scotland to want to remain there with him for the rest of her life.

Subtlety was not, he supposed, his strong suit.

He considered the direction of his questions for a moment. They certainly weren't leading to London, but the truth was a good part of his life was there. He fiddled with the pen for a minute, then looked at her. "I want you to tell me about that finishing school first," he said slowly. He paused. "And what you think of all this society rubbish."

She blinked. "Why?"

He considered. He'd actually planned to give her what was in his pocket in a more romantic setting, but perhaps there was no point in waiting. He wasn't sure the time was right, but it had bothered him that she'd looked at such loose ends the morning before. He wanted her to know where his heart was—even if he couldn't give her the details. He dug about in his pocket, then set a ring down on the table in front of him. He studied it for a moment or two, hoping he wasn't going about what he wanted in a way that was complete bollocks. He'd sent Gideon de Piaget into fits the day before by forcing him to wait an hour whilst he'd had the ring in question made over in a size that Madelyn had guaranteed would fit Sunny's right hand.

He put his finger on the ring, then slid it along the table, past Sunny's questions and his. He left it sitting in front of her.

"I want to know because I don't want you to agree to something you would loathe," he said quietly. "Whether I want it to be so or not, a goodly part of my life is spent as the face of my company. Not necessarily always in London, but unfortunately always in the public eye." He paused. "I want to know if it's something you can endure."

She sat very still, simply looking at the ring in front of her for far longer than he was comfortable with. He forced himself not to think about all the ways she could be deciding that his modern life was not to her taste.

She finally took a deep breath. "I learned to greet foreign dignitaries from twenty different countries in their own languages," she said. "I can name for you ten generations of all the royal houses of Europe and get all English titles correct on the first try. In my spare time, I learned all the useful plants that grew in the foothills near the campus." She looked at him then. "I think I could find lobelia just about anywhere, though I didn't learn that in Switzerland, necessarily."

He bowed his head for a moment, then he shot her a look from under his eyelashes. "You are a truly remarkable woman, Sunshine Phillips."

"And that's a truly remarkable ring, my laird."

He couldn't smile. "'Tis a wait-for-me ring, Sunny. I can't offer you anything else." He paused. "I would understand if you didn't want it."

She picked it up and looked at it. He had to admit it was a lovely ring, with diamonds that went all the way around it. He'd had it engraved on the inside, in Gaelic, so she wouldn't forget what was in his heart.

To Sunshine, the light of my life, I love you, Cam.

He watched her read the inscription and watched a single tear run down her cheeks. She wiped it away, then handed him the ring.

"I'll take it and wait, then."

It was with a profound sense of relief that he put the ring on her right hand, knowing he owed Madelyn MacLeod a very large bouquet of flowers. He leaned over and kissed Sunny on the cheek.

"Lose the lipstick," he suggested.

"Meet me in the loo."

"We'd never get out of it," he said with a smile.

"Probably not." She stared at her ring for quite a while before she looked back at him. "It is the most beautiful thing I've ever seen."

"You look at it, then, whilst I look at you, and we'll share that thought." He took her hands carefully in his, avoiding the scrapes that still weren't healed, then smiled. "Now, if you please, distract me with tales of Switzerland before I get myself in trouble in the loo. How did you find yourself there?"

She smiled, looking grateful for the distraction. "My parents had gotten teaching exchanges in Russia and didn't want us going to school back in the States unsupervised—even though I was almost seventeen and Madelyn just a year behind me in school—so off to Switzerland we went. My grandmother paid for it, but we were still definitely the bottom of the food chain when it came to family income."

"That couldn't have been pleasant."

She shrugged. "We survived. Well, I survived. Madelyn had a harder time. She refers to it as the Dark Alpine Period, if she'll even acknowledge she was there. Most of the time when I bring it up, she just takes a deep breath and walks away. I imagine Patrick didn't even know about it until after they were married."

"Why ever not?" he asked in surprise.

"Because she thought it was frivolous and wouldn't look good on her résumé. She'd always threatened to claim on her law school applications that she'd been homeschooled that year."

He ran his thumb over her ring for a bit, then looked at her. "And those things you learned? The society bit?"

"Never thought it would do me any good," she said with a half smile, "but I don't think I can think about it anymore without crying." She pushed a strip of paper his way. "Let's talk about something else."

He agreed without protest. By the time they reached Paris, he had learned that Sunny loved blue but not orange, the magical tingle of twilight but not the unrelenting heat of noon, bare feet instead of shoes, and Gaelic over German. He'd told her that his favorite color was also blue, his favorite place was home, and that his favorite thing to do was go through the purses of beautiful women he loved who wore skirts that were too short and throw out their lipsticks.

She'd laughed and promised to visit the loo in the station so he could be about it.

He wondered during that pair of hours if what he felt for her was something new, or an echo of loving her before. He came to no useful conclusion. All he knew was that he loved her not because he had loved her in a different life, but because she was light and laughter and the easing of his heart. He could scarce believe he'd survived all those years without her.

He prayed he wouldn't have to much longer.

It was early evening by the time he stood with Sunny just outside Alexander Smith's hotel room. It had been a perfect day spent rummaging through market stalls and hunting in out-of-the-way antique stores. Sunny had changed her skirt and shoes, he'd put on jeans he could breathe in, and he'd kissed her as often as he could behind obliging sellers of fruit and flowers.

He looked at her. "I love you."

She put her arms around him and hugged him tightly. "I love you, too." She sank back down on her heels and smiled. "All right, now that we're standing outside his door are you going to tell me whom we're meeting with?"

He clasped his hands behind her back. "He's an attorney, Alexander Smith. I had the misfortune of trying to fight him off in Manhattan several years ago, but I've managed to avoid him ever since. Geoffrey was the one who took his life in his hands to set this meeting up. I understand Alexander has given up his corporate raiding in the States to spend his time terrorizing poor, hapless Brits over here." He realized that she was looking at him in astonishment. "Have you heard of him?" he asked.

She didn't have a chance to answer because the door opened suddenly and the pirate himself stood there, dressed professionally in ratty jeans and a T-shirt that proudly proclaimed that *The Countess is in Charge*. He was missing his shoes and looked as if he'd just woken up from a nap.

"Hey, Sunny," he said with a yawn. "Slumming today?"

She disentangled herself from Cameron's arms. "Shut up, Alex," she said, leaning up to kiss his cheek. "Where's Margaret?"

"Trying to get the kids to bed. Go help, if you dare. Baldric's reading them the *Canterbury Tales* in the appropriate vernacular, but they're not impressed. Amery keeps bellowing for his Game Boy."

Sunny only laughed and walked off as if she hadn't a care in the world. "I'll see what I can do," she threw over her shoulder.

Cameron looked at Alexander in surprise. "You know Sunny?"

Alexander stepped back away from the door. "I'd be a lousy know-it-all if I didn't know it all, wouldn't I? Now, why don't you come right on in, my lord, and let's have a little chat."

Cameron walked into the room and felt more uncomfortable than he should have at the sound of Alexander Smith shutting the door behind him. The man scowled at him, then jammed his hands into his pockets in a gesture that was so reminiscent of Zachary Smith, Cameron had to do a double take. He realized only then that he'd obviously missed a very vital connection.

"You're Zachary's brother," he stated, dumbfounded. "And Elizabeth's as well, then."

"Boy, nothing gets by you, does it?" Alexander said with a smirk. He held out his hand and clasped Cameron's with a grip that was uncomfortably firm. "Now, before I deck you why don't you tell me why the hell you were mauling my sister-in-law out there in the hallway?"

Cameron pried his fingers from Alexander's because he thought he might stand a better chance of protecting himself that way. Damn it, when was he going to stop running into MacLeods, and half MacLeods, and MacLeods by association—all of whom seemed to think he had less than honorable intentions where Sunny was concerned?

"I don't suppose," he said slowly, "that it will serve me to point out that I'm paying you to pry into something besides my private life, will it?"

"Not when you're snogging with my sister-in-law while you're still engaged to Penelope Ainsworth it won't," Alexander said sharply. "Or has something changed in the past five minutes?"

"Nay, nothing has changed," Cameron said evenly, "but that's why I'm paying you all that bloody sterling, isn't it? So things *will* change."

Alexander folded his arms over his chest. "I suppose I should be curious how you can go from not knowing Sunny, all the way to really needing a good deal of privacy—which you'd damn well better not be looking for, by the way—in such a short time."

Cameron resigned himself to a rather long evening. "'Tis complicated—"

"Aye, it is, isn't it, my laird," Alexander growled in Gaelic, "when you arrive in the future with your head half bashed in and a dirk sticking out of your back."

Cameron gasped. He didn't mean to, but he couldn't help himself. "How—" he spluttered.

"Isn't that why you're paying my ridiculous fee?" Alexander continued on in Gaelic that Cameron would have bet his favorite horse Alexander hadn't polished so thoroughly in the current century. "To ferret out details your enemies don't want you to know so you can use them against them ruthlessly? Why in the hell do you think I wouldn't do the same in regard to *you*?"

Cameron would have answered, but he was saved by Sunny coming out of one of the bedrooms with a woman Cameron could only assume was the Countess of Falconberg. She was a lovely woman, obviously several months into a pregnancy and glowing because of it. She crossed over to her husband and pulled him away.

"Put away your blade, my love, and have pity on the poor man," she said. She reached out and took Cameron's hand in a grip that rivaled her husband's. "Lord Robert."

"Lady Margaret," he said with a smile. "What a pleasure."

Alexander wasn't smiling. Cameron felt Sunny put her arms around his waist, which certainly didn't improve things any. Alexander's expression darkened considerably.

"I don't imagine you stopped to think you could have solved this all before you dragged Sunny into the middle of it, did you?" Alexander demanded.

"Actually, he did think about it," Sunny said placidly. "He thought about it so much that he was willing to let me fly home day before yesterday. I'm the one who decided to stay."

"He should have had the backbone to strap you in your seat himself," Alexander said shortly. "It isn't safe for you to be anywhere near him, or couldn't he be bothered to tell you that, either?"

"Alex," Margaret began with a sigh.

"They're fair questions," Alexander said, still wearing a formidable frown. "He can answer them—if he has the guts to."

Cameron knew it wouldn't serve him to brawl with the man in his own living room, but he was damned tempted. He glared at Alexander. "The timing of this was not my choice, which I'm sure you know," he said slowly. "Now, why don't you consider the exorbitant sum I'm paying you to help me end my current troubles so I might wed your sister-in-law quickly and keep her safe?"

Alexander Smith told him quite descriptively what he could do with his money.

Cameron might have laughed, but he suspected Alexander was perfectly serious. Then he realized something else: Sunny had gone very still. He wondered about it, then realized with a start what he'd said. He had to force himself not to shift uncomfortably. He was actually rather grateful Sunny didn't have a blade to hand and he seriously hoped she wouldn't be able to get his out of his pocket before he could stop her.

"Sunny—" he began slowly.

"You said two days ago that you were going to marry Penelope!"

"Aye, I did say that," he began gingerly. He took a deep breath, then looked at her. "I hedged."

"And you couldn't have been *bothered* to tell me about that hedging before now?" she demanded. "You couldn't have dug deep for some sort of hint in that direction before you put me through *hell*?"

He would have tried to come up with something useful to say, but he imagined he wasn't going to have the luxury of enough time for that. Sunny looked as if she were torn between wanting to kill him and wanting to burst into tears.

"This should be interesting," Alexander said helpfully.

Cameron shot Alexander a glare, then turned a brief smile on Margaret. "Excuse us, my lady."

Margaret waved him away. "By all means. Take all the time you need."

"Which will no doubt be quite a bit," Alexander added with a snort.

Cameron suspected Alexander might have that aright. He took Sunny by the hand and hauled her over and through the first open doorway he saw. It was the loo, but he didn't care. He turned on the light, shut the door with his foot, then pulled Sunny into his arms before she could hit him.

"Damn you, Robert Francis," she gasped, her voice muffled against his shoulder. "Damn you to hell and back."

He closed his eyes briefly. "Sunny, I *couldn't* tell you."

She took a deep breath, then she burst into tears. He decided that he was through being the reason for it unless they were tears of joy. He held her close, soothed her as best he could, then waited for her to get hold of herself.

It took quite a while.

She finally dragged her sleeve across her eyes, then pulled his head down and kissed him.

She kissed him until he thought that perhaps she should stop. But when she started to pull away, he stopped her. He returned the favor so thoroughly that he thought he might have to remain in the bathroom quite a bit longer than he'd anticipated simply to recover from it. He tore his mouth away from hers finally, then clutched her to him and buried his face in her hair.

"I was trying to keep you safe."

"Damn you to hell," she croaked. "Or did I already say that?"

"Trust me, Sunshine, I've been there," he said, with feeling. "Every moment of every day for the past month when I couldn't have you in my arms."

"I don't suppose I want to know when you came to this decision, do I?"

"That I couldn't live without you, or that I wanted to wed you?"

"Either," she said. "Both."

"I knew I couldn't live without you from the moment I first saw you in Jamie's hall," he said, sighing deeply. "I knew I had to wed you—or at least try to convince you that you might want to wed *me*—the morning you rode back with me to my hall."

She pulled away and looked up at him in shock. "You decided *then*? And you couldn't tell me until *now*?"

He reached for a towel and dried her cheeks, then his own. "Didn't I tell you it was killing me to leave you?"

"I didn't think you meant *this*."

He took her face in his hands and kissed her softly. "What else could I have meant, my love?"

Her eyes filled with tears again. "I didn't dare hope for anything, actually."

He managed a smile, but it felt a poor one indeed. "I think, my lady, that I asked you to wed with me in another time, didn't I?"

"You don't remember that pseudo-proposal."

He smiled. "My head doesn't remember, but my heart always has."

She sighed deeply, then looked up at him. "Is it all this serious, Cam? As serious as Alex is making it out to be?"

He took her hands in his and turned them over. "Proof enough?"

"This was a fluke."

He shook his head slowly. "It wasn't, my love." He kissed her palms gently, then put his arms around her again. "Let's go see what he has for us. I'll add anything he hasn't discovered on his own, then you'll have the entire sordid tale laid out for you." He paused. "Just know, Sunshine, that I didn't keep silent because I didn't trust you, or because I was being perverse. I thought that if you didn't know anything, you wouldn't be attractive to anyone who might want to strike out at me." He paused again. "I was trying to protect you."

"You and your medieval sensibilities."

He smiled. "Aye."

She pursed her lips. "I wish I had a good secret to keep from you."

"You'll think of something. I'm sure it will involve lobelia." He looked at her hopefully. "A penance?"

She looked up at him seriously. "I'll think about it."

"And you'll wed me?"

"Is that a proposal?"

"Not offered here in the loo."

She leaned up and kissed him softly. "Then ask me later. I'll think about that as well."

He gathered her close, was rather grateful he felt nothing sharp going into his belly, then released her and turned her toward the door. "Let's go, before they think you've done damage to me."

She smiled at him as they left the loo, that same hesitant smile she'd given him that morning they'd walked to Patrick's. Only this time, he was much closer to being able to enjoy it legitimately.

It was progress.

He sat down next to her on the couch and looked at Alexander. "My apologies. Business, now?"

Alexander apparently thought Cameron had gotten what he'd

deserved, because his antagonism had disappeared. He actually smiled. "Whisky first, to help you recover?"

"I would love one, but I'll regret it and I need a clear head." He took a deep breath and reached for Sunny's hand. "Shall I take notes?"

"I'm a high-class operation," Alexander said with hardly a hint of a smirk. "I typed you up a few things on my Selectric."

Cameron looked at Margaret as Alexander went off to dig up his papers. "How do you put up with him?"

She shrugged. "We meet in the lists every other day or so. I put him in his place and we carry on."

He felt his mouth fall open. "The lists?"

Margaret smiled blandly at him, then began a discussion with Sunny about the advantages of settling differences thus. He looked at the Countess of Falconberg, dressed as she was in jeans and a T-shirt, and somehow still suspected there might be more to her than met the eye.

He leaned back against the couch and hoped that, considering what Alexander likely had to tell him, Margaret's birthdate would be the only thing to surprise him that night.

Chapter 27

Sunny looked down at the square diamonds that sparkled all the way around her finger. She wondered when Cameron had found her ring and what had possessed him to have it inscribed in a way that would leave her in tears every time she looked at it. It was truly exquisite, made all the more precious by the man who had given it to her.

Never mind that she was tempted to kill him.

She sighed, pulled her feet up onto the couch with her, and leaned against its back. No, she didn't really want to kill him. All she had to do was grab something too quickly or kneel down unthinkingly to have her hands and knees remind her that there were people gunning for Cameron who didn't mind who else they hurt in the process. Cameron had been trying to keep her safe and keep her close at the same time. She couldn't blame him for not being able to balance it perfectly.

She would have preferred to think he was overreacting, but she couldn't. If her hands and knees hadn't convinced her, the way Alex was practically salivating over the details he was spewing out would have.

She watched Alex's eyes twinkle as he divulged what was no doubt some salacious bit of something that he shouldn't have known. She liked him very much, partly because he was Zachary and Elizabeth's brother and partly because he loved his wife and was kind to his children. He was also ruthlessly intelligent and insatiably curious. She wondered, sometimes, if he knew when to turn all that off. Margaret seemed to survive it well enough, but Sunny imagined she hid the batteries to his laptop on a regular basis. Sunny loved him like a brother, but she couldn't have lived with him.

Cameron, though, was another story entirely. She made herself more comfortable and allowed herself the pleasure of looking at him. She couldn't say she was past the point of being a little startled by his beauty, but she now saw other things. She saw the hint of lines at the corners of his eyes, as if he'd been smiling a great deal or—more likely—walking over his land and squinting up into the occasional burst of sun. She could tell when something surprised him by the faint lifting of an eyebrow. She knew the complete absence of expression when he was digesting, or the way half of his mouth quirked up when he was either skeptical or amused in spite of himself.

She loved his laugh, his quick smile, his wry sense of humor. She could hardly believe that she might actually have what her heart had longed for so desperately for the past few weeks. She supposed she should have known what he was getting at when he'd asked her how she felt about London society, but as she had said to him in the bathroom, she just hadn't dared hope.

"Sunny?"

She realized he was looking at her. She smiled. "Forgiven."

He looked rather relieved. "No penance?"

"Well, I'm still thinking about that."

He smiled, reached up to tuck a bit of her hair behind her ear, then looked back at Alex. "Where were we?"

"Well, you and I were chatting. I'm not sure where Sunny was." He shot her a look. "Didn't you make out with him in the bathroom long enough already, or do you need to go back in for round two?"

Sunny threw a couch pillow at him. "You are an odious man."

Alex only laughed at her, then looked at Cameron. "She might be useful to you if she could just concentrate on something besides lusting after you."

Sunny smiled in spite of herself. "All right, I'll stop. What did I miss?"

"Just chitchat," Alex said. "I was unbending enough to tell your friend there that his little medieval secret is safe with me. I don't think I would have thought anything of him—given how polished and domesticated he is—if I hadn't endured my own share of time with a few medieval members of my household."

"Careful, husband," Margaret said, slipping her bare foot in between his. "Endured, indeed."

"And domesticated, my arse," Cameron groused. He looked at Margaret. "I'm almost a feared to ask about the tale I sense here."

"'Tis a very lovely one, actually," Margaret agreed. "Alex walked through a fairy ring near Jamie's keep and found himself in 1194—"

"Chained to your bed," Alex interrupted with a lazy smile

thrown his wife's way. He looked at Cameron. "She fell in love with me on the spot, of course—ouch, Meg," he said, wincing at Margaret's tug on his hair. "All right, the truth is I fell in love with Margaret right off, but I had to do some pretty fast talking to get her to return the favor. I won the right to marry her in one of King Richard's tournaments and it's been nothing but bliss ever since."

"Aye, it has," Margaret said, leaning over to kiss Alex briefly. "But I don't think there is bliss in the other chamber. I hear the cries of teenagers who believe they've been put to bed too early. I'll go see to it."

Alex watched her go, then turned back to Cameron. "So now you see that it wasn't really my superior investigating skills that led me to suspect you; it was recognizing the signs. Of course, you've been the topic of discussion over ale in front of Jamie's fire more often than you'd probably be comfortable with."

Cameron cleared his throat. "Indeed. And here I thought I was being so subtle."

Alex smiled. "You have been, actually, though you may want to see about making a little clandestine adjustment to the parish records in the village. I suppose you might also be interested in knowing that one of the reasons Jamie wanted to do the leisure center was he determined, as he does you know, that you'd been up at Cameron Hall for too many years without any brothers. He thought if he offered you a bit of business, you might come down off your mountain without your sword in your hand and join in our familial madness."

Sunny felt Cameron feel for her hand. She looked at him, saw the complete and utter lack of expression on his face and suspected she knew what he was thinking. All those years he'd been up there on his own, probably believing he was the only one living his particular experience, and all the time there had been men down the way who could have at least talked to him about it. She leaned close.

"A little visit to the bathroom?" she whispered.

He took a very deep breath. "Any more visits, and Alexander will start charging us rent." He released her hand, dug the heels of his hands into his eyes, then shook his head and looked at Alex. "Thank you," he said simply.

"You're welcome. I suppose I should also add that Jamie pushed you to meet with him about that same business when he did because he wanted you to meet Sunny and see if it dislodged a few pertinent memories. But I imagine you've guessed that by now."

"The thought had occurred to me," Cameron conceded. "I think, if you don't mind, I'd prefer a few unpleasant details now—lest I embarrass myself by showing undue and undomesticated emotion."

Alex laughed. "Heaven forbid. Let's get down to your business, then. I'm sure it'll make you feel much better."

Sunny watched him hand Cameron a thick stack of papers, which Cameron immediately handed to her.

"I think better just listening," he said with a smile, then turned back to Alex. "Go on."

Sunny flipped through the pages as Cameron and Alex talked. She hadn't realized Rodney Ainsworth had died so recently, or that he'd made Cameron the executor of his will. She couldn't imagine Nathan had been particularly happy about that. She wondered, absently, what Penelope thought.

"Here, Sunny," Alex said, handing her a thick manila envelope. "It's Lord Ainsworth's autopsy report. I'm no doctor, but I thought Rodney's decline was rather rapid considering his particular sort of cancer. I also thought it was very suspicious that no one was interested in finding out why. Then again, it is rather odd that Rodney's doctor has a daughter of marriageable age who is quite enamored of our good lord Nathan and likely wouldn't have much use for him behind bars." He paused. "Isn't it?"

"Unethical," Sunny said, shaking her head.

"But not impossible, as you well know. Take a look and see what you think. Now, Cameron, let's move on to something else. I noticed in Rodney's will that he left you a box filled with mementoes. What were those?"

Cameron shrugged. "Just a handful of things from his travels. They weren't valuable, if that's what you're after. Nathan could sell the whole lot and buy a cappuccino, nothing more. I imagine Rodney thought I would value them where his children might not."

"No hidden messages? No diamonds stuffed behind clan badges? No clues to buried treasure?"

Cameron smiled. "Wishful thinking, my friend."

"And you would know because you checked."

"I might have given them a shake or two."

Alex looked at him seriously. "I think you might want to do more than shake. I also think, as I'm sure you do, that there's much more to this than meets the eye. You've had a rather bumpy road since Rodney's death and I imagine you suspect Nathan and Penelope both of causing it—as well as suspecting both of them of coming after you—"

"Really?" Sunny interrupted in surprise. "Is that what you think?"

Cameron nodded gravely. "Aye."

"And you're still engaged to her," Sunny said in disbelief.

"Keep your friends in your hall and your enemies at your table, as my father was wont to say," Cameron said with a faint smile. "Unpleasant, but effective."

She shivered. "I can't believe this is what you're involved in."

"'Tis why I didn't dare tell you anything, lest you be drawn into it as fully as I was. Which you have been now just the same," he finished with a sigh. "And I'm sorry for it."

"I'll be all right," she managed, then she took his hand in hers and held it as tightly as she could bear to. It all made sense, now, and she couldn't really blame him for not having said anything. That medieval tendency to send the women back to the house while the men took care of the dirty work of battle outside still ran true in all the MacLeods. She couldn't have expected anything less from Cameron.

"How about another piece of the puzzle?" Alex asked. "You asked me to find out who's behind the trust that's buying up so much of Cameron Ltd., and I found a couple of names that might interest you."

Sunny looked at Cameron in shock. "Your business, too? Where does it all end?"

"Hopefully with us putting up our feet in front of the fire in Cameron Hall," Cameron said with a smile. "It's been a bit of a siege, actually, against me personally and against both my companies."

"And a not-unskilled one," Alex said. "Uncovering all the details took a bit of doing and, of course, more money to grease the appropriate palms. The trust is registered, after a handful of layers, to Nathan Ainsworth, which you already know, Cameron. Another ridiculous number of layers down, I found Penelope's signature. At the bottom of the pile is yet another name you'll recognize."

"I can hardly wait," Cameron said sourly. "Who?"

Alex looked at him tranquilly. "Tavish Fergusson."

"Tavish?" Sunny gasped.

"It boggles the mind, doesn't it?" Alex said with a laugh. "I didn't think he had the good sense to count the money in his till every night, much less be involved in any dastardly deeds."

"How in the world did he meet the Ainsworths?" Cameron asked.

"His youngest sister is a maid in Rodney's house," Alex said with a shrug. "That was pure chance, though. Vivian was going to school in London, waiting tables, and she met Rodney's house-keeper's daughter who told her there was a place for her if she wanted it."

Cameron shook his head. "I don't know how you find out these things."

"Friends in low places, usually, but you can thank Patrick for that last bit. After Sunny came home from points unknown wrapped in a Cameron plaid, he was eager to make certain his sister-in-law wasn't in love with a loser, so he put out his own feelers on you. He's also the one who provided you with that little dossier on Nathan's more disgusting habits and all the credit accounts of Penelope's that you don't know about but I'm sure she'll try to get you to pay off before you dump her."

"I can hardly wait," Cameron grumbled. "I can't understand, though, why they would bother with Tavish. He has no money."

"He's stupid, though," Alex said, "and could easily be used as a stooge for any number of things. Money laundering, diversion—"

"Poison," Sunny interrupted quietly.

Alex fixed her with a look. "Well, yes, as it happens." He nodded at the papers in her hands. "Better have a look at those labs, Sunny, and sooner rather than later."

"But why would anyone want to poison Rodney Ainsworth?" she asked.

Cameron shrugged. "Money? Power? There are many reasons why you might want the patriarch of a family out of your way."

"Especially if you're the son who's so deep in debt from horses and cocaine that you're willing to do anything to have your legacy on an accelerated schedule, as it were," Alex said. "Or if you're the daughter who clings to a lifestyle far above what she can manage financially but who would do anything not to have any of her friends know it." Alex leaned forward with his elbows on his knees. "I find it curious, Cameron, that Rodney dies and suddenly you find yourself besieged on all sides. You were the executor of the will, true, but the probate was very quick and the distribution of assets clearly defined. Neither Nathan nor Penelope stands to gain anything from your death—no matter what those trinkets you have might contain."

"Do you think they're vexing me out of spite?" Cameron asked.

Alex pursed his lips thoughtfully. "That's possible, I suppose, but it doesn't seem reasonable." He paused for another moment or two. "It seems to me that either Rodney's death was the cause of all your troubles, or Rodney's death was a means to distract you from what's going to become your real trouble very soon."

Sunny felt Cameron go absolutely still next to her.

"Indeed," he said finally.

"I can continue to dig for you," Alex said slowly, "but I'm not sure you want me stirring the pot any more than I have already. I've been discreet, but I'm not infallible." He paused. "I suppose I can see either Nathan or Penelope killing their father for the money—heaven knows they both need it—but that just doesn't feel right to me. They seem to be stringing you along, hassling you, trying to make you more miserable than lifeless—if you know what I mean. The reason why is what eludes me." He smiled. "Just who have you really irritated lately, Cameron, besides Patrick MacLeod?"

Cameron took a deep breath. "The list is long."

"I'll just bet it is," Alex said with half a laugh. "And on a more serious note, Patrick wants Sunny home. I'm not sure I shouldn't be the one to get her there since he tried to kill you the last time you met."

"I have no secrets, I see," Cameron said shortly.

"Oh, come on," Alex said, his eyes twinkling. "Do you think I could actually talk to Pat and *not* have him describe in the greatest of detail how he'd roughed you up? He said you were so terrified, you swooned right into Sunny's doorway and cold-cocked yourself."

Sunny found Cameron looking at her. "Will it bother Madelyn if I kill her husband?"

"It might," she conceded.

Alex laughed. "I think he might have felt bad about the last, but not *too* bad. He knows Sunny's fond of you, though, so I think once he's properly repaid you for whatever grief he thinks you've caused his sister-in-law, he'll play nice. He would, though, stand back-to-back with you right now if you needed him to."

"That's something," Cameron murmured.

"It is," Alex agreed. "I'm not going to tell you anything you don't already know, Cameron, but the people you're dealing with in London are very dangerous. Sunny could stay quite safely and happily with Pat and Madelyn. It would leave you free to concentrate on unraveling this mess."

Sunny watched them exchange a long look. She cleared her throat. "Don't I get to have an opinion?"

"Have a conversation with Margaret," Alex suggested, then he held up his hand. "On second thought, don't. She would just tell you to get a sword and sharpen it yourself. Instead, go talk to Elizabeth—or your sister. They would both tell you about the joys of pacing by the fire as war raged outside the keep." He looked at her seriously. "You know, Cameron's less likely to get himself killed if he doesn't have to worry about you."

Sunny looked at Cameron. "Well?"

"Alex makes a very good point," Cameron conceded. "Patrick could keep you safe and leave me free to do what I must. I'll come home as often as I can." He looked at her solemnly. "I lost you once. I couldn't bear to lose you again."

She looked down at the scrapes on her hands. She'd earned them even though Derrick had been following her. If she forced him to continue to follow her, he wouldn't be guarding Cameron. She couldn't deprive Cameron of that protection just because she didn't want to sit in front of the fire and wait.

"All right," she said with a sigh. "I'll go home. But you'll call me."

"Aye."

"And you'll hurry."

He put his arms around her and pulled her close. "I will."

"Have you two thought about just getting a room and getting this all out of your systems?" Alex asked with a laugh. "Sunny keeps looking at you like you're some sort of delicious, chocolate-smothered dessert she can't wait to stick her fork into."

Cameron glared at him. "You said you jousted for your lady wife, didn't you?"

"I did."

"I hope it hurt."

Alex only laughed briefly. "It did. Repeatedly." He rubbed his hands together. "Let me know what you find in Rodney's trinkets. And think about the other. I'm convinced Rodney's death was a red herring. I think if I were you, I'd be looking for the real deal to show up from another direction."

Cameron sighed deeply. "I will."

"Sunny, hand your lover there those papers," Alex said. "I want him to take a look at another thing or two before I kick you two out. You don't want to be wandering around Paris unchaperoned, now do you?"

Sunny exchanged a very grave look with Cameron, then went to say her good-byes to Margaret and the rest of the family while Cameron and Alex wrapped up the last of their business. She supposed he wasn't completely surprised by what he'd heard, but she had been. To think this was what he'd been living with . . .

No wonder he'd needed a refuge.

She stood near the door a few minutes later and watched him shake hands with Alex. He laughed at something Alex said and she smiled reflexively. She would have to tell Jamie at some point how grateful she was that he'd thought up the excuse of the leisure center—as much for Cameron himself as for her. He deserved to have souls around him who valued him, who were willing to stand by him.

She was very glad she had stayed.

$Half$ an hour later, she was walking hand in hand with Cameron and contemplating what she could do in Scotland to help Cameron. Maybe she would see what Rodney's postmortem revealed, then do a little research on her own. She was, after all, a grown woman. She could decide for herself what she should be doing.

And the first decision she would make was to never, ever take a shortcut through an alley.

She and Cameron were halfway down one when they were surrounded. Well, perhaps surrounded was too glorified a term for it. Three lads came at them from out of nowhere. Cameron cursed as he backed her up against the wall and put himself between her and the men.

It was so familiar, she almost had to sit.

But this wasn't medieval Scotland and Cameron didn't have a Claymore strapped to his back. He stood in front of her with his hands in plain sight and spoke calmly to the men in front of him. He spoke his French very poorly, which she understood immediately was a ruse. So much the better if their attackers didn't know he could understand them. She was tempted to reach into his pocket and pull out his phone to call Derrick, but realized that was unnecessary when she saw another shadow slipping along the wall behind the men. The calvary to the rescue, apparently.

"Say again what you want?" Cameron said, stumbling over his words.

"Money, *monsieur*," the lad said politely. "Keys to your car. Then your lady friend, after we're finished with you."

Sunny had watched Cameron leave his keys and his credit cards in the room's safe. She supposed he had money enough, but she doubted he would sacrifice them just to hold on to that. He pulled out a wad of euros and tossed it clumsily at the head lad.

Then he stopped making any pretense of being less than what he was. He took out the lad on the left with a well-placed fist to the face, then began to work on the one directly in front of him. Derrick came up behind the third man and rendered him blissfully unconscious. She closed her eyes in relief.

But when she opened them, she was looking into the face of the first man. Blood dripped down his chin and he looked as if he'd just lost a tooth or two.

And he had a knife in his hand.

She watched it come down toward her and was too stunned to do anything about it.

Chapter 28

C*ameron* heard Sunny's gasp and whirled around. He turned in time to see Derrick pull someone off her. She then stood there, pressed against the wall, taking deep breaths.

The familiarity of the sight slammed into him like a dozen fists. The déjà vu was so vivid, it was hard to separate it from reality. He could feel himself hopelessly outnumbered, killing men in front of him with a sword, secretly terrified that he would be slain and leave Sunny unprotected. Without warning, he saw another image laid over her. It was Sunny still, but she was wearing a homespun dress with a bloodstained bodice.

He looked at her in absolute shock. By the saints, she *had* been there.

Blackness clouded his vision suddenly. The next thing he knew, he was on his knees with Sunny's arms around him.

"Derrick, help me," she said urgently.

Cameron would have found himself on his face if it hadn't been for Derrick catching him before he fell. The pain in his head was absolutely blinding.

"Cameron, stiff upper lip until I at least pile the refuse up against the wall, aye?" Derrick said quietly. "Sunshine, what do they have of his?"

"Just money."

"I'll find it," Derrick said. "And I'll hurry."

Cameron could only lean his head on Sunny's shoulder and try not to puke on her before he could manage to get himself to a loo. He closed his eyes and wondered if it would be best to ignore the vision or let it wash over him fully and hope he survived it.

He hadn't come close to a decision before he felt Derrick's hands under his arms.

"Up you go, mate."

He was hauled to his feet, then Derrick and Sunny each took a side of him and walked him out of the alleyway and onto the street.

He knew that they had gotten into a cab with him, that Sunny had crisply informed the concierge at the George V that he had a migraine, not an excess of wine, and that they had somehow gotten him up to the suite and over to the loo before turning him loose.

"Do you want a doctor?" Derrick asked.

Cameron shook his head sharply, but that only made the room spin wildly.

"He'll be fine after he throws up and I work on his feet for a while," Sunny promised.

Cameron couldn't imagine that, but he wasn't going to argue. He shooed them out, then shut the door.

By the time he could think again, he realized he was not alone. Sunny was sitting on the edge of the sink, holding a cup of water and watching him. He took it, rinsed his mouth out, then flushed the toilet.

"I can't even blame you for this," he said hoarsely. "Unfortunately." He leaned over with his hands on his thighs. "I thought I was finished with this sort of business."

"I think it's temporary," she ventured, "but I don't know as much about head wounds as I'd like. Jamie could probably tell you more than I, given that he's spent so much time reading up on the subject. I think he did it in your honor, actually."

"The saints preserve me," Cameron said weakly.

She laughed softly. "Oh, just wait until he gets started sharing the little gems he's uncovered. You'll be eyeing the exits, believe me. For now, though, don't worry. A little reflexology on your feet will take away the pain."

"Thank you," he said with feeling. He managed to straighten and focus on her. "How long have you been there?"

"Not very long," she said. She pushed away from the counter. "I'll go get your jammies."

"I have jammies?" he asked.

"MacLeod dress plaid," she said with an innocent smile.

"You vile wench," he managed.

She laughed. "I'll be right back. Don't go anywhere."

He didn't think he was going to. He shut the toilet, then turned and sat down on the lid. Several minutes later he heard rather than saw Sunny kneel in front of him. Then again, he was too busy closing his eyes to really notice anything. He felt her hands on his shirt, unbuttoning it.

"Damnation," he rasped. "I'm too ill to enjoy this."

"Well, don't get your hopes up," she said, a smile in her voice. "You can take off the rest of your stuff by yourself."

He felt her slide his shirt down his arms and allowed it because he couldn't do anything else. He had to rest his face against his hands for quite a while before he thought he could sit up straight. He felt Sunny's hands, cool, against his bare shoulders.

"Can you do the rest?" she asked.

"Lass, if you take off any more of my clothes, I'll be in trouble," he rasped. He caught her as she got to her feet. "But you'll come lie down next to me tonight, won't you? Just to comfort me in my time of need?" He managed to look at her blearily. "Florence Nightingale would have."

"Derrick could be our bolster."

"Like hell he could," Cameron said promptly. He winced. "Is he still here?"

"Yes, pacing just inside the door. Want him?"

He put his arms around her and rested his head against her belly. "Have you told him anything?"

"Heavens, no," she said, sounding horrified. "I told him you get migraines from too much stress, but nothing else. Do you want him to think something else?"

Cameron managed to take a deep breath. "Not yet, though I daresay he knows more than he'll let on. He's Alistair's late valet's grandson, you know. What he likely wouldn't tell you is that he's my cousin as well."

"You have an interesting family tree."

He grunted. "Don't I, though."

"Well, if it makes you feel any better, the only thing that seems to concern him now is how green you looked." She pulled away from him. "Why don't you change and go lie down. I'll get Derrick something to eat."

"Ask him if anything is amiss, if you will."

"I will. Can you see to the rest of your clothes?"

"Are you offering to help me?"

She ruffled his hair affectionately. "If you're able to tease, then you're better. I'll leave you to it."

"I wasn't teasing," he called after her, but she was gone and the door was shutting.

He managed to get himself into pajama trousers and across the fifteen paces to Sunny's bed. He stretched out and closed his eyes, intending to rest for just a moment.

He hadn't realized he had slept until he felt hands on his feet. He opened his eyes and found Sunny sitting on the end of the bed with his feet in her lap. He groaned before he could stop himself.

"Sorry to wake you," she said. "You've been asleep for half an hour, but you were moaning. I thought it was best to do something about it before you woke up with a worse headache than you had already."

He would have responded, but she had begun in earnest to try to rearrange the bones in his feet.

"What are you doing?" he rasped.

"Taking the pain in your head away and working on your upset tummy as well. Close your eyes and relax."

He wanted to protest, but he found that he was having a hard time doing anything but melting into a pool of something that might have been himself at some point in the past.

She was miraculous. Lovely, saucy, and with the hands of a footballer. When he finally realized she had finished and that not only the pain in his head was gone but so was the nausea, he just couldn't muster up any energy for words.

"Pleasant dreams, my love," she whispered.

He realized she was whispering that in his ear.

"Gaah," was all he could manage.

She laughed and walked away. "Sleep well," she called.

He supposed he just might.

*H*e woke, looked at the clock, and saw it was midnight. He rolled from the bed and felt better than he had in years. He walked out of the bedchamber and found Sunny and Derrick sitting on opposite ends of the couch, chatting amicably. Sunny looked up when she heard him and smiled.

No disgust over his scars. No shudders over the marks of his past. Nothing but acceptance and a smile that had him walking over to pull her up off the couch and into his arms. He hugged her briefly, then sat down with her next to him. He looked at Derrick.

"You had a decent meal out of this, at least," he said pointedly.

Derrick only smiled. "I almost didn't after I listened to you sicking up your supper earlier. Only my excessively strong stomach allowed me to soldier on bravely and decimate what our lovely lady saw fit to order for me."

"*My* lovely lady," Cameron reminded him.

"The term was used in a particularly old-fashioned, vassal-ish sort of way, of course," Derrick said, straight-faced. He put his hands on his knees. "Now that you seem to be out of all danger of dying, I think I'll be on my way. Thank you for supper, Sunshine, and the pleasant conversation."

Cameron looked at him. "Go sleep in the other bedroom, Derrick, and make a decent night of it for a change. I think we're safe enough all holed up in here together."

Derrick hesitated, then shrugged. "As you will." He rose, stretched, then walked away. "Thank you for the bed, my lord. Nighty-night, Sunshine."

Cameron watched him go, then rested his head against the back of the couch and put his arms around Sunny. She leaned back against him and put her hands over his.

"How are you feeling?" she asked.

"Much better."

"Want anything to eat?"

He winced. "I don't think so quite yet."

She reached up behind her and smoothed her hand over his hair briefly. "Tell me what you saw."

"I saw you standing against a wall with blood down the front of your dress." He paused and took a deep breath. "Care to give me the details?"

She hesitated, then sighed. "You won't enjoy them, but I will. You and I had been sitting in the little healer's hut when you decided that perhaps I would be better off in the keep. We walked out of my hut and into a battle. It was you against probably a dozen men. At lease I think that's how many there were. I was too terrified to get an accurate count."

"Did no one come to aid me?"

She was silent for a moment or two. "No, no one."

He somehow wasn't at all surprised. "What happened to you during all this?"

"While you were standing one against at least a dozen, a man slipped behind you and threw himself against me." She took a pair of deep breaths. "I was holding your knife and he impaled himself on it before I could do anything about it. I didn't mean to kill him, but I think he would have raped me right there if I hadn't." She pulled away far enough to turn and look at him. "It wasn't an easy time to live in, was it?"

He shook his head slowly. "Nay, it wasn't."

She managed a brief smile. "After that, we ran back to the keep and you worked Giric over a bit. I think you enjoyed that."

"I wouldn't doubt it," he said wryly. He looked at her for a long moment. "My only regret in all this is that I can't recall every moment of every day I had with you. And that dwelling on the memories leaves me heaving in the loo."

Sunny leaned over to kiss his cheek. "I'm sure there was a backhanded compliment in there somewhere. Let me go make you some tea in repayment."

"Will it taste good?"

"What do you think?"

"I think this morning I never should have given you any money anywhere near a stall that sold herbs only you know the use for," he said grimly.

She only smiled at him, then went to boil water in a coffeepot. He watched her fuss with little packets of dried bits of weeds that he was certain would only make him heave yet again once they hit his stomach. He saw his life stretching out before him, full of light and laughter and all sorts of green things.

Bliss.

Assuming he could get past the current battle. He considered the things he'd learned in Alexander Smith's hotel room and supposed the thing that was most surprising was to realize where—or when—Alex's wife had come from. Perhaps there were more time travelers wandering around in present-day England than he wanted to think about.

The thought was a little unsettling, actually.

"Here's your tea," Sunny said several minutes later as she sat down next to him.

He took it gingerly. "That's what I'm afraid of."

"It will make you feel better."

"*You* make me feel better," he said honestly.

She put her hand to his forehead. "You're feverish."

"That's part of it."

"Drink it, Cameron, then go to bed," she said dryly. "You'll feel more like yourself in the morning."

"Are you coming along with me, Florence?"

She smiled. "If you like."

He did and he drank an entire cup of the vilest business he'd ever tasted for the privilege.

He had to admit, as the sun was rising, that the brew had been worth the price of its taste. He'd woken at dawn after a marvelous night's sleep, then spent a very pleasant quarter hour watching the light grow and reveal a woman near him who looked like a Botticelli angel when she slept.

It was inspiration enough to finish his current business as quickly as possible.

He rolled from bed, tested his stomach's resolve, then left the bedroom and shut the door behind him. He found Derrick pacing at the far side of the sitting room, talking quietly into his phone. Cameron walked over to the little dining table under the window, then called down for a hearty breakfast for two.

Derrick was off the phone by the time room service arrived. Cameron sat down with him and ploughed through a meal that Sunny most definitely wouldn't have approved of.

"Well?" Cameron asked as he pushed his plate away.

"Here's the news from yesterday," Derrick said. "Oliver said Nathan's lads were ballistic when they realized it was only him and Rufus making the very long car journey to Inverness instead of you. Rufus caught one and expressed a little displeasure with his fists. The leader escaped. The last one, Jim, had the misfortune of falling into Oliver's hands."

"Did he indeed?" Cameron asked with interest. "And how did things go for the lad?"

Derrick smiled. "Oliver took him to the pub, learned all his secrets, then ruthlessly used them against the lad first thing this morning when he woke with a mighty hangover. Then he threatened to have all of us beat the bloody hell out of Jimmy in succession if he didn't play turncoat."

Cameron sat back. "Inventive. What's it going to cost me?"

"The lad was making a hundred quid a day. He was rather breathless at the thought of three plus bonuses if he produced anything useful. Oliver pointed out to him that we had all Nathan's offices and phones tapped and that we would know if he betrayed us. And speaking of eavesdropping, I heard a very interesting conversation this morning."

"Did you, indeed?"

Derrick nodded. "I was listening in on Nathan's private mobile and heard him talking to a particularly Scottish-sounding character. I couldn't decide if it was a man or a lad attempting to roughen his voice to sound like a man." Derrick looked at him solemnly. "He was likely using some sophisticated masking device."

"Handkerchief over the mouthpiece?"

Derrick grinned at him. "Aye, my thoughts exactly."

"So, what did this master of vocal disguises have to say?" Cameron asked.

"He suggested that perhaps it was time they did a bit of poking around into your background." Derrick paused. "Something to call you to heel."

Cameron froze.

"Nathan said, and I quote, 'He's Alistair's nephew; what's there to find out?' And the answer was, 'He's much more than that.'"

Cameron had spent his life perfecting the ability to hear shocking things and not react. He'd done it when he'd learned of his father's death, lest the clan think him unfit to lead. He'd done it countless times in battle, lest his enemies think they had the upper hand. He'd done it for eight years in the future, lest everyone around him think he was completely barking.

Yet after all that, he couldn't stop his mouth from falling open now. "What utter rubbish," he managed.

Derrick only looked at him mildly. "I daresay. The lad hung up and Nathan spent a few minutes going on to himself about being forced to deal with all manner of drunken Scots, then he hung up as well." He paused. "You know, Cameron, I wonder if we're going about this all back-arsewards. I wonder if Nathan is behind all this trouble with your businesses after all." He paused again. "I'm wondering if it might be this Scottish lad who wanted it and he found Nathan to carry out the scheme."

Cameron felt a chill slither down his spine. He would have happily discounted Derrick's words, but they were too close to what Alex had said to be dismissed so easily.

"Cameron, I daresay you have a certifiable nutter stalking you. Didn't you buy off all Alistair's cousins and sundry distant relations before he died?"

"You know I did, because you helped me do it," Cameron said faintly. "Apparently we missed one."

"Shall I go dig?"

"Nay," Cameron said without hesitation. "Not yet." Nay, this might be something he needed to see to himself. He paused. "I'll do a week's worth of work in the next two days, then we'll go home and split up. Between the two of us, we might turn up what we need."

Derrick toyed thoughtfully with his fork for a moment, then set it down. "You look like you might manage it now. I wasn't so sure yesterday."

"I had a headache."

"I can understand that," Derrick said. "I saw what was left of your head all those many years ago. I'm surprised you have any wits left."

"So am I," Cameron said with a snort.

Derrick rose and stretched. "I'll go see what's happening outside, then let you know. The lads are waiting for us at the airport. Ring me and I'll have a cab waiting, shall I?"

"Please," Cameron said.

Derrick nodded, then left the suite. Cameron looked out the window and considered for quite some time what he'd just learned.

A Scottish lad?

A Scottish lad who knew enough about him to suspect he might be more than he appeared to be? He cast about for a reasonable explanation, but found nothing particularly comforting. It could have been someone with an overactive imagination, perhaps. Or, as Derrick had suggested, it might have been a disgruntled cousin looking for more money.

Or it could have been someone else entirely.

Cameron rubbed his hands over his face, then shook his head to clear it. It didn't serve him to speculate overmuch. He wondered, briefly, if he was making a mistake by sending Sunny home, then he pushed aside the thought. Nathan might have been talking to a Scottish sounding lad, but that was no guarantee the lad was in Scotland. It made more sense to think that mysterious lad would be in London where he could do more damage to Cameron personally.

All the more reason to get Sunny away from him.

He picked up his phone and dialed. It would serve him to have a very pointed conversation with Patrick MacLeod about the care and feeding of one Sunshine Phillips before she was there to argue.

A n hour later he was sitting next to Sunny with the Channel sparkling below him, watching her with a smile. She did not like to fly. Even knowing that they weren't going to be up much longer didn't seem to be helping her. He watched as his steward sat down in the seat next to Derrick, facing them. Ewan smiled at Sunny.

"How did he introduce me?" he asked, without preamble.

"More than stewardess, less than trustworthy," Sunny said, looking a little green.

Cameron glared at Ewan, who also happened to be his cousin an appalling number of generations removed, but Ewan only winked at him and turned back to Sunny.

"I am unsurprised. Why don't I give you the VIP tour of the plane? You'll be quite pleasantly distracted by all the reasons this Gulfstream is the obvious choice for the discriminating traveler with deep pockets like our good lord Robert there." He leaned forward. "Did he bother to mention that we're cousins? Or that he pays me slave wages? 'Tis a wonder I can keep food on the table, really."

"You do look a little emaciated," she agreed weakly.

Ewan laughed. "I raid the galley when Cameron's back is turned. You know, Sunshine, you shouldn't worry about the flight. Cameron's pilots are, as they will tell you without having been asked, the very best in the sky. But as I can see that might not reassure you, how about a whisky?"

"Aye, only if she wants to spend the rest of the flight in the loo," Cameron said darkly. "Ewan, leave her alone."

"No, it's okay," Sunny said weakly. "Distraction is good." She took a deep breath and looked at Ewan. "He flies a lot, doesn't he?"

"Several times a week," Ewan said, looking at her apologetically. "He can actually fly the plane, too, you know. When Penelope the Shrew is on board, he locks himself into the cockpit and leaves me to put up with her. Och, and now he's going to dock my pay again." He unbuckled himself and rose. "Come with me, Sunshine. I'd best get out of his sights so he forgets I'm on board."

Cameron shot Ewan a warning look, caught Sunny's hand on her way by and smiled at her, then sighed deeply and leaned his head back against the seat. He took a moment to enjoy not only his luxurious surroundings, but the fact that he could savor them without worrying about who might be creeping up behind him with evil intent. Derrick was sitting across from him, poking around on his laptop and listening raptly on his mobile to some conversation he no doubt shouldn't have been at the same time, and Sunny and Ewan were laughing in the aft cabin. He had never in the half dozen times he'd allowed Penelope on board had a decent flight. There had certainly been no laughter.

How Sunny had changed him and everything around him.

"She doesn't have a sister," Derrick stated, not looking up from his screen. "Available, that is."

"She doesn't," Cameron agreed.

"Damn."

Cameron smiled to himself. He looked up as Ewan brought Sunny back and gallantly offered her his arm to help her over Cameron's feet. Cameron reached out quickly and caught Ewan's hand before he could buckle Sunny in.

"I'll take care of that, lad."

"Just being useful," Ewan said innocently.

Cameron growled at him to sit down, then buckled Sunny in himself. He took her hand, then leaned his head back against the seat. He was tempted to close his eyes, but couldn't bring himself to. How could he, when he had Sunny to watch?

"How shall we pass the rest of the time?" Ewan asked brightly. "Poker? Gin? Robert Cameron trivia? I know all his most disgusting habits, you know. I see he's holding your hand, which leads me to believe that there's something going on here that I obviously haven't been informed of, but before it's too late, let me give you the truth. You can still run, you know. And I happen to be available, if you're interested."

"Ewan?" Derrick said with a sigh.

"Aye?"

"Shut up."

Cameron smiled. He felt Sunny squeeze his hand and smiled a bit more. Ewan commenced asking her all sorts of personal questions and she hedged with skill even a Cameron would have had to admire. Ewan promised her the truly appalling bits about Cameron himself once they'd kicked Cameron off the plane in

London and were headed on to Inverness. Derrick periodically called Ewan names, but that was nothing new. Cameron never failed to be impressed by the scope of Derrick's slanders. Things from each side of Hadrian's wall were given equal time and attention.

Thinking about things north of the border reminded him unhappily of what Derrick had told him that morning. He looked across the aisle out the window and wondered about that Scottish lad. Nathan wouldn't have had anything to do with a Scot without there having been a very compelling reason. Perhaps the lad was Tavish trying to be something he wasn't. Perhaps it was someone he didn't remember, someone he'd offended in the past so greatly that he was seeking revenge at any cost.

Perhaps it was Giric, come through the gate to make his life a living hell.

Cameron could hardly bear to think about the last.

He blew out his breath and consciously forced away thoughts about what he would face when he landed. Whilst he was happily captive for the next half an hour, he would allow himself the pleasure of his lady's hand in his and the companionship of souls who weren't trying to kill him.

Reality would intrude soon enough.

Chapter 29

Sunny sat at her sister's kitchen table and rested her chin on her fists. She'd spent a good part of the morning looking at Rodney Ainsworth's medical files. She suspected, not from the autopsy, but from the meticulous notes taken by the private nurse Cameron had hired to care for the man, that Rodney's death had definitely not been from either his cancer or natural causes. She didn't know either of his children well enough to know if they were capable of murder, but there had definitely been foul play involved. Each was as good a suspect as any, she supposed, though the thought of it made her a little ill.

As did the thought of Cameron having to be anywhere near either of them.

She looked at the discreet manila envelope in front of her, the one with all Rodney's medical records in it, and spared a very brief thought for what had struck her as she read through the file. If Rodney had been poisoned, which she suspected, there were perhaps dozens of places where his murderer might have obtained a poison.

A dodgy herb shop, perhaps.

There weren't that many herb shops in the area—dodgy or not. Tavish's was one. There was another up north, conveniently located next to a yarn shop—or so she'd discovered in the phone book. Cameron had suggested that she pass her time doing something that pleased her, and knitting certainly qualified. She needed yarn. If buying it allowed her a peek inside a previously unexplored herb shop, so much the better. If she happened to find something sinister, she would let Cameron know. If she found nothing, she would come back home and no one would be the wiser about her investigating things she probably should have left alone.

She stood up, then picked up the envelope and left the kitchen before she had to think any more about it. She tossed the envelope on her bed, then walked back down the hallway. She paused at the doorway to Patrick's office and saw Madelyn playing with Hope on the rug in front of the fire. Madelyn looked up with a smile.

"How're you doing?"

"I'm restless," Sunny said without hesitation. "I think I need to get out."

"I'll come."

Sunny hesitated. "I don't think you should."

"And neither should you," Madelyn said pleasantly, "but if you're getting out, then so am I. After all, it's Scotland. How dangerous can it be?"

Sunny supposed that was true enough. Outside of the odd encounter with medieval clansmen, she'd never run into anything else untoward.

"I'll put Hope in her carseat," Madelyn said, pushing past her. "Bank the fire, will you?"

"I need yarn," Sunny offered.

"Sure," Madelyn called back over her shoulder. "Hurry."

Sunny hoped she wasn't making a mistake, but really, it was Scotland. How dangerous *could* it be? She grabbed her purse, made sure her cell phone was in it, then banked the office fire before she went to look for her sister.

A n hour later she was driving north, happy to be out of the house and doing something besides sitting and stressing. The scenery was beautiful, she was in Patrick's Range Rover, which she knew wouldn't break down anytime soon, and she was wearing a ring on her finger given to her by a man who loved her. The sun was even shining.

Life was good.

"Where are we going?" Madelyn asked. "I'm assuming you have a destination in mind."

"I want yarn."

"That's what you said," Madelyn agreed. "What's your real destination?"

Sunny pursed her lips. "I'm really going for yarn. There might be an herb shop in the vicinity I've never been in before, as well." She paused. "I was thinking it might be worth a visit."

"Cameron won't like it," Madelyn said in a singsong voice. "You should be sitting by the fire, waiting for him."

Sunny shot her sister a look. "What he doesn't know won't hurt him, will it? And when did you get to be so medieval, Lady Benmore?"

Madelyn smiled. "It rubs off, after a while. Talk to me in a year and see if it hasn't rubbed off on you as well."

"I could only hope," Sunny said seriously. She took a deep breath. "I really do think we're safe, Maddy. I wouldn't have let you come with Hope, otherwise."

"I know," Madelyn said, reaching out to squeeze her hand. "We'll be okay.".

Sunny nodded, more to reassure herself than her sister. The bad guys following Cameron were in London, not Scotland. She and Madelyn would be safe enough for the morning.

She drove for another half hour, then slowed down when she reached the right village. She pulled to a stop in front of a shop that looked herby enough, then got out and waited for Madelyn to get Hope unbuckled. She walked with her sister into the shop, then had to close her eyes and take a deep breath.

Better than London exhaust fumes, definitely.

She looked around, then jumped when she saw the flash of someone disappearing behind a curtain behind the counter. Well, so much for being helped. She started to wander around, then squeaked in surprise when she realized there was someone standing right beside her who wasn't her sister. She put her hand over her heart and tried to catch her breath.

The woman was, Sunny decided immediately, a refugee from a fairy tale. An unpleasant fairy tale. She was lacking several critical teeth, she had a wart on the end of her nose, and her fingers were so gnarled with arthritis it was a wonder she could straighten them at all. Sunny fully expected to see her pull an evil looking wand out of her pocket and wave it over her and Madelyn both.

"What can I fetch for you ladies?" the woman cackled, reaching out with a bony finger to touch Sunny's hair.

Sunny managed a smile. "We're just here to sniff."

The woman frowned in displeasure, then muttered under her breath as she took herself and her black dress and scuttled back over to the curtain. Sunny watched her go and thought suddenly about the last witch she'd been convinced she'd seen. It had been that woman she'd encountered outside the yoga studio on the night Tavish Fergusson fired her. It was possible she was related to the old crone, but there was no way she was going to try to find out. She shivered and looked at Madelyn.

"I think I'm losing it," she whispered uneasily.

"Too much time with your nose in things that make you hallucinate," Madelyn said wisely. "Or maybe you're just having a bad week. Either way, can we go now?"

"Definitely." The trip was a bust anyway. No new clues, very scary proprietresses, and not a bodyguard in sight. She followed her sister outside and pulled the door shut behind her. "That place gave me the willies."

"I don't even have your kooky karma thing going and I agree with you. That was creepy. Yarn shop now?"

"Are you insane?"

Madelyn laughed. "Not today. Unlock the car, would you?"

Sunny did. "You know," she said slowly, "I think there was someone staring at us from the back."

Madelyn looked up from where she was buckling Hope in the backseat. "Want to go back in and investigate?"

Sunny looked at her in surprise. "Are you out of your mind? You have a baby!"

"I wasn't going to go back in *with* you," Madelyn said pointedly. "I was planning on keeping the car warmed up and ready for your hasty getaway. Actually, I think we'd be smart to just get back home before either Cameron or Patrick finds out we're gone. Pat wasn't going to be that long in Inverness."

Sunny got in, shut the door, and watched her sister click the locks. "Can you believe us? Modern, independent, tough women following orders like this?"

"I don't know about you, but I always feel slightly better when Patrick is standing between me and the door with a sword in his hands," Madelyn said dryly, "so I try to humor him when he asks me to stay put at home. Let's get out of here before he decides to use that sword on us."

Sunny snorted. She'd never heard Patrick come close to even raising his voice at her sister—but she wasn't going to press her luck. She turned on Patrick's car and started off through the village.

After a moment or two, a small gray sports car swung into her lane behind her.

Sunny watched it periodically, waiting for it to turn off, but decided that perhaps she was going to be followed all the way south. She glanced down at the fuel gauge, then looked for the first gas station she could pull in to. Patrick really didn't need any gas, but it was a good excuse to get off the road and take a deep breath. She looked casually over her shoulder to take in the sights.

She jumped when she saw the little gray car parked on the near side of the street in front of a block of row houses.

Damn it, she was going to hear a raised voice or two very soon. Maybe she shouldn't have objected so strenuously to Cameron leaving one of his men to look after her.

She was too far away for a particularly good view, but she could see a hat and sunglasses. It occurred to her, with a start, that it could be one of Cameron's men. She wasn't sure if she should be offended that he hadn't trusted her or relieved that he made an executive decision on her behalf.

She got back in the car and drove away, but kept an eye on the car behind her. The driver seemed to be making no secret of following her, consistently remaining a handful of lengths behind her. She waited for a bit longer, then pulled over into a turnout.

"Why'd you stop?" Madelyn asked her.

Sunny looked in her rearview mirror to find the gray car thirty feet behind her. The doors remained shut; the driver remained inside. Sunny frowned thoughtfully. "Nothing, really. I was just curious about someone behind us." She took a deep breath and saw a castle in the distance to the south, across the loch from where they were. "What's that?"

"It's the old Fergusson keep," Madelyn said in a very quiet voice.

Sunny felt Madelyn's shiver from where she sat. She understood that, actually. She didn't care who was following her, friend or foe; there was no way in hell she was staying anywhere near that creepy ruin of a castle. She gunned Patrick's car, sending gravel spewing behind her, and swerved back out onto the road, narrowly missing cutting off someone coming down the road south as well. She checked her mirrors for a bit, then relaxed when she found they weren't being followed.

Or she did until the gray car passed that southbound red Ford and took up its place behind her again.

"I think I should have listened to Cameron." She quickly shot her sister a look. "Don't tell him I said that."

"I won't," Madelyn said, wide-eyed. "What's wrong? Is it that gray car behind us?"

"I thought it might have been one of Cameron's guys, but now I'm not so sure. Let's call Patrick and see what he thinks. Maybe it's someone he knows."

Madelyn was already digging her phone out of her purse. She

called her husband, talked to him for a minute, then hung up. "He's doesn't have anyone following us—and he can't believe we're not at home in front of the fire. He's turning around, but said he'd passed Cameron heading home about half an hour ago. He thinks Cameron will get to us first and told me to call him and tell him where we were. Patrick will meet us at home."

"Does he think I'm crazy?"

"No, Sunny," she said nervously. "He doesn't."

Sunny took a deep breath. "I think I'd rather have Patrick come rescue us. Cameron's not going to be happy with me." She blinked. "He's supposed to be in London. I wonder why he's home?"

"Maybe he had a feeling," Madelyn offered. "It's that bad-guy antenna they all have. She frowned. "Why don't you have one? You would think with all that woo-woo business you have going on you'd be better at keeping us out of trouble than you are."

"You would think," Sunny muttered. She took a deep, steadying breath, then looked briefly at her sister. "Well? Are you going to call Cameron?"

"Don't you want to?"

"I'm driving."

"You're a coward."

"Whatever."

Madelyn laughed a little uneasily, then pulled the shocking pink phone out of the glove box. It started ringing before she could dial. She looked at the number, then swallowed uneasily. "Oh, look. It's Cameron. Obviously for you."

"I'm still driving."

Madelyn muttered something no doubt quite uncomplimentary under her breath, then gingerly held the phone to her ear and answered.

She didn't immediately drop the phone and Sunny didn't hear any shouting, so she supposed she was safe enough for the moment. Her sister finished her conversation, then set the phone down on the dashboard.

"Did you hang up?" Sunny asked.

"He asked me not to," Madelyn said. "He also said something about meeting you in the lists to settle your difference of opinion about what you should be doing when he's not five feet from you."

"I'll just bet he did," Sunny managed.

"He thinks he'll be to us in about fifteen minutes and said to just keep driving. He'll follow us home where you'll have the choice between rapiers and broadswords. I suggest throwing your arms around his neck and kissing him before he has the chance to think too much about either."

Sunny managed a smile. "He's a prince."

"He is," Madelyn agreed. "I think he's trying to instill a sense of confidence in us. I also think he's going to yell at you later. Again, jump right into the kissing. Works every time."

"Is this experience speaking?"

"Nah," Madelyn said easily, "Pat never yells; it's just an excuse. Then again, I never get into any scrapes with spooky old hags masquerading as herb shop owners. That's your domain, Sis."

Sunny wished it wasn't. She continued to watch the guy behind her, but nothing changed and his car didn't look any more friendly than it had earlier.

"How long has it been?" Sunny asked an eternity later, trying to keep her teeth from chattering.

"Fifteen minutes."

Sunny squeaked as a black rocket flew past her going the other way. She held on to the wheel tightly and tried not to look in her rearview mirror. She wasn't completely successful. She jumped a little when a low-slung black sports car passed the gray car and pulled in about eight inches behind her back bumper. Cameron immediately slowed down, forcing the car behind him to slow as well. Sunny would have waved, but she didn't dare take her hands off the wheel. She took a deep breath.

"I feel like I'm in a bad movie. Things like this don't happen to me."

"Have you been thinking unkind thoughts?" Madelyn asked weakly. "Brewing up nasty potions? Is it karma, coming back to bite you in the behind?"

"I'd have to give that some thought."

Madelyn reached over and squeezed her hand on the steering wheel. "You do that. And don't miss the turn. I'm ready to be home."

Sunny was as well. She took the turnoff for the village, then watched as Cameron followed her. The gray car continued on as if it had had no business with them at all. Sunny almost picked the phone up to ask Cameron if he didn't intend to keep following the guy, but she supposed Derrick or one of his other lads would do that. Then again, maybe she'd let her imagination get the better of her and it was all just an unhappy coincidence. It was

possible the driver of that car had pulled over to check a map
while she'd been getting gas. It was possible he'd been in a hurry
and that was why he'd followed her so closely.

It was possible she was becoming just as paranoid as Cameron
was.

It took her only another twenty more minutes to reach
Patrick's courtyard. She stopped in front of the garage and turned
the car off. She put her hands over her face and shook. The next
time, she would leave Madelyn at home. If something nasty happened, at least it would happen to just her. Then she would only
have Cameron scowling at her, not Cameron and Patrick both.

Before she had a chance to think about that too long, her door
was jerked open, her seat belt unbuckled, and she was pulled
bodily out of the car and set on her feet. She didn't even have a
chance to squeak before Cameron had hauled her into his arms.

"I'm not going to say anything," he said grimly.

"You don't have to," she managed, shivering as she threw her
arms around his neck. "We did find a suspicious herb shop up
north, though—"

He pulled back and looked at her with his mouth open, then he
shut his mouth and pulled her back against him. "Sunny . . ." He
had to take a deep breath or two. "Never mind."

"I'm sorry," she whispered. "It was stupid to go and even stupider to take Maddy and the baby."

"Aye, it was," he said without hesitation.

She closed her eyes and forced herself to relax. It helped to
have Cameron's arms around her. He was warm, solid, and holding her so tightly that she could hardly breathe. She felt safe for
the first time since she'd left him behind at the airport in London
the day before.

"I'm just the innocent witch up the way," she managed finally.
"Now look at me. Car chases. Muggings. Not being a mistress to
a man in a pricey black sports car."

He laughed, then bent his head and sought her mouth with his.
He finally lifted his head and smiled down at her. "We'll have
supper at Moraig's tonight and you'll feel more yourself. For
now, let's go inside and you can tell me what you saw."

"I will, but first tell me why you're home. I thought you would
be in London for a bit."

"I missed you," he said simply.

She smiled. "You didn't."

"I did. I'll tell you about it in great detail once I get past your brother-in-law. Look, here he comes screaming into his courtyard. I'm not sure who he'll want to kill first: you or me."

She looked at him sickly. "I wish I could laugh about that."

He hugged her tightly. "We've all ventured where we shouldn't have at one point or another, secure in our ability to survive anything."

"You?" she asked skeptically. "Surely not."

"I'll tell you about that singular occurrence later. I imagine Patrick has quite a few more ill-advised adventures to recount than I do. We'll ask him for a list. I'm sure 'twill make you feel better."

She looked over her shoulder as Patrick jerked Madelyn off her feet and into his arms. Sunny shot him an apologetic look, but he shook his head, then closed his eyes and held his wife close. Sunny sighed. She'd already heard a few of his more hair-raising escapades, so he probably didn't have much room to criticize her.

Sunny stood with Cameron while Patrick took Maddy and Hope inside, then she walked with Cameron toward the door. Before Sunny could get them inside, though, Patrick appeared. He stood in the doorway with his arms folded over his chest.

"Patrick," she began with a sigh.

He pulled her into a quick, tight, embrace, then pushed her into the house. "Your would-be lover and I have a thing or two to settle before I decide if he's worthy of you. Change your clothes, Cameron, then let's go."

"Patrick," she said in a low voice.

He looked at her for a moment in silence, then sighed deeply. "All right. He can come in and have something to eat. Snog with him all afternoon if you like, but then I will have at him. I promise not to leave him as bruised and bloodied as I did the last time."

Sunny smiled at him, then reached out and took Cameron's hand to pull him into the hall. He muttered something at Patrick as he passed, something that left her brother-in-law gasping.

"You'll pay for that insult," he promised.

"You'd like to hope so," Cameron said with a snort.

Patrick laughed out loud, then turned and walked off, shaking his head.

Sunny would have followed him, but Cameron tugged on her hand to stop her. She looked at him in surprise, then smiled as he held open his arms. She went willingly into his embrace, closing her eyes and sighing as he held her close.

She supposed she would have to surrender him to Patrick eventually, when she couldn't avoid it any longer. He and Cameron would probably make good use of the little meadow behind the castle, fighting, hurling insults and damning with faint praise exactly as Patrick did with Ian and Jamie. She would sit and watch, and be grateful for Patrick's generosity and good heart. Cameron deserved brothers who loved him, who would stand behind him, who would give him back part of the family he'd lost.

But she would also be very grateful for the day when they started a new family made up of just they two.

It was much later that evening when she sat with Cameron at Patrick's kitchen table, preparing to look at treasure. They'd intended to go to Moraig's for the evening but stopped halfway across Patrick's courtyard, exchanged a look, then turned without a word and gone back inside Patrick's house. She had Cameron—almost—and the comforts of the future all in the same place. After the morning she'd had, she just wasn't going to take any chances by crossing Moraig's threshold unnecessarily. Cameron seemed to feel the same way.

He pulled a wooden box out of his backpack and laid it on the table alongside his pocketknife. "I'm assuming there isn't anything hidden inside that's toxic," he said.

"Were you never curious about this stuff?" she asked.

"I was distracted by other things, actually," he said with a smile. "Rodney died a fortnight before I first saw you in front of Tavish Fergusson's, as you know. I glanced at what he left me, then shoved it all into my office safe and didn't think about any of it again until Alex suggested it might be useful."

Sunny looked at the things he was laying on the table. It was a rather unremarkable selection of touristy sorts of things: a very worn, wooden figurine; a small ashtray with a weighted cloth base; a nondescript Russian nesting doll, and a trio of porcelain elephants. Sunny looked at Cameron.

"You're sure you want to ruin these?"

"I found a letter from Rodney inside the box this morning telling me he was satisfied—and you'll appreciate this, I'm sure— that I had an affinity for old things and would know what to do with these when the time came." He smiled. "I can guarantee the pieces don't have any value in and of themselves. So, I think we should begin by crushing the elephants."

Sunny poached one of Madelyn's oldest dish towels and wrapped one of the elephants in it. Cameron put the lump on a cutting board, then took the cast-iron skillet she handed him and brought it down against the towel mercilessly. He unwrapped it, then frowned.

"Nothing here. Let's try another."

She handed him another elephant. He tried it with the same results. The final elephant was larger and it wasn't simply shards after it had been destroyed. Cameron picked up something that looked remarkably like a safe-deposit-box key and smiled.

"I should have known."

"But where's the box, do you suppose?"

"Probably cunningly hidden immediately adjacent to the box his children have already ransacked," he said with a snort. "I won't be surprised to find a letter inside telling me about a few pounds he tucked aside somewhere in Switzerland for use in keeping up the hall. He would have known Nathan and Penelope would run through their legacies in no time, and he wouldn't have wanted me to be responsible for maintaining his home after his death." He cleaned away the mess, then sat down and pushed the other things toward her. "You be the surgeon on the rest of this. I want to watch what might have been operating on me if we'd stayed in a different time."

Sunny smiled briefly. "You've already had that experience and you're probably glad you don't remember it. I'll cut, though, if you want me to."

He slid his knife across the table to her. She took a wooden figurine and managed to slice it open without too much trouble. She turned the body upside down and shook it.

Three dozen sparkling emeralds rolled across the table. Cameron looked at them thoughtfully for a moment, then handed her the Russian doll without comment. It had been glued shut, but she remedied that soon enough. She only got through three layers of doll before she hit the jackpot. She poured dozens of beautiful cut stones in a rainbow of colors onto the table.

Cameron sighed, then pushed the ashtray in front of her. Sunny cut it open and another large handful of unpolished rocks rolled across the table.

Cameron put his face in his hands for a moment, then laughed. "Ach, by the saints, I should have known."

"Valuable stuff?" she asked.

He pulled a jeweler's loupe out of his pocket and examined a few of the colored stones and emeralds. He set it down, then looked at the rocks. "The stones are exquisite, actually. They would fetch a good price from the right buyer. And the rest of these are uncut diamonds, probably from the mine Rodney's grandfather owned in South Africa. Their value would depend on who cut them and how well it was done, but it wouldn't be an insignificant amount of money, surely."

"Why did he give them all to you?" she asked in astonishment.

"Probably because he knew I wouldn't immediately sell them to buy drugs or shoes," he said with a sigh. He sat back and started to sort the stones idly into piles. "Well, this solves a bit of the mystery, I suppose, though I don't know why Nathan or Penelope would have thought I'd have these. I can't imagine they even know they exist."

Sunny wondered if he was thinking about what Alex had said—that Rodney's death was orchestrated to draw attention away from what was really going to happen.

She didn't particularly want to talk about that, actually.

"What did you think about the manner of Rodney's death?" Cameron asked, sounding as if he didn't particularly want to talk about any of it, either.

"I think the body would have to be exhumed to be sure," she said slowly, "but I feel fairly sure it was poison. There were striations on his fingernails that could have come from the chemo, of course, but they also could have come from arsenic."

He nodded absently, then looked at her sharply. "What did you say about his fingernails?"

"Striations," she repeated. "Of course, there was no proper autopsy done so we don't know what organs had failed, but his hands were a good clue. That, and the notes your nurse left. Why do you ask?"

"Because my uncle's fingernails looked like that," Cameron said faintly. "I thought it was odd when I buried him."

She felt a chill go down her spine. "What are you saying?"

He toyed with the gems a bit longer, then pushed them away and clasped his hands on the table. "What I'm saying is I think Giric followed one of us to the future. Me, I imagine, since he would have needed time to invent the sort of plan I fear he's been about."

"Surely not," she said faintly.

"I don't want to believe it, but I fear I have no choice. Derrick told me in Paris that he'd overheard Nathan talking to some Scottish sort of lad who'd advised him to dig into my background to bring me to heel."

"Oh, Cam," she said, feeling quite thoroughly sick to her stomach. "It has to be him, then, doesn't it? Who else would wonder anything about your past?"

Cameron lifted his eyebrows briefly. "I might have suspected one of those pesky MacLeod lads if this had happened six months ago. Clan rivalries, and all, you know."

"But now you know differently."

"Aye, I do." He smiled. "It helps to be in love with their witch, apparently."

She couldn't smile. "What are you going to do?"

"We'll sleep on it," he said with a sigh, "then see if an answer presents itself on the morrow. Perhaps we'll take the day and do a little investigating—together, this time. We'll start at Tavish's where you can intimidate him for me."

She pursed her lips. "Did Patrick tell you about the black eye I gave him?"

"He thought I should know whom I was standing to wed," he said solemnly.

"You look terrified."

He tangled his feet with hers under the table. "Well, since Patrick did tell me that he taught you everything you know about defending yourself, perhaps I should be." He reached out and dragged his fingers through the piles on the table. "What shall we do with our largesse here?"

"I don't know. And speaking of largesse, that's something we need to talk about." She paused, then took a deep breath. "You have too much of it. Alex gave me details."

And he had. He'd left her a little note in with Rodney's files, a note listing the number of Cameron's Swiss bank accounts and the approximate value of them when taken together.

At least 750 million pounds, Sunny, he'd written—with a smirk, no doubt. *Bet that'll send you to bed for the rest of the day.*

She looked up to find Cameron wearing that little smile she loved.

"I was hoping to wed you first, then give you the unpleasant tidings after it was too late for you to bolt."

She glared at him. "Don't laugh at me."

He apparently couldn't help himself. He leaned over, slipped his hand around the back of her neck, then kissed her briefly. "Don't be daft, woman," he whispered. "'Tis only money." He sat back and smiled. "Sunny, our children will have funds enough to satisfy that highway robbery called the death tax yet still be able to keep the roof repaired on the hall for a few years. If our little pounds see to that, then they've served their purpose, haven't they?"

She took a deep breath. "But I don't have anything to offer in return."

"Nay, Sunshine, you're wrong about that," he said seriously, "You have yourself and that is something you cannot put a price on." He reached for her hand and laced his fingers with hers. "If it will ease you any, I'll write you out a list of what it costs to keep Cameron Hall running each month. You'll not feel nearly so wealthy after that."

She found, to her profound surprise, that her eyes were burning. "Please let's stay in Scotland as much as we can."

"We will, love," he said. "And when we've a need to be elsewhere, we'll take those beautiful Highland meadows with us in our hearts. But aye, we'll be home as often as we can manage it."

She wanted to ask him if he actually thought he would ever be able to get out from under Nathan and Penelope, if people would stop hunting them both, if they would actually live happily ever after, but she didn't have the chance before his phone rang. He sighed.

"I won't be long. 'Tis Emily, no doubt with something I neglected to do."

She looked down at his left hand that was still wrapped around hers and trailed her fingers along the scar there. It was a little surreal, knowing she'd sewn that up hundreds of years ago as Cameron had taken a bath in a very medieval tub, yet there she was in Patrick and Madelyn's kitchen, listening to the same man talking on his cell phone to his assistant in London.

Life was very strange, indeed.

"Is that so?" he asked, raising an eyebrow. "Well, aye, I would be interested. Just let me know the time. And you let Oliver get you home tonight and sleep on your sofa." He listened for quite a while longer, then shook his head. "Emily, lass, for once in your bloody life do something you don't want to simply because I'm asking it. You can curse me all you like after the fact." He smiled. "Aye, I'm sure you will. Call me back when you have a time. Thanks, love."

Sunny looked at him as he hung up. "News?"

"A meeting called tomorrow morning by our good lord Nathan," he said, looking faintly surprised. "Perhaps he grows nervous. We've managed to turn his lads one by one except one particularly stubborn case and his chauffeur—and I'm not certain the driver couldn't be bought with enough sterling."

"So, you'll fly back in the morning?"

"Very early. I'll call you once I'm finished and we'll see where we stand. I assume you'll be sitting here in front of the fire, knitting. If you tire of that, you can sharpen a blade or two, just in case."

She smiled briefly. "How very medieval of you, my laird."

"Very," he agreed unapologetically.

"I could drive with you to the airport."

He started to protest, then stopped. "I suppose I could leave Peter behind with you. I'll have Derrick and Oliver with me, and Ewan can come along to be an extra pair of hands if I need them. But if I agree, Sunshine, I want your solemn word that once you drop me off, you will lock the doors and drive straight home. No following hunches, no trips to herb shops owned by any Fergussons, no running off to buy any fifty-quid dresses with all the money I put in your account this morning."

"You didn't."

"Your brother-in-law was eager to take a hefty fee for giving me the appropriate secret codes," he said dryly, "and actively encouraged the deposit. The man is a mercenary."

"He's repaying you for years of vexation from your ancestors," she said wisely.

"Likely so." He smiled, but his smile faded rather quickly. "I'm serious about the other, Sunny. I'll leave Peter to shadow you, but I want you to come back here without delay. Please leave me free to worry about things other than your safety."

She shivered. "I think I like medieval Scotland better."

"Don't wish that on either of us now," he said with feeling. "I'm far too accustomed to driving instead of riding."

"And you probably wouldn't survive without your daily dose of saturated fat."

"I daresay you have that aright," he agreed. "Nay, my love, let's stay in the future and rid it of things that might not belong."

It took her quite a while before she could speak. "Do you really think it's Giric?"

"I don't think I have a choice, do I? As improbable as it might seem, I fear he's involved."

"What will you do?"

"Draw him out," He smiled briefly. "But let us think on something else besides that tonight. Would Patrick let me sleep on his floor?"

She smiled. "He might even let you use the extra guest room. It's usually fairly free of ghosts."

He opened his mouth to speak, then shut it abruptly. "I'm not going to ask. I almost embarrassed myself this afternoon whilst we were indulging in a little swordplay. That bloody piper of his started up with his serenade and I think I might have made some sort of noise of surprise."

"Pat said you screamed."

He tried to scowl, but apparently couldn't manage it. He laughed uneasily instead. "Aye, I suppose I did. I'll be prepared for him the next time."

"You should feel flattered. Robert MacLeod doesn't play for very many people."

"Again, 'tis my affection for the MacLeod witch that earns me such fine treatment," he said with a smile. "I also brought my MacLeod plaid pajamas, just in case. That should earn me a decent night's sleep, wouldn't you think?"

"I should think so," she agreed.

"But not quite yet," he said, pulling her around the table and onto his lap. He put his arms around her and looked at her purposefully. "I think I should give that lovely MacLeod witch a small demonstration of my affection, aye?"

"Definitely," she agreed. As she had thought on more than one occasion, Cameron's mouth was a marvel. There was no sense in not giving it her full attention.

She didn't want to think about what he was up against, or the fact that he might very well be walking into a viper's nest the next morning. It could have been worse; it could have been medieval Scotland with Cameron standing against a dozen men with very sharp swords.

She hoped London wouldn't be as deadly.

Chapter 30

Cameron rode in the lift to the top floor of a modern office building in London and wished absently that he'd had a sword strapped to his back. He had his own lads all over the building in various capacities, of course, but that didn't do him much good if Nathan shot him right there in the boardroom.

He blew out his breath and bounced a time or two on the balls of his feet, just as he'd done for seventeen years of battle in medieval Scotland. He stretched his hands over his head, flexed his fingers, then sighed and shoved his hands in his pockets. There was nothing he could do now except hope he could refrain from calling Nathan names long enough for Nathan to blurt out things he didn't intend to in a fit of pique.

He walked down the hallway and went into Nathan's offices. He was charming to Nathan's secretary, an older woman whose mouth was perpetually drawn into a pucker of distaste. He couldn't blame her. He grimaced when he thought of the man as well.

He pulled a small box of expensive chocolates out of his suit coat pocket and deposited them on her desk.

"Not poisoned," he said with a wink.

She almost smiled; he was almost certain of it. She rose and showed him into the conference room.

"The best of British," she said under her breath.

Cameron smiled, but if there was one thing he most certainly *didn't* need, it was British luck. He walked in and saw nothing that he hadn't expected. Nathan sat at the head of a long conference table, flanked by a cadre of lawyers Cameron suspected dealt only in hostile takeovers. They had that sort of calculating, unfriendly look about them.

Cameron supposed if he'd had any sense, he would have been uneasy, but he'd been in like situations before and come away unscathed. After all, what did he have to lose, in the end? As long as he had his life, he could live quite happily in Moraig's hovel with Sunny. He could convince Patrick MacLeod to hire Madame Gies to cook at Benmore Castle and he and Sunny could mooch supper regularly. He could chop wood and keep them warm. The money didn't matter.

Of course, he had no intention of losing, but sometimes it helped to have a fallback position.

He came to a halt at the end of the table and looked at Nathan with a faint frown. "So many of your friends at this little meeting, Nathan, and so few of mine."

"Sit down," Nathan snarled. "This isn't a social call."

Cameron wandered over to the sideboard, looked for a bottle of water he was convinced hadn't been opened—and he tried half a dozen that had been sealed but were sealed no longer after he'd had done with them—before he cast himself down carelessly in the chair at the opposite end of the table.

"Then what in the world could this be?" Cameron asked, taking a swig of his water.

"Your notification of bankruptcy."

Cameron started to speak, then felt his phone buzzing in his pocket. He held up a finger to Nathan, then answered the phone. "Aye?"

"Bugged," Derrick said succinctly.

"What a surprise," Cameron said dryly. "I'd love to chat, but I'm in a very *important* meeting right now."

"Don't staple his arse to the table, mate."

Cameron laughed, then hung up and set his phone on the table. He looked at the lawyers, then at Nathan. "Bankruptcy?" he said, blinking innocently. "Is that all?"

Nathan gaped for a moment, then his expression hardened. "You think you're so smart, Robert, but this is no jest. I'm filing paperwork in the morning to make a formal tender offer for Cameron Ltd. You won't have control anymore tomorrow after noon, I imagine."

Cameron put his hands on the table and manufactured a look of surprise. "But how can you force me into bankruptcy just by buying up a few shares of my company?"

Nathan shot him a look of fury. "Don't be stupid. I'm buying *numerous* shares of your company and when I have controlling interest, I'll run it into the ground. You'll be so overextended, you'll have to sell everything just to cover the debts that will be in your name. You won't have enough money to keep your precious hall yourself. It'll probably be bought up by some Yank with more money than sense who actually *wants* to live in Scotland."

"Ah," Cameron said, with an exaggerated nod, "I see. Very clever of you. It begs the question why, though, doesn't it?"

"To teach you your place," Nathan barked, leaning forward, "among other things. You, daring to come south and sully *my* family with your uncouth self. I want you back in Scotland where you belong."

"If you want me to go back to Scotland, it seems a little unsporting not to leave me my house then, doesn't it?"

Nathan hurled a stapler at his head. Cameron shifted and it made quite an impression on what had been, a second before, a no doubt quite lovely crystal vase behind him. Cameron looked at Nathan's lawyers.

"Can't you control him?"

Nathan made noises of fury. The lawyers, to a man, began to shuffle paperwork importantly.

Cameron looked at Nathan thoughtfully. "Who gave you the idea to buy up so much of my company?"

"I planned it all myself."

"Bollocks," Cameron said bluntly. " 'Tis one thing, Nathan, to hate someone; 'tis another thing to hate so fiercely you're willing to risk your entire fortune—not that you have any of that left—on ruining a company the size of Cameron Ltd. It would make more sense to take over my company and run it yourself—and line your pockets as a result. There's more to this than what you're telling me."

"You'll never know what it is," Nathan said, "and it *isn't* your company anymore. Not after tomorrow morning."

Cameron rested his elbows on the table and studied Nathan for several minutes in silence. Well, he was missing something and he was damned if he knew what. Perhaps it was as Alex had said, that the whole assault was to vex him. He couldn't imagine what pleasure Nathan would take from that, but perhaps Nathan was simply incapable of sense and this was his madness on display.

Cameron suspected he could spend all day trying to understand that madness and it would be nothing but time wasted. Perhaps it was just best to put the final nail in the coffin and be finished. He put his hands on the table.

"Well then, let's get down to it, shall we? Did any of your gaggle of solicitors think to bring a list of *your* shareholders along to this little parley? I understand there's been quite a run on your stock of late. Especially this morning."

Nathan rolled his eyes. "Of course, you idiot. How stupid do you think I am—"

Cameron was quite satisfied he knew just how stupid Nathan was, but there was no point in saying as much. He simply waited for his words to sink in.

They did, then Nathan slapped his hands on the table. "What do you mean, this morning?" he demanded. "What does that mean?"

Cameron looked at the men on either side of the table. "I don't suppose you've had time to find out who owns—after all the layers, of course—all those charitable trusts, endowments, and hedge funds who have been buying up so much of Ainsworth Associates over the past fortnight? Actually, you can look for my name as well this morning on a rather substantial trade. I imagine I got quite a bargain."

"What are you talking about?" Nathan said in a low, deadly voice. "Tell me, if you dare."

"If you like," Cameron said easily. "What your lads here will find after quite a bit of digging is that the twenty-five percent of your company that you no longer own was bought up by various entities that are, in the end, mine."

"You didn't," Nathan said, his face mottled with rage.

Cameron looked at him coolly. "How stupid to you think *I* am, Nathan? I own controlling interest of your company now, which means you no longer have control of Cameron Ltd. Did you think I would allow you to ruin what my family has sacrificed for for *generations*, you pompous *git*?"

Nathan's lawyers went scrambling either for documents or for their phones. Nathan stood up and started shouting at them. Even his secretary opened the door to see what the commotion was about. Cameron looked at her.

"How were the chocolates?"

"Lovely, Lord Cameron," she said, the pucker turning into a species of smile. "Thank you."

Cameron smiled at her, then turned back to look at the chaos in front of him. He called out the names of a few charitable organizations, just to give the lawyers something to do, then realized his phone was buzzing. He picked it up, then went to stand against the wall where the caterwauling wasn't quite so loud.

"Cameron, where's Sunny?"

Cameron had expected Derrick. It took him a moment to realize it was Patrick. "What do you mean?"

"I haven't seen Sunny yet. You'd said she would be home by ten and it's quarter to eleven. Did you change your plans?"

"Nay," Cameron said, finding that his heart was suddenly not beating very well. "Have you tried her phone?"

"Aye. She's not answering, but that may be because she's afraid to pick up and possibly wreck your car."

Cameron took a deep breath. "Drive to Inverness for me—"

"I'm halfway there. I just wanted to make sure I wasn't over-reacting."

"Damn it," Cameron said fiercely. "I should have locked her in your bloody guest chamber. If anything's happened to her—"

"Don't panic yet. I'll do a little digging and get back to you."

"Where are Madelyn and your wee gel?"

"At Jamie's with him guarding the doors. I'll keep going and ring you in a bit."

Cameron nodded, hung up, and slipped his phone into his pocket. He'd seen Sunny back into his car himself. She'd still been sitting on the tarmac when his plane had pulled away, but promised she would go once he'd taken off. Perhaps she'd remained there a bit longer to read the car's manual. Perhaps Peter had done the unthinkable and allowed the battery of his mobile to run out.

Though that wasn't likely.

He leaned back against the wall and tried to relax as he watched the ruckus going on in front of him. Nathan currently had one of his attorneys by the lapels and was shaking him vigorously. Cameron would have enjoyed that, but he couldn't. He pulled his phone back out of his pocket and started to text Peter.

He was interrupted by the door opening. He looked up and cursed under his breath as Penelope came inside. He shut his phone and shoved it back in his pocket. Well, at least her hands were empty of liquids—or weapons. Cameron jammed his hands into his pockets and waited to see what she would do.

She looked at Nathan briefly, then walked over to him.

"Take your hands out of your bloody pockets, Mac," she said briskly, "and tell me what this is."

He ignored her first demand. "What this is, love, is your brother trying to ruin me."

She staggered. He'd never seen anyone do it outside films, and he was impressed by how graceful she was. She took her bag and brushed the glass off the top of the credenza with it, then leaned against it heavily and looked at him.

"Surely, not."

"Perhaps he couldn't bear the thought of you having to wed with me."

"He's no fool—" She shut her mouth with a snap and looked marginally embarrassed. "Not that I'm marrying you for your money, of course. It's just that Nathan doesn't have the brains to run Father's company. He certainly can't want yours."

Cameron lifted an eyebrow briefly. "I always find it surprising what people want—and what they're willing to do to have it. Commit robbery, perjury . . . murder." He shrugged. " 'Tis an interesting list, isn't it?"

Her mouth fell open. "You aren't suggesting that *I* would do anything of the sort."

"Of course not," he said smoothly, though he most certainly was willing to suggest quite a few things where Penelope was concerned. "Unfortunately, I imagine your brother's capable of those things and more."

Penelope looked at Nathan with a frown, then turned back to Cameron. "I'm finished with this conversation. Very depressing. Tell Nathan I came as he wanted me to. I believe he had house funds for me, but I can collect those later today." She looked at her brother for another moment or two, then smoothed her hand over her hair. "Don't bloody him on your way out. And remember brunch tomorrow."

Cameron suspected he wouldn't be there, but saw no reason to tell her that. He simply watched her go and wondered about her. She certainly hadn't leapt to her brother's defense. Either she knew he was guilty, or she was just as guilty as he was and she wanted to draw attention away from herself.

Or perhaps he had just spent too much of his life looking over his shoulder and now he couldn't distinguish friend from foe.

He would give that more thought later, after he'd finished with Nathan and after, ach, by the blessed saints, after he'd determined where Sunny was—

His phone buzzed and he answered immediately. "Aye?"

"Your car's on the side of the road, Cameron," Patrick said grimly. "Empty."

Cameron was particularly grateful for something beneath his backside. *"What?"* he asked incredulously.

"Peter's car is half crunched in a ditch behind the first. He isn't there, though there's blood on the ground by the door. Your Mercedes is clean, though the keys were still in it." He paused. "Odd, isn't that? It seems as though someone was more interested in vexing you than robbing you."

Cameron couldn't find words to use in expressing his astonishment and dread. Those had been Alex's exact words. He looked up to find Nathan standing in the middle of his frantic lawyers, simply watching him with a small, ugly smile.

And in that moment, he knew Nathan knew quite a few things he shouldn't have.

"I'll ring you again in five," Cameron said. "Get my car away from there, if you can. Leave Peter's for the bobbies to keep busy with. I have the feeling I'm not going to want any official help with this."

"Of course."

Cameron put his phone back in his pocket, then walked across the boardroom and rounded the end of the table. Nathan shrank back, then suddenly seemed to remember himself. He puffed out his chest.

"If you hurt me, my solicitors will testify to it in court."

Cameron moved aside a pair of sweating barristers, then looked at Nathan. "Where is she?" he asked quietly.

"Who?"

"You know who I'm talking about."

"Actually, what I know is who *you* are," Nathan said. "I have a friend who knew you . . . centuries ago."

Cameron wasn't sure if he was surprised to find his worst fears were being realized, or relieved that at least he now knew the face of his enemy. He smiled in his most bored fashion. "University seems that far ago, doesn't it?"

"I'm not talking about University," Nathan spat, "I'm talking about something else entirely and you know damn well what it is. Your particular background makes it a bit hard to have a legal birth certificate, doesn't it? And if you don't have that, I think you might not be entitled to several other things you currently enjoy."

Cameron saw several of the bloody barristers perk up their ears. He wasn't at all surprised, but he wasn't going to give them anything to gnaw on, either. He looked at Nathan in puzzlement. "What in the hell are you talking about, Nathan?"

Nathan leaned in closely. "I *know*, Robert."

"And I *know* several things about where your money has gone that would make your set of friends *and* your board of directors very uncomfortable," Cameron returned. "Would you like me to blurt a bit out now?"

Nathan did pale just a bit. "Best of luck proving it."

"You underestimate me if you think I can't," Cameron said quietly. "Now, before I beat the bloody hell out of you, tell me *where she is*. Kidnapping is a jailable offense, last time I heard."

Nathan lifted an eyebrow. "So's rape, last time *I* heard."

It took every ounce of self-control Cameron had not to throttle the bastard where he stood. The only thing that kept him from it was hoping that if he walked away, Nathan would do something to reveal where Sunny was—and Nathan couldn't do that if he was unconscious.

Cameron didn't want to think about Nathan being his only link to Sunny at this point, but he realized he had no choice.

He took a step back and looked at Nathan's attorneys. "Stick close to him," he advised. "You'll have plenty of billable hours trying to get him out of jail. Just hope the charges are limited to kidnapping."

Nathan started spluttering, but Cameron ignored him. He turned and walked out of the boardroom. He nodded to Nathan's secretary, then slammed his way out of the office. He ducked into the lift, then opened the second mobile Derrick had given him on the plane, the one that was dedicated to Nathan's private line. He didn't have to wait long. Nathan connected almost immediately with a voice Cameron hadn't heard before, a lad with a heavy Glaswegian accent. Cameron listened intently.

"Do you have her?" Nathan demanded.

"Aye. We're on the road now—"

"Shut up," Nathan growled. "Just get her there. I'm on my way. And keep your hands off her until I'm finished with her."

"I don't take orders—"

"You certainly do if you want to be paid!" Nathan bellowed. "Now, shut up and do as you're told."

Cameron listened to them curse a bit more at each other, then ring off. The thought had occurred to him, of course, that Nathan might have thugs in Scotland as well, but he'd never seen evidence of it. That lad he'd just listened to was not a Highlander, though, so perhaps he would make mistakes a lad raised in the hills might not, mistakes in following directions, or recognizing landmarks, or fitting in with the natives.

It was cold comfort, but he was willing to take it.

Vowing that he would make Nathan squirm until he passed out from the stress, he left the lift, dialing Derrick as he did.

"Hear that?" he asked.

"Aye," Derrick growled, sounding coldly furious. "Pat MacLeod called me, just so you know, so I'm aware of what's happened in Scotland. I've tried Peter repeatedly, but no answer. I've already called Ewan and had him ready the plane. What else can I do?"

"Call Oliver and make sure he shadows Nathan. I'll meet you at the airport."

"Aye."

Cameron hung up and ran outside to find George waiting for him. He jerked open the door and got in.

"Airport, George," he said briskly. "Please make haste."

"Of course, my lord."

Cameron dialed Patrick, who picked up on the first ring. "Nathan's had her kidnapped," Cameron said briskly, forcing himself to keep any emotion out of his voice. "They're on the road but I've no idea where."

"Do you have tails on these lads in Scotland?"

"I don't even know who these new lads *are*," Cameron said, helplessly. "They aren't Nathan's, or we would have known about them."

Patrick made a noise of frustration. "Think you they have anything to do with the gray car following Sunshine?"

"Nay," Cameron said slowly. "Whoever was driving that little Ford was easily intimated by me. Derrick looked for him in Inverness but didn't see aught. For all I know, it was a fool with one too many pints in him, following Sunny for the sport of it."

"Perhaps," Patrick said, sounding unconvinced.

"What of my car? Was there a sign of struggle? Any clues?"

"None, but I didn't dare take the time for a decent look lest the bobbies keep me where I didn't want to be."

Cameron could understand that. "You couldn't have done anything differently. I'm on my way home, but I'm leaving one of my lads behind to tail Nathan north. I can only hope he'll lead us to her."

"Are you certain he'll come?"

"Wouldn't you be?"

Patrick sighed heavily. "Aye, I would. Make haste, lad. We'll be on the road north. Do you need an extra car?"

"Aye, if you can manage it. I'll have Derrick with me."

"I'll have my Range Rover dropped off at the airport, then. Derrick can drive that and follow you up. Bobby's in your McLaren right now. I'll call you when I have other tidings."

"Thank you, Patrick," Cameron said, with a deep sigh. "If anything has happened—"

"Don't," Patrick said sharply. "You can't do a damn thing about it until you're here. She's tough as spring beef, just like her sister. She'll survive."

Cameron could only hope so. He thanked Patrick again, rang Ewan and had a brief conversation with him about haste, then hung up and closed his eyes.

He didn't allow himself to think.

A n hour later, he was standing at the door of the Gulfstream cockpit, watching the blue sky and finding it not nearly as soothing as he usually did. He'd changed into jeans and boots, much more sensible for tracking, but he wished desperately for a sword. He couldn't have been so fortunate as to have had Patrick bring an extra one along.

"Cameron, go sit."

He looked at his captain. "Marcus, fly this bloody thing faster."

"I can't go any faster, which you well know. We'll be on the ground in twenty minutes." He looked over his shoulder. "Sit your arse down, mate."

He cursed the man, a tough-as-nails former RAF fighter pilot, but did as he was bid. He looked at Derrick, who sat across from him.

"Anything new?"

Derrick had an earpiece in and was listening to his phone through it. He shook his head, then went back to listening. Cameron tapped his foot as the plane landed, but was up and pacing before they reached the hangar. He bounced on his heels until the first possible moment he could undo the hatch.

"Need any extra help?" Ewan asked.

Cameron looked at him seriously. "Can you keep secrets?"

"Please, Cameron," he said, rolling his eyes in disgust. "I'll go grab my gear."

Cameron leaped down the stairs and ran to his waiting car. The door opened as he approached and he slid in under the wheel.

"Thought ye'd want to drive," Bobby said solemnly from where he sat in the passenger seat.

"I do."

He waited until he saw Derrick turn on Patrick's lights behind him, then put his Mercedes in gear and left the airport. He drove very sedately through Inverness, calmly got as far out of town as he thought polite, then put his foot down.

Bobby only chortled.

"Call Pat," Cameron said briskly. "Find out where they've stopped and tell him I'm going to make a little visit to Tavish Fergusson's shop first."

"If ye say so, mate," Bobby said doubtfully. "Want me to stick 'im for ye?"

"After he's squawked like a plucked chicken, aye, I wouldn't mind."

Bobby seemed to find that to his liking and he wasted no time in telling Patrick what he would do if such an opportunity presented itself. Cameron found those thoughts of mayhem to be reassuring somehow. It also gave him something to think about instead of all the things that could be happening to Sunny whilst he was leagues away and unable to protect her.

He drove north as quickly as he dared. He had to slow for the odd cluster of sheep and the recurring little villages where he didn't want to run over any small children, but other than that, he flew.

"It'll go faster than this," Bobby remarked at one point.

Cameron shot him a look. "And you would know?"

"I would, mate."

Cameron would have answered, but he was too busy slowing down for his own village to do so.

Patrick was waiting for him outside Tavish Fergusson's sterile-looking shop. Cameron nodded to him, then jerked open Tavish's door and strode inside.

"I don't know anything," Tavish blurted out, flattening himself dramatically against the wall behind his counter.

Cameron stopped and leaned negligently against the opposite

side of that counter. "Why would I think you would?" he asked calmly. "Guilty conscience, Tavish?"

Tavish put his shoulders back. "You can't bully me."

"I daresay I haven't begun to try," Cameron said with a snort. "I'm curious, though, why you wouldn't think I was simply here for a few herbs. Or a bit of arsenic, if you have any."

"I don't sell that sort of thing," Tavish said haughtily. "I'm strictly here for the tourists."

"Oh, and we have so many of those," Patrick said sarcastically from his position at the opposite end of the counter. "Now, Tavish, my lad, we can do this easily, or you can make it all very difficult for yourself. Lord Robert and I have a few questions that we need answers for and I'm going to assume you'll be happy to help."

"I'll call my brother," Tavish squeaked.

"I suppose you could," Patrick agreed, "but then he'd know all about several things you might want to keep to yourself. Let's discuss those now, shall we?"

Cameron let Patrick take over and push Tavish as hard as he liked. He watched, wondering how long it would be before Tavish broke down and wept like a babe. He didn't suppose it would take very long. Tavish was, despite all pretense at manliness, a complete woman when it came to defending himself. He even dressed like a wench, what with his shirt unbuttoned halfway down his ches—

Cameron froze.

Before he thought better of it, he reached out, grabbed hold of the pendant Tavish was wearing, and yanked the thing over Tavish's head. He stared at the rough-hewn stone set in metal that lay in his hand and thought he might have to find a chair soon.

"Och, but that's mine," Tavish protested.

Cameron looked up. "Where did you get this?"

"None of your business."

Cameron had reached out and snatched Tavish by the shirt before he realized what he was doing. He refrained from shaking him until his teeth fell out, but he couldn't stop himself from pulling the man halfway over his very tidy counter. "If you don't want me to kill you here," he growled, "you'll tell me *where you got this*."

"It was a gift," Tavish gasped. "To ward off evil."

Cameron blinked in surprise "From a *man*?"

Tavish fought him off, pulled himself back over the counter to his feet, and straightened his clothes with a pair of jerks. "Of course not—" He shut his mouth, then looked horrified, as if he had said more than he should have.

Cameron could understand the horror. He looked at Patrick.

"North," he said. "She'll be north."

"How did you—" Tavish spluttered.

Cameron shot him a look. "I know you signed papers that put you together in a trust with Nathan and Penelope Ainsworth, a trust created to buy out my business. You'd better think of a damned good reason to have done that before I come back."

The blood drained from Tavish's face, his eyes rolled back in his head, and he slid down to the floor in a graceful swoon.

Cameron strode out of the shop and headed for his car. Damn it, damn it, damn it to hell. How could he have been so stupid?

"Planning on telling me anything soon?" Patrick asked pointedly from behind him.

Cameron spun around and looked at him. "We'll try the Fergusson keep. Trust me."

"Actually, Ian was planning to head that way. He might even be there by now."

Cameron cursed. "Tell him to be careful."

"He almost died in that dungeon, so he's always a bit ginger when scouting it out—even in the current century. Why do you think Sunny'll be there?"

"Because it isn't my cousin Giric we're looking for," Cameron said grimly. He spun on his heel. "Just trust me."

Patrick nodded shortly, then strode to his car. Cameron did the same, drove carefully out of the village and past the last house, then put his foot down.

He hadn't gone but a single bloody league before he'd blown past Hamish Fergusson's police car. He pulled over before Hamish even managed to get himself and his police car out from behind his usual bush. Patrick continued on, honking. Cameron glowered, then paced until Hamish pulled up behind him, his lights flashing importantly. He watched Derrick pull in behind Hamish and wait. Hamish got out of his squad car, hitched up his trousers, then marched over with a swagger.

"Here, now," Hamish began indignantly. "And where's that Pat MacLeod going in such a hurry! I say—"

"Shut up, you fool," Cameron snapped. "Shut up and for once in your life listen to something that might serve you."

Hamish gaped at him.

"I know where trouble is," Cameron said bluntly. "I will deliver the miscreants to you, unconscious and ripe for you to put in your pitiful little cells in the village, *if* you'll just keep off my tail and not blow this for me."

Hamish looked at him calculatingly. "Are you on the level?"

Cameron swore. "Stop watching so much telly, Hamish. Stay out of my way and I'll see that you're bloody famous and have all the glory for this. Now, what's your mobile number?"

Hamish wrote it down for him, then handed it over. His eyes were very wide. "There you go, my lord."

"I'll call you when I'm ready for you," Cameron said, slipping the paper into his pocket. "How many pairs of handcuffs do you have?"

"Handcuffs?"

Cameron resisted the urge to shake him. "Why don't you return quickly to the village," he began, with exaggerated patience, "collect all the pairs you might have, then hurry back to your bush and wait for my call. Can you possibly do that?"

"But your points—"

"Hamish!"

Hamish ducked his head. "All right."

"Trust me. 'Twill be worth it."

Hamish shot him a perplexed look, as if he found the thought of glory and fame to be just too good to be true, then apparently decided it was worth the risk. He marched back to his car, got in, then turned around to head for the village. Cameron threw himself into his car, pulled the door down, then gunned his McClaren back onto the road.

"Call Patrick," he said shortly to Bobby. "Find out where he's stopped."

Bobby looked at him, the phone already on his ear. "Up ahead a fair bit."

Twenty minutes later, Cameron saw Patrick's Vanquish pulled over on the side of the road. He pulled up behind him, then jumped out of the car. He heard other doors slam and knew Derrick and Ewan were running up behind him as well. He strode to where Patrick was leaning against the passenger side of his car, talking into his phone.

"Well?" he demanded.

Patrick held up his hand. Cameron wished he'd had a sword.

He wished he had kept Sunny with him. He wished a great many things that, at the moment, he couldn't change.

But at least he had lads on his side this time. Derrick and Ewan were standing with Bobby, and all three were watching him silently. Patrick slipped his phone into his pocket, then looked at him.

"Ian's found her. She's in the Fergusson keep." He paused. "You aren't going to like the next bit."

"Is she alive?" Cameron asked grimly.

Patrick paused, then reached out and put his hand on Cameron's shoulder.

"He's not sure."

Cameron had never been more grateful for twenty-eight years of living in medieval Scotland than he was in that moment. It was almost instinctual to take every emotion that didn't serve him and stuff it into a deep, silent place inside himself where it wouldn't get in the way of what he needed to do to survive. He threw his keys to Bobby.

"Get my car off the road. Derrick, take the other and follow him. Catch up to us on foot." He looked at Patrick. "Is it only Ian?"

"He has one of Conal Grant's lads with him, Andrew Mac-Dougal. Andrew has a rather interesting set of skills you might appreciate." He reached in his car, removed two wicked-looking dirks from the front seat, then handed his keys to Ewan. "Don't scratch my car or a dirk in your belly will be your reward. I think there might be an obliging copse of trees about a mile up. Use it for cover."

Ewan was, for a change, absolutely silent. He merely nodded, wide-eyed, took the keys, and walked around the car to get in.

Cameron accepted the sheathed dirk, shot his lads a last look of warning, then headed across the countryside with Patrick. It came as a pleasant surprise to find that Patrick had the same sorts of tracking habits he did, though he realized it shouldn't have. After all, Patrick MacLeod had lived a good part of his life in medieval Scotland.

But so had the Highlander keeping Sunny captive.

He closed his eyes briefly, then continued on, praying he wouldn't come too late.

Chapter 31

S*unny* wondered if she were dead.

Actually, that wasn't exactly true. She'd only wondered that as she'd struggled to come out of whatever drug-induced stupor she'd been plunged into. She now knew she was most definitely alive and quite uncomfortably chained to a wall in a ruined castle. She'd had terror flash through her briefly as she'd wondered if she'd perhaps driven Cameron's car into a time gate, been clunked over the head, and carried off to a medieval castle to rot forever.

Then she'd realized that the castle she was standing in wasn't an intact keep, it was the ruined Fergusson one, the bands around her wrists were actually handcuffs, and the souls watching her were dressed in modern clothes, not plaids.

It wasn't much of an improvement over what it could have been, actually.

She had to admit that when she'd realized where she was, she'd wondered if Hamish or Tavish—or both—had suddenly snapped and decided she should pay for all the perceived sins of the clan MacLeod over the years. She'd soon discovered that while it was indeed a Fergusson who had taken her prisoner, it was not a Fergusson brother. It was a Fergusson of a more medieval vintage.

Gilly Fergusson Cameron, actually.

Sunny had been very surprised, though looking back on it all now, she wondered why she hadn't seen it before. It wasn't that she knew Cameron's clan very well, but Giric had never seemed to her to have the smarts to pull off the kind of scheme that Cameron was trying to fight. She wasn't completely convinced that Gilly had that sort of cleverness, either, but it was hard to ignore the evidence standing in front of her. It was also hard to ignore the very unhinged look in Gilly's eye or the increasingly shrill tone of her voice.

The woman was stark-raving mad.

She was also, Sunny had realized once the stars had cleared enough for her to be able to see clearly, the black-haired witch who had been waiting outside the yoga studio that night Tavish had fired her. That realization had made her shiver so hard, she was still fighting the chills that went down her spine.

That was the kind of spooky happening she could most definitely do without.

Gilly was pacing on the opposite side of a yawning dungeon mouth in the floor of the great hall, speaking to her thugs in impressively coherent English sentences, and dressed in very unremarkable black trousers and white shirt with her dyed jet-black hair actually combed for a change. She presented a very reasonable picture. Well, except for the very sharp medieval dirk in one hand, the long syringe in the other, and the completely deranged look in her eye.

Sunny took a deep breath. She should have known she would come to a bad end with a Fergusson.

She closed her eyes briefly and wondered just where she'd gone wrong. Probably when she'd suggested she go with Cameron to the airport. Her second mistake had been to take Cameron's car home. She'd been nervous because it was touchy and jumpy and seemed able to do the speed limit in first gear alone. It had helped some to see Peter's lights behind her, but not much. She'd relaxed just a bit after she'd put Inverness behind her and gotten on a road with less traffic. There had actually come a point where she'd thought she would make it without trouble.

Then a big, black SUV had cut between her and Peter and tried to run her off the road. She'd thought it was just an aggressive jerk who'd had one too many instead of breakfast, so she'd spent a futile five minutes trying to outrun him. In the end, she'd pulled over because she'd just wanted to let him by. She'd heard the horrible sound of a car crunching and watched in her rearview mirror as Peter had been rammed into a ditch.

She'd started to try to figure out how to get the door open so she could go help, but changed her mind once she saw the rough-looking characters piling out of the SUV. In the ensuing panic, she'd managed to kill the car. Between trying to restart it and trying to find the locks for the doors, she'd managed neither.

The last thing she remembered was a hand going over her face and darkness descending immediately.

She supposed now that it had been a handkerchief soaked in chloroform to knock her out and some sort of narcotic to keep her out. She didn't feel well at all and desperately wanted to sit down, but her hands were above her head and the sconce that her chain was attached to was bolted into the rock more securely than she would have imagined possible. Even putting her full weight on it did nothing but make the handcuffs cut into her wrists. Unfortunately, she was getting to the point where she couldn't breathe very well.

And there was no sword-wielding almost-fiancé or brother-in-law in sight to help her.

Gilly suddenly barked at her men to go sit at the back of the hall. Sunny was faintly impressed to find that they did. She jumped when she saw that Gilly had come around the opening in the floor to stand immediately in front of her.

"I imagine Cameron will be here soon," Gilly said with a cold smile.

Sunny had a little shiver go down her spine at the sound of very medieval Gaelic coming out of Gilly's mouth. "How do you know?"

"Because Tavish called me half an hour ago to tell me that Cameron had been in his shop." She smiled easily. "He tells me everything, of course. I think I frighten him."

Sunny could see how she would, but thought it might be unwise to say as much.

"'Tis just a matter of time before Cameron puts the pieces together, of course. Whatever else he is, he is no fool. And he certainly wouldn't leave *you* in danger now, would he?"

"But he wouldn't have left you that way, either—"

Gilly backhanded her with the hand that held the knife. Sunny's head snapped around so hard, she dashed her cheek against the rock. She had never been struck in her life and the shock of it was so great, she could only stand there and gasp. It was the same sort of shock, she supposed, that one might have felt after having a very large bucket of cold water dumped over one's head while standing out in the snow. Only this hurt a lot worse.

"He ruined my chance to be mistress of Cameron Hall. I have quite a bit to repay him for."

"But weren't you that after Cameron left?" Sunny ventured.

Gilly shot her a look that had her wishing she'd kept her mouth shut.

"Giric wouldn't wed me," she said flatly. "He wanted me as his whore, nothing else."

"What an ass," Sunny said, before she thought better of it.

Gilly scowled at her for a moment, then relaxed just the slightest bit. "Aye, he was." She considered. "I suppose you're curious as to how I managed all this, aren't you?"

Sunny nodded gingerly. Maybe if she was very careful, she might actually convince Gilly that killing her was a bad idea. If she could just get her hands free, she might be able to get out of Gilly's way before Gilly pumped her full of whatever nasty thing she had in that syringe.

Gilly walked away, skirting the edge of the open pit. Sunny looked up, then cursed. The chain was not just hooked over the sconce, it was somehow hooked *to* it as well. There was no way to get herself free unless she was able to get out of the handcuffs and she could tell already that wouldn't happen without a key.

"Are you listening?"

Sunny nodded immediately.

"Giric found your little gate that led through the centuries," Gilly said, coming to a stop with her toes hanging over the edge of the dungeon mouth. "He came back home after a pair of months with a newspaper from your time, just to prove where he'd been."

"How clever of him," Sunny managed.

Gilly shrugged. "He wasn't, particularly, but he was thorough. He wanted to learn your tongue, then return to your time and simply slay Cameron. I thought there might be a better plan."

Sunny imagined that was true.

"So I waited," Gilly continued, beginning to pace, "until my firstborn son could hold the clan, then I killed Giric and used the gate myself. The MacLeod witch wasn't at home that night, which allowed me to help myself to a knife and clothing. I needed a place to live, though, and not on MacLeod soil, so I took shelter with an old woman who had no children. I repaid her for that shelter by finding herbs for her."

"The woman with the shop up north?"

Gilly pursed her lips. "Aye, and you almost found me, didn't you?"

"It was dumb luck," Sunny admitted. "And I didn't see you. But you were in the gray car, weren't you?"

"Nay, that was a lad working for me. I didn't want him to follow you, but he disobeyed me. He paid for that mistake with his life, of course."

Sunny had to force herself to breathe normally. Had she hoped Gilly might have some sense left in her? That had been a vain hope, apparently.

Gilly shrugged suddenly. "Since you'll be dead soon as well, I suppose there's no point in not giving you the rest of the tale, is there?"

Sunny had absolutely nothing to say to that. It took all her self-control to not beg Gilly to have mercy. But she was almost a Cameron and she suspected that even almost-Camerons didn't beg for mercy—not even when they were looking death in its demented eye. Besides, if she were really lucky, she might talk Gilly out of her plan. Maybe Peter would stop lying in a crumpled heap near her, wake up perky and clever, and they would both manage to escape before Gilly killed them.

Thinking about that was better than dwelling on whatever alternative she was sure Gilly had planned for them.

"Imagine my surprise when I realized soon after that Cameron was alone and you weren't anywhere to be seen." She scratched her cheek with the edge of her blade. " 'Twas baffling, so I decided not to act until I'd learned the truth. As time passed, I realized that I had come to the future a pair of years after Cameron had. I assumed that you would arrive eventually, so I waited. And whilst I waited, I thought about how to hurt Cameron best. I could see he valued his business, so I thought to strike there and let the rest come as it would. I looked for someone to aid me, then decided on Nathan Ainsworth."

"How in the world did you meet him?" Sunny asked in surprise.

Gilly shot her a cold look. "Do you think me incapable of presenting myself as a fine lady?"

"Of course not," Sunny said quickly. "It just seems so coincidental that you should have chosen Nathan when Nathan's father and Alistair Cameron were such good friends."

"And you think I didn't know that as well?" Gilly demanded. "I'm just as capable as the next Highlander of reading the paper."

"Of course you are," Sunny said with a nod. "I didn't mean to suggest otherwise."

Gilly didn't look particularly happy with that answer, but she continued on just the same. "I found Nathan at a racing track, losing enormous sums on the horses, and introduced myself as a distant relative of Alistair's. Once he knew I loathed Cameron as he did, it wasn't hard to convince him to help me. I've been work-ing off and on at Ainsworth Manor as a chef for the past three months." She smiled briefly. "That makes it easier to slip things into the stew, don't you know."

Sunny swallowed with difficulty. She wasn't at all surprised. It made her wonder, absently, if it had been Gilly to try to poison Cameron in the past, not Giric. For all she knew, Gilly had poi-soned Giric's father as well.

So much death. It was no wonder Gilly was crazy.

"I knew losing his business would hurt Cameron's pride," Gilly continued easily, "but in time, I realized that wouldn't be enough for me. I wanted to destroy his heart. I looked for you, but you still weren't in Scotland or England and I didn't know your surname. I finally saw your sister in the village a year or two ago. At first I thought she was you, but I soon realized my mistake. It was tempting to kill her, because I knew it would grieve you, but it wasn't what I wanted. I watched her marry that very handsome MacLeod lad and suddenly there you were as well." She smiled. "And then I knew the time to act had come."

Sunny closed her eyes briefly. Madelyn would have died and Sunny wouldn't have had a clue as to why. She swallowed, hard. "Your patience was rewarded."

"And it serves me still, for I'm patient enough to leave you alive now, when I can scarce keep myself from plunging my dirk into your breast."

"Why me?" Sunny managed.

"I already told you," she shouted suddenly. She took a deep breath, then visibly forced herself to calm down. "Because it will grieve Cameron to watch you die."

"But why do you want to hurt Cameron?"

"Because he never wanted me," she said in a low voice. "I wed Breac before I realized who I truly wanted was his brother. I never said anything to Cameron, but he should have known. I *willed* him to know, but he ignored me."

Sunny suspected that Cameron had been better off that way.

"I knew I was destined to be mistress of Cameron Hall," Gilly continued, "which left me with little choice but to have Cameron slain." She looked at Sunny archly. "I started that battle, of course. My kin were coming for Cameron, to repay him for not wanting me, to repay him for standing in the way of what should have been mine. And then Breac was stupid enough to take the blade meant for Cameron."

"But Cameron was going to wed you," Sunny ventured very hesitantly. "After that battle."

Gilly's change of mood was frightening in its swiftness. She drew herself up. "Do you think I would have lowered myself to have him then?" she said with contempt. "After he'd spurned me? After he'd killed my husband? After he'd looked at you as he'd *never* looked at me?"

Sunny could only stare at Gilly, mute. She was stunned to realize that Cameron had lost his brothers because of the machinations of the woman standing in front of her. She didn't doubt that Gilly had helped Giric turn the clan against Cameron as well. She closed her eyes briefly. So much death and sorrow all because Gilly had wanted someone who hadn't wanted her back.

Gilly sharpened the syringe with the knife. "So, here we are, waiting for your lover. He'll watch me kill you, then I'll watch him rot in some jail while I take over Cameron Hall and enjoy all the luxuries he takes for granted." She smiled. "I want him to suffer every day of every month of every year for decades to come, knowing what he had and what he lost." She looked absently at the needle she was sharpening. "I wish he would hurry so I could be finished with you."

Sunny opened her mouth to tell her that Cameron was probably not going to just walk in when she realized she was wrong. She realized that Cameron was leaning against the ruined edge of doorway nearest her. She suspected by the absolute lack of expression on his face that he'd heard quite a bit of what Gilly had just said.

He pushed away from the doorway and walked into the middle of the hall. He stopped ten feet behind Gilly.

"Hello, sister," he said calmly.

Sunny opened her mouth to warn him that Gilly wasn't alone, but she supposed he already knew that. She was positive of it when she watched Patrick, Derrick, and Ian slither through various other windows and doors. She could see other men slipping past other openings and guessed that the entire castle was now surrounded by men loyal to Cameron.

What a difference a few centuries made.

The skirmish with Gilly's men was very brief, but that didn't serve Sunny much. Gilly had leaped across the dungeon opening and grabbed her by the hair before Cameron could reach her. Sunny felt the prick of something against her neck. She didn't bother to identify what. A knife across her trachea, a needle in her jugular; it was all the same as far as death was concerned.

"Gilly, let her go," Cameron said easily. " 'Tis me you want anyway, isn't it?"

"After she's dead," Gilly agreed. "Or would it be worse for you to watch someone else have her whilst she lived still? These aren't all the men I have at my command, you know. Nathan will be coming soon and bringing others with him. Perhaps you would like to watch him and his men have her. Would that please you?"

"It would bother me," Cameron conceded.

Sunny looked at him, but his gaze was fixed on Gilly. She wished she could have gotten her hands down from over her head. Then again, she wasn't exactly sure how far she could run even if she managed that. She felt terrible.

"Get rid of them," Gilly spat, pointing to Patrick and the others.

Cameron made a motion with his hand. Sunny watched from her very uncomfortable position as Patrick, Ian, and Derrick made a very loud production of leaving. She could hear them cursing for quite a while before their voices faded to nothing. She didn't doubt they would double back and join whoever else was out there, but it wouldn't do her any good if Gilly slit her throat.

Soon, it was just her and Gilly by the wall and Cameron motionless in the middle of the Fergusson great hall. He was so beautiful, standing there with the sunlight streaming down on his dark hair, it was all she could do not to weep at the sight of him. She could hardly believe she was so close to having him, yet even closer to losing him.

"Since we're waiting for Nathan," he said carefully, "what shall we do to pass the time? Would you care to tell me how you came to be here?"

Gilly's hand tightened in Sunny's hair. "Don't distract me."

"I'm merely satisfying my curiosity," he said mildly. "I'd also like to know what it is you want. Besides me watching my lady suffer at Nathan's hands, that is."

Sunny found her head slammed back against the rock so hard that she saw stars. Well, at least Gilly had let her go. Gilly stepped away and stood at the edge of the dungeon pit. Sunny was enormously tempted to just try to kick her into it, but she caught the warning look Cameron threw her.

Let me handle this.

She supposed she didn't have a choice. After all, she was the one chained to the wall. She took a deep breath and tried to relax as she listened to Gilly repeat the story she'd given earlier. It was done without embellishment, so Sunny supposed it was accurate enough. Cameron didn't move, didn't try to rush Gilly, he just stood there silent and still. Gilly soon turned from telling her tale to berating Cameron for every imagined slight she'd ever suffered. And still Cameron merely stood there and listened.

But Sunny could tell he wasn't just paying attention to her demented ramblings. He gave off the same aura he had in the woods so long ago, as if he knew exactly what was going on around him. He shifted at one point so he was partially facing the door as well as Gilly. Sunny understood why a moment later when Nathan Ainsworth himself walked into the hall.

She couldn't see how this was an improvement.

Nathan was less impressive in person than in his pictures, and she supposed that probably bothered him quite a bit. It bothered her quite a bit that he had a gun in his hand.

Gilly turned to Nathan. "What took you so long?"

"I don't have a private plane at my disposal," Nathan growled. "I had to wait for the bloody shuttle just like everyone else."

"You'll have money enough very soon," Gilly said dismissively. "As you can see, I have gone to the trouble of saving his whore for you—"

"You did not," Nathan said in astonishment. "*I'm* the one who had her sent to you! Besides, I don't care about her. I'm here for *him.* Stay out of my way so I can kill him and have this over with."

"I don't want him dead," Gilly said sharply.

"I don't care what you want—"

Gilly advanced on him. "You fool, you couldn't have done this without my wit."

"And you couldn't have done this without my *money*," Nathan spat.

"Which you don't have any more of," Cameron put in. "Money, that is, Nathan. Not wit, Gilly. You have that and to spare, of course."

"Don't flatter her," Nathan said, his words clipped. "She's a backwoods Scotswoman who hasn't the foggiest idea of how to execute a decent revenge. I don't even know why I need her."

"Because I told you all his secrets," Gilly said in a low, very dangerous voice. "I told you he was the laird of the clan Cameron in 1375, that he traveled through time to get here, that he lied to have everything he has." She rounded the end of the dungeon toward him. "You would have *nothing* without me. And if you touch him, I'll kill you."

Cameron clasped his hands behind his back. "Thank you, Gilly," he said quietly, "for being on my side for a change."

That sent both Gilly and Nathan into a frenzy of shouting. Sunny flinched in spite of herself. She had thought nothing could be more dangerous than medieval Scotland, but she decided she'd been wrong. This was much worse. Cameron didn't have his sword, Nathan had a gun, and Gilly had no more hold on her sanity. Her shrill accusations were becoming wilder by the minute. At least she had turned her venom on Nathan. Even Nathan began to look a bit nervous.

"I say," he said at one point, taking a step back from her, "I'm all for a bit of housecleaning, but we have to make this seem like an accident."

"As you did with your father?" Cameron asked politely.

Nathan pointed the gun at his head. "What do you think you know?"

"He knows no more than you," Gilly said with a snort. "*You* didn't have the courage to kill your sire, *I* did. You wanted him out of the way and I saw to it, just as I saw to Giric's father for him." She spat on the floor at Nathan's feet. "I'm always forced to do things men won't. But everyone thinks *you* did it, Nathan, don't they? And if someone must swing for it, 'twill be you and not me. After all, you were the one who couldn't leave Cameron alone afterward, weren't you? I told you to wait and you'd have what you wanted, but you were too bloody greedy, what with your assaults on his office and trying to find him in deserted alleyways. I told you he was cannier than that, but you wouldn't listen."

Nathan's face was so red, Sunny thought he might be on the verge of a stroke. His hand was trembling so badly, he could hardly hold the gun.

"Do you actually think I'll allow you to spread any of that about?" Nathan said, sounding very agitated. "How would you like it if I killed him and ruined your plan, you stupid rustic—"

Sunny felt time begin to slow. She watched as events unfolded in a way that felt more like a movie running at a fraction of its normal speed. Maybe the drugs were catching up with her again or maybe she was growing dizzy from having her arms above her head for so long. She didn't know, didn't care, didn't want to watch, but she simply couldn't look away.

Nathan pointed the gun at Cameron's chest, Cameron pulled a foot-long dirk out from behind his back and flipped it so he was holding on to the tip of the blade, and Gilly rushed toward them both, her hands outstretched.

And just behind Nathan stood Penelope Ainsworth with a very large, very sharp rock between her hands.

She brought it down with crushing force against her brother's head.

Cameron flung the knife at Nathan as he turned to see who was behind him. The knife caught Nathan through the wrist, but the gun went off anyway. Gilly recoiled as if she'd been struck. Sunny watched her as she staggered around the edge of the dungeon opening. A red stain was spreading slowly over her chest.

And then time went the other way, moving so swiftly that Sunny felt as if the rest of the drama unfolded almost instantaneously. Before Sunny could blink, Gilly had reached her and stabbed the needle into her shoulder. She shoved the plunger home.

"Die," she breathed out, then she slid down and landed in a heap at Sunny's feet.

Sunny saw Cameron leap over the dungeon opening toward her. He caught her in his arms and jerked the needle free of her flesh before she felt her knees give way.

"I love you," she whispered.

"Sunny . . ."

"Don't let me go," she said, fighting the blackness.

"Sunny, stay with me. Stay with me!"

Darkness fell and she knew no more.

Chapter 32

Cameron caught Sunny as she went limp and lifted her up into his arms. "Aid!" he bellowed.

He'd hardly gotten the word out before he realized that Patrick and Derrick were already there on either side of him, working on the handcuffs that held Sunny's hands over her head. Once they had freed her, Cameron carried her around the edge of the pit, then sank to his knees with her in his arms.

"Go see to Peter," Cameron rasped to Derrick. He looked up at Patrick who was squatting down across from him. "What's the drug?"

"Ketamine," Patrick said briskly. "I found the bag just inside the door with the empty vials. Judging by the way your man Peter's breathing, I think he's had quite a bit. Sunny's had less, which is very fortunate." He put his fingers to her neck and looked as his watch for a minute, then put his hand against her forehead. "Let's get her back to Moraig's as quick as may be."

"You can't be serious," Cameron said incredulously. "Just what in the hell are you going to do there?"

"Let her come out of this without adding a whole host of other things to the mix," Patrick said evenly. "I know what I'm doing, Cameron."

"Against modern drugs?"

"Ask Bobby the former addict. I detoxed him more than once until he stopped being stupid enough to get high."

"I can't discuss the particulars right at the moment," Bobby said happily from the other side of the hall. "We have another collection o' unconscious lads outside, as well as this load o' refuse here. I've a bit to do to tidy 'em up for Hamish. Shall I bring 'em in and pile 'em all together, Pat?"

"Please do," Patrick said, rising. "I'll look quickly at Peter. You start for the road, Cameron. I'll fetch your car then meet you there in ten minutes."

Cameron couldn't move. He knelt there, cradling the woman he loved in his arms, and felt quite certain his heart was on the verge of breaking. She was bruised, her dark hair was tangled, her face exceedingly pale. He bowed his head and prayed, because he couldn't do anything else. If something happened to her, if Patrick was wrong and—

"Cameron, now," Patrick said sharply.

Cameron looked up. "I'm trusting you with what means most to me."

"I know," Patrick said seriously. "Make haste so I can take care of her properly."

Cameron picked Sunny up in his arms and turned. He almost ran Penelope over before he realized she was still standing just inside the door, looking down in horror at her brother. He didn't want to take the time to talk to her when time was of the essence, but she looked so devastated, he couldn't not at least offer her a brief bit of comfort. He walked over to her and stopped.

"Penelope?"

She looked up at him, her eyes full of tears. "I think I killed Nathan."

"His head is far too hard for that, love. Of course, he will wish you had when he wakes up in jail."

She took a deep breath. "But Nathan didn't kill my father, did he? It was that . . . that crazy woman over there, wasn't it?"

"I imagine so," Cameron admitted, "though I don't think Nathan will escape his part in it."

She shivered. "That woman said she knew you as well."

"Darling, everyone knows me here. That's what happens when you're laird of the hall up the way."

"But she said you were from another . . . time."

Cameron shot her a look. "Really, Pen. Too many romance novels in the bath, don't you think?"

She took a deep breath, then nodded. "You're right." She wrapped her arms around herself. "What now, Mac?"

"The bobbies will come and you'll answer their questions as best you can. I'll leave Derrick and Ewan behind to help you. Then at some point I'd like to talk to you about your father's company. Someone needs to redeem it."

"Who, me?" she asked, aghast. "Work?"

"Others have done so with great success."

She apparently couldn't even manage a glare. "It wouldn't matter, though, would it? Not with what Nathan's done."

"Penelope, your brother is a dangerous, vindictive lad, but I think the drugs have made those tendencies worse. The board will understand that, especially when I help them see the truth."

Her mouth fell open slightly. "You would do that for me?"

"Of course. After all, I owe you my life." He looked at her thoughtfully. "Why did you find yourself here, if I'm allowed to ask that."

She looked at him bleakly. "After I saw what Nathan was doing to you in his offices, I began to suspect him of less than charitable feelings for you." She twisted her hands together. "I wasn't sure what could be done, but when he left the building in a tearing hurry, I determined to follow him. I feared he would see me on the shuttle, but I was hiding behind dark glasses and a hat. There was also an obliging bloke next to me who seemed to raise his newspaper at just the right time whenever Nathan turned to look up the aisle behind him."

Cameron suspected that might have been Oliver. He would have to thank him for more than just shadowing Nathan and keeping Derrick apprised of the situation. He smiled. "Brilliantly done, Pen, truly. Today would have finished much more tragically without you."

She attempted a smile, but it was a sick smile indeed. "At least some good has come of it."

"And more will follow. I think I can guarantee it."

She looked at him silently for a moment or two, then looked at Sunny. She reached out and smoothed the hair back from her face. "She's beautiful. Is this the girl Nathan said you were seeing? Sunshine?"

Cameron wasn't surprised that Nathan knew, or that he'd passed on what he knew to his sister. "Aye. If it eases you any, I loved her years ago. I lost her, unfortunately."

Penelope considered. "And now that you've found her again, are you going to marry her?"

He nodded solemnly.

She took a deep breath, then let it out. "Very well, I'll call the newspapers tomorrow and cancel everything. I will try to paint you as the cad, but I don't suppose anyone will believe that."

"I haven't cheated on you, Penelope," he said gravely, "if that makes it any easier to bear."

"Saving yourself for marriage, Mac?" she asked tartly.

"Aye," he said, unable to stop his smile.

She snorted at him, then blinked when she realized he was serious. She pursed her lips. "Do you want the ring back?"

He shook his head. "Keep it. I'll settle your debts for you as well."

She looked a little taken aback. "Why?"

"Because, Penelope, that is what a gentleman does when he parts company with a woman, even a woman who has never loved him."

She had the grace to blush. "We have no secrets, I see."

"Did you think we ever did?" he asked mildly. He nodded to his right. "I believe there's a MacLeod lad over there who might be able to help you until Ewan and Derrick are finished with their business." He looked over his shoulder and met Ian's eyes. "Ian, would you take care of her?"

Ian nodded and walked over. "Happy to do so, of course. Lady Penelope, why don't you come sit over here away from the rabble. We'll have them bound long before they awake, then I'll see you installed happily in a comfortable spot for the night."

Penelope paused. "I hope she's better soon, Mac. And you'll call me about Father's company?"

He nodded. "Once Sunny's well, aye, I will."

She nodded, then walked away with Ian. Cameron took a deep breath, then left the hall with a considerable sense of relief coursing through him. A murder solved, an ex-fiancée exonerated, and nothing in front of him but the freedom to take the woman he loved home and cherish her for the rest of their lives. He supposed he would enjoy it—when he was sure Sunny would wake again.

He saw Patrick sprinting north as he continued east. Now that the blood wasn't thundering in his ears, he could hear that Sunny's breathing was very shallow and rapid. He cradled her close to him and walked as quickly as he dared toward the road.

He prayed Patrick MacLeod knew what he was doing. He wanted to believe that this was no worse than a medieval wound, but he wasn't sure he could. Modern life was, as he could readily attest, more dangerous in some ways than the past.

He quickened his pace and vowed he would give Patrick MacLeod an hour, but no more. If Sunny wasn't markedly better by then, he would take her to the hospital.

In the end, he gave Patrick three. Sunny had been unconscious for the first, fighting off tea during the second, and cursing during the third.

She was obviously going to be just fine.

He sat on the floor of Sunny's loo and stroked her hair as she rested her cheek against the cool stone of the floor and made use of an impressive string of vile names in an impressive number of languages. He supposed he should have felt relieved that she seemed to be applying them to both him and Patrick equally.

"Damn you both to hell," she managed.

Patrick clucked his tongue at her from where he sat leaning against the bathroom's door frame. "Really, Sunny. After all we've done for you."

"How long have you both been here?" she asked hoarsely.

"Since the very first hallucination," Patrick said unrepentantly. "It's been a glorious afternoon, really."

Cameron smiled at Sunny's less-than-gracious thank you. He also smiled at the fact that she had reached out and put her arm over his leg, and she was conscious enough to do both. He'd trusted Patrick MacLeod, but there had been times when he'd had his own string of vile curses to heap on Patrick's head.

But now Sunny looked as though she would survive, he was free of quite a few things that had been troubling him, and he could smell things cooking in Sunny's kitchen that had to have been imported from Patrick's house.

"Want me to shut out the smell?" he asked suddenly.

Sunny only groaned. "Nothing is going to make me feel any worse than I feel right now. Cam, I want you to take my brother-in-law outside and hurt him."

Patrick laughed. "Sunny, I only did what I thought was necessary. And of course none of it was revenge for that night I spent in your loo in Seattle, puking my guts out thanks to braving dessert at your table."

"You shouldn't have had three pieces of chocolate cake," she rasped. "Gluttony's a sin."

"So is lobelia frosting." Patrick looked at Cameron. "Best make her taste your dessert, Cameron, if you've irritated her."

"You hurt my sister," Sunny said weakly. "I owed you for the two weeks she spent bawling on my couch over you." She forced herself up so she was leaning on Cameron's chest. "You didn't have to put lobelia in that tea you made me. Unnecessarily vindictive."

"I knew you were going to throw up anyway," Patrick said. "No sense in not hurrying things along. It will cheer you to know that your beloved has already threatened to do damage to me—

repeatedly. I was, as you might imagine, not overly troubled by the thought."

Cameron snorted as he put his arms around his love. "Why is it every MacLeod ever spawned is so full of misplaced arrogance?"

"Because we're eternally charged with the task of bettering our Cameron neighbors."

"Are you two going to come to blows soon?" Madelyn said with a laugh, coming to stand in the doorway.

Patrick flashed his wife a quick smile. "Just keeping ourselves amused. Cam can take it." He looked at Cameron. "Sunny calls you that. Mind if we do, too?"

Cameron shook his head, though he was a little winded. "My youngest brother used to."

"Hate to tell you, laddie, but we're all older than you are." Patrick shrugged. "Perhaps you can count us as brothers just the same."

Cameron would have plunged a knife into his own chest before he let on how affected he was, but it took a moment or two before he could muster up a frown. It had been that sort of day. "I daresay I could." He cleared his throat roughly. "I appreciate the aid today, as well. I'm not too proud to say I needed it."

Patrick rubbed his hands together enthusiastically. "It was a pleasure, truly. If my sister's life hadn't hung in the balance, I would have been enjoying myself. I don't have much call these days for chasing down ruffians."

"Thank heavens," Madelyn called from the kitchen.

"You'll return the favor at some point," Patrick added with a smile. "Anything for family, aye?"

"Aye," Cameron managed. "Though I may have a hard time repaying you for your service to my bride today." He looked down at Sunny to find her watching him with one eye. He smiled reflexively. "Aye, beloved?"

"Tell me that isn't your idea of a proposal," she said. "Here in my loo?"

He shook his head with a smile. "Now that I'm free to do so, I'll choose a more romantic setting—"

She clapped her hand over her mouth suddenly. "Get out."

"Sunny—"

"Out!"

He didn't want to go, but she was surprisingly strong and

Madelyn was suddenly at her side. He was thrust out of the bathroom, Hope was shoved into Patrick's arms, and the door was shut and locked—all before he could protest. He looked at Patrick.

"I think we've been dismissed."

"I daresay," Patrick said with a grunt. He put Hope into Cameron's arms. "Hold my wee one whilst I finish supper."

Cameron looked down into big, bright green eyes, and found himself almost pushed to the edge of his ability to endure any more. Hope MacLeod didn't look terrified, or weepy, or as if she prepared to rear back and let loose a shout. She merely stared up at him for a moment, then popped her thumb in her mouth and began to stroke his arm with her other hand.

Astonishing.

"Your lad Derrick is pacing outside," Patrick said, standing and stirring at Sunny's stove. "Perhaps you'd best let him know his lady fair will survive." He looked over his shoulder. "Does he know anything about you?"

"Not as much as he'd like," Cameron said, "though I have the feeling that is about to change." He started to walk away, then frowned. "Is that the shower running? She shouldn't—"

"Well, 'tisn't as if you can help her, is it?" Patrick said with a snort. "Be off with you, lad, and let Madelyn see to her. Wrap Hope up before you go outside, though. 'Tis chilly today."

Cameron found a soft pink blanket, wrapped it around Hope, then sighed again as she burrowed against his neck and worked on her thumb. She smelled delightful and he couldn't help a brief feeling of contentment.

By the saints, when would he stop being so off balance with all these MacLeod females?

He took a deep breath, then opened Moraig's front door. He crossed Moraig's threshold with hardly a flicker of unease, then stopped when he saw Derrick leaning against the driver's side of Patrick's Range Rover, watching him.

"Very domestic," Derrick said with a smile.

Cameron shot him a disgruntled look, then walked over to lean against Patrick's car as well. A pity it wasn't the man's Vanquish. He might have had to sit rather firmly upon the bonnet in repayment for what he was certain would be an excruciatingly expensive repair of his own.

"You could have come in, you know," Cameron said.

Derrick shrugged. "I've been on the phone and I didn't want to disturb our lady. How is she?"

"Herself, finally, though I came close to killing Patrick MacLeod more than once until she was conscious. How does Peter fare?"

"Not well. Ewan says the docs believe he'll be there for quite some time to come."

"I wouldn't have admitted this earlier," Cameron said slowly, "but I think I would sooner trust Patrick than the physicians in Inverness. Perhaps you and I should endeavor to free the lad tomorrow and see what Patrick can do for him. Now, what of Nathan's lads?"

"As you know, we rounded them up before he entered the hall. I left them there in a heap." Derrick paused. "I apologize for not having stopped Nathan himself, though at the time I assumed you would want to see to him. I had no idea he had a gun, else I would have taken it away."

Cameron shook his head. "It worked out for the best, so don't think on it further. Handy that Penelope was there, wasn't it?"

"Very," Derrick agreed. "Oliver tailed her tailing Nathan, as I imagine you've surmised. He said she showed promise as a spy, but I don't imagine she'll make a career of it."

Cameron smiled in spite of himself. "I daresay not. Now, what of the others?"

"I promised young Jim a bonus for being so good in school and sent him back on his way before Hamish Fergusson arrived. Nathan's head lad was rounded up with the ones in the castle. Rufus is still tailing his chauffeur in London."

"And what of Nathan himself?"

"In hospital, under guard. He's conscious, but barely." He paused. "Oliver overheard him babbling about, well . . ." He stopped, then shifted. "Well, about traveling through time, or some such rot." He shot Cameron a look. "A little like what that unhinged woman was spouting inside the castle, actually."

"Rubbish," Cameron said without hesitation. He pressed on before Derrick could say aught. "What of you? What is your plan?"

"Now that you don't need me watching your back round the clock?" He shrugged. "I could fly back to London tonight, if you like, and see if I could be of some use to Rufus. Or I could stand guard here." He paused. "I could be fairly unobtrusive in a corner."

Cameron smiled. "I don't imagine Sunny would mind."

"Mate, our Sunny won't have a clue I'm there."

"Derrick, my lad, how many times do I have to tell you she's *my* Sunshine and not yours?"

"Another few, at least," Derrick said with a smile. He studied Cameron for a moment, then chewed on his words for a moment or two. "Have I ever asked you any personal questions, Cameron?"

Well, apparently he wasn't going to escape as neatly as he'd hoped. "Never," he said heavily, "in spite of all the times you've no doubt wanted to." He sighed. "Why is it I already know where this is going?"

Derrick shrugged casually. "I'm curious about that woman, the one who drugged our lady. Who was she?"

Cameron shoved his hands in his pockets. "My brother's wife."

"You don't have any brothers."

"I had two, at one point."

Derrick looked at him, clear-eyed. "When were you born?"

Cameron snorted. "What, haven't you read that big tome containing Cameron genealogy that lies in my solar?"

"I might have," Derrick said slowly. "I just thought there had been a mistake."

Cameron only shook his head slowly.

"Who are you?" Derrick asked faintly.

"You tell me."

Derrick took a deep breath. "You are Robert Francis Cameron . . . mac Cameron," he said with a shiver. "Born 1346."

"Who were my brothers?" Cameron asked calmly.

Derrick swallowed, hard. "Breac and Sim?"

Cameron smiled, then reached out and clapped a hand on Derrick's shoulder. "Spread any of that about, and I'll kill you slowly. But you can speak freely in front of Patrick MacLeod. He was born quite a bit earlier than I was."

Derrick swayed just a bit. "I don't believe it." He looked at Cameron in shock. "Time travel. What rot."

"Highland magic, my friend. Never doubt it."

Derrick shook his head. "I don't believe it." He paused. "At least I think I don't believe it." He shot Cameron a look. "It would explain quite a bit, though, wouldn't it?"

"I daresay it would."

Derrick rubbed his hand over his mouth. "I would like to talk to you about this in depth at some point. If you would be willing."

"I might," Cameron conceded. "I think I owe you that, at least."

"Mate, you don't owe me anything," Derrick said with a faint smile, "but you could humor me because I've been such a loyal vassal for so long. You could also teach me how to use a sword."

"Done," Cameron said without hesitation. Then he shot Derrick a look. "Loyal vassal, my arse." He pushed away from the car and walked toward the door. "Come in and hold on, lad. I think it will be a long night."

"As you will, my laird. Oh, and Cameron? You dropped something in the Fergusson hall."

Cameron saw the pendant in Derrick's hand and shifted Hope in his arms so he could take it. He looked down at it for a moment or two in the shadows and thought about it. Gilly had given it to Breac on their wedding day as a charm to ward off evil. Breac had never worn it, saying it bothered him somehow. He wasn't surprised that Tavish should have been oblivious enough to have felt nothing. It was even more abhorrent to him now that he knew what part Gilly had played in the battle that had resulted in Breac's death. Cameron handed it back to Derrick.

"Put it in my car, if you would, and I'll take it back to Tavish tomorrow. I don't want it on my land, though, and neither will the MacLeods."

Derrick shuddered as he touched it. "It belonged to that woman, didn't it? Was she a witch?"

"A Fergusson."

"Close enough," Derrick said, straight-faced.

Cameron nodded grimly. "I daresay. Let's go eat, before the thought overwhelms us."

Derrick only smiled, then accepted Cameron's keys. Cameron waited for him, then followed him inside Moraig's house, making sure he focused on getting himself over the threshold in the right time. There was no sense in taking chances when he was so close to having what he wanted. He probably should have argued with Patrick about bringing Sunny to Moraig's in the first place, but Patrick had insisted that Moraig's was the proper place to heal.

Cameron hadn't been able to disagree.

Half an hour later, he had finished combing out Sunny's hair for her and eaten a marvelous meal that Patrick had made from things thankfully not found in Sunny's refrigerator. He sat in one of the comfortable chairs near the fire and held Sunshine Phillips, dressed in Cameron plaid pajamas, on his lap. He listened to the conversation going on around him with only half an ear, preferring to concentrate on the woman in his arms. She wasn't nearly as interested in him, apparently, because she was sound asleep. He didn't blame her for it. It had been a long day.

He supposed there would come a time when he needed to digest what he'd learned that afternoon, but that would come later, as would an inquest into the events of the day. For the moment, however, perhaps it wasn't unreasonable to let himself enjoy the evening and leave the rest for the morrow.

He heard a knock on the door behind him and sighed in resignation as Ewan was invited in. Ewan made himself at home, as was his habit, and managed to win a bit of supper as well. Cameron watched as his cousin pulled up a stool in front of the hearth and sat down opposite him.

"Heard something interesting down at the pub," he said without preamble.

"Did you indeed," Cameron said sourly.

"Aye," Ewan said, his eyes already twinkling. "It was the fascinating tale of a medieval laird who let nothing, nay, not even time, stand in the way of his winning his ladylove. Care to hear it?"

"Can I stop you?"

Patrick and Madelyn laughed and told him to go on. Cameron sighed. Perhaps he would correct Ewan on the finer points of the story later on, when Sunny was awake and could help him. For the moment, he had his ladylove in his arms and time had deigned to wrap itself around them in the same place.

He wasn't going to complain.

Chapter 33

Sunny leaned back against the side of Cameron's car and watched as his plane taxied toward her. She'd almost grown accustomed to the sight of it over the past three weeks and had even flown with him a couple of times to London. She couldn't say she would ever be a happy passenger, but she supposed there would come a point where, as Cameron claimed, familiarity bred contempt. He could fall asleep before the plane left the runway and sleep all the way south until the plane touched down. She knew that because she'd watched him do it—but only once. The other time, he'd spent the trip simply watching her with a look of wonder on his face, as if he couldn't believe she had agreed to marry him.

But how could she have said no? He'd gone down on bended knee and offered her a very lovely, very discreet wedding band that mirrored her wait-for-me ring. It was only after she'd said yes that he'd handed her the enormous engagement ring that went with it.

He'd laughed at her sigh, then jumped up, hauled her into his arms and spun her around. He solemnly promised that from then on, he wouldn't buy her anything else and he would most certainly expect her to tend his garden daily.

What wasn't to love about a man like that?

She watched the plane come to a stop, then felt butterflies start up in her stomach when the door was opened and the steps let down. Cameron came loping down them immediately and the butterflies took flight. He slung his backpack over his shoulder and walked toward her, a smile on his face.

She pushed away from the car and ran to him, because she couldn't help herself. She threw her arms around his neck and held on tightly.

"I missed you," she whispered fiercely.

He laughed, but didn't release her. "I left yesterday morning, lass."

"So?"

He set her back on her feet, smiled, then bent his head and kissed her—very briefly.

"Hey," she said in surprise. "What's that?"

"Me, trying to keep my hands off you," he said honestly. "I think we're getting married in a day or so. I'm trying to avoid ravishing you until after that happens, actually."

"We're getting married *tomorrow*," she reminded him.

"Well," he said with a lazy smile, "if that's the case, then I suppose we might be a bit more friendly." He set his backpack down, then looked at her purposefully. "Come you here, wench, and let me greet you properly."

"*Wench,*" she said with a snort, then found that she didn't have much opportunity to complain about anything else. Cameron's mouth was just as much a marvel as it had been centuries ago. She shivered as he slid his hand under her hair and his other arm around her waist. Her only recourse was to hold on and hope she could walk straight after he finished with her.

"Get a room!" Ewan bellowed from across the tarmac.

Cameron lifted his head and looked down at her with a frown. "Has he been talking to Alex Smith?"

"I don't think he needed to."

Cameron threw Ewan a glare. "He will *not* be coming along on our honeymoon." He pulled Sunny close again and bent his head to hers. "Ignore him. Derrick will take care of him if he becomes too mouthy."

Sunny closed her eyes and smiled as she was greeted properly yet again. By the time Cameron lifted his head and was looking down at her with rather stormy blue eyes, she wasn't at all sure she was going to make it back to his car without having her knees buckle.

"I think you'd better stop that," she advised.

"Want to elope right now?"

She laughed uneasily. "We don't dare. The entire village is geared up for this monumental event, you know. You'd have angry Highlanders marching on Cameron Hall with pitchforks if you didn't show up in church bright and early tomorrow morning."

"I'll be your chaperon!" came a voice from across the way.

Cameron gritted his teeth. "I'm going to go kill him. It won't take long."

Sunny watched him walk over and exchange a few pointed

words with his cousin. Ewan only clapped Cameron on the shoulder, blew Sunny a kiss, then retreated back into the plane to do whatever it was he did to put it to bed for the night. Cameron came back over to her, shaking his head.

"They all have too much time on their hands," he said, picking up his gear and putting his arm around her shoulders. "I'm going to have to find something useful for them to do to keep myself from killing the lot of them. Derrick spent the last twenty-four hours lounging in my office reading my magazines and watching my telly, Peter loitered uselessly outside my office door flirting with Emily and my sixty-year-old secretary both, and Oliver sat on a chair in the hallway and apparently contemplated the wreck that is his life now that he has no call for trailing after evildoers."

She smiled. "Don't they want to go on your treasure hunts anymore?"

"That would require them to actually put on suits and look professional," he said with a snort. He opened the door for her. "I'll find something for them to do, since I was kind enough to see to a pleasant way to fill my own days."

She reached up and put her hands on his face. "Who are you kidding? You're a workaholic, Cam. You'll always have ways to fill your days."

He shook his head slowly. "Not anymore, Sunny. I've spent almost eight years keeping myself busy, but I'm ready for a change. I'll leave things as they are for a bit, but I'm going to find ways for us to be home more often."

"I have a garden to tend, after all," she agreed with a smile.

"I'd rather have you tending my heart, and that you can do anywhere," he said with an answering smile, "but I'll make sure you're here often enough to dig in the dirt as well." He kissed her softly. "Let's go home and get started on that."

Ten minutes later, Cameron was driving away from the hangar. Sunny reached out and put her hand on his leg because she simply couldn't stop touching him. It felt as if she'd waited for him for centuries, and now that the waiting was over, she couldn't quite let go.

He covered her hand with his, smiled, then turned back to getting them onto the road home. Sunny leaned her head back against the seat and closed her eyes. She considered again all the plans she'd put in place. It had been quite an undertaking to put together the wedding of the century in such a short time, but she'd tried to keep things simple and Emily had made things even simpler by being such a master organizer.

Sunny had found a seamstress in the village to make her wedding gown but left Emily to take care of everything else, including making a trip to Paris to buy Sunny a trousseau. Emily's taste in clothes was exquisite and Sunny had trusted she wouldn't buy her too many things that required nylons.

The rest of the wedding had been farmed out to village shops exclusively. It wasn't every day that the laird of the hall up the way found himself getting married. If there had been anything she could do to win the hearts and minds of the lads down at the pub and their wives, she'd been willing to do it.

"Any trouble on the way down?" Cameron asked, interrupting her thoughts.

"Hamish pulled me over for doing exactly one mile an hour over the speed limit—because he thought I was you," she said. "When he realized it was me instead, he almost made me late because he wouldn't shut up about what a right proper Highland lad you were, giving credit where it was due about the business with Nathan's men and your having been so kind as to keep his brother out of jail."

"Aye, that was good of me, wasn't it?" he asked sourly.

She laughed. "Tavish is an idiot, but not dangerous. He was trying to look important and got caught by people much smarter than he is."

"Well, he's damned lucky he's not in jail for being the conduit for funds between Nathan and Gilly. The only thing that saved him was that he believed that Gilly was his cousin."

"Which she was, in a certain sense," Sunny offered. "I imagine it also helped that he only stocks soap and not poison. I think we can safely assume that Gilly provided those things herself."

He shivered. "Aye, I daresay she did. She was nothing if not resourceful. If she hadn't been, Tavish likely would have found himself drawn into her madness as he was into Nathan's."

"Poor Tavish," she said with half a smile. "I think he's not cut out for either high finance or backroom dealings. What I do know is that he'll be singing your praises for quite some time to come. I just wish Hamish wasn't so thrilled about all this. I honestly think I'd rather have the points on my license that isn't quite a Scottish license yet but will be than listen to him for half an hour every time I leave the village."

He was silent for a moment or two, then he looked at her. "You don't have to do that, Sunshine," he said quietly. "Give up your U.S. passport."

She squeezed his fingers. "Cam, from the moment I set foot in the Highlands, I wanted a reason to stay. If I go back to the States, it will be for a visit only. If I'm going to take your name, I'm going to carry a British passport as well. Unless you're planning on putting me on a plane back to America at some point."

He shot her a startled look and almost broadsided a brick wall as a result.

She laughed. "I've waited my entire life for that sort of look on a man's face when he thinks about letting me go. Thank you. I'll even give Bess the odd curtsey for that."

He brought her hand to his mouth. "I love you."

"I love you, too. And I'll happily become a Cameron and all it entails. It will mean something to our children, don't you think?"

"I daresay, woman, that I need to find a place to pull off," he said hoarsely, "and show you just what I think."

"You just keep driving. We have a few last-minute details to take care of in the village." She made herself more comfortable in seats that were too comfortable to start with. "So, how did everything finish up in London?"

"As you might expect. Nathan is locked away at the moment pending a review of his sanity, which I hope will put him away for as long as he deserves. Penelope and I had a meeting with our brokers yesterday and stock has been happily put back into the appropriate hands."

"Is there anything left of Ainsworth Associates?"

He smiled at her briefly. "I wish I could say aye. She'll likely have to restructure the entire thing. Those Swiss accounts we found directions to in the safe-deposit box will go a long way to helping her with that, but the road will still be difficult. I think she'll be doing without quite a few luxuries for the foreseeable future."

"It builds character," Sunny said solemnly.

"Doesn't it though," he said, shooting her another smile. He looked back at the road. "The diamonds will help, which I imagine Rodney foresaw. Penelope insisted I keep a selection of gems and a pair of rough diamonds for you, an offer I accepted with my best show of graciousness."

"You're a very decent man, Robert Francis."

He laughed. "Aye, well, I was vastly relieved to simply be doing business with her instead of trying to escape an engagement with her. She didn't want to take either the money or the gems since her father had left them to me, but I assured her we both thought he'd done so as insurance for her." He smiled. "I think we can see her at social things and not worry about her cursing either of us. Isn't that a relief?"

"Absolutely," she agreed. She looked down at his hand around hers for a moment, then looked up at his face. "Do you worry about Nathan?"

"If I had any sense, I probably would," he said with a sigh. "Jamie showed me the what-absolute-bollocks stare he gives to anyone who talks to him about time travel. I've been practicing it. Want to see?"

"Of course."

He gave her a look that was so reminiscent of Jamie, she burst out laughing.

"Did it work?" he asked.

"I think you might want to practice a bit more," she admitted with a smile. "Or maybe you can just hope no one would dare ask you something that ridiculous to your face. It'll just be our secret, otherwise."

"And Derrick's, and Ewan's, and that whole MacLeod clan's," he grumbled. "I have never in my life trusted so many people with something of such import."

"Maybe you've never had so many people to trust," she said softly. "Time has made amends, Cam."

He took a deep breath. "Aye, it most certainly has, most gloriously. Now, what do we have on our calendar this afternoon that we might cancel so we can commemorate that bit of amends?"

She laughed. "Nothing, so drive on, my laird, and let's get all these last-minute details over with. I might be able to sneak out of Jamie's and meet you in the stables before dinner tonight if we do what we have to now."

He squeezed her hand, then had to concentrate on avoiding sheep-encrusted tarmac. Sunny was torn between watching the scenery and watching the man beside her. Cameron won. She'd seen Scotland before, and while she loved it, it couldn't hold a candle to the man sitting beside her.

Though she was profoundly grateful she was going to have a life filled with both.

"Not even half an hour?" he asked with one of those quick smiles she loved.

She sighed and pulled her pink phone out of the glove box. "I'll call Emily."

"I'll find a likely spot to pull over."

She laughed, because she was happier than she'd dreamed she would be and there was a man sitting beside her who loved her to distraction.

Time had made amends, indeed.

The sun had just set when Cameron pulled up in front of James MacLeod's hall in his Range Rover, dressed appropriately for the ceremony Jamie had no doubt made up just to do justice to the seriousness of losing his witch. He'd considered riding a horse to the current bit of business, but it was raining and he hadn't wanted any stray encounters with any time gates he didn't know about. Jamie's map, which he now owned a handmade copy of, was only good if the ink hadn't run because of the wet.

So to avoid any untoward journeys to time periods not his own, he'd driven. He was dressed in his medieval clothing because it had seemed fitting, and he'd brought his sword along with him because he suspected he might need it. He got out of the car and started to put his keys in his pocket only to realize he didn't have any pockets.

That was a bit of a problem, actually.

He sighed and tossed them on the seat, then shut the car door and hoped for the best. He strapped his sword to his back, wondered if he should feel slightly ridiculous, then cast aside the thought. No doubt everyone inside would be dressed just as authentically. As it happened, the only lights he could see outside were from torches. He might have thought he was in the past if it hadn't been for Patrick's black Jaguar parked next to Ian's red one. He took a deep breath, then climbed the steps and knocked.

Zachary Smith answered the door, as usual. He was dressed in rather authentic clothing himself with a rather authentic sword at his side. Cameron smiled.

"Nice."

Zachary flashed him a brief smile before he cleared his throat and put on a frown. "What is it ye want?" he asked in remarkably authentic Gaelic.

"I'm here for the MacLeod witch," Cameron said seriously.

Zachary stepped back. "Come inside and we'll see if you're worthy of her."

"Heaven help me," Cameron muttered under his breath as he walked inside.

Zachary laughed, apparently in spite of himself. "If it makes you feel any better, my lord, Sunny put her foot down about anything interesting tonight. She said we'd done all the damage we were allowed to last week."

Cameron grunted at the memory. Jamie had invited him over for a bit of swordplay and Cameron had found himself running through MacLeods and their various and sundry relations—one right after another. He hadn't complained, because his prize had sat on a bench against the wall and watched the entire time. He would have gone through weeks of such torment to have her, and he'd wanted her to know as much. She'd done him the very great favor of giving him a massage after the fact under the very watchful eye of Patrick MacLeod himself, so he'd counted the day well spent.

"I assume I passed the test," Cameron said pointedly.

"I let you in, didn't I?" Zachary shut the door, then stepped back. "After you, my laird."

Cameron looked into the hall and had to stop for a moment and fix the scene in his memory.

The entire cast was standing near the fire. Jamie, Elizabeth, and their children; Patrick, Madelyn, and Hope; Ian, Jane, and their two wee ones; Alex, Margaret, their children, and Jamie's bard; and Zachary standing next to his sister, with Jamie's minstrel Joshua standing next to Zachary. Sunny's parents were there as well, both busily jotting down what Cameron could only assume were Gaelic idioms they would want to discuss at length later.

Linguists to the core, as he'd already found out during supper with them earlier in the week when they'd ruthlessly grilled him on whatever suited them in all the languages he claimed to speak. They were interesting, to put it politely. They had consented to his taking Sunny to wife, though, and for that he'd been grateful.

He was also grateful for the little group of souls who were apparently there to represent him: Derrick, Ewan, and, the saints preserve him, Emily as well. She didn't look too terribly surprised by what she was seeing, so he supposed he could add yet another soul to the tally who knew his most private secrets.

And in front of them all stood Sunshine Phillips, the only light he had in his life.

Jamie stepped forward and folded his arms over his impressive chest. "What is it ye'd be wanting, Cameron?"

Cameron inclined his head just the slightest bit. "The MacLeod witch, if you please."

"And if I don't?"

"I'll be happy to satisfy you over blades," Cameron said without hesitation. "Again."

Jamie shot Sunny a look over his shoulder. "I understand I've had as much satisfaction as I'm allowed." He pursed his lips. "Well, I suppose I'll see how you plan to take care of her, we'll look over a document or two, then I'll see if she'll have you. Though I want it noted that *I* would have preferred another go with swords, myself." Jamie leaned forward. "You'll have to keep on your toes with this one, Cameron. She'll run roughshod over you if you're not careful."

"I'll keep that in mind," Cameron promised.

Jamie looked at Zachary. "Fetch chairs, brother, and let's be about this."

"Always me," Zachary muttered under his breath. "Someone please grow up soon so I can be done with all this fetching."

"Derrick is likely about your age," Cameron said with a smile. "Ewan, as well."

Zachary nodded toward the two of them. "Come help, then."

Cameron watched his lads troop along after Zachary and found himself slightly surprised to see they were both wearing very medieval gear as well. Sunny's doing, no doubt. He had to take a deep breath before he dared look at her. He caught her eye and was the recipient of a tender smile. He supposed she didn't know there were tears leaking out of her eyes.

He suspected he might be close to it himself.

Once chairs had been brought, Jamie nodded and everyone sat, Jamie's family around him and Cameron's around him. Sunny sat next to Jamie, dressed in a lovely black dress that reminded him quite a bit of the memory he had of her standing in Moraig's doorway. It didn't make him queasy this time, for which he was profoundly grateful.

He honestly couldn't have said what he and Jamie discussed, though he supposed he'd given a decent accounting of what he would bring to the marriage. He accepted the ridiculous sum Jamie had dowered Sunny with, vowing right then to find a way not to take it. He certainly didn't need the money, which Jamie damn well knew. But there was pride and tradition involved, so he didn't balk. Not yet.

A Bible was produced and he signed along with Sunny. Then Jamie placed her hand in his and gave her to him freely.

Cameron looked down at her and felt a little weak in the knees. "I see a threshold over there."

Jamie harumphed. "Handfast with her if ye will, lad, but ye'll not take her to your bed until after ye've knelt with her before the priest tomorrow."

Cameron squeezed Sunny's hand. "It's at least a step in the right direction."

"I'll take it gladly," she said with a smile.

So he led her over to Jamie's door, opened it, then took her out onto the top step. He pledged himself to her, listened to her do the same, then he took her in his arms and kissed her as thoroughly as he dared with a hall full of witnesses.

Then he let out the breath he felt like he'd been holding for eight years. "I love you," he said, gathering her close. "I don't want to let you from my arms ever again."

"One more day and you won't have to."

"We're going to have a sleepover tonight at your sister's house," he vowed. "I'm not taking any chances."

She leaned up and kissed him softly. "I agree." She pulled away and took his hand. "We're not quite finished here. You have one more thing to do."

He blinked. "I do? What?"

"Come back to the fire and you'll see."

He walked back inside the hall with her, shut the door behind him, then walked over with her to the hearth. She put him in front of it, looked at him with a smile, then slowly sank to her knees before him.

He gaped at her for a moment, then reached out to pull her back to her feet. She shook her head.

"Hold out your hands, my laird."

Ach, not that. He had to drag his sleeve across his eyes first, and he wanted to protest, but he didn't. He supposed it wasn't every day a man had his betrothed wife kneel before him and pledge him her fealty. If she was determined, he wouldn't forbid her. He supposed, though, since he was being so agreeable, she could overlook the tears that ran down his cheeks.

Sunny kissed his hands, then rose.

And then Derrick took her place and knelt as well.

"Bloody hell," Cameron managed.

Derrick looked up at him with a smile. "Is that part of the ceremony, mate?"

Cameron rolled his eyes because it was easier than blubbering any more. He took a deep breath, then accepted Derrick's fealty. He accepted Ewan's in turn, though he would have been the first to admit he was having a hard time seeing very clearly and he had to rely on his ears to identify the lad in front of him. By the time Emily had knelt before him and put her hands in his, he was a complete wreck.

He pulled Emily to her feet after he'd accepted her loyalty, then put one arm around her and the other around Sunny.

"Anyone else?" he asked gruffly. "Whilst I'm completely unmanned here?"

"Oliver has a question or two for you," Derrick said with a small smile. "As does Peter, if you can imagine it. When next you see them."

Cameron sighed. "Perhaps I might manage a better showing during the next round."

"Ale," Jamie announced. "And juice for those so inclined. And we'd best start dinner before our good lord Robert makes us all weep."

Cameron was soon distracted by many manly slaps on the back from the male relations, kisses from his future sisters-in-law and cousins, and an offer from Ian's son Alexander to sneak off for a happy hour passed playing Legos. He was terribly tempted by the last, but managed to secure a rain check.

At length, he found himself standing next to Jamie as tables were set up for supper. He clasped his hands behind his back and cleared his throat.

"Thank you, Jamie, for your part in all this." He had to pause for quite a while before he trusted himself to speak. "I would have lost her forever without your aid."

Jamie clapped him on the shoulder in a friendly fashion. "If I don't keep watch over the fabric of time and all the romantic particulars it produces, who will?"

"I daresay," Cameron said, managing a smile. "No one better than you to do it, of course."

"Aye," Jamie agreed modestly.

Cameron was half tempted to ask Jamie why he thought Moraig's gate had gone awry and left him coming forward so much sooner than Sunny, then thought better of it. That was a question better left for another time—perhaps after he'd been safely wed to Sunny for a year or so. Perhaps there wasn't an answer. Perhaps 'twas merely Fate taking a hand in his poor life to give him his hall and his love, together in a time of marvels.

He pushed aside those thoughts for contemplation at a later time, then turned back to Jamie. "You know, I might have a small way to repay you later, if you like. My grandfather fought against your son Jesse for years, you know."

Jamie blinked. "Nay, I didn't know that."

"I'll tell you of the more noteworthy skirmishes, if you like."

Jamie cleared his throat roughly. "I'd have those, aye, but perhaps not tonight. Your betrothed is scowling at me. Perhaps she fears I will make you draw your sword, after all."

Cameron laughed and shook Jamie's hand, spared a brief moment to consider the absolute improbability of standing in the MacLeod keep in any other century with his poor form unpierced by dozens of MacLeod blades, then went to retrieve his beloved, who was indeed giving Jamie a warning look.

The rest of the evening was passed most pleasantly with supper and conversation and he found himself soaking up the warmth of family that he hadn't had in years.

It was all because of Sunny.

A handful of hours later, he was sitting with her in front of the fire in Patrick MacLeod's great hall. He held her on his lap and trailed his fingers through her hair. His heart was so full of things he'd never expected to feel, he simply couldn't find the words to speak.

He counted his blessings instead. First and foremost, he had a woman who loved him, who accepted him and wanted him because of what he was, not in spite of it. He had a little clan of four souls who had gathered around him that night and vowed to stand behind him no matter what. He had other souls who were loyal, if not a little less knowledgeable. He had the money to keep the roof at Cameron Hall fixed far into the future and to buy Sunny the occasional fancy supper and the odd fifty-quid dress.

"Wed me?" he murmured.

She met his eyes and smiled. "Yes."

"I may keep asking you that for a few years."

"And I'll be happy to answer you the same way every time you ask, even after the fact." She touched his face. "Happy?"

"Very. The only thing that will improve upon that is the right to carry you to my bed, but we'd best not discuss that right now."

She laughed. "Probably not." She kissed him softly, then crawled off his lap and held down her hands for him. "The doors are locked, the gates are secure, and I need my beauty sleep."

"Heaven help me," he said. "I can hardly keep my feet as it is."

She smiled and pulled away from him. "Be here in the morning?"

"Aye."

He watched her as she walked away, then waited until he'd heard her door close before he walked down the passageway and poked his head into Patrick MacLeod's study. Patrick was sitting in front of the fire with a book in his hands.

"You can go to bed now, my lord chaperon," Cameron said dryly. "She's gained her bedchamber unmolested."

Patrick shut his book, then banked his fire. He came to the door and put his hand on Cameron's shoulder.

"You're worthy of her."

"High praise."

"Aye, it is," Patrick agreed. "You know, I wouldn't allow you to have her if you hadn't earned it. Now, just don't run out all the cold water in the morning when you shower, aye?"

Cameron pursed his lips. "I'll do my best."

Patrick patted his cheek rather too firmly, just as Breac had done scores of times, then laughed and walked away.

Cameron watched him go, then smiled to himself and sought his own bed. He was very grateful indeed for family.

But he was grateful for Sunny most of all.

Epilogue

Sunny walked up the stairs from the great hall to the wing of the keep that had been first built in the sixteenth century, remodeled in the eighteenth, then further improved by Cameron a handful of years ago. She'd had five months to become accustomed to the castle being her home, though she supposed she would never walk through the great hall downstairs without some sort of chill running through her.

Time travel did that to a woman, she supposed.

The door to Cameron's solar was half open, so she didn't bother knocking. She peeked inside and found Cameron and Zachary sitting in front of the fireplace, pouring over plans on the coffee table. Cameron looked up and smiled at her.

She stumbled, but caught herself before he could get to her. He caught her by the arms.

"You're not wearing heels, love. Why so unsteady?"

She leaned up on her toes to kiss him instead. "It's just you, as usual."

"I feel the same way." He put his arms around her. "Do you need something in particular, or am I fortunate enough just to have the pleasure of your company?"

"I missed you," she admitted. "I've been out in the garden, but it seemed a little lonely, so I decided to come in and see what you were doing."

He lifted an eyebrow. "Nothing I couldn't cancel."

She smiled. "Could you?"

"Have a seat and I'll make that happen."

She pulled away and went to sit down on a stool near the coffee table. She smiled happily at Zachary. "We're still in our honeymoon phase. Sorry to give you the boot."

"Well I've had him for almost two hours, so I imagine my welcome has been sufficiently worn out anyway," Zachary said dryly.

She looked at the plans spread out on the table. "Are you working on something for the trust?"

"The Cameron/Artane Trust for Historical Preservation?"

Zachary said with half a laugh. "Yes, actually. I'm wondering, though, how it is your husband got his name first on the list?"

"His charm is legendary," she said, unable to keep from smiling. "Not even Gideon de Piaget is immune."

"Fortunately, since it got me the job of head architect. I will continually praise our good lord Robert as loudly as possible for that alone."

She smiled. "So what's your first project?"

"A little remodel on a cottage near Wyckham." Zachary frowned thoughtfully. "I can't understand the significance, but Gideon seems particularly determined to do something about it. They're going to pay me buckets to take care of it, so I'm hardly going to complain."

"Don't sell yourself short. You have a good feel for old things."

Zachary smiled blandly. "I have quite a lot of hands-on experience. It's really amazing the things you can learn after college, isn't it?"

She laughed. "Knowing how much time you've spent with Jamie on his little jaunts to the past, I would have to agree. So, what will you do after you finish with the cottage?"

"Talk Gideon into letting me get my hands on Wyckham Castle, which is conveniently next door." He rubbed his chin thoughtfully. "It's owned by the Earl of Seakirk, who seems to be related to them, though I'm still not quite clear on how. If Gideon can put in a good word for me, I'll be satisfied. It's a spectacular ruin, though, with great bones."

"Are you camping out in that castle while you're doing all this work in the winter?" she asked, surprised.

He shook his head with a smile. "I've done enough camping over the years with Jamie, thank you just the same. Gideon's wife owns an inn that isn't too far, but what I'm really angling for is a chance to hang out at Artane for the duration. Who knows what sorts of things I'll turn up in the attic?"

"Be careful," Sunny said lightly. "Curiosity killed the cat."

Zachary shot her a look. "Sunny, Artane's just a nice old pile of stones that Gideon's ancestors managed to keep in the family. There is absolutely nothing of a paranormal nature that's ever gone on there. Gideon promised me that."

"He's probably lying," she said without hesitation.

Zachary laughed. "Probably. It doesn't matter, though. I've seen it all."

"I imagine you have. So, when do you start on it?"

"It probably won't be until February, most likely," he said. "I'm flying home for Christmas, then I have a couple of projects to finish up in London before I sign on exclusively with the Trust. I'm hoping to get back to Artane by the end of January and show Gideon the plans. Cameron seems to like them well enough, so I'm hoping for an equally positive reaction from the English side of the equation."

Sunny looked up as Cameron sat down on the couch. He winked at her, then looked at Zachary.

"Ten minutes, lad," he said briskly. "Talk fast."

Sunny smiled as he hustled Zachary through whatever final discussion he wanted to have. She propped her elbows on her knees and her chin on her fists and just watched the man who was husband, lover, friend, and the one who stole her breath every time she looked at him.

She still had a hard time believing she was his.

She'd thought she couldn't love him any more as she'd knelt before him and pledged him fealty. She'd thought her heart would be as full of him as possible when she'd knelt beside him in the village chapel the next day and bound her life to him.

And then he'd brought her home to his keep.

He made her his sweetly and tenderly so she would, as he'd said, look back on her first night in his arms with satisfaction and pleasure.

And once that was behind them, he'd stolen her breath and hadn't bothered to return it since. Patrick had warned her that Cameron was intense and she was in for it if she gave herself to him. After five months in Cameron's life and his bed, she could personally attest to the truth of that statement. But she had no regrets. He lived and loved with equal fervor and she was grateful for both. She supposed real life would intrude at some point, but she hadn't seen any signs of it yet.

After they'd spent a month honeymooning in all their favorite places in Italy and France, they'd come home to Scotland, but somehow it still felt like they were not quite back to reality. Even though Cameron ran miles every morning before she was awake and had half his day over with before she managed to unstick her eyelids from each other, he still pulled her into his arms every chance he had.

For herself, she had started work on the book she'd been

wanting to write for years, a book that would reflect not only what she knew but what she'd learned from Moraig. She'd also spent hours cooking with Madame Gies, riding over Cameron's land with him, tending his garden.

She'd even learned to survive the other half of her life that was spent in London. She had found herself photographed at parties and invited to society lunches. She'd eventually learned to decompress with George on the way back to the house Geoffrey Segrave had convinced Cameron to buy next to his own. She'd found that her expectations for a life with a man who was satisfied with a nine-to-five job had been completely taken over by a man who managed hundreds of millions of pounds during the day and couldn't wait to be in jeans and bare feet after the day was over.

And whether they were in London or Scotland or any number of other places where Cameron went to do business, she carried with her in her heart thoughts of walking through Highland meadows with the man she loved next to her.

It was so much more than she'd expected.

She came back to herself to find Zachary standing up suddenly. He winked at her.

"I've been dismissed."

Cameron laughed and reached up to shake his hand. "Show yourself out, won't you? I have a date with my wife."

"Someday the doorbell will ring for me," Zachary said with a sigh, rolling up his drawings. "I'll call you when I know something new."

"You do that," Cameron said, reaching for Sunny and pulling her up onto his lap, "just not this afternoon. Shut the door behind you, there's a good lad."

Sunny felt herself blushing furiously, but Zachary only laughed and did as he was asked. She looked at Cameron.

"How's your afternoon look?"

"Pleasantly empty. What did you have in mind?"

She shrugged, but she couldn't help but smile. "I just wanted to talk to you for five minutes."

He looked at her purposefully. "And what in the world will we do with the rest of the day once your five minutes are over?"

She laughed. "I'm sure you'll think of something."

"Go lock the door," he said purposefully. "I'll have come up with an idea or two by the time you return."

She got up and walked over to lock the door. She returned to the fire and found herself pulled back into his arms.

"Talk fast," he suggested.

"You only have one thing on your mind," she said breathlessly.

"That's what happens when a man waits eight years for the woman he loves," he said with one eyebrow raised. "Or it might be I'm still trying to get your black Paris miniskirt out of my system. I'll give it a bit of thought and let you know. But still talk fast."

"All right," she agreed, "if you'll stop kissing my neck. It's very distracting."

He sat back with a heavy sigh, but a smile was tugging at his mouth. "All right. I'll give you five."

She smiled hesitantly. "I'm planning a little party next week." She paused. "A sort of dinner party."

He looked at her in surprise. "You?"

"Well, yes, me." She paused, wondering how he would take what she had in mind. "There might be haggis."

He relaxed visibly. "I see. What's the occasion?"

"Your birthday."

He looked so shocked, she wondered if he was displeased or not. Then he began to blush.

"Well," he said finally, "I see."

She put her arms around his neck and hugged him tightly. "You're very sweet."

"So you keep telling me. Who are the guests?"

She pulled back and smiled at him. "The usual suspects. MacLeods, in droves. John Bagley. Emily, of course. Derrick and a couple of others who vow they will show up in disguise and you'll never recognize them. I think Bobby's coming as Odo the Clown."

Cameron laughed, apparently in spite of himself. "I'm not sure if I should thank you or shout at you."

"You never shout at me."

"Well, then I suppose I'll just thank you," he said with a hesitant smile. "This is very unexpected. I feel certain I'll fidget uncomfortably all night."

"It isn't brunch," she pointed out. "How bad can it be?"

"Point taken." He looked at his watch. "And your five minutes are up."

"That wasn't five minutes."

"My watch runs fast. Come here, woman, and distract me from what you just told me before I squirm anymore."

She was quite happy to oblige him. He had, after all, cancelled his afternoon for her.

It was very late in the evening of his birthday when she found herself lying with him on the thick rug in front of the fire in his solar with her head on his shoulder. The party had been everything she'd hoped for. Cameron's hall had been full of villagers come to raise a pint to him: old men he had listened to, old ladies he had been kind to, younger souls who he'd taken the time to befriend. Sunny had issued a general invitation and been slightly surprised at how many had taken her up on it. It had been worth it, though, to see the grave smile on Cameron's face.

He had fidgeted quite a bit as well.

Once the villagers had gone, it had been just her family and his gathered around him, teasing him, toasting his health, congratulating him on actually managing to survive long enough to win such a fine witch.

And after that, it had been just Madelyn and Patrick who lingered behind with Hope, sitting with them in front of the fire in the great hall as Madame Gies and her lads cleaned up.

And then, an hour later, it had been just they two.

Cameron had sat next to her for a bit, holding her hand and running his thumb over the wait-for-me ring he'd given her. Sunny had watched him, grateful beyond measure that he was hers. Body, heart, and as much of his soul as was acceptable to heaven, as he would have said.

And then he'd led her up the stairs and into his solar, where he had loved her until she was, as usual, breathless.

But now she'd caught her breath and she had one last thing to give him. She leaned up on her elbow and looked at him.

"I have a present for you."

He tangled his fingers in her hair and smiled up at her lazily. "I think you just gave me my present. And more than once, if memory serves."

She smiled. "It's actually more something I want to tell you."

"Is it a good something?"

She pursed her lips. "What bad could it possibly be?"

"You're leaving me for Tavish Fergusson?"

She laughed, then sat up. "Not a chance. I'll be right back."

"Hurry."

She smiled at him, then wrapped a plaid around her and went to fetch from their bathroom what she'd been hiding under feminine protection products Cameron wouldn't have come near if he'd had a sword at his back. She held it behind her, walked through their very medieval-looking bedchamber, and back down the hallway to his solar. She shut the door behind her, locked it, then walked over to the hearth. She knelt down on the rug next to him.

"Ready?" she asked.

He sat up. "I'm not sure."

She handed him the pregnancy test. "Congratulations, my love. You're going to be a father."

The blood drained from his face. She caught him, then realized he'd planned that. He pulled her down with him, rolled her over so he was leaning over her, then he bent his head and kissed her.

"I'm speechless," he said, sounding slightly awestruck. "When can we expect this pleasant arrival?"

"I imagine in mid-summer," she said, smiling as he gathered her into his arms.

"Thank you," he whispered.

"Thank *you*," she returned, pulling him down and holding on to him tightly. "Thank you, Cam, for giving me the Highlands. And a beloved Highlander to go with them. And lovely summer days full of your endless meadows of flowers."

He lifted his head and smiled at her. "And the rain?"

"It is Scotland, after all," she said with a smile. "And I do love the rain."

"And me?"

She put her hands on his face. "I love you best of all. Shall I show you?"

"I'll show you this time."

A pair of hours later, Sunny watched him sleep by the light of the fire and contemplated her life.

She thought back to the night when she'd first touched him, when she'd been sitting in front of the fire in Moraig's house, listening to the rain on her roof and desperately wanting a reason to stay in Scotland. A simple man with a decent job and a bit of a garden would have been inducement enough.

Instead, what she'd gotten was a man who was intensity personified, land to roam over on long, flower-strewn days of summer, and a beautiful castle to curl up in on long, fire-warmed nights during the winter.

She supposed there were times when it just was best to not get what one had planned for. She closed her eyes and put her arm around her love.

Life had a way of providing so much more.

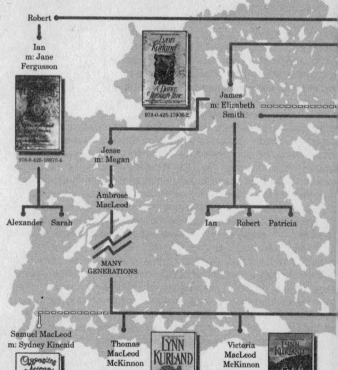

Robert

Ian
m: Jane
Fergusson

978-0-425-16970-4

James
m: Elizabeth
Smith

978-0-425-17906-2

Jesse
m: Megan

Ambrose
MacLeod

Alexander   Sarah

Ian   Robert   Patricia

MANY
GENERATIONS

Samuel MacLeod
m: Sydney Kincaid

978-0-515-12865-9

Thomas
MacLeod
McKinnon
m: Iolanthe
MacLeod

978-0-425-18197-3

Victoria
MacLeod
McKinnon
m: Connor
MacDougal

978-0-515-14127-6

MACLEOD

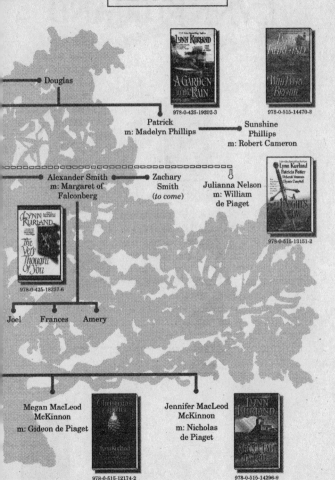

Douglas

Patrick
m: Madelyn Phillips ━━━━━━━► Sunshine
Phillips
m: Robert Cameron

978-0-425-19202-3

978-0-515-14470-3

Alexander Smith ━━━► Zachary
m: Margaret of   Smith
Falconberg   (to come)

Julianna Nelson
m: William
de Piaget

978-0-515-13151-2

The Very
Thought
Of You

978-0-425-18237-6

Joel   Frances   Amery

Megan MacLeod
McKinnon
m: Gideon de Piaget

Jennifer MacLeod
McKinnon
m: Nicholas
de Piaget

978-0-515-12174-2

978-0-515-14296-9

family lineage in the books of
Lynn Kurland

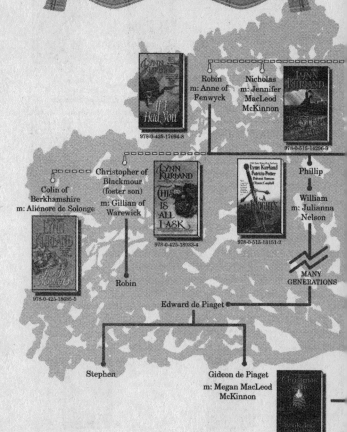

Robin
m: Anne of
Fenwyck

Nicholas
m: Jennifer
MacLeod
McKinnon

978-0-425-17694-8

978-0-515-14296-9

Christopher of
Blackmour
(foster son)
m: Gillian of
Warewick

Phillip

Colin of
Berkhamshire
m: Aliénore de Solonge

978-0-425-18033-4

978-0-515-13151-2

William
m: Julianna
Nelson

978-0-425-18685-5

Robin

MANY
GENERATIONS

Edward de Piaget

Stephen

Gideon de Piaget
m: Megan MacLeod
McKinnon

978-0-515-12174-2

DE PIAGET

978-0-425-16514-0

Rhys de Piaget
m: Gwennelyn
of Segrave

Amanda
m: Jake
Kilchurn

978-0-515-13348-8

Miles
m: Abigail
Garrett

978-0-425-15542-4

Isabelle   John   Montgomery

Kendrick
m: Genevieve
Buchanan

978-0-425-18238-3

Mary

Jason
m: Lianna
of Grasleigh

978-0-515-13362-2

Richard of
Burwyck-
on-the-Sea
(foster son)
m: Jessica
Blakely

978-0-425-17107-3

Robin   Phillip   Jason   Richard   Christopher   Abagail Anne

Thomas
MacLeod
McKinnon
m: Iolanthe
MacLeod

978-0-425-18197-3

Victoria
MacLeod
McKinnon
m: Connor
MacDougal

978-0-515-14127-6